COSMIC CONSCIOUSNESS

Mike Longmeadow

Cosmic Consciousness

Copyright © 2019 by Mike Longmeadow

Editing: Terry Stafford

Cover art by: Marcus Castro

Library of Congress Control Number: 2019912512

ISBN

Paperback: 978-1-64085-837-4

Hardback: 978-1-64085-838-1

Ebook: 978-1-64085-839-8

"*If it be true that there can be no metaphysics transcending human reason, it is no less true that there can be no empirical knowledge that is not already caught and limited by the a priori structure of cognition.*"
—C.G. Jung, *The Archetypes and the Collective Unconscious*

CHAPTER 1

As Dr. Frank Cutler emerged from the biochemistry lab clutching an envelope, he had trouble containing his excitement. His face was frozen in a smile that would have scared Freddy Krueger, and he had a spring in his step that made him look as though he was skipping. He got to his office as fast as he could without running. Once inside, he closed the door, shut the blinds, and sat at his desk. Taking in what was probably his first real breath since walking out of the lab, he started hysterically laughing and crying at the same time, holding his documents as if they were his own children. Dr. Cutler couldn't bear the thought of this being true and knew at that moment that the end was near. As he regained his composure, he opened the envelope to reassure himself of what he had found out.

Contained in the three pages he was holding, was the confirmation that, of all the possibilities of evolution, the human being had been nothing more than a parasite-ridden being that had managed to dominate existence over time, invading and killing whatever it latched on to. The disappearance of the dinosaurs, generally thought to have been caused by a giant meteor was, in fact, a mass infection by a single-minded parasite, focused on destruction, that had infected a small and hairy monkey-looking being. These hairy beings could take over a given territory within months and follow, without question, the parts of the brain that regulated instinctual actions. By use of tools and weapons, they pushed the dinosaurs back into small pockets of land, isolating the herbivores, inciting them to overpopulate and eat everything they could until they died out from starvation. Out of food, the predatory dinosaurs began to attack each other, and within a generation, they had all disappeared.

This was a place where the most well-disguised beings were the unique survivors. Snakes and alligators were proof of this, as they were among the handful of species able to resist the virus that took over the earth. The sea remained intact for a long time, sharks and giant octopuses attesting to the survival of some creatures who once roamed the earth freely. But now, even the sea is under siege, the hairy monkey having evolved into what we now know as human. With its evolving technology, humanity has found new ways to plunder the deep waters of our planet. Dr. Cutler was almost shaking; his life's work finally coming to fruition. With this proof, he could now convince the dominating oligarchy that he could help them strengthen their hold on power. His belief that humans were nothing more than the product of an infected DNA was now stronger than ever. Dr. Cutler picked up the phone and called Dwight Como. As the phone was ringing, Frank knew he held the ultimate argument to that would finally convince the heads of the controlling oligarchy to move forward. Dwight Como picked up the phone.

"Come now. I have the proof you asked about. And bring your documents." Frank hung up without waiting for Dwight's answer.

• • •

"Hello? Hello? God damn it!" Dwight slammed the phone down and abruptly started shaking.

What kind of proof was Cutler talking about? After a moment, Dwight decided to go without telling anyone. He didn't want to have to answer questions about his association with this freaky scientist. He grabbed his briefcase and left, not knowing he would never return.

The outside air felt almost alien compared to the stuffy mass of dust they refer to as air in that small hiding place of theirs that he and his colleagues affectionately called little HQ. Dwight and his colleagues were attempting to combine neuroscience, particle physics, and anthropology to find the evolutionary link that could explain the rise of human dominance. They had made some advancements in the understanding of certain realities, studying how information traveled after major discoveries, such as fire or the wheel. How these advancements affected the social fabric and how the evolution of science gradually placed mystical and religious beliefs on the back burner. But they had yet to find any explanation for why certain major discoveries were achieved at the same time across the globe. In a time when there was no practical communication between the different nations that populated the earth, it was difficult to understand how ideas were transmitted from one part of the earth to the other.

Dwight Como believed in the presence of an energy field that permeates the earth and carries electromagnetic waves which transport ideas and thoughts around the globe outside of the physical body. Although the math showed the possibility of its existence, he and his colleagues had yet to find any tangible proof. While they were accumulating data to understand how communication worked in ancient times, Dwight had been contacted by Dr. Frank Cutler, who needed his knowledge in anthropology to confirm a theory. Dwight had been secretly meeting with Dr. Cutler in hopes of unlocking something that would help him and his colleagues confirm any part of their theory. He didn't tell the doctor about his current research, limiting his interactions as a consultant to him at first, integrating any new data to his group's experimentation in hopes of furthering his own research.

Dwight took in a couple of deep breaths and felt a change in the air. He looked around. The old neighborhood felt the same but appeared different, a slight but visible glow or shadow covering everything with a sombre filter. The clock on the church tower read three o'clock, but it seemed more like early evening to Dwight, with people and buildings casting long shadows. He wanted to go but was too captivated by the darkness enveloping everything. As he watched the people walk along the narrow streets, he noticed some who seemed out of place, either not of this time, or somehow not of this place in the universe. Some were oblivious to the bleak environment, going to wherever they were going, head down, shoulders squared, walking with purpose. But some were visibly troubled by their surroundings, looking lost, confused. Dwight noticed one man who had what appeared to be a round hat but was in fact his head. The glow around him gave off the impression he had a hat on. His skin had a greenish, sickly hue. Dwight shuddered as he forced himself to start walking. The sick man then noticed Dwight and instantly became excited, his eyes lighting up. The man rushed to him, his bulging eyes appearing like two light bulbs with a fly caught inside. When the man stopped in front of Dwight, he wasn't sure what to do. Although this man was probably nothing more than a street bum, he was a little out of focus, wrapped by vapors, like the ones you see when you look down a hot street in the summer, which gave Dwight some pause as he tried to make sense of this impression. The man stood there and had yet to ask for change, his mind undeniably elsewhere. Then his eyes straightened out. He looked straight at Dwight and spoke, his voice strong and crisp.

"The answer is clear, you must make the right choice!"

Before Dwight could ask him what he meant, the man was off and running, disappearing into a blur. Dwight ran after him, but as he turned the corner, the man had disappeared. Dwight noticed a door closing slowly in front of him. It seemed deeply ensconced in a brick wall. Instinctively, Dwight went to knock on it. The door was large, thick, and ancient looking. He used the brass door knock hanging in the middle. Even though it seemed to him like he was hitting a brick wall, the wood that made up door was almost petrified, and the deep echo of his knock suggested a large empty room inside. The door stayed ajar, then reopened a little, creaking on its hinges while simultaneously growing more and more out of focus, making Dwight a little nauseous. There was another man behind the door who looked as though he were a hundred yards away, even though he was right there holding the door ajar. Dwight strained his eyes to see clearly, trying more and more desperately to make sense of what was happening, a panic cramp settling in his bowels, making his head spin. The man at the door was Dr. Frank Cutler who was looking at him while balancing a small object in his left hand. Dr. Cutler was mumbling something that Dwight couldn't understand, but as he stood there, the mumbling entered his mind, rendering him unable to move. Dr. Cutler's hand came to lay on his head, the mumble now clearer.

"Relax, empty your mind, let me in." Dr. Cutler repeated the mantra until Dwight's consciousness was no longer present.

Dwight felt his mind slip away but couldn't do anything about it. He was caught in a strange limbo between the sleeping and waking world, witness to both, limited to existing as a passenger in each realm.

Dr. Cutler, certain Dwight was open to receive orders, continued his chants, now directing his thoughts.

"You will assist me in my research."

Cutler repeated the phrase ten times, then finished programming his victim by waving his hand across Dwight's face.

"You will wake up when you see yourself in the doorway," he whispered.

Dr. Cutler pulled back from the door, and in an instant, Dwight recognized himself in the man holding the door and stepped back, out of breath. The door slammed shut the moment the man holding it let go, but right before it closed, Dwight heard himself utter these two words; "choose diligently".

Trying to understand what happened, he found himself on the sidewalk looking at a brick wall, dumbfounded. A passerby deposited some coins in Dwight's hand, which snapped him back to reality. The dark cloak was evaporated, and the bright afternoon sun shone once again. The old nineteenth century three story buildings were back to being charming in their assorted colors, each a personal reflection of its owner's tastes. Dwight had grown up in this neighborhood, and had seen it change from a blue-collar, grey-looking, hard luck neighborhood to a hip, colourful and trendy district. He felt that he could almost see himself playing cops and robbers with sling shots and plastic toy guns around the empty buildings, a "for rent" sign in every second window. He then realized how much he missed his childhood friends, who mostly were forced to move as the rent went up, catering to a new clientele. He had been fortunate enough to inherit his family home, although his university salary would have been enough to stay in the neighborhood. Feeling he was losing grasp on his mind, he sat on a bus stop bench to try to make sense of everything that happened, gradually regaining his composure. He decided to keep all this to himself for now, his mind feeling like mush. If someone was to ask him about his day, he wouldn't know what to answer. A balanced mind was needed before he could talk to anyone about this. He knew something had happened but wasn't able to pinpoint what that could be. Suddenly, Dwight felt an uncontrollable urge to share everything he knew with Dr. Cutler. He got up and went to gather his research, now focused solely on the task at hand, a distant voice trying to resist Dr. Cutler's hypnotic programming in the back of his mind.

CHAPTER 2

"Tell me, who are you?" The man asked Engella Iblis, clasping his hands together and leaning in to listen.

Any time Engella had to relate her life experience, she would almost always fall into a pessimistic view of the world. But here she was, being asked to do just that. Fighting the cloak of darkness her mind was trying to create, Engella proceeded to recount her life story.

Born into a loving family, Engella Iblis was propelled into the foster family system after the death of her parents in a car accident. She had bounced from home to home from four to nine years old, each new place turning out to be temporary. It didn't take long for her to realize that people live by their own standard, their own belief, excluding any outer influence to protect their own. She's not a foster child who had to carry around horror stories from her time bouncing around, but that time did serve as a basis for her understanding of the human condition—what makes the soul and mind tick. At a time when kids her age were learning how to hopscotch, she was learning how to read a person, how to know if the person in front of her was trustworthy. She didn't question why this was happening to her; her young mind was way too busy trying to make sense of everything.

She was first placed in a temporary home after the car accident that killed her parents, where she spent nearly a year. Both of her parents were orphans, so there was no family to turn to. The people in the first home helped her get her head above water as she tried to wrap her young mind around the notion of life and death. They supported and guided her through the emotions of her loss until she found her feet under her. Within a couple of months, as she was finding some comfort—some balance—she was moved to a new family that was supposed to become permanent. Even though she knew the situation was temporary in the first home, she found herself facing her second loss within the same year. She knew there was little chance she would see the first family again, and so, she tucked away her feelings once more and adopted a cold and analytical view of her new surroundings. Doing this helped her cope with the sense of abandonment she felt in dealing with this harsh reality.

In this home, where she was from five to seven years old, she had to learn to fend for herself. There was no verbal or physical violence, but no love or tenderness either, as the eight children living in the home had to find their way. The "parents" felt this was the best approach to teach the children to survive in the unkind, brutal, real world. Their take on social survival was that the only way for a person to advance in life was by stepping on someone else's toes. They applied that logic to the home, which created a strange crisscross of affiliations in the family, as the children naturally split into two groups.

In her new family, Engella was witness to the possibility of the co-existence of different points of view. One foster sister had set her mind to selling lemonade and set up a lucrative little street corner business, giving her some pocket money that the others didn't have. But her money was her money—no sharing. Opposite to her was the foster brother, who was mowing neighbor's lawns for cash and sharing every penny. Engella chose to keep an emotional distance from both sides and learned practical household chores to stay in touch with all her foster-siblings. She could already make a mean omelet at six years old, and she soon became the morning cook for the kids in the house, a role that gave Engella some solace in her confusing and harsh childhood.

The foster family was soon declared unfit due to the loss of employment of one of the parents. The children in the home were once again spread around to other families. Engella hadn't created a deep attachment to any of her foster brothers and sisters, but still felt the deep sting of a bureaucratic decision ripping into the social fabric of the family, as dysfunctional as it appeared.

The next six months were the worst Engella had ever lived. She ended up in a temporary foster family once again, but this time, a litany of contradictory rules made life unbearable. There was no way for a child to obey all the rules all the time, so there was always someone being reprimanded—generally more than one. The punishments were isolation from the family for twenty-four hours, with nothing but a small batch of fruits and vegetables to sustain themselves until the next day.

Engella grew to like the isolation and made sure to break enough rules to stay there as much as possible, but without incurring the more severe punishments, which were more painful. That is where she discovered the contentment that is attained by meditating, although she didn't know it at that point. All she wanted was to be alone. A numb darkness fell over her soul during that time. How could these parents be considered fit and not the others, the sole difference being current employment?

During her long hours isolated from the world, she confronted her darkest thoughts, contemplating possibilities a child shouldn't envision. The emotional tsunami she was holding back since her parents' death was now surging forth, slow and powerful. Sometimes she thought about her own death, considering the notion that her demise would go unnoticed and could end this pointless life of hers. Other times, she dreamed about running away, thinking that she was on her own anyhow and needed no one to help her. Gradually, she let herself slip deeper into her darkness, creating a separation between her and the world around her, which gratified Engella's wish to be alone. By that time, Engella was undeniably aware of the dual nature of the human soul. She had seen kindness and virtue but also malice and dishonesty. At eight years old, she was already aware of the duality of human existence but didn't yet know how far that notion would take her.

Once again, she was placed in a new foster home after her time in the house of rules and isolation. She landed in a welcoming, warm family. Engella didn't stay in her dark place for long, being pulled out by tenderness and understanding. She embraced this new family, joyfully surrendering herself to the love that permeated the house. She ended up being adopted by the family and spent the rest of her childhood and adolescence in a loving home where she was encouraged to explore the world and be curious. Gradually, she built a personal philosophy around the notion that what we want is distinct from what we need, trying to learn of her own limits about what is acceptable or desirable. During her late high school years, she decided to head into sociological studies with a minor in anthropology. She considered that the life that had been hers prepared her for that academic pursuit and threw herself into it headfirst.

Her time in college was somewhat forgettable as she lumbered through her courses, feeling uninvolved, looking for some truth which never materialized. As she came upon the end of the studies for her bachelor's degree, she stumbled upon the works of Carl Jung and Wolfgang Pauli[1]. It helped her rediscover her interest in the duality present in every human soul. The search for light, the fight against dark, the acceptance of both—her realization that both are necessary. She remembered that during her high school years, she alternated her behavior from open-minded friend to all-out bitch, studying people's reaction to her changes, studying their willingness to expose their dark side. That was her first foray into trying to understand the duality that inhabits us all. But getting limited results, she let it slide, ultimately forgetting about it altogether, as the social pressures of maintaining a balanced front overcame her wish to explore the social psyche around her.

With her focus renewed, she concentrated her master's degree on this theme, her essay on the duality which governs us all accepted on the condition that she push her research further, as she could not show enough coherent arguments to uphold her thesis satisfactorily to her peers. One professor chose to become her mentor and suggested she broaden her research base to accumulate more data to corroborate her theory. She decided to explore a wide variety of faiths as a basis to try to uncover why humans try to keep their spiritual realities apart from their practical realities. There she was, some years down the road, her post-doctoral essay on hold, meeting with a Yaqui sorcerer.

"That's all nice and good, my dear, but I didn't ask you what happened to you, I asked you who you are." The village sorcerer was looking at her intently, Engella noticing a slight smile on his face. He seemed genuinely amused by her story.

"Oh, well... I've always lived by the idea we are a product of our lives, so who I am is intrinsically entwined with what happened to me."

Engella felt he was testing her credibility, still deciding if he would accept "the interview" for her post-doctoral essay.

"True, but life will always be what you want it to be." He paused and changed the subject. "How did you find me?"

The question caught Engella by surprise.

"As you know, I've been on a philosophical pilgrimage, gathering data to finish my thesis. Traveling from temples to churches to mystical sanctuaries only succeeded in making my thesis look convoluted and confused. But during my time in Mormon territory, everything changed. By then, I thought I was going in circles, not finding anything of note that could add any real content to my essay, contemplating the possibility of quitting. Then I had a strange dream in which a man approached me, pulled me out of my dream, and carried me to this place."

"You need to come here," he said, standing next to a rusted road sign indicating the village. Without a doubt, the most realistic dream I've ever had. Everything that happened from the moment I met the man until he vanished felt like I was fully awake, although I knew I was in my dream."

"Hmm. And you came without question?" The sorcerer asked, his half-smile still present.

"Well, that experience was the first time I couldn't explain what had happened with logic, plus I felt it was in line with my thesis research, so I thought, why not. A new perspective is always welcome."

"Why not, indeed," chuckled the sorcerer.

He then became more serious for a moment, his eyes no longer smiling.

"You have been sitting there for half an hour now, and you still haven't asked me."

"Asked you what?"

"Anything; my name, why you're here, how old I am, what the weather will be like tomorrow."

He was smiling broadly by now, and Engella took this as a sign he was warming up to her.

"What do you mean, why I'm here?"

"Now there's a question I can answer!" He exclaimed joyfully. "You are here for your next phase, my dear. By answering my call, you have shown yourself ready to explore new realms. My presence here with you confirms that."

He looked giddy from the excitement it gave him.

"You're here to teach me?" Feeling the conversation was about to take a mystical turn, she decided to play along.

Engella had become accustomed to having some form of metaphysical dimension slipped into the conversation by the spiritual leaders she has met, and felt this was no different.

"Oh! I cannot teach, but you can learn plenty." He looked straight at Engella. "You are the one person who can overcome your limitations. I can guide you and help you, but I cannot teach you anything. You alone can learn what is necessary for you."

"What does that even mean?"

Engella felt thrown back to the lost little girl she was when her family vanished, her emotions wanting to boil over. She narrowly managed to overcome the emotional onslaught, as the sorcerer looked at her, appearing to take pleasure in the discomfort he created.

"It means what you need it to mean to understand."

"Are there different results for each person? How will I know if what I've learned is valid?" Engella wondered out loud.

"No, everyone comes to the same result, but the path followed is different for each person."

"Okay." Engella knew she was in the right place. For once in her life, she felt she was where she needed to be. She took in the sense of calm this feeling procured and took a deep breath. "All right then, let's start at the beginning. What's your name?"

The sorcerer smiled at this. "Now we're getting somewhere. My name is Rafael Durango, and I will be your counsel during your exploration. Let me show you your room." Rafael got up and left the house without checking if Engella was following.

He showed her a small room with minimal accommodations. A bed, a dresser, and a chair were all the furnishings the room contained. Grey plaster walls and a small window completed the picture. Rafael waved her in, bowing his head in a salute before leaving without another word. Engella found herself sitting on the side of the bed, part of her at ease with the situation, part of her in complete disarray. She began to tap at the dust on the floor with her feet, observing the mini dust clouds dancing in a ray of sun coming in through the window. She had no idea what Rafael meant when he said she was answering his call. Was it him in her dream? She had remembered the name of the village when she woke up, but that was it, as the rest of the dream reverted to a distant feeling. But the one thing she knew is that was where she needed to be for the near future. She had little knowledge about those people, if only that they were persecuted as much by the Spanish as the Mexican governance that followed. She had no idea how much knowledge this tribe possessed and how much they were willing to share with her.

CHAPTER 3

Dwight felt ambivalent as he walked down the street, his mind split in two. He knew that as soon as he met Cutler, he would give him all his research, a decision beyond his control. But a small part of him was fighting the idea, coming in like a distant echo in the depths of his mind. What had Cutler done to him to make him willingly give away years of research and all the information he was using to map the human anthropological evolution. Dwight watched himself walk towards Dr. Cutler's office, unable to control his impulse, as if he was beside his own body. The images of the strange man and his strange meeting with Frank Cutler were already hazy, distant, although the event had happened moments ago. Dwight knocked on Dr. Cutler's office door, still unsure after the strange experience he had observed. Frank Cutler called him in, his head buried in the piles of paper spread across his desk. Dwight walked in and immediately felt the nervous energy emanating from Frank. This helped Dwight get a grasp on his consciousness, although he felt his mind was still at the mercy of the commands inserted into him by Dr. Cutler.

"You said you have some sort of proof," Dwight said, attempting to control his profound need to hand over his work right away.

Frank didn't react. This emboldened Dwight, never a fan of being ignored.

"Frank, what did you find?" Dwight firmly insisted, feeling he was gaining more control.

This time Cutler raised his head. "We are nothing but a parasite, my friend." Frank's eyes were bulging from lack of sleep—the deep, dark circles accentuating the redness in them.

"What do you mean?"

When Dr. Cutler laid his eyes on him, Dwight felt himself losing control over his actions and decisions once again.

"I've tracked a bacterium all the way back to the origins of life on earth, and I believe it controls our deepest desires." Frank paused to add dramatic tension, studying Dwight to see if the hypnosis had taken by analyzing his reaction. Satisfied with what he saw, he continued as Dwight looked emotionless and empty.

"It's an extremophile parasite that had developed the capacity to travel in space by the way of meteorites. Travel through space broke it down to a micro cellular level, which gave it the chance to latch itself onto the DNA of the first thermophile bacteria[2] that populated the earth. The parasite found its way into the DNA structure that formed the first multiple cell organisms, starting to eat its way through everything it could, using life on the planet against itself. This is a parasite in the most classical sense, eating away at its host until it needs to move on. That same bacterium is present in human

DNA to this day, which explains most of humanity's destructive behavior."

Frank, continued his rant, almost talking through Dwight, happy to listen to his own voice.

"We are guided and manipulated by this bacterium to exercise dominance over anything that crosses our path. Its dominance over our decision-making had led us to believe we have free will, which is a fallacy. Now I believe I can target and cut it from our DNA. By isolating and destroying it, we can begin to influence the course of humanity's future by inserting what we consider to be right in its place. But before I can go ahead with my plan, I need your anthropological knowledge to confirm the evolution of the parasite in our system over time to secure the funding."

Frank was out of breath at this point. He looked at Dwight, waiting for an answer, a reaction, even if he didn't expect one. Dwight was visibly overcome by the flood of new information and had trouble keeping his head on straight, his brain unable to analyze anything.

Dwight was fixated on Frank's eyes, they were bulging and darting all over the place. He could barely absorb the information being presented to him. In his current state, he was unable to sustain a conversation, let alone understand what Frank was telling him. Dwight was, at best, confused. A part of him cursed the fact that he couldn't resist the temptation to give away his research. The briefcase at his feet was calling him to pass on the papers contained in it. Using every ounce of concentration he had left, he managed to stay put. In a flash, Dwight saw himself with Dr. Cutler as he was being hypnotized, realizing this is where his urge to help Cutler came from. Then, fully aware of what was happening to him, Dwight took a seat, remaining silent, trying to ward off the hypnosis.

• • •

Observing Dwight's demeanor, Frank noticed that he seemed to be resisting his call to hand over the research. He thought he needed to perfect his hypnosis techniques for the project to advance properly. Although Dwight wasn't as docile looking as he wanted, Frank decided to continue.

"You see, if we remove something from the DNA structure, it must be replaced with something else before its internal system fills in the blank DNA strand with empty cells, therefore weakening the whole structure. If we can do that, we can manipulate the people to do our bidding, so to speak. Can you see the impact we will have?"

Frank leaned in on Dwight as he said this, almost screaming by now, his hands firmly on the desk. He leaned back to calm down. "Look, I need your expertise so I can develop a plan and find proper funding for the project. The anthropological aspect is necessary for me to understand how I can use the empty DNA strand to our advantage. I want to coax humans to ask for it, not impose unilateral rules. Let humanity believe they are constructing the future through our little intervention without the knowledge that they are being manipulated. I believe if we do this, we can be the heroes of future generations, the ones who unlocked a better life for all. Science fiction books have dreamed up different futures, but not one comes even close to what can happen in our reality. We can design the future to our liking, with some help, of course."

"How does the human anthropological evolution play into your theory?" Dwight asked, his voice unrecognizable to his own ears, sounding as if they were blocked with cotton.

Frank paused, surprised that Dwight was still able to understand his ravings under hypnosis. He took a mental note of this and continued.

"For me to get the necessary funding to continue with this project, I need to convince my potential investors with something more concrete than my theory alone. I'm aware it's a rather strange theory, and even though I have the science to prove it, I need something more recognizable to the common mind for the investors to fully buy-in to the project. This is where anthropology comes in. With the appropriate timeline, you can show our investors how humans have systematically taken over whatever space they occupied—how any resistance to our presence has been annihilated. This would confirm the science I have, which proves the parasite has influenced our behavior over time."

As he spoke, Frank studied Dwight's demeanor, noticing his gaze was now clearer. Too excited and filled with pride, Frank decided to continue even if Dwight seemed more alert.

"The fact we can instill thoughts or desires in the DNA structure to direct a person's decision-making is secret and must stay that way for now. I'm bringing you in because I need your research, and I need to bolster my theory with some social sciences before I present it. Neuro-science is still in its infancy, making it useless for now, and I don't believe particle science can help a layman understand the depth of this discovery. Now we have anthropology, which can quantify the level of destruction this parasite has brought upon the planet."

Frank now understood the hypnosis was partial and decided to open up a little on the ins and outs of the project to help convince Dwight.

"You want me to quantify destruction levels? How exactly do you expect me to do that?" Dwight asked, more clearly than he expected, hoping to hide his growing awareness.

He had now regained all his composure, the controlling haze that dominated him before having evaporated. He studied Frank's demeanor, looking for a hint of . . . anything. Was he crazy or sane? He didn't care at this point. Dwight decided to remain as static as possible, trying to mimic the behavior he had under the influence of Dr. Cutler's hypnosis. At the realization his question could be perceived as doubt, he continued. "All right, I'll help, but I will need my research papers with me to be able to give you what you need."

Frank found Dwight's appearance had changed drastically. His eyes looked clear now, his elocution flawless. Had the hypnosis failed, or was this Dwight's brain adapting to his new mental state? Unfazed, he reached into the bottom drawer of his desk.

"This calls for a celebration!" He poured two glasses of whiskey and offered one to Dwight. He gulped it down.

The revelations made by Frank coupled with his strange hypnosis experience, along with the shot of whiskey, pushed Dwight over the edge as he started shaking as if his body was freezing cold. He was already doubtful about the research he was doing with his colleagues at the university, feeling they were hunting unicorns, but was now placed before a far more outlandish theory and didn't know how to react. Then the giggles caught him. He descended to hysterical laughter. Frank looked at him impassively, waiting for the laughter to subside, thinking the outburst was a side effect of the hypnosis. Dwight's hysteria dwindled, leaving him to catch his breath and blow his mucus-filled nose. He managed to regain his composure enough to organize his thoughts, wondering if he should tell Frank he was no longer under any outside influence. He decided to play along, feeling that if he resisted, he was at a disadvantage, since being in Frank's laboratory made him an easy target.

At that point, Dwight knew two facts for sure. One; since Frank had revealed his master plan, there was no going back. The only possible outcome was to collaborate or die. And two; the lengths to which Dr. Cutler had gone to include Dwight were far beyond anything sane, which meant the consequences of a refusal could be catastrophic.

"How long do I have?" Dwight asked, staring absentmindedly at Frank, trying to look like he was still controlled by an outside force.

Frank seemed satisfied that he still had Dwight under control, the blank stare having returned, a confirmation the hypnosis was still holding. Frank proceeded to explain that he needed to chart the human invasion of the planet through history. By way of anthropology, they could prove beyond any doubt that the parasite has been the main motivator in the existence and evolution of humanity—how any great discovery has systematically been used to destroy or control. It would show how humans spread over a territory the same way a parasite latches on to a host, starting with a central infection which could be defined as our cities, that spreads in all directions, which could be called urban sprawling. It's the way we eat away at each available resource until it's exhausted. Frank was convinced the history of these elements would combine with his own research to show how the bacterium controls every part of our existence.

CHAPTER 4

On the fifth day, Engella woke up with her muscles screaming for mercy. She had been placed on a training regimen that was harder than anything she had ever experienced. Normal exercises done in abnormal ways. Push-ups on slippery rocks near the river, jogging at midnight with no flashlight, meditating in the blistering noon sun. Engella was covered with bruises and scratches all over her body. Rafael walked in.

"Ready?"

"No," Engella said, her teeth clenched from the pain. "Can you please explain to me why I'm being subjected to this training? I mean, if you're to tell me about the teachings of your people, why do I need to be pushed so hard? I've noticed other people from the village follow this regimen, why can't I simply take notes and be on my way?"

Rafael looked at her with his head cocked sideways, unsure of why she asked the question. "Well . . . if you want to be witness to the energy that surrounds us, you must first adhere to a strict training regimen to have the physical ability to absorb all of the information. What is awaiting you is far beyond anything you can imagine, and if I let you advance without being properly prepared, you will not be able to absorb the information because your physical body will abandon you before you can understand. But you know this. If not, why would you have let five days pass before asking me?"

Engella was surprised by the question, and for a second, she forgot about her pain. "What energy are you talking about?"

As Engella asked her question, she fought back the vague images or mirages she saw when meditating or praying, which she had always classified as normal hallucinations. Her adherence to logical thinking always led her brain to make sense of nothing with something. Rafael began to explain the goal he had with the initiation he was imposing on Engella.

"For over fifty generations, the sorcerers of the Yaqui people have searched for a higher consciousness. About two generations ago, a sorcerer came to the realization that the way we see the world is distorted by the world around us. Our inner perception changes according our outer environment. We spend every ounce of our available energy to adapt and conform to the environment we call reality."

Rafael paused to make sure Engella was listening. Seeing she was focused, he continued,

"The thing is, this energy can be used elsewhere, if you accept that there's more than one level of consciousness. The reason I am subjecting you to this physical training is that the same sorcerer, who discovered the levels of energy, was also swallowed by the sheer majesty of what he discovered. Since he was out of physical shape, his energy dissipated into the cosmic void when he travelled there. He could not concentrate enough power from his body to stop the dissipation since all his energy was used to simply stay alive. He became the first of what are called lost souls. His spirit self, still present in the dream realm, became adept at attracting others and swallowing their energy, letting them forgo the physical world and thus live eternally. Feeling lonely, he convinced other initiates to join him in the other realm, creating a small army bent on destroying a person's subconscious for their own survival."

Engella raised her hand, Rafael taking it as a signal to stop. She settled herself more comfortably, sensing this could take a while. She then waved her hand in a circle, indicating to Rafael he could continue. Smiling at her refusal to speak, he continued.

"Except it's not eternal. The lost souls need to absorb a person's subconscious to survive the same way we need to eat in the physical world. They have accomplished this by constantly scouring the dream realm, searching for troubled souls. They recognize these souls by the lack of light emitted by them."

Rafael stopped when he saw Engella's eyes widen, he reorganized his thoughts before adding, "As you will come to know, each person's subconscious is free from the physical constraints of the conscious reality as it travels in the dream realm under the guise of a ball of light. That light is our subconscious, which the lost souls attract by creating a distortion around them. This distortion attracts troubled souls, who are in search of a sense of calm. The troubled soul is generally happy to stay in the warped cloud as it simulates a state of bliss. The lost souls then absorb the person's subconscious energy, inhaling the emotions attached to their memories from the physical body, rendering the person listless, in a sort of waking coma."

Rafael stopped, wiping his face with a wet cloth, trying to hide the tears that began to stream down his face as he spoke.

"The lost soul's physical body remains in a complete coma as long as its subconscious energy travels in the other realm. We watched them become skeletons, as all we could do was keep them hydrated by pressing a wet cloth over their mouths. Over time, their body died but didn't decompose, the subconscious energy keeping it whole. We tried to travel to the other realm and reason with them but only managed to enlarge their numbers. Our community didn't want this to become reality, as we sat bedside with our unconscious comrades, unable to intervene. This being a new evolution in our existence, a new set of practices was imposed. I accepted to guide you based on the strength of your spiritual quest and your innate capacity to interact in the dreaming world. Others have been contacted before you, but their lack of response showed us they wouldn't be able to develop their capacity to the level we need. If you're not strong enough, the lost souls will either integrate you into their ranks or absorb your energy, rendering your physical body useless."

Rafael looked at Engella with a loving smile, trying to lighten the mood. "We will soon begin a more spiritual approach. But for now, you need to continue your training," he said, lending a hand to help her up. "When you're able to wake with no pain, we will press on."

Two weeks passed, each morning less and less painful. The midnight jog had become her favorite time of the day. She was able to feel the ground around her, seeing it as one would if using night vision goggles, and was no longer tripping all over the place as they jogged.

Engella had come to understand this was not solely a training for her body. She needed to learn to become fully aware of the energy that surrounds us. During the noontime meditation, she had developed the capacity to shield herself from the sun's heat by redirecting her energy and thoughts to ascend to a higher level of consciousness, occasionally catching a glimpse of an ethereal presence around her. Nonetheless, Engella was also becoming more and more anxious as time passed, expecting some sort of spiritual illumination to occur. But none came, training and discipline relentlessly filling her days, leaving no time for daydreaming. As the third week loomed, Engella broke down. She opened her eyes, no longer able to sleep, but found herself paralyzed in bed, unable to move anything other than her eyelids. Panic set in as her breath became short and irregular. Engella didn't know where it could be coming from. Tears began to stream down her face, launching her into an uncontrollable sob that violently jerked her body. As she cried in her bed, she felt incapable of confronting another day of training. Rafael knocked on the door, Engella barely able to utter a sound to call him in. He walked in, smiling.

"Embrace the moment," he said. "You are perceiving your dual nature. Before I can take you on your journey, you must first gain control over this part of you." Rafael walked out of the room without another word, not giving Engella any chance to talk.

She remained petrified in her bed, her thoughts swirling in every direction, her mind screaming bloody murder from the paralysis. She remembered the sense of abandonment she felt every time she was transferred to a new foster home, the anger she felt before the sense of injustice this engendered, the anxiety she felt when facing a change of home. Everything was challenging her sanity. Every maddening discussion she had with a spiritual leader, that always ended with something like, "You must first have faith," or "Your salvation is in your devotion," came back to her. She felt waves upon waves of anger and despair, wanting to go back to each of these so-called spiritual leaders and spit in their self-righteous faces. The anger rose, filling her mind with murderous intentions as she let the rage spread to every pore of her body.

"Embrace the moment." Rafael's voice suddenly rang in her mind. She managed to fixate on that thought for an instant. At once, she felt a sense of calm spreading over her, going down through her torso. She gradually regained control over her body but remained in bed, exhausted.

The rest of the day was devoted to concentrating on each volatile thought that tried to jam her mind, attempting to understand, accept and use the energy irradiating from it. Overcome by the onslaught of memories that came to her at first, Engella used every bit of her concentration to acknowledge each memory, each emotion. Anyone who came in the room at that time would think she looked like a crazy person in her bed, laughing, crying, screaming at each memory that invaded her mind, accepting and loving each one as a part of her. A sense of profound calm gradually returned to her, as Engella managed to regain some composure, at least enough to breathe normally again. She knew she had passed some sort of mental barrier and felt ready to take the next step with Rafael. As the sun went down, Engella stepped outside to look at the stars. The weight she had felt in the pit of her stomach all her life was now gone, making her feel more complete than she ever had.

CHAPTER 5

Frank was ready to present his findings and secure the funding he would need to press ahead, professing to have found a solution to many of humanity's problems through DNA manipulation. His research complete with the addition of Dwight Como's anthropological analysis, there he was, starting his presentation to a group of men representing the Dark Matter Initiative. They are a group that has managed to infiltrate every level of power in the world political stage, who are dedicated to controlling humanity's destiny to their own advantage by any means necessary. The group was mandated by the powers in place at the beginning of the 20th century to survey fundamental research in particle physics. Their goal was to intercept all research and extract any useful elements that could be used to consolidate their hold on industrial, corporate, religious, and political power. Within a short period, members of the Dark Matter Initiative understood that they held the key to the future and seized power on all levels of authority in the world. There they were, listening to Dr. Cutler's idea that could offer them the possibility to solidify their stranglehold on the levers of power.

"Humans have spent the greatest part of their existence doing nothing more than trying to survive, or rather this is what is believed. Throughout history, there's plenty of evidence of humanity's fight for survival—from natural causes such as the ice age, the great plague, or important climate variations that forced millions to move, to situations created by humans themselves such as war and famine."

Dr. Cutler paused, wiping some hair from his face, glancing at his audience to see if he had gotten their attention. "The thing is, in the periods of time when the dangers of extinction were minimal, humans have made it a priority to take over any given territory. Fighting for it, exterminating everything believed to be useless that came across their path, abusing everything that was considered useful. Destruction is an integral part of the history humans have traced over time. If not by way of war between tribes and civilizations where millions, probably billions, have exhaled their last breath, the destruction has come by way of abuse of the natural resources."

By then, Dr. Cutler noticed the men before him were leaning in, visibly interested. He was too invested in himself to realize the interest being manifested at this moment was caused by the fact that the men representing the Dark Matter Initiative were wary of the direction the presentation was going. Frank, oblivious to this, continued his presentation proud that he had caught their attention.

"Methodically, humans have eaten away at everything that is deemed useful to them. This has been happening since the beginning of time, to the point of provoking the disappearance of, or greatly diminishing, certain essential resources. Fish is a prime example, as certain types of fish have vanished, while for others, their numbers are down so low, they risk disappearing as well. Meanwhile, humans have made a habit of constantly casting aside anything considered useless. Attesting to that are the many "cleansing" operations that occurred over time. Some operations consisted of hunting animals that are considered dangerous, to the brink of extinction. Other times, we have seen attempts to eradicate entire populations of people on false pretenses. Poisons were created to kill and exterminate all insect life, even using the same poison against other humans on occasion."

Frank was getting dangerously close to overstepping his limits with the group, the men before him began to squirm in their seats, coughing. Frank thought they may be somehow threatened by the presentation. Unperturbed, he continued, confident that if they listen long enough, they will see the benefits of his plan.

"Over time, humans have developed societies where cohabitation became a possibility through the creation of laws and moral constructs, which your group, and others before, have been mandated to enforce by the powers in place throughout history. But with this social design came the necessity to organize spiritual thought more cohesively, so the moral boundaries could be contained within a controllable, confined space. By eliminating any ability for the people to follow their own spiritual paths, it became possible to control entire populations with messengers declared to be the purveyors of truth. They would have the responsibility to choose what they told the population, telling the people what was needed to keep the threads of society nice and clean. This reality lasted for centuries, as the spiritual guides, books, or any knowledge that could help humans ascend to a higher spiritual level were concealed from public scrutiny, labeled as dangerous. These societies moved blindly into the future, unaware that the forces which governed their existence came from their own imposed beliefs, sometimes to the point of their own extinction."

Dr. Cutler paused, conscious of the fact that his presentation could be interpreted as an accusation against the oligarchy that had dominated human existence for the past 2000 years. But he was there to solidify their hold on power, not erode it. At that point of his lecture, he needed to be careful not to lose their interest. The men sitting across the table hadn't moved much since the start of the presentation, but Frank could feel a wave of annoyance coming from their side of the table. Confident he could drive home his presentation, he continued.

"As knowledge became more available to the public, spiritual dominance over the people wasn't enough anymore. From what I've gathered, this is where your group comes in. You have been at the forefront of scientific exploration, guiding the research to meet the oligarchy's needs first. I was surprised to find out this was accomplished without casting aside the religious leaders in the group, although it's understandable considering they still hold dominance over a handful of humanity's flocks.

"By integrating the three main religions into their fold, the Dark Matter Initiative had managed to overcome the creation of a religious resistance. They then solidified their hold on power by nourishing the scientific thirst for knowledge that began to emerge in the population, isolating their religious beliefs. Based on the newly accessible information, humans have forged out a new conviction based on the reality displayed by science. This new certainty has displaced the notion of religious faith towards the reassuring possibilities of scientific truth, where many answers are still waiting to be discovered. I believe this has caused your group to extend beyond its zone of comfort, and this is where I can help you. I hold the key to humanity's future, and with your help, it can become a reality. Your power will be absolute after my plan is in motion."

Dr. Cutler, sensing he had erased the sense of annoyance that had developed around the table, went in for the kill.

"I believe I can change a person's DNA to fit the parameters imposed by the oligarchy's needs. After my intervention, the people will not only be at your service, they will beg for your guidance. But before we can begin to transform the people, we'll need to convince them that this operation is a necessity. Otherwise, we'll be forced to face a revolution, which would only make things that much more complicated. The faith we will need to instill in the population regarding the procedure I propose will need to have religious overtones to function properly. In recent years, most scientific advancements have been based on nothing more than theories. As elegant as they may be, this can breed doubt in the layman's mind. Between a scientific theory and a religious belief, the only real difference is mathematics. That's an avenue we can use to construct the base of our philosophy to convince the people. We have reached a crossroads where belief in the institutions that oversee the efficiency and productivity of society is plagued with doubt, and that needs to be addressed."

Frank took a glass of water and drank while looking at his audience, trying to see if he had managed to pique their interest enough for his project to take flight. One man was busy typing on his phone, which gave Frank a boost of confidence, convinced the man was sending a positive message. He had to push on. He had come too far, and the fate of his project rested on their approval.

"I want to clarify at this point that I'm not looking to participate in the decision-making process of the oligarchy. Once the modifications have been applied to humanity's DNA structure, my sole wish is to enjoy a comfortable retirement, along with the distinction of making the greatest discovery of all time."

This last comment generated a snicker from one of the men, who expressed his doubt to Cutler. "We're still far from that at this point, don't you think? You speak of creating faith towards a profound transformation, but you have yet to convince us you own more than a theory." He stared down Cutler who stood his ground, a smile appearing on his face.

"You're absolutely right, sir. Visual aids are always helpful, aren't they?"

The man leaned back in his chair while Frank walked toward the door and opened it to let a man in.

"This man has been reprogrammed to follow my every instruction. Although his actions are limited to simple orders for now, with your help, I know I can develop a more complete version of this."

Frank turned to the man he brought in and asked him, "What do you need?"

"My needs are yours," the man said.

The men across the table started to whisper with one and other, a sense of excitement filling the room. Frank then asked the intrigued assembly, "Do you have a request for our friend?"

The men convened and began to discuss it. Their whispers were so low, Frank couldn't make out what they were saying. One of the men turned to Frank.

"One of our scientists has gone rogue, we need him neutralized."

Frank was unfazed by their demand. The fact that they were using another scientist to try and scare him didn't work. He was even expecting something like this to happen.

"Very well. Give me his information and I will send my soldier on his way."

A second later, Frank received all the pertinent information to get the man the group wanted to be silenced and sent the reprogrammed soldier on his way. "It shouldn't take too long. We can wait here, if you like."

Dr. Cutler had omitted the fact that the man he sent out was actually hypnotized, not transformed. He chose not to divulge this information in fear that he would be ridiculed, hoping the hypnosis level would be strong enough to carry out the task. Once he secured the funding, he would probably let them in on the secret. The conference room was bathed in a dim sunlight, the tinted windows helping to reduce the glare coming in. Everyone was waiting in silence, some men shuffling through papers, while others tapped away on their phones, informing their bosses of the progress of the meeting. An hour went by and Frank's phone vibrated. Proudly, he showed the men his phone screen, that read, "it's done," along with the picture of a dead scientist.

"As you have probably surmised by now, this man is programmed to hunt. In the future, we will be able to program a person for any task." Dr. Cutler looked at the men and added, confident in his proposal, "Do we have a deal?"

CHAPTER 6

In the short time since her arrival in Yaqui territory, Engella had attained a level of understanding of her own energy aura that went far beyond anything she had ever experienced. The fact that she was able to run in the surrounding fields at night and be able to "see" the ground still blew her mind. She had developed the capacity to have waking dreams, which showed her a strange and wonderful place, although she could only bear witness to her surroundings, unable to move in this realm.

"It's a simple exercise," Rafael had told her. "All you need to do is find an object you can concentrate on, keep your focus entirely centered on that object as you fall asleep, and you will wake in your dream looking at that same object."

As far as teaching goes, this explanation was one of the most detailed Rafael had given Engella since she got here.

"Can it be my hand?"

"Anything at all, even imaginary. If you have something to focus on, you're good."

Since that conversation, the days had become somewhat routine, and the moment she thought she was to be initiated into the possibility of traveling in the dream realm, she was ordered to leave the village. Rafael explained that she needed to see the world with her new understanding of the energy that surrounds us before proceeding further. She was to re-enter her world with the knowledge of her duality. It would help her become aware of the energy we dispense to adhere to social protocol. It would force her to fully commit to her own energy, as the proximity to many people would teach her to be more aware of herself. She must evolve to the point of understanding the indestructible force that embodies our existence and find a way to travel back to the village in the dream realm.

Engella knew that she would need to spend time away from the village. The problem with this theory is that she didn't feel ready to reinsert the "real" world. This village is where she felt most at home. As she was about to share her thoughts with Rafael, he entered her room and began to share his own before she could tell him how she felt.

"You must know that the world we call reality is nothing but an illusion. It's become this way because of the way humanity has interacted with the dream realm. Energy doesn't react the same way in this place because we've cultivated our relationship with the dream realm. In the rest of the world, over time, an image of what civilization should be like emerged from the collective unconscious.[3] That single image then found its way to everyone's subconscious mind, obscuring the bigger picture for each individual."

Rafael was talking as he was packing Engella's bags.

"The sense of certainty we feel at times, that moment when we say to ourselves 'this is home,' comes from the fact that we are attached to a specific point of energy in the field that surrounds us. When that energy corresponds to someone's vibrations, that person feels at home. If each human could define his connection to the energy field instead of letting the physical environment dictate it, the world would be a different place."

Engella laid in bed, contemplating the same discolored blotch on the ceiling she has looked at since getting there. She turned to face Rafael.

"What you're telling me is the same as other religions and beliefs. The one new thing you've shown me is to acknowledge every emotion or thought I might have and embrace them as my own. You talk about energy fields but can't show me. The waking dreams I've had can be nothing more than a fabrication from my mind. How is that different from a priest telling me to believe in God without question by showing me miracles that are nothing more than still unexplained scientific experiments?"

"What do you remember from the dream that brought you here?" Rafael asked absentmindedly. He looked around to make sure he didn't forget anything Engella might need in her bag.

"Not much," Engella said. "I remember there was a light or a glow coming from all around. And I remember the road sign near the village. The rest is pretty much a blur. I have notes I took after waking up, but I don't know what they mean"

"And the waking dreams?"

"Same, I can see my hand, the ground at my feet, but the rest is blurry at best, like looking at the stars through a light cloud cover."

"Well, you need to be able to see the blur with more clarity before I can help you evolve to the next phase of your existence. Exploring the other realm is dangerous at best of times. So, being able to see is paramount to a person's survival." Rafael stood up, ready to go.

"There. Your bag is packed. But before you leave, come with me." He brought Engella to a hut in the middle of the village and invited her in. There were cushions set up in a circle in the middle of the hut. She chose one and sat on it.

"There's something I can show you before you leave." Sitting down in front of her, Rafael held out a small bowl filled with a reddish, pungent liquid and gave it to Engella. "Call it a guided tour," he said with a malicious smile in his eyes.

Engella grabbed the bowl and took a sip, repulsed by the smell.

"Drink it all in one gulp," ordered Rafael.

Engella hesitated, the smell of the liquid gagging her. Taking a deep breath, she swigged down the liquid. Her body immediately started to tremble, a burning sensation going from her throat down to her bowels. She felt the need to lay back as she could sense her mind trying to leave her body. Her weightless self elevated to the sky as if propelled by an invisible impulse. As her conscious spirit left the house, she could see her body lying down on the floor. "Am I dying?" she asked no one, feeling her body abandoning itself to the burning sensation, which was now spreading through her veins, warming her bones. The feeling that enveloped her was the same one she had when her stepfather would tuck her in at her last foster home where she discovered happiness. She wondered if she would feel her physical body within her conscious spirit, but the thought was pushed away by an all-encompassing sensation of pure bliss as her spirit floated further away.

Engella, now free of the constraints of her physical body, was unable to do anything other than float. She looked down at the earth and was blinded by the discharge of light every single object was emitting. It looked like a radar weather map, but she knew she was looking at the energy fields Rafael had evoked. She was conscious the whole time as she marveled at the show of lights before her. Blinded by the sheer brightness of everything, she felt as though she was in a dream, but she was fully conscious and present, even more so than in the waking dreams. As she began to see through the bright light, Engella could make out small pops of energy appearing randomly on the ground, some blending into the sea of lights that covered the ground, others reaching up to the edge of the atmosphere. Engella began to feel pangs of fear as she remained suspended in the sky. She wrangled the emotion, transforming it into one of wonder and amazement.

It changed the picture before her, as the abstract strands of light covering the ground morphed into a clearer picture. She was able to distinctly see the different sources of light radiating from the ground. Every living object was radiating its own light, each glowing at different intensities. Some were floating aimlessly. Others seemed to be following an organized pattern. She noticed an energy burst that emerged from the ground, aiming itself directly at her. As it reached her, the mass of erupted energy stopped and began dragging her down. The speed of the descent accelerated exponentially as she mustered all her energy to try to embrace this powerful force. But the fear paralyzed her thoughts, her mind certain she was falling to her death.

She felt the weight of her body during the fall, making her fear grow stronger. A guttural, weak sound came out of her mouth, but it was enough to stop the plunge, her spirit now floating over her body in the room where Rafael gave her the dreaming liquid. She awoke abruptly in the hut, covered in sweat, sprawled on the floor, cushions spread out as if she had having seizures the whole time. Rafael, who was sitting in a corner waiting for her to regain consciousness, seemed startled by her sudden awakening, springing to his feet as if someone had pressed a button.

Engella started shaking from exhaustion. Rafael placed his left hand on her forehead and his right on her stomach, then started to hum a soft melody. The shaking stopped right away, his humming somehow reaching his hands, making them vibrate. Engella progressively regained some poise, trying to understand what had happened, trying to classify the event in her mind. The sheer immensity of what she saw went far beyond her understanding of the spiritual mind. Rafael finished his soul massage and patted her on the shoulder.

"Okay!" she said. "Everything is energy. I get it."

Rafael smiled, tapping his index finger on his forehead as a goodbye gesture. She wasn't sure she would ever see him again, the training imposed by Rafael having no time table. He told her she would know when the time had come to return to the village. Trying to make sense of her hallucinations in the hut, Engella reverted to her habit of internalizing to analyze. She then returned home, not knowing what to expect.

She arrived at the city a changed person, feeling like an alien discovering a new civilization. She was a little disappointed to realize that she didn't physically see anything differently. A tree looked like a tree, and a person was a person, unlike the blasts of energy she perceived after drinking the potion in the hut. She did find some comfort in the fact that although she couldn't see the energy, she could feel something around her. It permeated the air but remained invisible, like the perfume would envelop you in the middle of a lavender field. Engella could feel vibrations coming off different people, and as she was beginning to be able to see the vibration emitted around her, the phone vibrated in her pocket, a stark reminder that she was back in "civilization."

"Wow. You answered!" Ayla screamed, forcing Engella to pull the phone away from her ear.

Engella met Ayla Karemi went she was trying to figure out a way to integrate some notions of mystical thinking in scientific research. Since Ayla was a particle physicist, Engella thought she would be the perfect person to talk about the link between particles and the energy that surrounds us. She found in Ayla, the open mind she was looking for. From the moment they met, their friendship had grown exponentially. Reticent to collaborate at first, Engella had embraced Ayla's child-like curiosity and helped her enrich her research, curious to see where she would go with these notions. Engella was happy to have found a kindred mind in Ayla.

"Hi. Yeah, I was out of range for a while." Engella said. "I hope you weren't worried."

"No. More like impatient. I need to see you. I might be on to something big. Come to my place as soon as possible."

Ayla was talking so fast, Engella understood one out of two words. "Okay, let me drop off my bag at my house, and I'll come over."

"No. Come now. I know you travel light. You need to hear this right away." Ayla then made kissing sounds and hung up.

Engella tried to recapture the moment she was having before the call, but everything was back to its bland physical real self—no cloak of mystical perfume anywhere—nothing but grey reality. But her disappointment was short-lived since she was happy to see Ayla right away. If there was one person with whom Engella could share her experience, discuss it, and make sense of it all, it was Ayla. Ayla's excitement on the phone had influenced Engella, who was then almost running.

CHAPTER 7

When she began her bachelor's degree in particle physics, Ayla Karemi thought she was going to head into the experimental side of the research. She had grown up with a great interest in the inexplicable, always looking to find an explanation to anything that piqued her curiosity. At a young age, she would search for the answer to simple things, like where the water in the tap comes from, or where the sun goes at night. As she grew, Ayla became more and more interested in metaphysical phenomenon and began to study the work of astrologers and psychics, trying to see if there's some truth outside the obvious limitations of those who are pursuing "the reading of someone's future." Seeing this, her father helped her direct her energy towards science, telling her there's nothing in the divination arts that would be able to explain anything other than a vague possibility of a brighter future. He introduced her to the world of particles, which blew Ayla away. She plunged into the study of the marvelous and strange world, latching onto each theory as if it contained the ultimate truth. Even though she was entering middle school, she approached the 12th grade math and science teachers at school to learn the basics of the theories and formulas that populated the infinitely small world of particles.

As she grew up, the science teacher took her under his wing, impressed by her capacity to understand the chaos of particles. He offered his help, putting together experiments to test the theories she wanted to explore. For the first experience, Ayla wanted to explore the double-slit[4] experiment, which demonstrates that when a photon goes through the two slits of an opaque plate, you can either know the entryway or the point of arrival of the photon but not both. That went on sporadically from 9th to 12th-grade, her trials staying pretty basic since the school didn't have the equipment to perform many of the experiments related to the particle world. When she left high school, Ayla's goal was to become a researcher at the CERN supercollider. She sent her application to Stanford, hoping to make her dream a reality. The university was impressed with the large variety of science projects she had pursued during high school. Her capacity to show her understanding of different quantum theories in her presentation letter convinced the committee to accept her in the physics program and offered her a full scholarship.

The first year was a big letdown, as Ayla found herself studying the basic theories once again—something she had done in detail over the past years with her teachers in high school. She plodded through, repeating to herself this was a new beginning, that she was on the right track, hoping she might come across some unknown information she might have missed. But as the second year rolled around, Ayla felt cornered into something she hadn't expected. She was surrounded by closed minds. Those presumed scientists were bent on proving a theory right or wrong based on the logic of their own opinion, not facts. They found ways to direct their research so it showed the information necessary to confirm their calculations. During that second year, she saw a number of her colleagues get stuck in their research, primarily because they wouldn't dare explore a theory outside the confines of existing science, limiting their results to what we already know. They would sometimes add a minor detail or two to an existing theory but never made any real advancements.

Ayla began to question her journey in experimental physics, gaining greater interest in theoretical physics as time passed. Under the advisement of one of her professors, she continued her degree to the end, choosing to do her masters in particle physics philosophy. The professor who advised her to finish the bachelor's degree in experimental physics became her master's mentor. Intrigued by her academic journey, he became interested in assisting Ayla in her pursuits. He admired her resolve to push the boundaries of the scientific method. She would approach any problem with a way of thinking contrary to most of the accepted methods used by the scientific community, usually hitting a dead-end, but on occasion, creating a small breakthrough. Her master's degree referred to the possibility of accepting the chaos that is the particle realm in a way that could enable a fresh approach to its understanding. It means letting the mind wander to unusual conclusions, opening the possibility of finding answers in esoteric fields of thought.

She started her master's research by exploring a theory called the Pauli-effect.[5] This theory was famously linked to physicist Wolfgang Pauli, who was reputed to have experimental machinery break down when he was close by. She argued that in the same way, humans carry a specific chemical combination that reveals itself through pheromones, they also carry a distinct energy signature that affects the world around them in chaotic ways. To demonstrate her theory, Ayla extrapolated in her new mathematical formula that the electrical signature of a person was the variable that affected the chaos of the particle realm. She hoped to demonstrate the unexpected results some people experience with inanimate objects from time to time. In her memoir, she argued that by limiting our research approach on a scientific basis alone, we limit our discovery potential by at least half. By opposing different points of view to any given theory, the breakthrough potential will at least double, if not more. Her mentor was 100% behind her in this venture. But he recommended that she be careful, the ideas she was conveying would undoubtedly cause a loud backlash.

"As soon as you even evoke the notion of mysticism, a lot of people won't even read the rest of your essay," her mentor warned. "Be supremely cautious in the formulation of your ideas and be sure to show how you can apply scientific rigor to the line of thought you're implying. If you indisputably define the difference between mystical philosophy and mystical practice, I think you'll be okay."

"I'm not trying to suggest we use crystals and pyramids to find answers. You know that."

"I do, but you need to make sure anyone who reads your essay sees the same thing."

Dr. Robert McCann, Ayla's professor, was considered somewhat a rebel in the Stanford circles, as he often accepted master's theses that would be rejected by other professors. What he saw as scientifically applicable could sometimes be considered by other researchers too different, even inconsequential. In his defense, this approach did open new avenues in particle research. As a result, his method produced a highly successful rate of theses, as some of his students created more concise mathematical formulas, thus opening new avenues in the particle world. But the university board also saw that a good number of his students produced nonsense, causing many headaches for Dr. McCann, as his methods were constantly being questioned. Despite this uncomfortable situation, his philosophy was that pure science should be open to all possibilities in the sole pursuit of knowledge and advancement. His mantra was, "limitations of the mind breed prejudice, which in turn induces ignorance."

"Preaching to the choir, sir," Ayla said. "For now, I haven't begun to write my essay. I'm concentrating on making sure I get all the necessary credits for the master's."

Ayla had already suffered run-ins with some colleagues when she suggested they use different approaches to their problem. She was already the crazy one in the department. She didn't need anyone to bring her down before the project was finished. She knew that her doctoral scholarship hinged on the essay.

She built her theory around Wolfgang Pauli's work on synchronicity and the number 137,[6] which was coined the "cosmic number"[5] for its supposed significance in reuniting the speed of light with Planck's constant. She was careful to include the science behind it all, referring to Richard Feynman and Enrico Fermi to solidify her argumentation, and to omit the work that was also put in by Carl Jung on the subject, fearing his input was too mystical. Her essay was accepted without question, although some members of the reading committee expressed concern over her suggestion that science and mysticism have grown closer with the discoveries made in particle physics.

Ayla worked hard through her doctorate, trying to find a workaround to the limitations of Cartesian thought that plagued particle research. As she was developing her thesis, she was constantly challenged by professors, even colleagues, about her research. Some of them going as far as questioning her motives. It had degenerated into bullying in some cases, as she began to receive mean, insulting emails, "presents" sent with malicious intent, like an esoteric book on the supposed use of quantum physics to look into the future with a card that read, "leave us be, go and join your kind." Ayla had to continually justify her research to everyone, her mentor and one other professor being the only ones encouraging her to pursue this avenue. As much as she leaned on the works of Pauli, Feynman, and Fermi about synchronicity and its mathematical existence, she was still viewed as a wild eyed, naïve young girl. One professor even went as far as telling her that whatever she submitted, she would get two out of four credits for the course, probably less. He told her he thought her pursuits shouldn't even be evoked in a serious place like this. But all the noise left her unfazed, as her doctorate was nothing but a pursuit she embarked on to gratify her curiosity. If someone felt bothered by her research, that was their problem, not hers. As she reached her mentor's office for her weekly meeting, two colleagues walking by threw insults her way under their breath as they passed her. Ayla had pretty much heard it all by then. She walked into the office without a word and shut the door.

"I have to say, I admire your resolve," Dr. McCann said as she sat for their meeting on the advancement of her thesis. He was not one to stay silent if challenged.

"Yeah, well, if they want to make themselves feel bigger by belittling me, it's on them, not me. Anyhow, I've come too far, this research needs to be completed, whatever the result," she said, rifling through the documents in her bag, trying to find the latest results to share with him.

Ayla had always been a distracted scatterbrain. But she always managed to keep everything together by way of spectacular instinctual intelligence that helped her see order in the chaos she created. Anyone who went to her office only saw disarray, but the chaos was precise, although inefficient. Dr. McCann waited for Ayla to find what she was searching for in her bag. He was used to her thought process, knowing her paper shuffling indicated some mind shuffling as well. He sat back in his chair, admiring her mind at work, a smile spread across his unshaven face as he congratulated himself in supporting her.

"Ah! Here we are," she said. She went right into it. "You asked me to look at the possibility of integrating horizontal causality into my research to strengthen its scientific value. You argued that this might show the possibility of quantifying the chaotic randomness of vertical causality. I followed your cue and based my premise on the notion that the cause and the effect present in horizontal causality are separate. It is the ideal approach to be able to visualize the vertical force that comes into play when it activates the horizontal reaction. Unfortunately, I believe this will remain obscure in the end, because it's all theoretical. But I'm certain that further investigation into this line of research will certainly help experimental physicists create more precise experiments in the future. But I don't know if I'll ever have the chance to see any form of an experiment that could corroborate the theory in my lifetime. The science behind this knowledge is still too far from practical application."

Ayla stopped, looking at Dr. McCann for some encouragement.

"I'm not surprised; you're introducing a new philosophy. It takes time to include new ideas and apply them. But this does give you ammunition to explain your goal to understand both the how and the why, because this is where you stand now. The science you show is solid. I'm not worried about that part. What worries me more in your thesis is the notion you introduce, suggesting our minds are linked to an energy field. By making this assertion, you also suggest freewill is somewhat of an illusion. You state that our decision-making process is influenced by our immediate environment, that we do nothing more than constantly adapt to the changes that happen around us. It is a sensitive subject matter, though I must say your math is good, elegant, and complete. Now, you need to find a common link between your research and existing science that won't destroy your theory."

Dr. McCann had always been Ayla's lighthouse, as he constantly managed to direct Ayla's mind in the right direction. He went on.

"You could visit some meditation centers, speak with yoga masters, or something along those lines. It could help you crystallize your ideas and give you a clearer picture to finish your thesis. I admire the rigor you have put into your work, but now I think it's time for you to explore the chaos a little more." He gave Ayla a phone number.

"This could be an avenue. Her name is Engella Iblis; I believe she could help you understand the chaos."
***

As Ayla threw herself into a mystical pilgrimage, her goal was to find common ground between the different faiths that permeate humanity, whether mystical or religious. Her thinking was that within the resemblances, there's a hidden link to a greater scientific comprehension of anything and everything. During one of her library expeditions, Ayla called Engella Iblis to meet up. Ayla was surprised the first time they met. The woman she met carried a strange, enigmatic vibe. They had met to discuss Ayla's exploration of mystical research patterns or ways she could integrate the spiritual thought process with the scientific one, as per Dr. McCann's suggestion. Engella was tall with shoulder-length brown hair that fell over her face, like curtains on a window, the curls in her hair following her facial structure to a tee. Her brown, almond eyes were soft, inviting. Their softness spreading to her round, light brown face, her mouth seeming to carry a permanent half smile. But what hit Ayla wasn't the physical aspect of Engella's beauty. The calm, pure energy emanating from her carried a surprising amount of power. Ayla's heart swelled in her rib cage just by standing in front of her. Her scientific mind went straight to the notion of chemistry between people, the natural exchange of pheromones. But she had never felt it to such a degree. Born into a Buddhist family, Ayla had learned to always search for a middle ground, a balance. The power of Engella's energy overwhelmed Ayla beyond anything she had ever felt, but she managed to keep a straight face while her brain went spinning out of control. A mixture of sexual appetite and intellectual curiosity fought over control of her consciousness. She took a deep breath, trying to keep her mind clear. She had no idea how her life was about to change.

"Professor McCann tried to explain your process to me, but I think it fell beyond his field of understanding," Engella said in a matter of fact tone.

Ayla was surprised that such a strong, authoritative-sounding voice could come from such a soft-looking face. She instantly felt akin to this woman. Although their life paths were surely different, Ayla felt an attachment to her.

"What you're looking for won't reveal itself in a lab or a math formula—at least not in the foreseeable future," Engella continued. "You'll probably have to turn to a different approach if you want to understand a little more. I believe I can help you with that if you're interested. But I can help you on the condition that you accept the reality that will manifest. Come with me."

Engella grabbed Ayla's hand and all but dragged her to Lake Lagunitas near the golf course, never letting go of her as they weaved their way through the university corridors. Out of breath, Ayla stumbled along until they arrived at the edge of the lake. Engella then continued her explanation.

"As the water flows, it carries the elements and nutrients necessary to the health of the lake, be it from the rain or an underground water source, right?" Engella didn't let Ayla answer as she continued.

"In that same way, the electromagnetic energy our thoughts and desires emit is attached to a field, or a lake, that absorbs the energy and redistributes it to all, nourishing people's thoughts and desires, influencing social behavior. Thing is, a person needs to be introduced to this reality to be able to see it, and there's no formula or experiment that can show when someone is ready to be initiated. I feel you're ready to see more, but first, we need to get you in shape. Right now, there's no way you can reach the required energy level to see."

Engella fell silent, looking pensive. As first conversations go, this one was certainly the strangest Ayla had ever had. "I don't know about another reality," she said. "My hope is to incite any particle physics researcher to diversify their research patterns—to look at the science with a new lens, if only to see if anything changes."

Ayla wasn't sure delving any deeper into this line of thought would help in any way, but Engella's assured tone intrigued her. It seemed as though Engella had been waiting to intervene somehow.

• • •

When they began the training, Ayla met with some religious leaders and yoga gurus that talked to her about a different reality, but always withholding the possibility to see or explore that reality physically. Even with meditation, the best Ayla could hope for was a small glimpse into the subconscious. Engella was hinting at the possibility of consciously exploring quantum levels of existence, and that piqued Ayla's curiosity to see how far she could take her. They spent the next weeks training hard, Engella putting Ayla through the motions without any remorse, explaining the importance of having a strong, fit body to explore what lies behind the reality curtain. Relating everything Rafael had taught her, Engella kept a strict training regimen. Every time Ayla would complain about the pain, Engella would answer this was necessary.

Following in the footsteps of Rafael's training, Engella would give away a snippet at a time of what would follow the training, helping Ayla maintain her level of motivation and keep going. Engella then initiated Ayla to midnight jogging. The first time they left the house, ready for a jog, Ayla thought they would stay on the well-lit roads and eat away at the kilometers on the streets. Engella had brought her to the coast of the San Francisco Bay, where the shadows overpower the feeble lights emanating from the park nearby. Ayla spent most of the first nights falling on her face, tripping on every little bump, scraping her knees and elbows to the bone. Engella snickered at this, telling Ayla she needs to learn to feel the ground around her without seeing it, that it's a necessary part of the learning curve, adding morsels of her own experience. It made Ayla angry and confused, but she kept her focus, each morning feeling she was getting closer to what Engella was planning. If anything, Ayla thought she would at least be ripped after this and hung on to that thought when her body screamed for mercy. Her fascination with Engella never swayed during this time, as they grew closer with each passing day, developing a family-like bond, a deep trusting love.

One morning, Ayla woke to a strange smell in her apartment. A strong, pungent odor that grabbed her by the throat, almost making it hard to breathe. She walked into the kitchen to find Engella hard at work over the stove, producing the aroma.

"I believe you're ready," Engella said without looking. "What I'm about to show you will change everything. Let yourself go, and you'll be fine. If you try to resist, the energy you create will attract dark energy. That's all I will say. I don't want to influence your experience."

Engella spoke as she was preparing the potion that Rafael had given her before she left her Yaqui friends.

"You want me to drink that bitter thing?"

The pungent smell didn't seem to affect Engella, who was whistling while preparing the concoction. "We'll have to let it cool a little, but yeah, ideally in one big gulp." Engella was smiling broadly, which worried Ayla a little.

"What can I expect?" She asked, trying to buy some time, still deciding if she would go through with it.

"Don't know, it's different for each of us. But one thing you will be exposed to is the energy field I have told you about and its connection to each of us. How you interpret what you see is all based on your own life experience, so there's no way for me to even try to guess what you will see. Here you go." Engella handed Ayla a small bowl with the pungent liquid.

Ayla looked at the bowl in her hands, unsure. As she had during the whole process, she leaned heavily on the notion of the four noble truths of Buddhism her father had instilled in her during her childhood. He had spent her whole childhood insisting on them: truth is suffering, truth is the origin of suffering, truth is the end of suffering, and truth is the road you follow. He also insisted on the three existential characteristics. Nothing exists independently, nothing is permanent, and no single phenomenon can fulfill our urges because everything is in constant change. Bringing the bowl to her mouth, she felt herself coming full circle, having started in the throes of spiritualism, moving to the cold calculations of science and then returning to the spirit realm as she gathered her courage to down the bowl of strange, reddish liquid.

Within moments, Ayla's mind was submerged in a tidal wave of energy that seemed to emanate from the depths of the earth. The wave was seeping out of the ground and reaching for Ayla's spirit body, invading her soul, pushing away any possibility to adhere to a coherent thought. Ayla saw the kitchen, her twisted body on the floor, and Engella watching her as her spirit self was unceremoniously thrust toward the sky. In a fraction of a second, Ayla found herself floating on the edge of the earth's atmosphere, carried by an overflow of her own memories that seemed bent on pushing her into deep space. Ayla, her mind in agony as she alternated between bliss and panic, was desperately trying to hold on to one thought, any thought, so she could begin to regain control over her conscious mind.

The memory of her first meeting with Engella popped into her mind, and Ayla latched onto it. She found herself watching their meeting from the perspective of a fly on the wall. She saw herself and Engella with the library bathed in unnatural light. The two figures stood before each other, but no one seemed to be speaking or doing anything at all as they looked at each other, waiting. Feeling she had some control over her mind, Ayla attempted to get closer to the two figures. As she approached, both turned to face her, and their gaze propelled Ayla's spirit body into space beyond the atmosphere, as she found herself looking at the earth from afar. Floating aimlessly in weightless space, Ayla understood her spirit body possessed some mass. If not, she wouldn't feel the weightlessness of space. This realization acted as a balm on her as she began to analyze her surroundings with a clear mind. The earth was magnificent, its blue hue emanating far into the darkness of space. Obsessed by the beauty of a storm forming in the southern hemisphere, Ayla was too focused on the cloud formations to see the specs of light floating around the edge of the atmosphere. Her focus on the storm caused her spirit body to begin its descent to earth. It started slowly at first, giving her time to admire the formation of some storm clouds. Ayla began to feel her weight as she gained speed upon touching the atmosphere. As she accelerated, she felt her mind slip away once more while the specs of energy floating around the edge of the atmosphere enveloped her and thrust her toward the ground. As fast as she was propelled toward the sky, Ayla found herself on the floor, looking at the ceiling, bathed in sweat. Engella bent over her, a smile on her face.

"Pretty cool, huh? Next time, you need to be able to go on your own."

As she was saying this, Engella had already placed her hands over Ayla's forehead and stomach. She quietly hummed, her hands vibrating under the chants. Exhausted, Ayla let Engella do her thing as she slipped into a deep, dreamless slumber, unaware she was smiling as she fell asleep.

CHAPTER 8

Heading home after his eerie encounter, Dwight was still dizzy from all the new information Dr. Cutler gave him and took a long detour. He was worried that his mind was still on some spell, and he wanted to make sure he was himself again. During his long walk, he tried to make sense of the vision he had of himself in the doorway, trying to tell him to be cautious. Was it related to the cloak of darkness he had perceived in the air earlier when he was going to his meeting with Frank? He had spent his life flying under the radar. He was always analyzing everything, never divulging more than was necessary to the person in front of him, keeping his cards close to his chest. Even though some would say that his behavior had isolated him from the world, most of the time, he didn't mind. When he had to collaborate with someone for something more than the usual social interactions, he would feel displaced, as if he was not useful.

This feeling of isolation began at a young age. As long as he could remember, Dwight's parents were solely focused on their careers and were too busy to relate to their only child. For them, their family was nothing more than a business transaction in their books. That model of education left Dwight having to fend for himself in his free time, his parents providing only the necessities related to the practical aspects of life. They showed no real emotions around him, captivated by their own life, which caused him to grow up an angry child, prone to outbursts for no reason. But Dwight's behavior wasn't noticed by anyone who could have helped him at the time, isolating him even more into a world where he saw everyone as nothing more than tools to be used when necessary. And now here he was, sitting in the park, his brain splintered by the overload of information thrown at him. He would need to undertake this research without any guarantee that Dr. Cutler would acknowledge his work, as it had happened too often before. If Frank was telling the truth, or even a partial truth, he couldn't let his name be erased from the research. It was too important. Having those thoughts reassured him, he knew was no longer under any controlling mind spell, and he began to relax at last.

Looking up at the rare, visible stars in the city sky, Dwight let his mind wander, searching for a sliver of understanding to help completely dissipate the thick, murky fog that invaded his mind. He let his thoughts travel back to the single most fun thing he liked to do as a child, visiting the civilization museum. As far back as he could remember, he would relish in letting his mind wander into the era depicted in the display set up by the museum. He would escape the pressures of daily life with dreams of what everyday life was like for the people in past times. He would give himself good, important roles in those dreams, obscuring the fact he was alone in this world, freeing him from the emotional constraint loneliness induces. Although he always liked exploring a new presentation, the permanent exhibits at the museum were the main reason Dwight chose to study anthropology. With them, he was able to deepen his knowledge of any given time in history, igniting a lust for learning. After his first visit, he began to bring a notebook and jotted down specific information, then went home to start his own research so he could deepen his understanding of a given society.

By the time he was in high school, he had started noticing errors in some of the displays. Tools used at the wrong time, pieces of decorative clothing set up on the wrong person, minor details that went unnoticed, although relevant. These inaccuracies didn't disturb the balance of the presentation, so the visitors didn't notice it. He started to catalog the mistakes he had seen, and after compiling enough evidence, he informed the museum authorities of his findings. It became his first brush with scholarly injustice. The museum director arranged to have Dwight's research sent to the museum's committee of experts, who made the proper adjustment to the defective presentations. After closing the museum to accomplish all the changes, the director organized a big reopening to publicly unveil the modifications applied by their committee, naming and thanking a long list of the specialized workers that helped them to realize this project in such a short time. He intentionnally omitted Dwight's contribution, worried the presence of a teenager on the committee would diminish the museum's reputation. The museum director knew that if Dwight came forward to denounce his absence from the list of contributors, nobody would believe the claim of a teenager. Dwight felt foolish after the

speech of the museum director, realizing that all that
man had said to him was a lie. The director had asked
him for all his research so the museum could create a
dossier accessible to all, giving visitors access to the extra
information he brought in. He told him his approach
could even be used in the future to analyze artifacts
and create a more precise past for our ancestors, letting
him believe that he would be part of the process in the
future. Dwight had handed his work over, his chest
swelling with pride, without keeping a copy at home.
But the museum committee erased Dwight's name
from the research, not wanting to be called out on the
fact that a high school student found some errors in
their presentations. As much as Dwight had tried to
contact the director, it soon became apparent that he
would never receive credit for his work. While he was
still reeling from the injustice suffered at the hand
of the museum, he got an F at school for allegedly
committing plagiary in his schoolwork. It happened
in history class for an assignment on the history of an
ancient society to be picked by the students themselves.
Dwight had done an extensive study of the Celts from
their origin to their conversion to Christianity around
the fifth century. His teacher did not believe a high
school student could come up with such a complete
assignment and refused to acknowledge the work as
Dwight's. Even if his teacher was not able to cite any
exact text from which Dwight had plagiarized, his F
remained. What hurt him the most was that his parents
sided with the school. After that day, his mother asked
to see every assignment Dwight had to do for school so
she could verify there was no more plagiarism. The rest
of his school year was pretty much a wash as Dwight
descended into depression, turning in weak reports so
he wouldn't be accused of copying any more. His grades

slipped enough for him to be forced into summer classes if he wanted to graduate to the next level.

• • •

That is where he first met Engella Iblis. They were fifteen in his summer class, so Dwight thought that he could hide in the group and slide by unnoticed. The teacher was a young woman who was hired by the school to survey the class and make sure the students behaved—nothing more. Even though she was there to keep an eye on them while they were doing the imposed schoolwork to pass the class, Engella took Dwight under her wing right from the beginning and didn't let him close himself off for the duration of the classes. For Dwight, even though he was taken aback at first, it seemed as if they knew each other since forever. The warmth he felt when he was around her had melted away all the doubts he had created in his mind before entering the classes. In four weeks, she reignited his passion for knowledge. With the love and support she displayed, he took in the lessons of the past year as a warning to be more alert as to who he can trust. Engella had shown him that some confidence could be attributed to someone, but that trust must never be given for no good reason. She had made it clear from the start that she believed in him, and that faith was enough for Dwight to open up to her. He shared his deepest fears as well as his highest hopes, like he never had before to anyone in his life, discovering in Engella the support he never had with his family. When he told her how much he hated being around people, but that at the same time he didn't like the feeling of being alone, she listened, doing nothing more than guiding him to his own conclusions with no judgment and plenty of loving tenderness. That relationship had a profound impact on his life in those short four weeks, changing something in him on a primal level.

That summer propelled Dwight to become one of the most renown anthropologists in the world. While he was still working through his bachelor's degree, the assignments he turned in were so detailed they attracted the attention of museums all over the world. They came to him asking for his insight on unidentifiable archaeological discoveries, hoping he could shed light on the true origins of those artifacts and understand what they were holding. He had found solace in the recognition he was receiving, although it didn't properly meet his ego's needs, the underlying childhood anger still festering within him.

At that point, he was living his life in a blind frenzy, blazing his way through university, going from project to project, ignoring any sign that he was becoming more isolated, as he limited his interactions with others to a professional rapport. He finished his bachelor's degree a year in advance and then effortlessly completed his master's degree. The university offered him a tenure position right away, not wanting to lose him and his fame to another school. Dwight was oblivious to the university's motivation to retain his services and continue to profit from his research. But even if he had known, he wouldn't have cared. As long as he could pursue his research without being bothered, he was a happy man. But the lack of intimate human contact took its toll over time. Dwight dealt with the pressure the isolation caused on his psyche by barhopping in search of any and every girl who accepted his invitation to spend the night with him. Feeling warm skin on his own a couple of times a month was sufficient to keep him going for a time. The simulation of intimacy it produced was enough and gave Dwight a sense of purpose to his existence, where he could imagine he was leading a normal life.

He felt those rare encounters as a balm on his usually solitary life, as every night he had with a sexual partner carried the secret hope it would evolve to something more. It invariably ended in deception and caused Dwight to create a sociopathic view of relationships, his heart having bled dry. It drove Dwight to slip further and further into a deep psychic hole, his isolation bringing on some paranoia as he saw every colleague as a potential adversary who could at any moment steal some of his research and use it for their own gain. Regardless of his way of life, he was established as *the* world leader in anthropology, and he was steadfast in maintaining that title; it represented the one thing that was his alone.

● ● ●

The air was getting cooler in the park, which brought Dwight's mind back to the present moment. He tried to remember what he could have missed during his previous encounters with Frank, going through every detail of their meetings. Cutler had approached Dwight at first with empty promises and verbal contracts, unaware Dwight's paranoia would cancel any attempt at striking up a new friendship. After the failure of his first endeavor to convince Dwight, every following effort to communicate by Dr. Cutler was limited to phone or email, keeping his interactions simple, seemingly not wanting to spook Dwight. That told Dwight that Cutler desperately needed his research for some project, but he didn't understand the implications before today. For a time, the communications stopped, and during that time, Dwight met Sofia, unaware she was a hypnotized agent working for Dr. Cutler. She was to seduce Dwight and let him believe they started a relationship. Her end goal was to steal the anthropological research and bring it to Dr. Cutler. Except things didn't work out as planned for Dr. Cutler. When they were out on their second date, Dwight and the hypnotized woman crossed paths with Engella Iblis. Dwight distinctly remembered that the moment he saw her, everything else went out of focus as he worked at finding a way to evade his date and join Engella. He could remember how Engella's presence made him suddenly wary of the woman he was with. She was loving and affectionate, but it seemed forced. He chose the restroom as his escape route since it had two separate doors. He stayed in the restroom for a couple of minutes, and after cautiously making sure his date was waiting at one door, he exited the other to look for Engella.

Dwight would never see Sofia again. But at that moment, it was the last thing on his mind. As he left the club they had entered, he saw Engella waiting nearby, waving him over as he excitedly accepted her request. He ran to her, the high-strung high school kid he once was taking over his mind. As he reached her, he didn't know what to say and gave her an empty-headed stare. She smiled. A broad, authentic smile that warmed Dwight's soul, flashes of summer school racing through his mind. He stood before her in silence, admiring her commanding presence, amazed that she was now more beautiful than she was during the summer classes. She reached out for him to take her hand. As soon as they touched, Dwight was shocked by a surge of energy beyond anything he could ever imagine. It felt like a lightning bolt traveling from his fingertips through to his toes. He was petrified in place, Engella still smiling as she stood there. Dwight felt her energy reach every cell of his body and then burst into an uncontrollable combination of tears and laughter, shaking. He slumped to the ground, unable to stand, and Engella let go.

"I'm sorry," Engella said "I didn't expect you to react this way." Dwight was starting to regain some composure as he sat, attempting to understand what had happened. "A lot has taken place since we last met, I'm not sure where to start, so why don't you tell me what you've been up to?"

Dwight was too busy regaining control over his mind to notice she had asked him a question. She saw his mind was still clouded and continued, feeling he was somehow ashamed of something. "You don't have to worry about my approval. If our lives are crossing now, it's probably because its necessary and part of both our evolution."

Dwight snapped back into consciousness. "Evolution, huh? Funny; you're the second person to talk to me about that. I suppose you'll say you hold some sort of key to the future?" He suddenly felt angry, disappointed. The one person he had trusted in his life was now spouting the same kind of nonsense Frank had presented to him. "Because let me tell you, I'm not someone to join a cause because someone tells me it's the way to go."

"That's why I love you," Engella said, dissipating Dwight's disappointment in an instant. "Thing is, there isn't one single answer, but I can guide you to recognize the energy around us if you're interested."

A handful of people had told Dwight they loved him, but this was the first time he felt it. He didn't know what to do with this feeling, his heart wanting to pound right out of his chest. Unable to utter a single word, he leaned in to hug her and started to cry again, years of anger and isolation pouring out with his tears. She accepted the hug and stroked his hair, not saying a word. It lasted for a good fifteen minutes, passers-by not noticing them as they isolated themselves from the world in their embrace. As Engella felt Dwight calming down, she began to loosen her hug, pulling back a little to encourage Dwight to do the same. She decided at that moment he was someone she should introduce to Rafael someday.

"You know," Engella said. "When the summer class we did was over, I knew we would meet again. Your presence here, at this point in my life, along with your reaction to our meeting, is a confirmation for me that I'm on the right path. As for you, I can help you find the reason for our reunion, but you alone can decide the direction you want to go with this." She looked at him affectionately. "Your insecurity towards others can be your saving grace at times but keep your eyes open. There are some genuine people out there, and you could miss them."

Since he started his studies in anthropology, and even before that, Dwight's goal had always been to make sense of the past so that we may advance into the future with confidence. Even if he had become somewhat of a hermit since entering university, his faith in humanity was somehow intact, and he hoped his research would help humans understand the past more clearly. In the last year or so, he had lost that confidence, surrounded by wannabe scientists and researchers who only wanted his fame to rub off on them. His chance meeting with Engella that night reignited that old feeling.

When he entered university and began to trace out humanity's anthropological map, he genuinely thought he was helping humans evolve through his research, at least on a social scale. To some extent, he thought he had become capable of predicting what physical evolution we could expect as humans based on the tools we use, the beliefs we adopt, and the social constructs we create. He opened his mind to the fact that it wasn't a coincidence that two people had approached him in a short period to propose solutions to humanity's evolution. It created a break in his mind that incited him to begin a more personal research, a journey that could enlighten his choice. He would leave the university. Still ensconced in Engella's arms, Dwight was triggered to get up when he saw two strollers walking by, looking at them, dusting off imaginary particles as he clamored to his feet.

"I've got to think about it," he bluntly told Engella, a distant feeling of paranoia returning to the pit of his stomach, which he hated.

"I understand," Engella said, also getting up. "Should we meet again, I'm sure it will be for the right reasons." She then turned and left, leaving Dwight to his own devices without another word.

"Wait! Shouldn't we exchange phone numbers or something?"

"No need. If we have to meet, it will happen." She walked away gracefully, Dwight's mind spinning, not sure he could regain control at this point.

He watched Engella disappear into the dark alleyway. He was wedged in place, unable to put one foot in front of the other, unable to adhere to a coherent thought, his brain concentrated on keeping his vital functions in order. He knew that night had brought on a new chapter in his life, but he didn't know how to begin the exploration of the new reality. The coolness of the evening helped Dwight with his recovery as he saw his date exit the club, looking for him, causing Dwight to disappear. He gathered himself and headed home using dark alleyways to stay out of sight. He decided to sleep on his decision and let the morning tell him what he must do.

The next morning, Dwight made sure he was nowhere to be found. Before disappearing, he sent a message to Frank Cutler, telling him he would send him the work as it progressed but would be unavailable for some time. He told his neighbor he would be gone for a while, telling him he had a big project to embark upon and would not be home for a few months. The owner of the grocery store that was on the first floor of the building was the last person Dwight spoke to in person before he disappeared. He left no forwarding address and no phone number. That morning, Dwight had decided to work both sides, for now, not yet certain of the outcome on either side. He woke up with a need to find the answers on his own, packed a light bag and left, not knowing where he was headed.

CHAPTER 9

Zorina Smith was meditating in her room when her friend walked in, grunting to signify his presence as he entered the room. She took this as a challenge on her concentration and remained focused on her meditation, ignoring his presence. He smiled and sat in front of her, settling as comfortably as he could, ready to wait. Zorina stayed true to her mantra for the next two hours, at first, voluntarily ignoring, then forgetting about her friend in the room. As she emerged from her meditative state, she was surprised to see him waiting there.

"We need to advance the plan," he said. "We need you to attend some speed dating evenings to recruit more potential supporters." His face was serious, even angry.

Zorina had never seen her friend in this state and it disconcerted her a little. The serenity meditation usually gave her had already been swept aside by the urgent energy she felt coming from her friend. She was part of a small group that called themselves the collective unconscious allegiance—a loosely affiliated group of mystical and scientific researchers who are dedicated to finding a peaceful path for humanity to follow. Their work was a multi-disciplinary quest, as they search for ways to use the psycho-electric energy that surrounds us to help humanity reach its full potential. The group was focused on developing the philosophy and practices that would carry humanity to a more elevated state. The logic behind their research was to cut off the dark aspects of our existence, our souls, by adopting a lifestyle devoted entirely to the light, or in other words, all that is good. They rationalized that if humans are devoted to searching for the light, the darkness that clouds our souls will no longer have a foothold on our consciousness, bringing humanity to an era of peace and pure bliss. They believed they could wipe out the notion of war, of consumerism, of greed; they believed they could erase the feeling of emptiness that plagues most people; they believed they held the ultimate truth that would bring on an era of equality, of growth of the soul that would guarantee a brighter future for all. This belief had become a conviction over time, causing them to lose sight of a bigger picture—distorting their knowledge as they committed the ultimate crime of forcing their research to fit their theories.

Each meditation was a source of great understanding for Zorina, although she was never able to define what the insight was the moment she awakened from it. On any other occasion, she would let her mind wander freely after a session, letting the insight she experienced settle in her subconscious. But this time, she felt pressured to speed up her process; there was an emergency. She was a recruiter for the group. Her special gift was her extreme sensitivity to other people's receptiveness to outside energies. What she liked to call her blessing, helped her weed out those who have closed themselves off from the outside world. Through mental and emotional limitations, some people made it impossible for anyone to get close. Zorina would eliminate them as candidates, as too much time would be dedicated to breaking down their internal walls. The immediate needs of the allegiance had to be centered on candidates who were open to the energies that govern our lives, which Zorina was able to identify. The quickest way she had found to try to assess as many people as possible was attending speed dating soirees. Most people made a conscious effort to be a little more vulnerable during those evenings, which made Zorina's work that much easier.

"How bad is it?" She asked her friend.

"The initiative has recruited more soldiers. We're more in danger than we've ever been."

His look was sullen, defeated, but Zorina refused to think the allegiance had reached their end. She left her friend in the room and got dressed to go on her recruiting run. Heading to the bar where the speed dating event was taking place, Zorina couldn't shake a murky feeling of dread that was anchored in the pit of her stomach. She was nervous by nature, but this feeling carried threads of reality with it. As she reached the bar, she noticed two men next to a dark-colored car looking in her direction. She ducked behind parked cars to avoid being seen, slipping into the bar as discretely as possible. Once inside, she peeked out of a window to confirm what she saw. The two men's eyes were red, a light glow emanating from their eye sockets accentuated by the dark bags that gave their faces a tired, stressed look. Zorina observed the people crossing their path and saw that no one else noticed their eyes, ignoring them as they walked by. She decided to continue her evening and would later inform the group of what she saw. This is probably part of the reason why her friend was so tense. If the dark matter initiative had found how to control people, the time had come to step up the allegiance's agenda and start recruiting people who can fight back.

Zorina settled at a table and waited for the bell to so she could start the interviews. The bar was decorated with valentine-like decorations. Red hearts of varying sizes hung from the ceiling, and red flowers adorned each table, the contrast accentuated by the white linen cloths covering the tables. Some syrupy R&B served as background music, which did nothing but emphasized the decadent atmosphere. The participants would have five minutes to connect with the person in front of them, after which a bell would ring, prompting everyone to change tables and start another five minutes with someone else. One after the other, she encountered dull, empty men uniquely focused on scoring a one-night stand, checking her out the same way you choose a piece of meat at the grocery store. The energy they exuded was nothing but a nebulous and thick cloud of perfume and pheromones. As she moved through the tables, becoming worried she wouldn't even find one person that night, she noticed a man at the next table. His energy was calm, and he seemed out of place, which was a good thing Zorina thought.

"Perfect." She muttered to herself. The guy in front of her arrogantly puffed his chest.

"Glad you like it." He said, dusting imaginary crumbs off his chest, making his pectorals dance.

"What?" Zorina looked at him strut in his seat and wondered if it was worth it to help these people in the end. She decided to ignore him and observed the man at the next table, waiting for the bell to signal the switch, eager to get away from this sexual shark. Making it clear to her current partner she was ignoring him, Zorina leaned in to listen to the conversation at the next table.

"Christopher Saddleton is my name. I love oranges, cats, summer storms, and movies that move me." Christopher said. He noticed the woman at the next table had leaned in to listen, which made him uncomfortable, but he pushed on.

God, this speed dating shit is wrong, Chris thought to himself, every part of him screaming to bolt out the door. His mind was boiling in disbelief before such utter stupidity. But he had a thousand dollar bet riding on this soiree that he couldn't find a date outside the comfortable surroundings of his corner bar. More important than the money, he didn't want his friends to be right.

"I'm Cindy Travers. I love romance, surprises, plush toys, and the occasional trip to the islands; any island. How old are you, Christopher? And do you exercise?" She looked at him, trying to decide if he was buff enough for her to commit.

"Wow! Right to the point, huh? Well, I'm twenty-eight years old, and I stay in shape, playing hockey and training at home on occasion. How about you, Cindy? How old are you?" Christopher thought he could instill a sliver of common sense by throwing the question back at her.

"Oh! But my age is irrelevant; I'm whatever age you need me to be," she said with a coy smile, twirling a strand of hair in her fingers.

This is ridiculous. I won't survive the evening, and it's gonna cost me a grand on top of it, he thought to himself. Christopher looked at the giant clock on the wall, grandmaster of each minute, and decided to wait the last fifteen seconds he had with Cindy in silence. She looked at him, a little perplexed but not surprised, and waited with him. She didn't mind, anyway. He was too lanky for her. She liked shorter men. When the bell rang from the mighty clock, every guy was to move one table to the left, and each girl, one table forward. The organizers said this maintained a randomness necessary to the success of the evening. Christopher did as was required and sat down in front of an enigmatic, brown-haired girl, the one who leaned in to listen to his conversation, who had defied the rules and slid one table sideways, pushing away the next candidate with a mean glare. The rebel's eyes were clear, brown, a slight almond shape giving them a permanent smile. But there was also a profound determination in them that Christopher found deeply attractive. He was convinced she would be able to stare down a cat with such intensity. She had symmetrical features, each one both beautiful and strong, making him wonder what she was doing here. Christopher felt a wave of excitement as he found someone he wanted to get to know. He was worried he didn't groom enough before coming here, wondered if he was in a good angle for the lighting, then laughed at himself, trying to calm himself down. He chased the weirdness away and started his little introduction speech, except this time, he was nervous. Zorina had noticed he stiffened up at her sight and gave him a soft, calm smile to try and help him calm down.

"Christopher Saddleton is my name. I love oranges, cats, summer storms, and movies that move me." Then added, "and I'm twenty-eight years old, and I like to play hockey." He squirmed in his seat, feeling like a twelve-year-old kid in a basement party trying to ask a cute girl to dance.

She looked at Chris, at first with a fierce determination, seeming to scan him. Within seconds, she relaxed and smiled, which blew him away. A glow radiated from her as her face lit up, her eyes turning to lasers as she pierced Christopher's facade, digging deep into his soul. Already thirty seconds had passed.

"Hello Christopher Saddleton, will you help me?" Although she was asking a question, she spoke it in a neutral tone, apparently certain of his answer.

"Sure . . . but how?" Christopher felt he was losing control of his movements, Zorina's eyes penetrating every thought in his mind.

She lowered her eyes and took Christopher's hand, and as soon as their fingers touched, he felt a jolt of energy travel through his body, and as her grip tightened, her pupils had dilated, obscuring any trace of brown. When their eyes locked once again, she hypnotized him almost instantly, her gaze entering his mind and freezing his brain entirely. It felt as though he could carry out basic functions like breathing, but somehow, he became but a visitor in himself, the body acting upon some other force that overwhelmed his consciousness.

"Don't worry. I won't hurt you," she said soothingly, aware that Chris could hear her but could do nothing about it, and they got up to walk out together.

What she didn't prepare for was the fact that when two people get up to leave together, it sets off a "victory bell," and three spotlights turn to the new lovebirds as they exit. Everyone started clapping, raising the anticipation level in the room as everyone now expected to find a mate. As she guided him toward the exit, she kept whispering in his ear, "one foot in front of the other, take your time." When they reached the door, his arm began waving to the people in the bar on her simple command, "wave." They walked out together, hand in hand, and Chris couldn't celebrate the fact that he saw his two friends, who were staking the place out to see if he could get a date. Then, there he was, the winner of the bet, one thousand dollars each, unable to celebrate.

She guided him to her car, sat him down delicately on the passenger side with a simple "sit" command, then got in herself. Before starting the car, Zorina took his face with both of her hands and kissed him. Chris felt his mind rushing back into its place during the kiss. Re-entering his body created confusion in his mind, much like the way he feels when he awakens from a dream that was too real, too palpable.

"My name is Zorina Smith. You may not understand what happened, but please understand that you are in no danger for the moment." She caressed his face with the back of her hand as she spoke. The calming sensation was instant and complete.

"What do you mean, for the moment?" Christopher was relieved to feel his mind was coming back, and he was asking the right questions.

"I mean that if I'm right, you are the right one for the job, and no harm will come upon us."

Her face then became serious as she looked into her rear-view mirror. It seemed to Christopher that she was on the verge of panicking as she clumsily put the car in gear. She released the clutch, jumping and bouncing out of the parking space, apparently not used to stick-shift cars. They bounced along until she got to the third gear. This time, she managed to let go of the clutch with ease, and they smoothly gained more speed. As Christopher gathered his thoughts, he peeked back and caught a glimpse of two guys getting in a car, their eyes fixed on the car Zorina was driving.

"What if I'm not the right one for the job, as you say?" Christopher asked, not sure he wanted an answer.

"I think you already know the answer to that," she said, keeping her eyes on the road as she spoke, both hands firmly on the steering wheel.

"Well then, for the sake of both of us, I think there are two guys following us in a blue sedan."

"I know," she said, accelerating.

She searched for the car in her rear-view mirror, hoping she had already lost them. The headlights following them were still visible, and she let out a deep, guttural "fuck!" She then stepped on the gas, the car rolling dangerously as she turned the corner almost on two wheels. Looking at Christopher, she knew his mind was reeling. He couldn't stop looking into the rear views and shooting panicked glances toward the rear. Then suddenly he calmed down. This excited Zorina, who was relieved she had chosen the right person. The two red-eyed men were gaining on them. Zorina was too busy fighting the manual clutch to keep up her momentum. But as the men got closer, Chris wanted them to catch up, hoping for a fight.

"Slow down." He said.

He wanted to come face to face with them, although her stress level was telling him it wouldn't be a friendly game of rock, paper, and scissors. He needed this for some reason.

"Go into the next alley," he told Zorina. She looked at him and saw in his eyes that everything would be fine. She knew Chris was in complete control, his mind clear, his muscles tensed up.

She swerved into a wide alley that went into a small yard, a single, dirty light bulb generating a dim light on the dark, moonless night. She stopped the car in the shadow created by a large garbage dumpster.

"I believe you know what you must do," she said, caressing his cheek as she spoke. "I can feel your deep-seated need to confront these men, as I know you feel in your soul. Don't be afraid to let it flow through your veins; it's the only way you can win."

Christopher said nothing and got out of the car when he heard their vehicle entering the yard, almost crawling, their headlights out. He stepped into the light, and at once, they stopped their car and got out. They began to approach him, and he noticed what had grabbed his attention earlier; their eyes were red, like the ones you see on a Polaroid picture. On any other occasion, he felt certain he would've freaked out and ran, but there he stood, feeling utterly calm, almost serene. He then slipped back into the shadow to attract the men toward him, happy to have worn black to this "soiree." A smile appeared on his face as the two men split up, satisfied they took the bait. Each man went around either side of the dumpster. *Perfect*, Christopher thought as he squatted, ready to pounce. The first one decided to look inside the dumpster, giving Christopher the occasion to flip the heavy steel top, crushing his head on the side. The crunch of the red-eyed person's skull breaking reminded Christopher of the sound a potato chip makes when you bite down on it. As the body slumped into a heap, no longer receiving commands from its brain, it hung from the side of the dumpster, only hanging from the skin. The other one leaped from the back of the dumpster, and all Christopher had to do was punch him straight in the throat as he turned to face the man. The agent fell, gasping for air, and Christopher then grabbed a brick lying nearby on the ground and with no remorse, crushed his skull with three swift cracks at the back of his head. The third shot buried the corner of the brick into his skull, and the guy stopped moving. Almost instantly, Chris started shaking violently, realizing what he had done. Zorina came to him and wrapped her arms around him, soothing Christopher with her voice in his ears. "Breathe. It's over. Breathe." She repeated this over and over until he stopped trembling. She helped him up and sat him back in the car. As she drove away, there were no hiccups with the clutch this time. Christopher fell asleep almost instantly after catching his breath as she drove him away to a new life.

• • •

When Christopher awoke, he was in a small, well-lit room in a single bed with white sheets. The sun was starting to hit his face, which is what woke him in the first place, and he laid there, trying to remember what had happened the night before. Zorina went into the room, at first peeking to see if Christopher was awake and entering when she saw his eyes wide open. She sat on the side of the bed, looking at him with what he saw as deep affection, her hand caressing his chest through the sheets.

"I knew you had the capacity," she said.

"Capacity?" His throat was dry as sand.

"Yes, capacity. You see, we are surrounded by energies that are far beyond our realm of comprehension, that are available for anyone to use and channel. The calmness you felt come over you yesterday was a small part of it. We are a group dedicated to bringing this realization to humanity, except we are under siege from another group dedicated to controlling the people to serve their own greedy needs. They've always had the advantage in numbers, but now they produce the people like the two men we saw last night. Did you see their eyes?"

"I did." He remembered how seeing their eyes had strengthened his resolve. "What are they? Robots?" His voice was rasp from his dry throat.

Zorina went to get him a fresh glass of water that Christopher downed in one swig, feeling the water rush down his throat to his thirsty body. As he thanked her for the water, Zorina continued.

"They aren't robots. They're soldiers from another group, opposed to ours. We're not sure how it's done, but men like those we saw last night have begun to appear lately, and it's worrisome for us. We think they're programmed somehow, probably by hypnosis, and their unique goal is eliminating our group from existence. The fact you saw their eyes means you have the capacity to see and feel the infinite energy of the universe, which tells me I made the right choice last night."

"And what group might you be in, my dear?" Christopher tried to look disinterested, forcing himself to keep a certain distance from the outlandish theory she was exposing. "I mean, you say they program people, but last night didn't you use some sort of programming on me?" Zorina remained stolid as Christopher continued. "You didn't try to stop me killing these men, and if anything, you encouraged me to do it. Here we are the next morning, and for some reason, I feel normal, no trauma, no remorse. Although I killed two men last night, every ounce of my body and soul was telling me I was doing it for the betterment of mankind. How's this not programming?" Christopher's anger rose in him as he spoke, now determined to get some answers before finding a way out of here.

"I am part of the Collective Unconscious Allegiance, and our duty, at this time, is to protect the collective unconscious from decimation by the forces that have governed our world for too long. These forces want to pull people as far away from their true nature as possible to control society's decision-making process. But if everything goes as planned on our end, we can reconnect with the universe. Then we, as humans, will regain contact with the earth's energy core, which will obliterate the darkness that pollutes our souls and liberate the light. If they retain control over the choices we make, nothing will change, and the earth will surely erase us from existence in order to survive."

"When you put me in the trance so you could control my movements for us to leave the speed date thing, you were using the surrounding forces, is that it? Because, you know, had you asked, I probably would've said yes."

Christopher was seething, his face was stern, showing his deep hurt he felt to be used as a pawn the way he was. The methods used by the other group that she was belittling were the same as the ones she used on him at the bar. Except she had been completely honest up to this point, so he decided to listen to her a little more before deciding if he would stay or not.

"Probably can't be an alternative in a situation like this one, and I'm sorry if it scared you. But I had to try it to see if you were sensitive to the energies, and the quickest way for me to find out was to hypnotize you, sort of. Just so you know, had you not been sensitive enough, a part of you would've instinctively fought the energy displacement, and you wouldn't have been able to follow me as easily. Worst case, you would have looked too drunk to others, and I would've accompanied you out before letting you go home."

"But that's not what happened," Christopher said, racking his brain to find something coherent he could adhere to, still trying to understand.

Zorina then proceeded to explain that the group's theory and philosophy are based on Carl Gustav Jung's research into the collective unconscious. What happened to Christopher the night before pertained to Carl Jung's relationship with Wolfgang Pauli, a physicist with whom Jung discovered that the energy surrounding us was nothing more than matter waiting to react. They had kept the results of their findings secret, fearing a serious backlash from the scientific community because of the mystical component in the theory. But they did reach out to some colleagues to discuss the theory's validity. A small group of scientists corresponded on the subject until a consensus was reached on the inapplicable nature of this theory. It had no real scientific value, albeit an elegant mathematical formula. The correspondence diminished until it died out, Carl Jung and Wolfgang Pauli, the only two remaining believers in the theory earth is wrapped up in a psycho-energetic energy field. Even they gradually drifted away from this research, as other more interesting scientific endeavors beckoned them. Parts of this research were uncovered by the founding members of the Collective Unconscious Allegiance, and that's why May '68 in Paris or Woodstock in '69 happened. Two men and one woman, all former students of Jung, pooled their knowledge with two theoretical physicists and managed to create a wave of peace that they sent through the earth's energy-mass by way of profound meditation, which caused a wave of synchronistic events to occur to a large mass of people at one time, leading to what now people call the "hippie era."

"What the hell do you mean by that?" Christopher asked, almost screaming. But Zorina didn't react and continued.

"Things should've gotten better from that point. Today, we should be collectively at a new level of consciousness, but something was missing for the transformation to be permanent, and that's what the Collective Unconscious Allegiance has been working on ever since." She then fell silent, her gaze cast on the floor.

As outlandish as the story was, Christopher couldn't stay mad at Zorina. Everything about her told him she believed what she was saying, although a big part of him was still very wary of her explanation. He was curious to see where this was going, so he spurred her on. "What's the latest on the research?" Christopher ventured, feeling his anger was turning into curiosity.

She didn't answer right away, and he didn't push for a quick response. Zorina sat on the edge of the bed, her eyes filling tears. "One of the men in the group turned on the others after meeting with a person who showed this man how the energy could be used to manipulate masses to their own personal advantage. He left with the research, leaving the others with nothing. We now know this person was a member of a group called the dark matter initiative, and they have been one step ahead of us ever since. All we've managed since then is to regain the level of knowledge we had when this happened."

She fell silent once more, her gaze transfixed on an empty spot on the wall. Christopher desperately wanted to ask a slew of questions, as he raised his hand. Zorina ignored it and continued her history lesson, her voice beginning to break up.

"In the last months, the allegiance had to split up and go work underground, because the dark matter initiative began to relentlessly pursue our members with the soldiers you saw last night, bent on eliminating the group."

"Why dark matter initiative? Where does dark matter come into play? And why the Collective Unconscious Allegiance? I feel we're in the middle of some sort of dungeons and dragons' game and I'm not sure where I fit in." Christopher's face turned red, showing his his anger rise to his throat once more. He got up to get his jacket and leave.

She looked at him with stern eyes but didn't stop him from grabbing his coat. She tried to answer Christopher's question. "We think they control every aspect of scientific research, but regardless, names are meaningless, they are nothing, words reunited to form an image, create an existence. If we do not name them, they don't exist, which would create more chaos. I need you to listen, so you can understand what I'm trying to explain." Her tone had changed to that of an angry parent as she looked at him with her mouth pinched, and her cheeks flushed.

"I am listening." Christopher said with a firm tone. "And if I understand correctly, you have been hiding as a nameless group with a name, but now they've gotten your scent, you're in trouble, and you need soldiers." Christopher was sitting next to Zorina, his gaze fixed on hers, challenging her to contradict what he said.

She eased a little, traces of a smile returning to her face. "You're perceptive, that's good. Yes, we need soldiers. The group had never thought about the need for defensive tools since we have always strived for peace. We experimented through meditative sleep, trying to use the Neutrinos crossing the earth's path to carry the astral body in the ethereal realm. Thing is, the initiative was informed of our experimentations. Since then, they've launched an all-out attack on us in the physical reality and have eliminated at least half of our people. Some are dead, some have seen their minds broken beyond repair, reduced to being psychiatric cases wandering the streets, homeless. Most of this was accomplished by traditional means, like causing accidents or programming assassinations, but now they seem to have new agents who can track and follow someone."

"Okay." Christopher said in a raspy voice his throat dried up again as she described the two men from the night before. "And now, today, what's the situation like?" He asked, feeling he had been pulled into something he couldn't escape.

She looked like a doctor trying to find a way to tell his patient he has a month to live. "I'm sure about you and me and my friend, that's all. I don't know if any others are still alive. But I would guess we have about ten or fifteen people left."

His jaw dropped. "And they are how many?"

"Hundreds, if not thousands," she said without hesitation. "But much weaker. One of us is worth a hundred of them," she added, hoping to ease the tension. "Look at what happened last night."

Chris remained flabbergasted, unable to speak. She pushed on.

"The thing you must understand is that their beacon is darkness and hatred, and like the two you killed earlier, they are predictable."

"Kind of like zombies," Christopher thought out loud. "But what about the state you put me in last night. Can I call on it any time? Is it something I need to conjure?"

"You're sensitive. You saw their eyes. If the need arises, you will know what to do. Your conduit is open now."

"How will I recognize the situation?"

"You'll know."

Christopher could tell that was the end of that conversation and kept silent. He was busy trying to understand how his life could have changed so much in such a short time, knowing there was no going back to his old life. Zorina reached into her bag, pulling out a leather-bound book with nothing on the cover, but it looked old and worn.

"Here, read this." She gave him the book and then pushed him aside to lay in the bed, seemingly falling asleep almost instantly, her breathing becoming slow and deep in seconds.

He started reading, not sure of what he was about to find.

CHAPTER 10

Frank Cutler walked into the office building with his heart pounding out of his chest. He was there to present his final plan to a group of representatives for the dark matter initiative, including envoys from the major religions who were invited at Frank's insistence. He was convinced his plan would work but persuading the initiative members to loosen their purse strings, each one among the wealthiest people on earth, is always touchy. Frank was aware his plan could be regarded as complete nonsense, although he had left their first meeting with a good feeling, which helped boost his confidence. Adding the religious leaders to the fray was a risk, but a necessary one. He believed his documentation would be enough to incite enough interest for the project to move ahead, but he needed to stay alert. His hypnosis experimentation alone could justify a hefty budget, which, for some reason, gave him even more confidence as he prepared to face his ultimate test. If they refuse, his project would be dead in the water, with his reputation on the line, and possibly his life.

The members of the dark matter initiative didn't like having people walking around with knowledge that could impede their plans, so Dr. Cutler needed to make sure he convinced them on that day. He exited the elevator at the top floor of the building, the doors opening to an open office space with floor to ceiling tinted windows covering the back wall. Frank walked up to a large, oval, cream-colored table. He was alone on one side, with eight people looking at him on the other, their faces hidden by the shadow they cast as the sunlight pierced through the windows, creating the dark silhouette. But Frank could still make out their eyes, that looked like dark cavities but carried a glimmer. The rest of their faces were out of focus, which made him cringe a little as he pulled out his documents and spread them in front of him. It appeared as though their eyes were powered by some unseen force, making them glow somehow. Frank pushed away that thought and settled in the middle seat as he passed along a copy of his plan to each person before him. He plugged in his computer to project some visual aids during the presentation and then chose to stand, feeling he could control his nerves a little better this way.

"If you're ready, I will begin the final presentation for the project I submitted that will prove without a doubt that the future of humanity is in our hands. With this presentation, I will prove we have the tools to usher in a new era, where business opportunities can be created, planned, and executed with almost no risk. We can create a world where spiritual guidance can be coordinated and organized to a degree never realized by any religious group. If you have any questions during the presentation, please keep them for the end. There could be an answer to your question along the way."

Frank settled in the middle seat of the table, still working at keeping his nerves in check. The eight people in front of him had yet to move, their motionless, glowing stares burning through Frank. He cleared his throat and began to read.

"This document will prove the necessity we have to seize the opportunity to regain full control over humanity. My research has unveiled elements that can show us how to use a previously untapped energy present in every human in ways that will help us keep and even solidify our control over the population. By extension, we then also control the resources bestowed by the earth for our profit alone and have the power to dictate the people's spiritual leanings. In the plan that will divulge in the following pages, I will try to explain what this energy is and how we can use it. I requested this meeting before you finished your analysis because I believe we are in a vulnerable position, as knowledge about the information contained in the document is spreading. I believe it's our duty to make sure we are the guardians of this power by overseeing all research related to this. If not, the next human evolution could exclude the initiative."

The other men at the table squirmed in their seats at this last comment.

"But should we manage to meet this goal, we will be able to preserve our position at the top of the hierarchy created at the beginning of this century." Frank cleared his throat before continuing. "I believe the solution is contained in our DNA. During my research, I have bared witness to a disturbing new reality that could explain our evolutionary motivations. The missing link. This link is the key for us to be able to impose a stranglehold on the aspect that dictates everyday life, be it social, political, or religious."

Frank looked at the men across the table, unable to read their reaction, making him cringe a little. He continued, still unsure of the outcome of the meeting, but trying to keep a steady tone in his voice to hide his nerves.

"It's imperative that we keep this information confined to the people present in the room until we are ready to activate the project. I believe you understand this is a sensitive matter, and should this news leak out to the public, there's no way for us to predict what the reaction would be. We must make sure we have the population's confidence before going ahead with the project. A concerted effort will need to be accomplished by each one of us to work together to carry out this monumental task. I've been informed of certain fringe elements of your organization that have gone rogue since our last meeting, leaking information and sabotaging projects in the name of humanity. With this new knowledge, we will be able to reign them in and reprogram them. They can become our first official test subjects, and you will see how potent this discovery can be."

As he spoke, Frank noticed that the group was leaning in, undoubtedly interested in his suggestion to reign in fringe elements. It gave Frank a substantial boost in confidence, and he continued, his resolution now stronger than ever as he stood once more.

"I plead to you to read this document diligently, as it's the basic architecture for our new evolution as leaders of humanity. Like many times in the recent past, the initiative must adapt to stay at the top of the food chain. The initiative is led by the group who organized the modern political system that tricked people into thinking they were making a real choice, calling

it democracy and thus maintained a hold on authority over the people for decades. In more recent times,
when the people started to ask for more money in their
pockets, a debt-filled world was created, producing an
illusion of richness, forcing the people to do what we
told them if they wanted to be able to maintain the
level of comfort they had grown accustomed to. This
system has held up until today, and now we are at a
new threshold as people believe they are becoming
aware of their mystical selves. Except this time, we
are the ones wielding a weapon, not the people. So far,
your control over the masses has been maintained by
using psychological and neuro-scientific knowledge to
keep social unrest at a minimum. But this method has
proven to be onerous, as fringe elements resistant to
the influence constantly create more chaos. With the
weapon I'm proposing, we can now gain control over
a person's innermost instinctual necessities and guide
them according to our needs. By way of a rather simple
procedure, we can dictate a person's deepest wish and
thus keep control over society by programming the
people to fit our needs at any given time."

Frank grabbed a handkerchief and wiped his forehead as sweat began to pool at the edge of his hair. He
looked around the room at the others, ready for his final
push. He clicked on a document on his computer, and
a graph was projected on the wall.

"The human DNA is corrupted. The weapon I speak
of will work at this level. The graph I have projected
will help you understand the depth of our intervention."
He coughed. "I'm sorry, but my throat is parched, and
there's nothing I could add to the document you have.
I will let you read the following pages, which contain
the information you will need to understand the depth

of this change. As stated earlier, this must stay secret, top-level security."

Again, Frank looked at the group gravely.

"As you read, please be aware that I have withheld some essential information to assure my own survival." Frank paused, trying to measure their reaction, getting nothing. "I'm fully aware of the methods used by the group to cut out potential rivals, but you must understand I do not want any position of power in the next phase. I only want to be recognized as the great discoverer of the missing link, which will guarantee me a quiet and prosperous life. As you read the document, be aware that in the case where you would be interested in continuing, I will then include the missing parts of the research."

Frank stopped speaking and looked at his audience. The eight representatives had taken many notes during his presentation, which he found encouraging. Frank knew this was the moment he had been waiting for and needed to be confident looking. If they surprise him during the question period, and he wavers even slightly, they might leave, and Frank would be back to nothing. More than that, they could decide to kill him here and take what research they have and try to make a go at it without him. Frank felt a bead of sweat on his forehead again, unsure if he should wipe it away, wondering if it could be viewed as a sign of weakness.

"I suggest reading the chapter on the tools that will be used; it should give you a clear picture of the requirements needed to carry out this task." Discreetly wiping away the sweat as he sat, Frank Cutler awaited his fate in silence.

As the men finished reading, one by one, they closed their document and crossed their arms, waiting for their colleagues. The presentation now complete, Frank was relieved to see no one had left. Then each representative began to pack up their stuff and leave, each giving Frank a calling card, saying someone would contact him soon. Two of them stayed behind. One presented himself as a lawyer sent by the corporate consortium; the other hovered behind as if observing.

"This document is interesting, Dr. Cutler, and I will, without a doubt, send it to our consortium, but I need to ask why do you use the pronoun "we" so profusely? You are not a member of our group. You have made an intriguing discovery, but as you stated yourself, you are but one person." The corporate lawyer looked at Frank with intent, obviously trying to intimidate him.

"True, but I'm the only one that has the key to the future," Frank said, sporting a cocky smile. "And you need me to interpret the findings so that we may use them appropriately. By the time you know enough to get rid of me, you will have retained so much power over the people that you will most certainly have forgotten about killing me. I will have settled somewhere, reaping the immense benefits of my discovery, and you will be busy pulling the puppet strings of society."

Frank looked at the lawyer, unable to refrain from smiling, feeling he had won, that they were convinced. The lawyer changed his stance, opening himself up by uncrossing his arms.

"All right. What else do you need from us?"

Frank's enthusiasm went up a notch at the question but managed to restrain himself and started to explain that he needed more laboratory space, keeping as calm a voice as he could, his excitement boiling over. The corporations have most of the land, so they could begin to make sure they have all the strategically important sites before construction begins. As he did with his research, Frank only gave the information the lawyer needed, keeping the knowledge that his own laboratory is already set up to begin procedures close to his chest. He knew his life was on the line if he naively gave all the information away. The groups of power in place didn't stay there by being magnanimous, after all, and Frank needed to be careful. He knew he had passed a major obstacle to the accomplishment of his plan. He had to make sure the next phase goes without a hitch.

"There's one person you should probably track down. His name is Dwight Como," Frank told the lawyer. "He knows a lot, and I wouldn't want him to step on our toes as we move ahead." Frank had no intention of sharing any part of the spotlight. Dwight's work had helped Frank develop his theory, but he had to be silenced.

CHAPTER 11

August was by far Ayla's favorite month of the year. The trees are at their densest, creating a green partition with the deep blue of the late summer sky as if someone had managed to trace the tree line with a thin black marker to add to the contrast. The air was thick with floral perfume and pollen, the plants and trees reproducing in a quantum chemistry dance Ayla reveled in. As she dreamed about the biological particle dance happening before her eyes, Ayla let her mind go back to her research. Since her experience with Engella, she was constantly revising her scientific insights, often finding she was looking at the wrong place.

In her research, she came to the conclusion that the search for dark matter is going in the wrong direction. The calculations and models created to that point in time to detect dark matter, for example, were molded together based on known math. That caused a slew of problems, the most important being the fact that the research had become stagnant, some scientists even evoking the possibility there's no dark matter. Others kept the research going, declaring that a single particle could be the essence of dark matter, thus limiting the research to looking at one particle at a time, each time revealing a small part of the answer. But each new piece of the puzzle was incompatible with the previous one, making them run in circles as they chased partial theories. She had the inspiration to explore her theory sitting in the park one summer day two or three years ago, as she tried to visualize the chemical dance that was pollination. In her thesis, she argued that every quantum particle that permeates the space around us works together to produce the deep, dark blackness that is over 70% of space. No one particle is responsible for maintaining the cohesion, as every particle that exists in outer space spreads unevenly across the galaxy.

Which particle is present in which part of space varies according to gravitational exposure, other gaseous and spatial anomalies. When she was in the park that summer, she managed to visualize the pollen flying around. That day was windy, and she saw that the pollen followed a random pattern. It surrendered its future to the elements present at that precise moment. The pollen doesn't wait for a specific wind strength to release itself into the air; it merely does. Invisible and infinitely light, this creates the unseen chaos that becomes natural beauty, as all the different types of pollen fly up together in the wind in a chaotic orgy. The rain then comes to infuse the ground with the mixed chemicals. According to the availability of light, ground minerals, and other factors, the pollen present at that specific emplacement will then yield the beauty we call nature by producing a specific flower or plant. Ayla took that burst of inspiration and tried to apply it to quantum particles. As she advanced in her thesis, it became clear to her that this was a good track to follow. It could even explain certain space anomalies that didn't fit in the accepted limits of what governed the universe by including a chaotic element in the calculations. By finding a basic constant of the variation of elements present, we could calculate the percentage of each element present at any spot in space. At the same time, she suggested that using a mystical approach to certain problems afflicting particle physics could help the community evolve on some theories governing the research for the last forty years. It didn't mean abandoning all logical thought and process. It meant looking at a situation with wonder and amazement, including far-fetched thoughts that go beyond the scientific process, accepting a force greater than ourselves that we can't yet see. She argued that it would help the scientific community make progress, as the particles behave in ways that are alien to our physical world and must be observed with new eyes. Instead of trying to force their existence into the implacable logic of practical physics, she suggested we look at their chaotic existence with admiration and let it divulge itself to us. As she traveled in her mind, Ayla recalled how her mentor had fought her during the whole process, keeping her from delving too deeply into the mystical aspects, always making sure she never left the scientific process behind. She wondered if she had ever thanked him for that. His input stopped her from leaning too heavily on the mystical side and even helped her absorb Engella's teachings without losing it. She remembered how proud she was when she handed in the final version of her thesis. In the end, all her arguments had enough scientific basis to be published, although the mystical leanings of her essay would certainly cause an uproar.

Once public, her essay received criticism beyond any common measure. The simple suggestion of exploring avenues outside of the accepted limits decreed by science to help further the research created more noise than she had anticipated. Colleagues were avoiding her as much as possible, isolating her from the scientific community as she tried to further her theories without any outside help. It became a chore to look at her email inbox that was constantly filled with mean, hateful messages. But somehow, she was okay with this. She became certain, over the time it took to write the essay, that she was on the right track. What she needed to do then was to apply some methods to the theories she proposed to prove the validity of her claims. But how? Her background was entirely scientific since high school, and even if she stood by her essay, some doubt had arisen in her mind since it had been publishing. Her inability to find any practical research patterns combining science with mysticism took its toll. On top of that, the backlash was much more virulent than she had expected, and even though she never relied on the opinion of others to justify her work, she wondered how she could be the one person in the world who's right. What kept her going was that she wasn't looking to be right; she was looking to open the research to more possibilities, even wrong ones. In the end, she knew some of her work would be recognized.

She sat at her computer to start to erase the hate mail. One by one, she "erased the rage," as she liked to say, clicking away at the emails, taking a second on each to make sure she wasn't erasing the rare important message. "Fraud," "interloping bitch," and other well-meaning hints populated the subject lines that gave Ayla enough information to know not to open those messages. Then came one email that didn't carry hate in the subject line.

It held only three words. "We believe you." She opened the message, unsure of what to expect. It read:

Let me begin by stating right away; we are not a cult. The following message may seem like we are trying to coerce you into a cult-like group, but it's not the case. Please read through before making your decision. Should you delete the message before you finish reading it, you can expect to meet someone from our collective soon; we desperately need to speak with you.

The Collective Unconscious Allegiance is a research group focused on finding a solution to the understanding of the universe. It's composed of scientists and mystics of all callings, each dedicated to deciphering the truth to our existence. It has been created under the guise of Carl Jung and Wolfgang Pauli's theory on synchronicity and the existence of an energy field that permeates the earth. The collective unconscious that they suggested does exist; we have found it. The network of energy that surrounds the earth holds all the knowledge we have accumulated over time. All the thoughts, memories, and emotions of people around the world are transformed into some form of animistic, primal energy that wraps around the earth, which in turn influences our personal subconscious, which then influences our conscious mind. In 1967, we were able to implant the notion of pure love using a combination of scientific equipment and mystic people to influence society's decision process. Since that time, many problems have plagued our existence. For example, much of our research was looted some years ago, but we have continued, nonetheless. Recently, our group has been under immense pressure, which has caused our numbers to diminish greatly. Because of the limitations this has created, our efforts to continue the research are very slow. We may sometimes happen on surprise discoveries, but our lack of resources limits the possibility we have to use that knowledge.

What we hope to achieve is to awaken humankind to the notion of a collective unconscious. We believe that if humans are aware of the existence of a collective unconscious, all will be able to gain a deeper understanding of everything around us. As an example of our experiments, we believe our 1967 intervention accelerated what has become identified as "the hippie era." We had attempted to introduce the notion of pure love into the energy mass by way of group meditation. But it lasted for a limited time because we also believe that our implant didn't penetrate the energy mass; it rode it like a wave. That is why the era was so short-lived, as the energy we tried to instill evaporated after a short time. Since then, we have devoted our research to find out how we can penetrate the energy field to be able to infuse it properly and bring in a new age of light for humanity.

After reading your essay on the possibility of merging mystical and scientific research, we believe you could be our missing link to finding a solution. Your interpretation of how to try to merge the two lines of thought is in alignment with our methods, and we believe both have much to gain from this association. You do not have to promise anything; our hope with this message is to speak with you to compare notes and see if our intuition is correct.

Take your time to think about it. If you have not answered the email by next month, we will try to contact you in person. It's important that we meet. Humanity's future rides on this.

The Collective Unconscious Allegiance.

Transfixed by her computer screen, Ayla didn't know what to make of it. It could be interesting to join a group like this one, but with what was going on around her, this had all the makings of a practical joke. "The hippie era?" she thought out loud, incredulous. Ayla decided to answer by imposing some conditions of her own. If this was a practical joke, it might dissuade them.

Let me start by thanking you for reading my essay with such an open mind.

Without question, I'm interested in meeting, but I must first develop my trust in your group before we can collaborate. My current research is time-consuming, meaning I will be at my office most days next week, but not available to travel. Tell me when would be best for you, and I will make sure to be at my office that day.

Sincerely,

Ayla Karemi

Ayla clicked *send* and sat back, almost expecting an answer right away. After waiting for about five minutes, staring at the inactive screen, still trying to make sense of the email, she turned her attention to seeking out who could have done this as a practical joke. Respect for her work was generally pretty low, and she didn't put it past anyone to go this far to try to defame her. Her main suspects were colleagues from the theoretical department. They felt directly attacked by Ayla's affirmations, and as much as she tried to explain that she wasn't discrediting their theories and that she was trying to help further the science by alternative means, they persisted in their hostility toward her research. As she started to make a list of suspects, planning to confront them in person, she received an incoming email notification. She clicked to see what it was. The group had already answered her email.

Good to hear from you so fast,

There's no problem for us to meet you at your convenience. Today, being Monday, we have sent Zorina Smith to meet with you. She should be arriving soon. Should you be absent, she will return every day until you are present. She will have the necessary information for you about our expectations, and you can ask Zorina any question you might have, we have nothing to hide. We are aware you will need time to analyze the data, but please be mindful that the situation is time sensitive, as others are also hard at work trying to unravel the secret to use the unconscious as a weapon. The search for light continues!

Ayla's instincts instigated her to hide, waiting for the person from the group to arrive, still unsure if it was legitimate. If she even remotely recognized the person they call Zorina, it would confirm a practical joke. Ayla was still undecided if she would confront the person or not if that was the case. Forcing the rising paranoia to the back of her mind, Ayla thought that this could also be the beginning of something great, her anticipation growing with every minute.

Someone knocked at the door. Ayla jumped, surprised, and went to the door, her heart pounding. It was a fateful moment. When she opened the door, it would either be a pie in the face or a new adventure. She stood at the door, unsure. She stood there for at least thirty seconds, trying to think of something to say when she opened the door. Split between the paranoia of being laughed at once more and the enthusiasm of finding kindred spirits, she remained behind the closed door, looking at a vague shape in the tinted glass. A second knock startled her, and she precipitously opened the door without thinking. The woman standing there was unknown to Ayla, which relieved her beyond what she expected, a wave of pressure lifting from her shoulders. She stood there in silence, a small part of her still a little skeptical.

"How can I help you?" She asked, her mind blinded by the sheer brilliance the woman exuded. Ayla had felt this once, with Engella Iblis, but now she also saw the brightness she had only felt before. It washed away any doubt about a possible practical joke, Ayla was now more excited than ever.

"I'm Zorina Smith, you should be expecting me," she said, extending her hand.

"I was, and I'm relieved this was true," Ayla said, shaking Zorina's hand.

"What do you mean true?"

"It's not important. Let's look at the documents you have."

Zorina pulled out a leather-bound book along with some folders filled with papers containing formulas and theories on the group's venture towards the unknown.

"The book is our manifest, should you be interested, and the folders are theories and formulas you can compare to your studies to see if we are compatible." Zorina looked up at Ayla, "I know you are still analyzing my presence here, deciding if you can trust me. But let me reassure you, we don't contact anyone without first evaluating whether an association is possible. Your research is directly in sync with ours. And now, standing before you, I also know you are open to the energies. I shouldn't be telling you this yet, but I feel you have already reached that conclusion. We are encircled by an energy field that influences our existence, and we believe we can use it to better the lives of all humans by learning to manipulate it."

Even if Ayla was in the throes of almost uncontrollable excitement as she scanned the documents, seeing real science, real math, she decided to keep her meeting with Engella secret for the time being. Her paranoid brain convinced her Engella could be an emergency contact if this adventure went sideways. She accompanied Zorina to the door, thanking her for the documents.

"Give me a week. By then, I should be able to make more sense of how we can work together."

Ayla had regained her composure but was still fascinated by Zorina's presence, seeing a glow around her that she didn't see on other people. She felt as though Zorina could read her energy, unaware of the role she had with the group.

"Perfect, I'll inform my people. I'm confident this will continue." As she turned to leave, Zorina added, "Your energy is beautiful, follow your path."

After Zorina left, Ayla locked her office door and proceeded to begin reading the documents that were brought to her. She juggled with the idea of contacting Engella but chose to wait, wanting to clear her mind first. She left the manifest aside, wanting to explore their science to see if it made sense first. The research encouraged her. They had made a decent effort at encompassing and tying together different approaches to their research, and Ayla saw where she could help them. Their attempts were still limited to current knowledge, current theories. She could help them go beyond known science. The mystics in the allegiance were making the same mistakes as the scientists by limiting their search to what they already knew.

Her background in both science and mysticism would help her explore their research and possibly find areas where she could add on. It would ultimately open new avenues in research presently classified as pointless, which excited her. Their theories and formulas showed Ayla they were missing some critical information. Satisfied that she was not a victim of a prank; Ayla locked the documents in a filing cabinet and left the office. Engella was there waiting in the corridor.

"Came to tell you I'll be away for a while," Engella said.

"Okay, but why come to my office to tell me? You could have texted," Ayla said, almost flashing back to her earlier experience with Engella, her senses still hypersensitive after her meeting with Zorina.

"Don't know, I felt I had to. I'm going to India, and I don't know when I'll be back. Guess I wanted to see you before I left." Engella then stepped in to hug Ayla. "I'll try to keep in touch," she said, releasing the hug and walking away.

Ayla stood in the corridor, watching Engella leave, confident they would meet again. As she left her office, she noticed two people who seemed to be observing her. A spark of fear appeared in the pit of her stomach. They turned to follow her as she weaved through the corridors toward the exit. Ayla accelerated her pace, trying to find a spot where she may hide and wait to see if the two people were following her. She got outside and hid behind a trash container, squatting down to make herself as invisible as possible, and waited. Seconds later, the two people appeared at the corner wall, looking around for someone or something. The woman turned toward the trash container, freezing Ayla in place as she began to walk toward it. Ayla stopped breathing, remaining as still as possible. The woman stopped not two feet away from Ayla and began sniffing around like a predator searching for its prey. Ayla was transfixed by the woman's animalistic behavior and didn't see the man going around the container. He grabbed her by the shoulder, his other hand expertly covering her mouth to muffle a scream. The woman kept watch as the man secured Ayla by using police like tactics, painfully neutralizing her. He pushed Ayla to the ground holding her arms behind her back, one knee pressing down between the shoulder blades, her face against the asphalt under her. The woman came over and gagged Ayla as they carried her to a car they had signaled over. They shoved her into the back seat, the man sitting next to her. The woman got in the front seat.

"Dr. Cutler needs to see you," the woman said as they drove away.

CHAPTER 12

Frank didn't have to wait long for an answer from the initiative. Within days of the meeting with the representatives, he was granted access to an ultra-modern lab so he could demonstrate his theory. He was to carry out the demonstration before a committee mandated by the initiative to confirm the possibilities exposed by Dr. Cutler in his presentation. That meant a group of twelve scientists representing the three levers of power: political, corporate, and religious, would assist in the procedure. Frank's chest swelled with pride. He had reached a major milestone in his plan. But he needed to navigate the next phase with caution. From this point on, Frank needed to be sure to be in complete control. The second they felt they could proceed without him, there's a good chance he would be terminated. He needed to reach a certain threshold—a point in time where his input was no longer a necessity, with most of the population under control. He could then fade out of the picture and reap the benefits of his venture. Frank knew he was playing with real power, standing right at the center of the ultimate conspiracy. Once the new system was in place, he would be in the clear, but for the time, that was the moment where he felt the most exposed and vulnerable. He needed to make sure he could leave the lab after the demonstration. There was a real possibility that he could be sequestered in the lab by force until everything was complete.

He chose to show how he hypnotizes people to do his bidding, become his soldiers. That, in itself, was a great accomplishment, and he intended to show them how this greatly benefits the group. If they question it, he would argue they first need to build an army, in case the resistance is stronger than anticipated. As he was gathering the documents needed for the meeting, he locked away his main documents in the floor safe he had installed, closing the trap door that fit flawlessly into the tile flooring in his office. He was very proud of his work. If someone comes looking for it specifically, there's a good chance it won't be discovered, with the trap door hinges disguised as tile grout, making the door practically invisible. The danger lay in someone taking the time to feel the floor, as the trap door was ever so slightly spongy, giving away a millimeter at most. But even then, they would still need to crack the safe, equipped with a double combination. It could probably be opened with an explosion, but the force necessary to open the door would be so strong that it most certainly would destroy its contents as well—not to mention the whole house. Frank's transport arrived on schedule to take him to the initiative lab.

They drove for at least an hour, heading east, by which time Frank was hooded and asked to lay on the floor. His heart rate spiked at the panic caused by the hood. He was certain he would never see his lab again. The drive lasted another hour, and with his eyes covered, he lost track of their general direction. They could just as well be heading back to the city, and Frank wouldn't be the wiser. He concentrated on keeping his head on straight, mentally preparing for a fight if they decided to try and keep him prisoner. They then entered a dirt road, Frank suddenly being bounced around on the floor of the vehicle from all the potholes. As they slowed, a faint farm smell infiltrated the cabin, which didn't reassure Frank one bit. Being far outside the city all but confirmed to him, they weren't going to let him leave. They stopped, and he was escorted out with care by the man who had been sitting next to him. The place smelled of damp hay, Frank guessing they were in a barn. He began to comprehend the possibility that he would be a prisoner in this place, already planning an escape in his mind. After being dragged along for a few minutes, he was directed down a long flight of steps, after which they descended many floors in an elevator, his heart beating rapidly the whole time. The elevator doors opened, and Frank's escorts removed the hood. An impressive array of neon lights blinded Frank for a second as he fought to regain his focus. They were in a plain, grey corridor lined with brown metal doors.

"They're expecting you in room 137," one of the escorts said, pushing Frank from the back, urging him down the corridor.

"Here we go," Frank said under his breath.

They walked down the corridor to Door 137. Frank took a deep breath. Everything hinged on today's demonstration. His apprehensions toward becoming a prisoner placed him on full alert, having become extremely wary of being accompanied to such an isolated place. He entered the room into an antechamber to the lab, visible behind the glass. It had more subtle lighting than the corridor, the main source of light coming from dentist lamps focused on two people who were strapped into massive chairs. Frank was relieved to see the subjects they had seized seemed apt as they squirmed in their seats, wide-eyed and afraid. That meant the initiative were willing to play along for now. Frank felt his worries melt away as his mind began to focus on the task at hand, and he entered the lab. He proceeded to shake hands with the two scientists already present. Once inside, Frank was amazed by the equipment present. He was elated that they had taken the time to read the whole document but was surprised at the speed at which they had put all this together.

"How will this work?" one of the scientists asked, jarring Frank from his daydream.

Frank looked at the scientist and smiled. This man had not yet read the documents—that much was clear—and he mentally congratulated the initiative for their level of paranoia.

"Well, first things first," Frank said, feeling light as a feather. "We must initially create an army of submissive soldiers bent on realizing our every wish. With them, we will make certain no one else tries to interfere with our work. This will take a few days, after which we can start to wipe out any resistance to our plans." He paused, scanning the room to see if they were accepting his premise.

"How do we create the soldiers?" another one of the scientists asked.

"Simple hypnosis," Frank said, quickly adding, "Except this one is deep, almost irreversible. With my methods, a person is a servant to the wish we impose in their mind."

"Why not do a mass hypnosis?" a voice thundered through the speakers that were hidden around the room.

Frank looked for a window to see who was talking but only saw cameras. The fact he couldn't see the speakers added to the surreal, godlike presence of the voice.

"Because with that kind of hypnosis, their capacity to be productive members of society is greatly diminished. This would affect the economy in general since no one would be able to participate in the economic construct, basically being zombies. It would systematically destroy everything you've built. It would make your presence, and mine, useless. What keeps the economy going: war, selective famine, and the chase for profit would become obsolete, voiding your power. There would be nothing to control, nothing to manipulate."

"And why use this method today?" The voice seemed even louder in the speakers. Frank had a feeling the real scientists were behind that speaker, observing from a distance. The ones around him were probably security agents instructed to act in case he tries something.

"Because, before we can firmly institute the obligation to subject the people to DNA manipulation, there's a strong chance we will meet some resistance. The soldiers we create today will be implacable, unstoppable machines that will make sure all rebels are captured and silenced. We can then program their DNA to accomplish any task we need them to do, and I guarantee they will like it. For now, looking at the subjects you have brought me, I can say with confidence, they will be highly effective soldiers."

Frank's confidence rose as the voice from the speaker stayed silent after his last intervention.

The scientists present in the lab didn't have the knowledge to fully understand his plan, and for some reason, this reassured Frank he would be okay in the end. The fact the scientists were security agents meant the initiative took him seriously, possibly even feared him a little, which excited his ego. As long as he gave the powers in place fundamental control over the whole of the human population, he knew they would keep their end of the bargain. But should the transformation stumble, even a little, Frank knew his life was on the line. He needed to make sure he remained an integral part of the operation and not become a loose end.

Frank approached the man tied up in a chair. He was visibly scared, sweat running down his face, his eyes bulging. Frank placed his hands on either side of the man's face. The man spat at Frank, but his mouth was so dry, all he could sputter were small droplets of salt.

"It's going to be okay. Soon, you will be in the throes of ecstasy and will have forgotten about the fear you are experiencing." Frank turned away from the man and said to one of the agent-scientists, "We need to prepare some medicine."

They left the man tied up and afraid as Frank showed the scientists how to prepare the hypnotic tonic, a Valerian root-based concoction, being careful to stay in the camera's field of vision so the real scientists could see. As they returned to the man, Frank explained the need to make sure the patient consumes the right quantity of potion.

"Since most patients refuse to swallow directly, I have chosen to use intravenous injection to ensure they receive the right dosage, which is based on their weight. If we give them too much, they fall into a stupor, and if we give them too little, the hypnosis is temporary." As he spoke, he set up the IV drip. "It should take about half an hour," he added as he leaned on the table behind him.

As they waited for their patient to show signs of the potion taking hold of his mind, Frank proceeded to explain the importance of implanting their suggestions at the height of the trip they are going through to have full control afterward. He illustrated how to observe the eyes, and once the iris is black, obscured by the expanded pupil, it's time. "When this occurs, there's a five-minute window where we are talking directly to the person's subconscious. Once the person wakes up, they will be at your service.

"Once they are hypnotized, it's important to have somewhere they can sleep off the buzz. Their bodies are exhausted and need some replenishing." Frank looked up at the cameras. "I suggest a medical set up, so we may speed up their recovery."

The man began to show signs of the potion taking effect, his pupils expanding. He then began to mumble incomprehensibly. Frank approached the man, placing his hands on each side of the man's head once again and waited. He held the man's gaze for minutes on end, observing the iris as it grew, obscuring the brown of the eye, millimeter by millimeter. The man was descending joyfully into the psychedelic dream concocted by Dr. Cutler, his confused mumbles becoming erratic screams of joy. Frank explained to the scientists that some people react joyfully, while other subjects freak out, screaming bloody murder, but they rarely stay calm.

"There's no difference in the method of hypnosis, the only thing needed to succeed resting on the notion to implant ideas at the height of their enthrallment, be it joyful or fearful." As he was explaining the notion of implanting ideas at the right time, he remarked that a missed opportunity carries no real danger. It merely propels the person being hypnotized deep into a psychosis, making them useless, and you must start again with someone else. One of the scientists commented that it should be easy to find new candidates, that there's no shortage of desperate people out there. The other scientists all shared a hearty laugh at this, except Frank wasn't laughing.

"At this point in the project, we must take every precaution to be as quiet and invisible as possible. If we start kidnapping people left and right, it will make our work that much more complicated. The social psychosis of many unexplained disappearances is to be avoided since we plan to design a case of social hysteria to our advantage to facilitate the establishment of the new DNA program. Should there be a general panic right before we begin, the resistance will be stronger from it. Now follow me; our subject is ready."

Frank returned to the bound, but much calmer, man. His eyes were bulging, irises black, the pupils seeming to act independently. One of the scientists ventured a question.

"Does everyone calm down when its time?"

"At last, a decent question!" Frank blurted as he rolled his eyes. "Yes, they all reach the same state. As I said before, the eyes are the key. Even if the subject has reached a calmer state, if the color of the iris is even slightly visible, the procedure won't fully work." Frank turned to the bound man. "Listen to my voice." The man's eyes began darting around so fast it didn't seem humanly possible. "You are useless without us. You are subject to our desires. We are your masters now. You will obey and act upon our orders. You will have no other desire than to fulfill our demands."

Frank repeated those words over and over for about five minutes. As the man slipped into a coma-like state, Frank stopped and turned to the scientists. "In about an hour, he will emerge from the anesthesia. He can be untied, and a bed should be prepared for him. We can use intravenous hydration while he sleeps." He looked up at the cameras. "I believe we will need two to three hundred soldiers to assert full control during the transformation."

"Noted," the speaker blared before going silent for good.

"Now, how do I get back home from here?" Frank asked, looking to the agents around him for an answer.

CHAPTER 13

After a full day of waiting for flight transfers in three different airports, Engella finally arrived in Bhopal. She had gone there after receiving a letter from Dwight by way of traditional mail, inviting her to a village in India.

Hello Engella,

Let me begin by saying that our reunion stirred up long-forgotten emotions I thought belonged in the past, and I thank you for it. My life had become a constant chase for the next research grant or pursuing a new discovery, which left a chasm in the middle of my soul that I couldn't even see. Your reappearance has caused an emotional tsunami in my mind and my heart, causing me to question everything, and once again, I thank you for that. After our reunion, I left the university to travel in search of a new home. For no obvious reason, I had an attraction for India, and what I discovered is the reason I'm writing to you. The village I've found is like nothing I've ever come across in my anthropo-logical research. Their way of life encompasses beliefs from a wide philosophical range. I don't like using this word, but this is the closest approximation of a perfect society I've ever come across. You must come and join me here.

Engella was smiling as she read the letter, a beautiful example of his capacity to jump from one subject to the next without losing his train of thought. He finished his letter with directions to the village, stating that by coming here, she could deepen her knowledge, "advance her quest," as he put it in the message. The directions he gave were vague, saying the village was in the middle of a park called Satpura National Reserve, with an X on a paper map indicating the "exact" location of the village within the reserve. The airport in Bhopal was rather small, and she had no trouble finding the taxi stand. She asked the driver who approached her how much it cost to get to the nearest train station.

"Where do you want to take the train to?" the driver asked in perfect English, which carried a melodic tone, making it sound as if he was singing.

"Satpura National Park," Engella said, showing him the crudely drawn map Dwight had sent her. The driv-er's face lit up.

"I can take you directly, madam. Sixty rupees an hour. It's a five-hour drive, so 300 rupees total, and believe me, you will much prefer the comfort of my taxi over the crowds on the train; if it's even running today. If you choose the train, its 150 rupees for that distance, plus the forty for me to take you to the train, plus another forty or fifty rupees to get from the train station to the national park. It's not a big difference, plus I can initiate you to my music during the trip."

As he wrapped up his well-rehearsed speech, he began to place Engella's luggage in the trunk of his taxi without waiting for her response.

"Why not?" Engella said, taking a seat in the back of the taxi. "And take the scenic route while you're at it." Engella felt at ease with the driver, feeling thankful she found him so easily.

"It will be a pleasure, and may I invite you to sit in front. It's a long trip, and the comfort is far superior in the front. My air conditioner doesn't reach the back seat that well on hot days like today."

Engella took her place in front. "If it's okay with you, I'd like to leave the windows open. I like the warm air."

The driver acquiesced to her preference and pressed a button on his dash that opened all the windows at once. As they left the city of Bhopal behind them, they came upon what looked like a small country dirt road, and Engella asked the driver if they could take that road. He told her it would prolong the trip a little, but she wanted to take in some scenery, sick of looking at clouds from the airplane window. The driver obeyed, turning on the road, which seemed to disappear into the forest. As the taxi entered the small opening in the trees, some low-lying branches smacked on the windshield, with a branch slipping in the open window, cutting off a flower from it that landed on Engella's lap. The flower's perfume filled the cabin as she attached it to her hair. Looking ahead, Engella admired the thickness of the forest adorning both sides of the road, the dark green of the trees smattered with spots of color coming from low-hanging flowers and fruits.

She then spotted a bunch of macaque monkeys joyfully leaping away from branch to branch at the sight of the car, putting a smile on her face as she leaned back, rested her head, and looked out the window. The bright

sun was replaced with a semi darkness due to the tree
cover which cooled the air. The trees almost obscured
the sky as they drove through the luscious, green arch.
With the air chilled by the shade of the trees, the cabin
became cooler, prompting Engella to cover herself with
a light blanket she pulled out of the bag she kept at
her feet. She then angled her head to have the wind hit
her in the face. The smell of flowers in the heavy forest
humidity mesmerized Engella, who closed her eyes and
breathed in the fresh air.

She knew Dwight was right to invite her here.
Whatever happened once she reached her destination
would be positive; she was certain of that. Her gut
feeling was that she was heading for something major,
although she couldn't put her finger on it. It bugged her
a little. She had become adept at reading the energies
that surround people. But this time, albeit Dwight's
letter, there had been no dream, no premonition of any
kind to give her a clue of the events that would follow.
After reading the letter, Engella had tried to search her
waking dreams for any clue, but to no avail. They rolled
along in silence as the taxi stayed on the tree-arched
road for about an hour, the driver also taking in the
scenery, pointing to different birds with a child-like
smile on his face as they flew by. Engella felt like she
had entered a new life; her turbulent youth, the travels
that led to the Yaqui Village, her strange relationship
with Dwight, her meetings with Ayla, and everything
in between was now far away, as if from the life of
someone else. She noticed some more monkeys eating
fruit, comfortably settled on different branches of a tree,
watching them go by. She couldn't help but wonder if
they were from the same family as the ones she saw
when they entered the forest. The taxi then emerged
from the trees, the hot sun flooding over them once

more. The driver accelerated a little since the road had become smoother. He asked if they should roll up the windows to get the AC going.

"Take your time," Engella said. "I've got plenty to pay you, don't worry. But if you want to roll up the windows, go ahead." She felt the same lightness of being as she does after meditating and wanted that feeling to prolong itself."

"Just a nudge faster, we still have many hours to drive," the driver said with a smile. "When the road is nice, slow does not suffice. It's a saying at my taxi stand. Most of my customers are business people, and they want me to get to their destination as fast as possible. So, it's a bit of a reflex to speed up. I will try to be careful with the gas pedal. Poke me with your elbow when you want me to slow down."

The driver was happy to be compliant with Engella's desires, calculating the extra rupees he would cash in on this fare. Even if he stayed the night at a hotel, this fare alone would still be more than some days in the week. As if reading his thoughts, Engella asked him, "Are you going to spend the night before returning? It's a mighty long drive to do at night, and it's already mid-afternoon. By the time we get there, it will be dark."

The driver laughed. "You sound like my wife. She doesn't like me driving at night outside the city, so we have an understanding that if I get an out-of-town fare in the evening, I will return the next morning. I've already texted her."

"In that case, I will pay for your room. You've been so nice, I want to repay somehow, and a tip won't be enough." Engella was fascinated with the fact that she was not able to see the driver's energy, but she liked his vibe.

Since receiving Rafael's teachings, she had developed the ability to see a person's energy, or at least feel it. But the driver didn't transmit anything Engella was able to detect, other than he looked like a good person. If it bothered her a little at first, she let it go in the end, feeling at ease with this man.

"Oh! No worries madam. A distant relative administers a hotel near the national park, and he always gives me a discount, so it won't be a hassle." The driver felt a little uncomfortable from Engella's offer but tried not to let it show.

"Good. So, it won't be too expensive for me," Engella said with a smile. She then turned her head, simulating a nap so the driver wouldn't be able to argue. He smiled and drove on.

The ride continued in silence for hours, the driver giving Engella brief history lessons about a building or a monument along the way. They arrived at a village in need of gas. The gas station looked like any other in the world, with a big yellow canopy covering four gas pumps with a convenience store attached to it. Engella went to the store to fill up on snacks for the rest of the trip, urged on by her hunger. The village was called Bari, situated at the foot of a hill, with Hindu temples sitting at the top of each peak overlooking the village. The village itself was time-stamped in the past, the style, a mixture of Hindu and old English architecture. Some modern edifices were sprouting up where a house or a business might have burned down or otherwise been destroyed. But, Engella felt a sense of contentment permeating the village. What she saw told her there was no sense of urgency to modernize in this little town. Looking at the people strolling along at a leisurely pace, their life unpolluted by modern stress, she admired the stubbornness it probably took to resist modern development. As she observed the villagers more intently, she noticed modernity wasn't absent; it had been selectively used to their advantage. As in the rest of the world, everyone had a cell phone, and commercial transactions were computerized. But the difference resided in the fact that life had not accelerated. The villagers had learned to use the technology to help without letting it bully them into more "productivity," keeping a traditional way of life in a modern setting. People walked around; heads held high, not buried in their screens. She was still daydreaming as she entered the convenience store, her mind getting sucked back to the present by a hip-hop song with Bollywood beats blasting from the speakers. The store was filled with washer fluid, oils of all kinds, but no food was in sight. There was a bored young man at the cash register. Engella walked up to him, not sure if he understood English.

"Where can I find the snacks?" She asked, pronouncing each word exaggeratedly and miming the eating gesture, bringing her hand to her mouth.

"Market," the guy said, pointing behind him with his thumb. "And I understand English, by the way," he added, looking a little insulted.

"Thanks, and sorry if I offended you." Stopping to listen to the music, she added, "love the music by the way." Engella left the store a little embarrassed and headed to the market next door, as the guy at the cash register was bobbing his head to the beat. He gave Engella a "gang sign," twisting his fingers in strange ways to acknowledge her good taste in music and to show he was not offended.

The market was a series of small shops, each with its specialty. Engella spotted a street cart with dried fruits and mixed nut bags. She bought a large bag of each, ready to get back on the road. When she got back to the taxi, the driver saw the bag in Engella's hand.

"How much for the bag?" He asked.

"Forty-five rupees."

The driver laughed. "You got swindled." He got in the car, ready to go.

They left the village and got back on the main road, gobbling up the snacks in a heartbeat, both hungrier than they had anticipated. Engella almost regretted that she didn't buy more. They were on an asphalt highway, eating away the kilometers, Engella deep in thought as the scenery crawled along sluggishly, a warm haze visible on top of the trees that spread beyond the horizon. Since Rafael had taught her to see, her life had changed drastically. Her ability to feel, see, understand the energy surrounding us gave Engella a level of awareness that she had grown accustomed to. But since her arrival in India, she had been cut off from her abilities. Everything around her was nothing more than what it represented: a tree, an animal, a rock. No energy pulse, no glow, or any form of energetic emanation for Engella to see or feel. She was back to needing her five basic senses, which was fascinating to her, as she realized she had not relied on them for a while. Even if this gave her some anxiety, she knew it would be okay; something told her this was going to be a great adventure.

"Have you ever heard of the Soochit Karana[7] tribe?" she asked the driver.

"Yes, aren't they the group of illuminated oddballs living in the tiger sanctuary?" He looked at Engella. "Is that where you're going? Because correct me if I'm mistaken, but you don't seem like someone who would live by their beliefs. Don't misunderstand, they are good people, but every time I hear of this village, what I hear doesn't correspond with what I see in you." He asked his question with no malice in his voice, which raised a little doubt in Engella's mind.

"I don't know if their belief system is for me. That's what I want to find out." Engella waited for the driver to continue, but he didn't, and Engella left it at that. They rolled on.

They drove through farming fields that spread to the horizon until the driver slowed the car, coming to a stop near a farm, and pointed. "From what I know, the village you seek is more or less five kilometers in that direction." The driver stepped out of the car to stretch; the total is 400 rupees; do you want to pay cash or credit?" he asked, pulling out his cell phone in case she chose plastic payment.

"Cash, 500 rupees, plus 150 for your room." Engella looked around. "Aren't we supposed to be in a national park? How come there are farms all around?" Engella was loading her packsack on her shoulders, tying the straps tight as she spoke.

"We need to use protected land, because the usable yet unprotected farmland is invaded by urban development or industry and rendered useless. Thing is, tigers roam these lands, which makes the farmer's work that much more difficult." He looked her in the eyes. "Keep an eye out for them, by the way. If you see one, don't run, but try to get as far from it as possible." He bowed slightly. "It's been a pleasure, madam. Should you need another taxi ride, I would be honored to be your driver."

He got back in his taxi. Engella called out to him. "I realize I haven't yet told you my name. I am Engella Iblis; it's been a pleasure to meet you."

"But what's a name if not a designation for administrative purposes. I like your energy, and that is enough for me. Take care, Engella Iblis." He waved out the window and drove the taxi away, leaving Engella on the side of the road. After watching him disappear over a hill, she headed in the direction indicated by the driver.

The night was moonless and dark, but Engella felt her extrasensory sensations coming back to her, feeling the ground under her feet without looking down. The trees had a slight glow to them, flooding the forest floor with a greenish hue. She was smiling broadly as she saw the forest as you would when using night vision goggles. She became giddy, the excitement of renewing with her capacity to see, making her impatient to find the village. Looking up at the sky, seeing it covered with millions of stars, she realized the last time she saw so many was in the Yaqui Village in Mexico. It reassured and inspired Engella to push on and find the village as fast as possible. She looked at the paper map Dwight had given her, deciding it had no real value as she stuffed it back into her pocket.

CHAPTER 14

The two kidnappers drove Ayla to a housing compound hidden behind a thick patch of trees with nothing but a small, almost impassable dirt road leading to it. From there, they led Ayla to the main part of the village—a group of cottages that were placed in a circle. They occupied about three hundred square feet for each parcel, and there were about twelve of them surrounding a small park. Ayla laughed at their feeble effort to create a civilization in this essentially natural environment. They were surrounded by forest, but the way the cottages were oriented suggested they did everything in their power to obscure that reality. The cottages all faced each other in a way that when the inhabitants stepped out, they were in a simulated urban setting, the view to the forest obstructed by the houses and the row of cypress trees that circled the compound. Ayla saw a barn behind the cottages, probably a remnant of a past colony on these lands.

She was bad at orienting herself and had no idea where they had taken her, even though she wasn't hooded. The general surroundings indicated to her that she was on some sort of farmland, but should she escape from her captors, she wouldn't know which direction to go. As the car slowed, Ayla thought she noticed some movement in the surrounding cypress trees. It looked like someone was walking in a crouched position, but she decided to discard it as the glimmer of a bird's wing, concentrating on trying to figure out what was going on. The car came to a stop, and the man sitting next to Ayla stepped out while the woman went over to Ayla's side and opened the door. They were almost gentle in their demeanor, helping Ayla out of the car with care. Ayla noticed their eyes seemed transfixed on something, thinking they must be under the influence of some sort of drug. Although they were cordial, they remained silent, pushing Ayla towards one specific cottage without restraint, their walk almost a jog. Each cottage in the circle had a hobbit-like feel. The buildings were wood construction; small windows carved out of the wall on each side of the doors, which were marked with a symbol Ayla didn't recognize. The cottage they were bringing Ayla to was different, also made of wood, small windows and a marked door, but were heavily decorated with flowers that carpeted the ground around the cottage and a thin path leading to the front door. It had a sign she could read. *Fundamental Peace Corporate Retreat.* The woman entered, followed by Ayla, who was being pushed by the man who followed behind. They entered the reception area of the complex.

A counter facing the door was flanked by two display units filled with pamphlets about the activities offered at this retreat. The types of yoga the pamphlets proposed along with the name of the place told Ayla this was some sort of meditative retreat—probably for one corporate conglomerate as the pamphlets all had the same logo. Before she could ask her two chaperons what they were doing there, the woman opened a trap door on the floor behind the counter and directed Ayla down the stairs. They went down one flight and entered a cement basement, which was empty, except for the elevator door on the far wall. There were no buttons to call the elevator. The three of them stood there, waiting. Ayla took it as a possible moment to act and bolted for the exit, running back to the stairs before the two escorts could react. She reached the trap door but found it impossible to open. It seemed bolted from the outside. She sat on the stairs, discouraged. Up until that point, she had been holding on to the thought that this would somehow turn out okay, but as she looked at her situation, it felt as though her life was in danger. The two hypnotized agents approached Ayla, each grabbing one arm and yanking her down the stairs, banging her head on the low ceiling in the process.

With blood streaming down Ayla's face from the cut on her forehead, they returned to wait at the elevator door holding on to Ayla this time. She was dizzy from the smack on her head, not sure she could stand on her own if she wasn't supported. The elevator doors opened, and they entered, Ayla's feet dragging behind as she found herself unable to walk. There were no buttons inside the elevator. The doors closed, and the cab began to go down, Ayla feeling her feet almost lift off the ground as it descended. The elevator stopped abruptly, causing Ayla to throw up in her mouth. The taste of the blood that had come from her forehead slipped into her mouth, causing her stomach to churn out another wave of bile, this time with enough force to spray the floor. As Ayla was hacking and coughing with puke still hanging from her mouth in long strands, she was dragged to a room furnished with a large conference table.

Happy to be seated, she clumsily pawed at the glass of water on the table, the dizziness playing with her depth perception. Ayla was handed a washcloth to clean away the blood on her face. Her dizziness fading, she realized she was in a large laboratory. Through the conference room windows, she could see the equipment all around them, her curious mind returning with a vengeance as she wondered what the equipment could be used for. From her vantage point, she could see every part of the laboratory, which was arranged in a circle around the room, much in the same way the cottages were organized in a circle around the small park above ground. Ayla had no idea how far underground they were but judging by the speed the elevator seemed to be going and the time it took for it to stop, they were deep. She tried to channel her newfound knowledge of the energies Engella showed her but found she was frozen in place, unable to think coherently. Blood was still oozing out of the gash on her forehead as she dabbed it with her soaked washcloth. Then, a door opened, exposing another part of the laboratory for a second, Ayla noticing what seemed like cages behind the man who was coming out. Did she see people in the cages? Ayla couldn't be sure, as the man closed the door behind him before she could make out what she saw. He was an older man who visibly didn't care about the opinion of others when it came to his grooming habits. His hair, fighting for position on his head, the nose hairs lunging out of his nostrils, and his unkept eyebrows giving his stare a crazy vibe would scare any child. But his demeanor was calm, composed, confusing Ayla's instincts. Unable to get up to shake the man's hand, she managed to greet him with a nod.

"Good day, Miss Karemi. My name is Frank Cutler. I'm terribly sorry about the way you were forced to come to me, but you must understand, time is short. Your research on challenging scientific philosophy to new modes of thought has attracted my attention, and I would like to include it in my research. It will help to further it and propel you to celebrity status. But I do have questions about your methods." Ayla felt her clarity returning, so she risked an aggressive reply. "You couldn't have called me? I mean, this feels a little over the top. If you wanted access to my research, you could have asked." She felt it wasn't the right question but needed time to make sense of the situation.

"True, I could have simply called." He looked at her intensely, his eyes bulging a little. "But the situation we are facing has forced my hand. You see, my research is going to help humans reach a new level of consciousness, and my current task is to group all the research that could help the cause. At this point, you must understand that I am proposing a complete buyout of your work. You will not be able to continue it unless you join my cause. I kidnapped you because I couldn't take the risk that you run away with your research after my call. Should you refuse, I'm obliged to inform you that I will have to extinguish the risk you represent by isolating you here forever." Frank paused, exhibiting a defiant smirk. "But if you accept, you are free to go. My two soldiers will drive you home, and you will give them your research, so we may continue the project. If you don't cause trouble, I may even cite your name in the pages of the research." He added that, hoping to appeal to her ego.

"I don't see the freedom in your proposal, but I guess I don't have much of a choice," Ayla said, feeling the nerves get to her, weighing the possibilities she had to escape if they held her there.

She concluded she would need to agree to the terms offered if only to get out of that bunker. Cutler had been clear on that point. She mused on the fact that she was facing an impossible choice, hearing her friend Dwight Como telling her these choices were the rare free-will moments we face in life. The rest is nothing but social conjecture and peer pressure on a grand scale. But she felt this wasn't one of those free will moments. She had already decided that once outside with the two guards, she would look for a way to escape.

"Freedom of choice is a lure, my dear," muttered Frank, as if he was reading her mind. "People need to know what is expected of them for there to be any chance of happiness in the world, and I expect to realize this accomplishment within the next year." With an almost indiscernible movement of his head, Dr. Cutler ordered the two agents to flank Ayla.

"Once you give your work to my agents, you will forget this ever happened." His gaze was fixed on her as if he was trying to hypnotize her, but it did nothing more than make her uncomfortable.

Someone with a laboratory as advanced as this one probably had a lot of resources, Ayla thought. *Better be careful*, she told herself. She got up, ready to leave. "We need to go to three places to get everything. It might take a while," She said.

She looked at Frank, gauging his reaction, looking for any hint that could give her more on the man. He smiled crookedly, proud of himself for convincing her. *There*, she thought. *Narcissist*. She knew what to do. She changed her demeanor to give him the impression she was admired him.

"I'm sorry if I seem perplexed," she said, "but I must admit, I'm a little star struck to be in such a well-equipped lab, plus it's clear you know where you're going. The fact you need my research to advance yours is such an honor, but to possibly have the chance to be cited would be a crowning achievement for me." As she was speaking, Ayla noticed Frank's chest puff up a little. She continued, feeling she knew the response. "Should you need my help at any point, I am available to join your team." Frank cut her off.

"No need, everything is in place," He said, no emotion visible on his face.

"Why do you need my research in particular?" she asked, regretting it right away.

She wouldn't get an answer. Frank became serious and remained silent. He got up and signaled the two agents to go with Ayla to retrieve her research. Before they left, he grabbed each one with his hands on each side of their face and seemed to give them orders. All Ayla could pick up was what he said after each order. "Do you understand?" It sent chills down her spine. Frank left by the same door he came in, and this time, Ayla was able to see clearly that the cages behind the doors were holding humans. She promised herself to avoid being imprisoned there and followed her two puppets obediently. As they emerged in the miniature housing complex, she began to take mental notes of the environment, trying to recognize some natural features that could tell her where they are. She knew she needed to get away from her captors first, but she couldn't just take off running at that point, still unsure of their exact location.

"Where do we need to go first?" the man asked. Ayla, surprised to hear his voice, directed them to the university. Being on familiar territory should help her find a way out.

As they drove away from the compound, Ayla let her mind wander as she always has when a situation becomes too complicated. She let her thoughts take over without limitations, childhood memories crisscrossing with science theories, family souvenirs popping in her mind during a philosophical musing. These random thoughts often brought her to an epiphany, which she desperately needed. Allowing her gaze to get lost in the far away horizon, she found herself comparing the offers made to her. Ayla had always believed scientific advancement was her main goal, and from what she had gathered so far, the one she faced was the mother of all discoveries. She felt this one was akin to the discovery of something fundamental, like fire, or the wheel, but an ominous feeling seemed to hang over the man at the laboratory. The future of humanity was in the hands of these two groups and Ayla had no idea if she could trust either of them. She needed to contact Engella somehow, and sooner rather than later. As they reached the highway, the woman said a car seemed to be following them. The man exited on the following ramp to see if the car followed them, which it did. He then began to take smaller and smaller roads, the car staying behind them, getting closer. Ayla felt a pinch of dread take hold in the pit of her stomach as the driver accelerated on the dirt road. The car behind them drove up to the bumper. After hitting the bumper twice, making them swerve, it leaned on the bumper once more and began to speed up, pushing the car. The man lost control within seconds, doing a 180-degree spin into the ditch, landing backwards. Ayla's neck snapped back on impact, giving her a severe whiplash. Despite the danger she might be in, she couldn't help but think of the pain she would feel the next day as the car following them stopped on the road. The two guards tried to exit the crashed car. A man got out. Dazed and confused by the crash. Ayla felt the man's energy: bright, powerful, all-encompassing. He looked like an angel to her, his inner light shining from every pore in his body. The energy he emitted told her he was here to help her escape. The two agents extracted themselves from the car and approached the man on the road, slumping to the ground as soon as they reached him. The man came down the ditch to help Ayla. He was a young man, his face illuminated by joy, a serenity that soothed Ayla's mind. She climbed out with his help.

"Hi, my name is Christopher Saddleton. I'm here to help you get away from these things." As he spoke, he climbed up the ditch to his car in an instant, opening the passenger side for Ayla, still clambering up, fighting the softness of the ground and the dizziness of the crash. He reached out his hand to help her up. They got in his car and they drove away.

"What happened back there?" Ayla asked. "They fell to the ground for no clear reason."

"They're hypnotized, so all you need is a command that will leave them inoperative, and you're good to go. They should wake up in about an hour, their commands erased. By the time they return to the compound, we will have disappeared."

Christopher looked over at Ayla, worried she might be hypnotized as well, and not sure how to react if the deactivation command didn't take with her.

"First, how do you know about that place?" Ayla asked. "And second, were you in the bushes when I arrived there? It felt like someone was watching us." Her inquiry reassured Christopher since a hypnotized person wouldn't ask those questions.

"That was me. I received a message from the Collective Unconscious Allegiance when they found out you were captured. I would've acted faster, but I had to wait for you to leave that place, because had I tried to free you at the compound, it would have been far more complicated."

"And if he had kept me in the bunker?" Ayla asked, knowing the answer.

Silence greeted her question.

"Good thing I played along with him then," she said, leaning her seat back to rest her neck.

"You can sleep a little," Christopher said. "We have a couple of hours."

Ayla tried to rest, but sleep didn't come right away. Knowing she had to recover everything related to her work before they "disappeared," as Christopher said, she pondered the possibility of leaving without retrieving her work. She didn't know why Frank Cutler wanted it, but she knew she didn't want him to get his hands on it. Anyone who kidnaps a person to propose a no-win deal is up to no good; that much is evident. As they ate up the kilometers, the laboratory fading from her mind, Ayla's fatigue became unbearable weariness. Unable to fight it, she let her body get heavier, sinking into her seat, the stress incurred in the last hours fading away. The energy emanating from Christopher was washing over her, the calming influence complete and profound, as she slipped into a deep sleep.

CHAPTER 15

Engella was sitting on a rock at the edge of a forest that surrounds crop fields. She was drinking water, taking in the many fragrances as she thought about Rafael. Looking around, she tried to find traces of a path or any sign that could give her a direction to follow. She took small sips of water, concentrating on the water entering her body, feeling it spread to every molecule of her being, making sure she was well hydrated before entering the forest. Engella did this until the container was empty. Wanting to refill, she noticed a stream nearby. She squatted and dipped her canteen in the stream after taking a sip with her cupped hands to be sure the water was clean. As the canteen filled, something moved in the trees. She looked up and saw two eyes shining through the leaves and heard a deep breathing sound. The hidden beast moved, revealing its head—a tiger. Thinking she should be afraid, Engella felt unnaturally calm, and the tiger seemed to pull its head back as if motioning

Engella to follow it. It then disappeared again in the trees. She got up, trying to keep track of the tiger that was moving through the forest at a fast pace, not worried if Engella was following or not. Almost running, she kept pace with the feline, speeding through the forest as if in broad daylight, the green hue emitted by the trees illuminating the forest as if it were daytime. She was jumping and hopping along joyfully, feeling a sense of liberation.

She stopped. There was no more noise, either from the tiger or anything else. The forest had gone silent. Engella shirked behind a tree, crouching to listen more intently at the forest, feeling a pang of fear grabbing hold of her consciousness. Rafael had taught her to listen to the silence—to listen for that which is unheard, to listen for the vibrations. She tried to apply the teachings but felt overwhelmed by the sheer immensity of the journey that brought her here. Still crouched behind a large tree, Engella began to concentrate on one thing at a time to regain the calm she needed to keep moving in the forest. She first slowed her breath, pushing the fear away. She then focused on the deafening silence around her and picked up on an ever-so-slight vibration in the air. It seemed to come from the top of a small hill ahead of her. She stood and began climbing. The hill was much steeper than she thought. She needed to get on her hands and knees to keep her balance while staying focused on the vibration, which was increasing in strength. Coming close to the crest of the hill, she noticed a glow coming from the top—a light yellow glow reminiscent of a small campfire. Engella stopped to listen. She felt the vibrations in her chest, vigorous, powerful, and she knew she had found the village. Looking around for the tiger, she couldn't see or even feel it anywhere near. She thanked it for guiding her, her voice dissipating into the forest.

She then climbed over the crest of the hill, which revealed a small village. A serene calmness enveloped the area, most of the villagers sleeping at that late hour. Sparsely placed lanterns created just enough light to move around without running into walls. Small houses, some made of wood, others with brick, along with the occasional makeshift tent, were haphazardly scattered around with no identifiable path through the huts and houses, forcing her to weave through with no discernible direction. Engella sat on a bench under a lantern, taking in the palpable dreaming vibrations of the sleeping people. The energy they displaced raised Engella's spirits, her soul celebrating her arrival with ecstatic elation. *This is nice,* she thought. Engella heard a door open. As she turned, a man came to greet her. He spoke in a low voice, seemingly out of respect for the silence that permeated the area.

"Happy you made it," he said, "Rafael told us you would come here. I'm delighted it turned out to be sooner rather than later. We need your Help." He looked at her with a smile that could be used as a poster that represented bliss—his whole face lit up with joy.

"My name is Jolan Tamer. I represent the village on the spiritual plane. You must be Engella Iblis."

"I am. How do you know Rafael?"

"We haven't met in person, but we have crossed paths in the dream realm. During one of our encounters, he told me of you, and since that time, I have been probing the dream realm for your presence, so I could follow your progression."

"That was you, huh? You know, since leaving the Yaqui Village, every time I would have a waking dream, I couldn't shake the feeling something or someone was

COSMIC CONSCIOUSNESS   141

watching me. I had become convinced the lost souls were
watching me, waiting for an occasion. I even stopped
having waking dreams for a time with the hope that
the feeling would disappear on its own. Why didn't
you show yourself? We could have saved a lot of time
getting me here had you done that."

Engella said this with a twinge of anger, but chased it
away, wanting to keep a positive outlook on the situation.

"This is my new home. I feel it in my bones." She
choked a little, and before she could continue, Jolan
cut in.

"You had to find it yourself. My curiosity towards
your evolution was selfish, which is why I didn't show
myself to you." Jolan's face became contrite like a child
caught with his hand in the cookie jar. It lifted what
little doubt Engella still had weighing on her. She had
no anger, no doubt, no apprehension about her presence
here. She felt so light she grabbed a branch from the
bush next to her, afraid she would rise to the sky.

"Rafael told me something similar. But the process
creates so much doubt; I came to a point when I thought
I might abandon it. But, now that I'm here, I know
the effort was worth it." Engella looked at Jolan. "I'm
guessing you sent the tiger?"

"No. But I felt it, which woke me. I soon realized
you were in our forest and that the tiger was guiding
you here, so I decided to await your arrival. During the
next day or two, we will help you settle in; then, we can
begin the work that brought you here."

A speck of light broke the horizon as they spoke,
announcing a new morning. As the sun rose, Engella
was treated to an array of colors emanating as much
from the flora, which abounded around the village as
the houses and tents adorning the grounds. She noticed
there were no numbers on the doors, but each one was

embellished with a different drawing, apparently indicating who lived there. The joy filling Engella's mind and soul was almost unbearable, as the village awoke slowly, people emerged from their homes, some going directly to the kitchen to begin cooking breakfast, others preparing the tables. Music began to flow out from the back of the terrace, where the tables were spread out cafeteria-style. A mixture of guitars and flutes were jamming—the melodic flute, banging drums, and the grubby sounding guitar merging into a lyrical sound that floated through the village calling the people to breakfast. Jolan offered Engella his hand to help her up, and they joined the people heading for the food court. Walking to the dining area, Engella took in the energy emanating from everything in the village. She was overwhelmed with all the joy. She had never felt so profoundly touched before. Even when Rafael showed her the existence of the other realm, she didn't feel as complete as she did at this moment.

Jolan interrupted her amazement. "You said this felt like home. But keep in mind that the task you are to carry out has no guarantees. Your actions could mark the end of our village."

Engella was offended by his suggestion. "What do you mean, the end of the village?" "If you're looking for a scapegoat, I will have to decline to help you." Engella's jaw was tightening as she spoke.

"You misunderstand me," Jolan said in a calm voice. "The village has faced extinction in the past, and we have always found a way to overcome. We face a dire situation once more, but no one can predict what the outcome will be. I want you to be fully aware of the implications, which is why I'm telling you this. Time is short, and at some point soon, you will be needed elsewhere, which means we need to act fast. The energy from our tree has begun to pulse again, and it needs our full attention."

"Tree?"

"You will see it soon. It's a tree of life[8], one of a few that remain. Their existence has always been classified as legend, but they do exist. Ours was reduced to a stump in the fifteenth century by the forces that still control human existence to this day. Its destruction was an act of war against the village, but also against the knowledge that will elevate humans beyond the limited scope of physical reality. After the destruction, a select group of members of the tribe were tasked with preserving its existence over generations. For generations, our people have patiently waited for it to be reborn, nurturing its roots, feeding its appetite for psychic energy. Your presence here gives me hope that we have reached a turning point in our existence—that our hard work over the centuries has been rewarded."

"Why my presence in particular?" Engella, although aware of her capacities, was always bashful when she was celebrated.

"From what Rafael has told me, and from what I've observed, I believe you have the capacity to engage its vibrations. If you manage to do that, a new age will rise. That is your task."

Jolan was, in many ways, like Rafael, with his matter-of-fact tone mixed in with a floating sensation of ecstasy that surrounded him. The difference was that Jolan also radiated something dark and menacing—like he knew about a dark secret.

Engella smelled the food as they approached the buffet at the food court, her nostrils consumed by the richness of the aromas. She found herself breathing in the spice-filled air with unbridled delight, her appetite screaming for mercy. In the previous twenty-four hours, she had eaten one airplane meal and the trail mix bag she shared with the taxi driver. The odors filling the air made Engella hungrier than she had ever felt in her life. As she and Jolan arrived at the dining room, an impressive-looking spread greeted them. Engella could choose between a varied choice of salads, sausages, and eggs, each spiced a different way. Grabbing a plate, she wondered why they would prepare so much food for such a small village.

"I'm surprised there's so much food. I would think less than half of that would nourish the village, no?" Jolan smiled at this.

"Yes, we don't need as much. But after our meal, the excess will be packed up so we may trade with neighboring villages for different resources. We trade what we don't need for what we do. Our cooks are creative, and our food is in demand in the region, which is why, at almost every meal, an excess is produced for trade. The residents who take care of the kitchen are magicians; believe me. Their effort alone helps keep the village fully stocked. Their contribution has given us the opportunity to trade our excess for some luxuries—like the tables in the dining room, for example."

"Okay, then." Engella stopped listening while she tried to choose a meal. She was going back and forth between the tandoori eggs and the tomato, cucumber, and onion salad that gave out a strong coriander aroma.

The woman behind the counter chimed in to break her indecision. "You can have a little of both, you know. You aren't limited to one element." She was smiling and speaking in the tone of a mother encouraging her child. Engella extended her arms, holding an empty plate, nodding at the suggestion. The woman filled her plate with some eggs and some salad.

Engella sat to eat, acknowledging the people at her table with a smile before diving into the food, practically inhaling it. The others laughed as they ate at a more typical pace. Satisfying her hunger was the one thing on Engella's mind as she ate in silence, not noticing the commotion she caused around her. Engella downed a glass of water after her meal, feeling the energy filling every pore, every cell in her invigorated body, every ounce of food turning to pure vitality. She looked around the table and saw she was the only one who was finished, even though she was the last to sit down. She leaned back on her chair, content.

"My name is Engella Iblis," she said to the people around the table. "I've been invited here by my friend, Dwight Como. But it seems my presence here was anticipated, although I'm not yet sure what my exact role is." She let out a loud belch, generating a hearty laugh from the table. Engella sheepishly apologized.

"No need. That belch had an exuberance that you must not deny." The man speaking to her wrapped his arms around Engella's shoulders to hug her. "Welcome," he said.

Engella felt a lifetime of weight soar from the depths of her soul up to the sky, disappearing into space, liberating her spirit. Every ounce of pain, every fleeting moment of unease her life had produced was lifted, then dissolved into the clouds. The feeling was almost too much to bear for Engella, who began to cry silently. The man who hugged her smiled at this, his demeanor calm as he held her hand, which helped her let go of her tears. This helped her take full advantage of the new sensation of freedom as she avidly embraced her newfound liberty. The feeling of lightness was accompanied by a sensation of heightened senses. She looked around the village, noticing things she had previously missed. A light glow emitted by the houses, the roots from the bushes and trees making the ground pulse the same way as it does in her waking dreams. She tried to reassure herself that she was not dreaming, feeling a jolt of pure energy from the earth as she sat. "How am I able to see this while I'm awake?" Engella Mumbled almost inaudibly.

"It's the tree," the man said. "By the way, my name is Stephen Balder, but you can call me Baldy." The man had a thick head of red hair, his face almost hidden by the bush on his head.

"I'm guessing the name is ironic," Engella said. His sensible demeanor helped her return to the present reality.

Her comment created an instant burst of laughter around the table that spread to the other diners. The conversations then became animated, loud, happy. Baldy looked around the grounds, appearing almost surprised.

"It's been a long time we haven't felt this much joy in the village. Thank you for bringing it to us," he said as he hugged her again.

Engella backed away a little that time, her urban reflexes kicking in—the same way she did when she was a child. She would create a strong bubble around her when living in densely populated areas. But as Baldy held his hug, Engella felt his love envelop her, and she abandoned herself into it, feeling his tears on her shoulder.

They hugged and time stopped for a moment. She didn't want the moment to end. She felt the pure love emanating from Stephen, and she reveled in its warmth. Engella broke off the hug first, uncertain about the duration. Stephen let her go, and as he did, whispered into her ear. "Once again, thank you for being here."

A noisy, joyous brouhaha began to arise around Engella as everyone participated in the cleaning up process, some clearing the tables, others packing up the leftovers for trade with the neighbors before scrubbing the kitchen clean. Engella joined in with the clearing of the tables, ending up as a dish dryer in the kitchen.

"It's awesome how everyone spontaneously pitches in like that," Engella said to the woman working next to her.

"It's like that for common tasks." the woman said as she scrubbed a pot. "But for the bigger tasks that need some education or special knowledge, such as hunting or scientific research, each is free to follow their personal tastes. There's but one limitation to this; when it's time to choose, certain essential tasks might be in urgent need of extra hands. In those cases, a person will be asked to choose in accordance with the needs of the village. What generally happens, though, is that someone already assigned to another task will agree to change, looking for a challenge, or bored with their current task. If someone is forced to accept an unwanted task, they will be free to change as soon as someone else can take their place. They often become well respected in the community for the selflessness of their actions." The woman continued to rinse out the sink after the dishes were done.

"All I can say is, wow. And there's never any animosity between people about their choices?"

"Oh, sometimes," the woman said. "It can get ugly. But we have a round table every week where we can hash out our differences. If you see all this joy around you, it's because we accept the existence of pain and sadness. We don't turn it away, facing it to love as much as we love joy and happiness. Whichever energy you face in a day, if you love it entirely, it will become positive energy.

There's no light or dark, only love. See you around, dear," she said, patting Engella on the shoulder as she left.

"Yeah, see you around."

Engella was floored by this conversation. She remembered Rafael telling her she would find her way to a new home after her sojourn in the "civilized" world, but she never expected her new home to be this awakened, so attuned to another concept of reality. Everyone had left the food court, leaving Engella alone. She looked around, not sure where to go. She spent the rest of the day walking around the village, taking in the sights and sounds of her new reality. In the early evening, Jolan Tamer emerged from a large tent and came to Engella, inviting her to sit at the table with him.

"I hope the others didn't scare you away," he said, smiling. Engella sat in front of him, still trying to absorb everything about her new surroundings.

"Not in the slightest," she said. "More so, I believe you're right about my presence here."

"I know I am," he said, furrowing his brow. "Let me show you where you can set up your home." They got up, and Jolan guided her through the twisting paths of the village to an empty spot of earth. "Here is your parcel."

"It's empty." Engella chuckled.

"True," nodded Jolan. "This way, you can build it any way you see fit. The first night is always a little strange as you can imagine, being naked under the stars, but I will get some blankets for you if you want." As he turned to leave, he added, "tomorrow we can talk, rest for now."

Jolan left Engella in her small plot of land without waiting for her answer. As silence descended on the village, the dim light of the moon began tracing shadows around her. Engella settled on her spot of earth, lying on her back, looking up at the stars, so distant yet still our guides through time. She was trying to imagine where the walls of her home could go. She sensed she had found a new family and wanted to build something that would show that. A man brought over some blankets that Engella spread on the ground, looking to define the limits of the walls of her home. She played around with them for about two hours. When she laid herself on the ground, she fell asleep as soon as her head touched the self-made pillow that she fashioned with the leaves from the massive croton plants bordering her lot. The nocturnal noises coming from the forest around her spoke of rich diversity with sloth bears noisily walking by scrounging for food, the more discreet felines skittering by in the bushes, producing almost no sound. The sounds were the lullaby that she carried with her into her dreams.

Engella was surprised to emerge in the dream realm, having made no conscious effort to go there. She realized her mind had already created a personal rendition of this new evolution. She entered a fantastical world made of floating trees, shining flowers, and roaming animals, some advancing, nose to the ground, others running in groups. Rafael was there as well, appearing to be waiting for her.

"A rather chaotic place," he said playfully. "But at least it makes you easy to find."

"How do you mean?" Engella asked, still trying to get her bearings. She hadn't traveled that far in the realm in a long time, and it took her a moment to set her head straight.

Telepathic communication had always perturbed Engella a little, and she needed a moment to acclimate. She mused that the long absence from this realm accentuated the weird sensation, and that helped her gain a foothold on her consciousness. Rafael explained what he meant. "When you left the village after we first met, your energy signal was moderate. If someone had been looking for you in the dream realm back then, it would have been an impossible task to locate your energy signal. But now, by working on your capacities in the physical world, you have become a beacon in the dream realm, shining above all other sources of energy the same way a lighthouse would. Once I saw your energy pulse starting to grow, I came to visit on occasion, fascinated by the fact that your presence here wasn't even necessary for the energy to grow."

Rafael's floating ball of energy stayed silent for a second before continuing. "But in recent days, something peculiar happened. Your energy pulse became brighter, which I took as a sign you were going to return soon. As I awaited you here, witnessing the birth of this new reality you were creating for yourself, I was amazed at your aptitude to assimilate new elements of your life into this realm." Rafael's spirit body quivered a little. "Thing is, you are visible to all in the realm, even those with ill intentions. You need to control your light if you don't want to be assaulted by a lost soul."

Engella, sensing her energy stabilize as Rafael spoke, felt more emancipated than ever in this realm. She realized how much her power had grown. "My light is for everyone and everything," she said. "I won't obscure a single photon." She was surprised at her own firmness but embraced it wholly. "Should a lost soul invade my space, I will love it. Should a malicious being assault me, I will embrace the battle. I will not hide; my time is now."

Rafael's figure quivered a little more, as he dropped out of focus. "I need to return close to my physical body for now; it needs my energy. I came over to welcome you back to the realm. Should you need some help in the upcoming battles, send a signal my way; I will come."

Rafael's likeness then disappeared, fading out of focus until Engella saw the house she lived in during her time with the Yaquis. She didn't understand what he meant about the upcoming battles but didn't linger on that thought. She turned her spirit-self to face away from the Yaqui Village. Before her stood a wooden house, each plank painted a different color, flowers adorning each side of the fabric-made front door, with three pane-less windows around the house. A small ladder led to the roof, where Engella found a pile of colorful cushions. She laid herself down, looking up at the stars. *This will be my home*, she thought, as she let her spirit-self dissolve into a dreamless sleep.

She awoke as the first rays of light broke the horizon, excited to get started on her house. She had noticed a workshop-like tent the day before and went straight there. One side of the tent had piles of uneven pieces of wood stacked in a pile with a sign in front that read, "Serve Yourself." The other side of the tent had some tools spread on a makeshift wall. There was a motley choice of hand tools. The wall was devoid of power tools, although there was plenty of space to add more equipment. Engella took a handsaw, a hammer, and some nails then returned to her "plot of land," as she liked to call the ten square foot site that was her new home. As she went back to the workshop to gather some wood, three other people were picking through the wood.

"Do you have a preference on plank length?" a woman asked as Engella walked in the tent.

"Um, no. Are you picking wood for me?"

"Yup. We saw you exit with a handsaw and a hammer, so David, Thiago, and I decided to help you while we wait for breakfast to be served. My name is Naina."

All three had their arms full, so Engella hurried to pick her own pieces while her three new friends went to deliver the wood to her house. As she returned with her arms full, Engella found the wood the others brought piled up carefully, but no one was in sight. Today it was a food bell calling the village to breakfast. Engella added her wood to the pile Naina had made and joined the villagers for the feast. Today's special was a tandoori lentil soup chock-full of varied vegetables or freshly caught hare, prepared in a rich mushroom sauce served with rice. As Engella sat with her newfound friends, she inhaled the wondrous smell of the hare on her plate. The smell was delicious and nutritious in itself, but before digging in, she felt she had to ask around the table.

"How come you guys eat meat? I mean no disrespect, but the vibe I get from this place led me to speculate that it's a vegan area."

"Meat is food as well," one man said, his mouth full of hare's meat. He took a moment to swallow his bite before continuing. "But we are careful never to eat meat prepared under duress. What I mean is that any meat that was first imprisoned, tortured, and slaughtered has no life value in it, so we stay away from it. The meat we eat we must hunt, after following specific guidelines to ensure we don't eradicate any animal from existence. We also have some cows and goats who live in the surrounding area, but they are not fenced in. If they choose to stay, we cultivate their meat once their life cycle has expired. This meat has lived free and died according to a natural order and is thus full of life, vitality. In our search for balance, it's also important to recognize the presence of the tiger and other predators around us and leave some meat for them around the village. The tiger is our protector, but it's also the governor of the forest, something we must respect. When everything is accomplished following a natural order, it's easy to preserve the balance."

As he stuffed his mouth with more food, Naina picked up the explanation. "It's the same with vegetables. Any veggie that was raised in giant fields, inundated with pesticides, has no life in it. We have small fields to the north for some fruits and vegetables, but we usually deal with local farmers who practice multiple resource farming, which preserves the earth's fertility and offers a large variety of crops to select from. To them, we are nomadic hunters and gatherers, and our products are generally well-received. For us, they are sedentary workers of the earth who help us achieve our goals by helping us keep our kitchens fully stocked.

"It has worked this way for generations. All we need to do to continue this trade is to be open and receptive to the needs of the surrounding villages and respond to them. In the history of our village, we have been purveyors of wood and other natural resources, teachers, laborers, and now we supply the adjoining villages with high-quality food. What is expected from us in the future is unknown, but we will embrace whatever is demanded from us unless it goes against our nature, which has so far never happened. Now, let's go look at your home and start putting up those planks." Naina grabbed Engella by the hand and pulled her away from the table, At the same time grabbing Engella's plate. "Finish it on the way," Naina said. "I'm curious to see what you will build."

CHAPTER 16

Christopher had gotten off the highway as fast as he could, choosing to pass through every single little town on their route. When Ayla asked him what he was doing, he explained that this way made it easier to see if they were being followed. By using this route, there was no way for a car to follow them without being spotted at some point. Ayla, impatient to reach her office to recover her documents, decided to take in the scenery to try to keep her mind off the urgency eating away at her nerves. They passed through every town, Christopher taking the time to turn into the small residential streets as if he was heading to one of the houses. To pass the time without losing her mind, Ayla played a game she hadn't done since childhood, to keep herself from screaming at Christopher to go faster. She would spot a house, analyze the condition of the home's landscaping, and try to imagine the life being lived in that house based on what she saw. As Christopher turned into a small street,

Ayla spotted a house up on top of the hill they were climbing. The yellow paint on the house was beginning to crack in some places, one specific window almost falling out, it seemed. The grounds around the house were littered with a mixture of crabgrass and small plots of flowers. Without a doubt, they had been tended to until not so long ago. The flower beds were still giving out beautiful blooms all over the grounds, fighting the crabgrass for position.

"It must have been beautiful when the garden was cared for," Ayla said, whispering to herself.

"What must have been beautiful?" Christopher asked, his eyes almost permanently fixed on the rear-view mirror. He noticed a police car had taken an interest in them since their arrival in that little town, making Christopher nervous.

"The yellow house up ahead, it's a game I play when I get bored in a car."

"How does it work?"

He was happy to have a conversation to focus on, hoping to keep his paranoia in check. The police car will surely let them go once they leave the town.

"Well, you pick a house in town or a car on the highway, and based on what you see, you try to imagine the life of the people inside. The yellow house, for example, has tattered paint and an abandoned front lawn that was well maintained until not long ago. There's a window seemingly in bad shape on the left, which tells me they don't have the money to fix it. But the good shape of the front lawn also tells me the people living there liked to care for it before, but something happened. The paint looks a little old, but still carries a pop, which tells me the house was painted about five or ten years ago. All this leads me to believe the main breadwinner of the house fell on hard times, and hard choices were imposed by their new situation. For example, do they fix the window or pay the energy bill? Do they spend money on the upkeep of the garden or buy eggs? I believe the family living there has suffered a great loss and find themselves buried under the gargantuan task of keeping the roof over their heads. The size of the house tells me it's a family of four or five members, and the generally decrepit state is caused by the fact that the children are not old enough to find a job to help them stay afloat, as shown by the toys spread around here and there."

Playing this game really did help her relax as she let her mind explore the different possibilities of life in the yellow house.

"Plus, I think the parents told their children to finish school before worrying about bringing in some money," added Christopher, happy to play along. The police car had turned away, so he was breathing more easily. Ayla smiled.

"There you go. Yeah, I like that. The father or mother was working in a local factory that closed, and now, they want their children to climb above factory working. The house suffers, but the scholarly evolution of their children is in good shape. Yeah, I like that."

They had passed the house by now, but Christopher added, "There seemed to be a small shed in the back. I imagine some sort of activity is going on in there as the parents try to find new sources of revenue."

"Hmm, alcohol or auto repair?" Ayla asked playfully.

Christopher didn't answer; he was back to scanning his rear-view mirror. His face had turned deadly serious, Ayla surprised and frightened by the uncompromising look on his face. He muttered something unintelligible and hit the gas pedal, sinking Ayla into her seat as the car took off. Her heart sank, and she was unable to ask Christopher what was going on, busy holding down her stomach, now up in her throat. He turned on a dirt road using his handbrake and hid the car in some bushes. He got out to cover the visible parts with more leaves. As they were both covering the car with leaves and branches, Christopher grabbed Ayla by the shoulders and pulled her down brutally. She held back a scream of surprise, knowing he heard or saw something. She buried herself down to the ground as a brown car passed slowly, its passengers obviously looking for something. There were two men in the car. The one in the passenger seat seemed to be looking at a screen, perhaps telling the driver what direction to take.

"Shit! They have our GPS location," Christopher mumbled. "Come on, they'll be back soon." He grabbed Ayla, and they penetrated the forest behind them. Christopher directed them to a stream. "We'll have to walk in the water to erase our footsteps, I hope you don't mind getting your feet wet."

"We gotta do what we gotta do, I guess." She smiled and stepped into the stream, the cold water filling her cotton shoes. The water was cold, but she didn't even feel it, her mind focused on running away from their pursuers.

As they jogged along the stream, they heard some shouting that came from where they left the car. The two men had run into the forest behind them, breaking branches along the way, causing Ayla and Christopher to pick up their pace. As they jogged along the stream, they could tell the two men were staying close behind.

"You said they tracked the GPS. Is it possible they put one on me while I was in the laboratory?" Ayla asked Christopher. He stopped abruptly.

"You're right. We need to get you some new clothes. It looks like there's a farm ahead. We can find something for you there."

"I've got a better idea," Ayla said as she began to undress. "Help me find some large leaves and vines. I'll be fine. I took wilderness survival classes, and I think I can manufacture some temporary clothing."

They found what Ayla needed, and within minutes, she was dressed in a leaf-made poncho held together with vines pulled from a tree. They went up a hill to a small cave Christopher spotted while they gathered the leaves and vines. They laid low, waiting for the two men to appear. Christopher felt his muscles tense up the same way they did in the alley with Zorina. The two men clumsily waded through the stream bed, cracking branches and splashing their way ahead, making no effort to be silent. One of the men came upon Ayla's clothes as he followed the directions given by his screen. Realizing they had lost their target, they both looked around for a clue, but without the GPS to follow, they lost all their bearings. After about five minutes of searching, they left head down, and went back the way they came.

"At least we know these guys can't track us without a GPS," Christopher whispered as he got up, keeping an eye in the direction where the men came from. "We left a clear trail coming up to this cave. If they can't see that, we should be okay if we stay low. They'll surely send more adept hunters our way, but we've bought some time for now." He turned to Ayla. "Where do you need to go first?" She looked at the leaves covering her body.

"First, I need actual clothes. This poncho is comfortable, but I don't think it qualifies as low profile." Christopher burst into laughter at this.

"Man, your capacity to stay in the present moment is fascinating. In the Allegiance, most of the people I speak to talk about the future, what's coming, our need to believe. For me, it's always rehashing the past, trying to find where I went wrong, so I don't repeat the same mistake. With you, there's no need to believe in any ethereal future or mistake-filled past because there's nothing else but the now." He paused, seemingly deciding if he wanted to tell Ayla something secret. "You know, I've heard about a place in India that would be perfect for you if it really exists. I think that's where we need to go." Christopher looked around, trying to see which direction to go next. Lost in his thoughts, he hadn't noticed Ayla was already on her way, heading for a farm she saw through the leaves.

"Wait! What are you going to tell them? Don't we need a plan?" Christopher yelled, running to catch up.

"Don't know yet," Ayla said. "Guess I could play the role of a kidnapping victim or be the victim of a practical joke. We'll see when we meet the inhabitants."

"Yeah, that one," interrupted Christopher. "Playing kidnapped will attract the police. If you convince them that your anger is focused toward some imaginary mean friends, we should be good."

As they approached the farm, Ayla and Christopher stayed inside the tree line, observing the grounds to see if there was any activity, trying to decide if it was safe to advance. While Christopher looked for any sign of trouble, Ayla played her travel game to help her decide—a sprawling house surrounded by agricultural fields. Well maintained, the house on the top of a hill, the blue and white paint scheme making the house glow in the sun. A porch, furnished with some swings, a chess table, and two long benches on either side of the main door, wrapped around the house.

"A happy family, generations of farmers, proud and successful. They will be goodhearted," she decided. Ayla looked over at Christopher and nodded. She got up and went to sit on a bench next to the door and waited. A dog watched her approach but didn't move a muscle, content to follow her with his eyes as he laid in the shade. Thanking the gods for this underperforming guard dog, Christopher went around the other side of the house, hoping he wouldn't run into anyone. He was to play the discouraged friend looking for help, but he never could play any other role than his own and feared he would blow their cover if he had to speak to anyone.

He came around the house and saw Ayla sitting on the porch bench, waiting. She looked like a forest nymph in her leaf and vine poncho, her bare feet dangling an inch above the ground. He stayed back a little, admiring the way the sun kissed her dress and caressed her skin. The light breeze was making the leaves dance on her, reinforcing the forest nymph impression. She noticed him looking at her and smiled. Christopher felt his cheeks blush. He didn't know where to stand, feeling like a teenager caught staring at a girl in class. She waved for him to join her, and he sheepishly sauntered over, feeling his face and ears becoming red and hot. He sat next to her. She took his hand and looked at him with an angelic smile, which dissipated his discomfort instantly. The smile told him everything would be okay. He fell in love at that moment, remaining silent as his heart grew in his chest. Ayla, her mind already thinking of the next step they should take, broke the silence.

"We'll wait here another half hour, and if nobody comes, or if we don't hear any activity in the house, I'll go in and take some clothes. I'm sure the door is unlocked; it feels like that kind of house. Do you have any money on you? We should leave something to pay for what we take."

"No cash, but this could work." Christopher pulled his wallet out and removed a prepaid credit card. "I use these types of cards so no one can keep track of me by following my purchases. I buy them in bulk. My friend, who works at a convenience store, always orders an extra batch for me, so I can't be associated with a specific card. I pay them back by doing odd jobs." He looked at the card in his hand. "This one's for a hundred dollars, but I have another for two hundred if needed." Ayla kissed him on the cheek, grabbed the hundred-dollar card, and went into the house.

Christopher marveled at the fact that her first thought was to pay for whatever they would take, feeling his heart swell even more in his chest.

"Keep an eye out," she said as she entered the front door, unlocked as she predicted.

Christopher waited on the porch, taking in the view, dreaming about the possibility of having this life. Looking out at the fields, imagining they're his, his mind constructed the life that would be if this was his reality. He always wanted children, and in this world, he would have four, two boys, two girls. He would show them the farming business but would let them choose freely if they wanted to stay. As he was delving deeper into his dream, he noticed a car drive by. It stopped and turned around. Christopher instantly got up and entered the house, sliding along the wall. Once inside, he peeked out the window, spying on the suspicious car. It slowed as it approached the house. Christopher could make out two people in the car but couldn't be sure they were the same pursuers.

"Ayla, get what you need. We have trouble!" She walked down the stairs without making a sound. "Stay low," Christopher whispered. As the car entered the driveway, someone in the car lit a flashlight and pointed it at the house.

"Do you think it's them?" Ayla seemed almost excited at the prospect.

"It's our pursuers alright, but not the same men," Christopher said. "Stay quiet. I'm pretty sure they haven't seen us."

The two men got out of the car, split up, and went around the house, each covering his side.

"Can you deprogram them like you did before?" Ayla asked. She was ready to enter battle.

"I could try, but they don't all have the same command. I had to give it a shot on the side of the road; we were cornered. Right now, they don't know we're here. If the command doesn't work, it could be the end for us. We should wait, and when they leave, we'll find transportation." Ayla slumped down a little, disappointed there wouldn't be a battle.

Since her run-in with Dr. Cutler at his laboratory, Ayla felt as though she was at war, but she didn't know against what. Nor did she know how her research could have sent her down this path, but she knew that for whatever reason, her research was dangerous to someone. Their two pursuers made their round of the house with no discretion, making plenty of noise as they progressed. The dog barked at them at first, then went silent. Ayla feared for the dog's life, and both men reached the porch, peering in the window that decorated the top of the door. The door handle began to shake, but it stayed shut. Christopher had locked it when he went in. The two men decided no one was home and went on their way. As the car left the driveway, a deafening silence overpowered everything around them. Ayla felt the silence like a pressure wave on her head, the lack of sound crushing her skull.

"We need to find Engella Iblis," Ayla said, desperate to break the silence.

"Your documents first," Christopher said. "We need to get to them before they do. If they have hounds on us, it means it's important."

"Hounds? As in bloodhounds?"

"Yeah, they have different levels of hypnosis. The ones we call hounds are unrelenting when they must find someone, and they don't need GPS. We believe their senses are heightened. They are only used when the situation becomes critical. The ones you met at the laboratory are easier to evade. They have a specific task and can't overcome that programming when the situation becomes chaotic around them. Other than that, I don't know much about them. I do know they are hellbent on eradicating the collective unconscious allegiance, as members of the collective have disappeared, then turning up dead while others have vanished for good. I'm part of a cell of three people, and we don't know how many others are still alive." Christopher then fell silent.

As he gathered his thoughts, Ayla was already busy searching for something that could help them get away from there as fast as possible. She spotted a small bowl next to the front door with a small shiny object lying in it. It contained a key set with a car company logo stamped in one of them. She tugged at Christopher's arm, indicating to him she was heading outside. He pulled her back.

"We can't use the doors. I'm sure they booby-trapped them, and as soon as someone walks through, they'll be back within minutes. Our only chance to get out of the house is by using a second-floor window. They didn't have time to set the trap on those windows."

Ayla was smiling. "Wonderful! I love an adventure. Do you think they had time to set a trap on the garage? There's a shed behind the house that probably contains the car that goes to this key." She showed Christopher the car keys.

"Well, I don't believe we have much of a choice," Christopher said. "At least, it will get us closer to your documents. Then we can leave the country."

They went through the master bedroom window since it gave them access to the porch overhang to help them get down without having to jump. Once on the ground, Christopher pointed out a small piece of tape at the bottom of the front door. It had a small wire going through it, which was an emitter. If they had opened the door, it would have broken the seal, and a signal would have been forwarded to the two hounds, or any other hypno-robot tasked with finding them. Reaching the garage-type shed, they both looked around for a piece of tape or anything that could be interpreted as a snare. Nothing caught their eye, so Christopher laid down a simple plan.

"Alright, there doesn't seem to be anything on this door, but we might have missed it. So, before we open the door, let's try to slip in and make sure the car can start. Help me up to the roof. I saw a trap door access up there when I looked in the window."

Ayla obeyed without question and helped Christopher by giving him a leg up. He clambered up with some difficulty, cursing the nails sticking out of the wall. As he reached the roof, the trap door was already half-open. Ayla threw the keys up to him, and he slipped into the garage. The key had a Honda stamp, but the car was a mishmash of different car parts. A Ford hood, Mazda logos on the tire rims, and god knows which other brand for the doors. *Great. Like this thing's gonna start.* Christopher thought. He got in the car, causing it to creak and moan as he sat. The dashboard was as eclectic as the rest of the car, with three company logos decorating the interior. He inserted the key and closed his eyes. He turned the key once. The car began to cough. He gave it a little gas, and right away, the motor lit up, generating a deep grumble that surprised him. It felt like there was a lot of power under the hood. Before he could get out of the car, Ayla had already opened the garage door and joined him in the front seat.

"This baby sounds awesome!" Ayla was beaming.

To her father's dismay, she had always had a keen interest in muscle cars, and the sound of this one injected her brain with a big dose of dopamine. As they drove off, Ayla was squealing at the sound of the motor revving up, feeling like the little girl she was when her father reluctantly took her to car shows. Christopher kept the drive slow and methodical like before, but as they grew closer to the city, it became clear the car wasn't bugged since no suspicious-looking cars had appeared in the rear-view mirror. Ayla didn't mind the time it took, basking in the low rumble of the engine, the vibrations massaging her soul. She felt like she was inside a giant metal purring cat. The sensation led her mind back to her childhood. Then, abruptly, she realized she might not ever see her family again. She was surprised at how little that thought affected her mood. She couldn't shake the feeling of elation that chase gave her. She looked at Christopher, admiring the way the sun danced around his face. Ayla had never experienced this kind of attraction to someone and wanted to explore it with Christopher. But they first needed to get away from this place, this country. Ayla directed Christopher to the university first. If Dr. Cutler wanted to seize her documents, the first place he would look would be the university. Her safe should be hard enough to find for them to reach the university before the "hounds" found the documents. She left nothing on the university computer since her friend, Dwight Como, had told her about his work being hacked. But the safe had some important USB keys and papers that Cutler and his army could bury, which would set her research back as she would need to reconstruct her findings and theories.

Once in the city, Christopher proposed that they switch modes of transport, as the car they were in would attract unwanted attention. Ayla unwillingly accepted, giving the car a last kiss on the hood as they left. "Thank you for the ride." They headed for a subway station nearby and opted for the lead cabin on the train, both keeping their backs to the far wall, observing the people, looking for any sign of trouble. They got off one station before the university, choosing to walk the rest of the way. Christopher chose a convoluted route again, constantly peeking back to see if they were being followed. They reached the university with no problem, and the more they could advance without any issue, the more Christopher got nervous.

"I don't like this," he muttered. "Even if we're not being followed, we should have been able to spot some agents patrolling. They're surely looking for you around here."

"How would you spot one?" Ayla asked.

"Depends. If you're able to see psychic energy, they have red eyes, like on a Polaroid picture. If you can't see, you can look for a general feeling that they're out of place somehow."

"Like that guy?" Ayla pointed to a man standing at the top of a set of stairs like a club bouncer, his hands crossed in front of him, scanning the grounds with an intimidating look, except there was no club entrance behind him.

"Yeah, like that. Do you see the eyes?" Ayla looked at the man, but he had sunglasses on, which added to the awkwardness of his presence, but they didn't allow Ayla to see his eyes.

"Um, he has sunglasses on." Ayla looked at Christopher dubiously.

"Sure, but you can still see a glow emanating from the edges. Don't worry; it's different for everyone. Some see the eyes. For others, it's something else. Something made you look at him. You just need to find out what that was, and you'll know what to look for."

"I'm not worried. I've seen enough to understand that there are different kinds of powers at work. I can take care of myself. Let's get to my office so we can get out of here."

Her return to the university filled Ayla with dread, the memories of the heckling she was subjected to all coming back to her at once. As they walked the university halls to her soon-to-be former office, the jeers she was exposed to when she was working on her thesis were still present in the walls. Colleagues would take the time to stop her and point out the error of her ways with arrogance or threw insults at her from across the hall for everyone to hear. Her saving grace had been her mentor, Engella Iblis, who both encouraged her to keep her focus on the process and not to let the noise dampen her spirit.

As they entered her office, a sense of calm returned to Ayla, proud of the fact that she was able to protect her office space, feeling like she entered a haven each time she went in. In there, she was able to concentrate entirely on her research, obscuring the caterwauling going on beyond the door. Her desk was placed facing the door. That way, if someone entered, she could see them right away, with two file cabinets adorning either side of the door, acting as imaginary guards. There was a small kitchen set up in the corner next to the desk, with a coffee maker, a mini-fridge, and a microwave, along with a small round table and two chairs. Ayla left the middle of the office empty. She called it her reflection spot. She would sit lotus style in the middle of the office and meditate when she needed to ponder a problem. There was a small red X on the ground to mark the center of the room. Christopher took a seat at the table, waiting for Ayla to retrieve her documents. She stood in the middle of the office, seemingly captivated by something in front of her. All Christopher could see was a blank whiteboard. She realized he was waiting and broke out of her fixation.

"Sorry, I was taking everything in since this is my last visit here. Looking at the board, I wondered if I remembered to erase it before I left. If I didn't, someone was here. Let's see if they found the safe." Ayla bent down and pressed on the side of her desk, following a precise pattern, and the top popped up, revealing a trap door.

"Did you forget to erase your board often?"

"Sometimes, when I knew I was coming back soon."

"And what kind of information would someone find on it?"

"Nothing much. Bits and pieces of my research, what I was working on that day." Ayla turned the safe knob, expertly going through the combination. She made one final turn, and the safe clicked. Still thinking about Christopher's question, she continued talking. "I was trying to remember what I was working on the last time I was here." Christopher could barely hear what she said as she buried her head in the safe.

Ayla smiled and sat up, holding five USB keys. She handed them to Christopher and went back in to pull out some documents, a disheveled pile of papers and files ready to collapse at any moment. Ayla expertly manipulated the papers and slipped them into a brief-case, not dropping a single sheet in the process.

"There. Let's go through the desk drawers to be sure, but that should be it from here." She stopped. "Oh! Grab the baklava in the mini-fridge; they're too delicious to abandon."

Christopher complied without question, pangs of hunger beginning to hinder his concentration. As he bagged the baklava, he slipped one in his mouth, pro-voking a wondrous explosion of honey and happiness, causing him to stop and savor the moment. The delight this little dessert gave him almost brought tears to his eyes.

"Where do you get these?" He asked Ayla, his mouth still full.

"A little shop about five minutes from here. The nicest baker you'll ever meet. The croissants aren't bad either, but no one on earth can equal his baklava."

"You said it," Christopher mumbled as he swallowed the snack.

They left the office and headed for Ayla's apartment, so they could leave this godforsaken city. Ayla noticed the same man as before, now guarding an invisible door at the indoor common area. She nudged Christopher and nodded toward the hypnotized oppressor. They slipped back into a corridor that led to more offices and an emergency exit.

"We're going to set off the alarm by going through here. Get ready to run," Christopher told Ayla.

"Go right when you exit. There's a park nearby," she told him, holding her briefcase like a football. "There are thick bushes where we can hide if necessary."

Christopher placed his hands on the bar to open the door and took a deep breath. They nodded their readi-ness to each other, Ayla's heart beating out of her chest.

"Quick, I hear him walking this way," she told Christopher.

He pushed on the door handle setting off a flashing red light above the door, the sole indicator the alarm had been tripped. They took off like two teenage shoplifters running from a mall cop and headed for the park Ayla spoke of. As they reached the central plaza, Ayla pulled Christopher towards a clump of thick bushes to their left. They dived in, digging themselves in to disappear while they waited for the agents to come looking. They both worked at calming their excitement and breathing, trying to become as silent as possible as they lowered their heart rate. It took about five minutes, during which Christopher cursed himself for stopping to hide. But the club bouncer finally came around, surveying the surroundings, sweeping the ground with his eyes for a clue toward the direction they might have taken. Ayla felt her heart stop, worried they punched a hole in the bushes that could attract the agent's attention. Christopher was fixated on the target, like a hunting dog ready to pounce. He placed his hand on Ayla's shoulder,

"Stay calm. I can hear you breathe."

Ayla pushed away her worries, applying the breathing techniques she had mastered since childhood, slowing her breathing until it became silent. The club bouncer walked toward their position, zeroing in on the exact spot they entered the bushes. Christopher dug in his feet, ready to bolt. He nodded to Ayla to get ready. The bouncer stopped right in front of them, apparently trying to figure out where they might have exited. He saw the hole they punched to get in but seemed to be looking for an alternative explanation, not satisfied they could have entered the bushes. Christopher grabbed a stone on the ground and threw it behind them. The noise attracted the attention of the agent, and as soon as he went around the bushes to look, Christopher grabbed Ayla's wrist and pulled her out, running back toward the university.

"Won't there be other agents there?" Ayla managed to blurt as she was pulled abruptly along.

"No. By now, they've spread out in every direction. Our best bet is going back. That way, we end up behind them, and we can coordinate our movements by observing their operations."

They slipped behind a wall, Christopher looking back to see if the agent had caught their scent. With no one in sight, he took Ayla by the hand and began walking at a normal pace. Ayla didn't understand why he took her hand but didn't mind at all. She liked the idea of walking around hand in hand. They walked along, looking like any average strolling couple when Ayla spotted two university colleagues walking toward them. One colleague, she didn't know very well, but the other was a major bully. She tugged at Christopher for them to go around, not wanting to confront anyone. Christopher, understanding her discomfort, gave her a wink as they approached the two men, the bully looking surprised to see Ayla wasn't scampering off. As they got close to the men, Christopher started talking.

"I've got to say, Miss Karemi, without your insight, there's no way we could have solved the equation that's been stumping us for so long." As Christopher said this, Ayla observed the bully's reaction, her ego inflating as she saw the man's face go from a mean smirk to surprised, to disappointment. Christopher continued. "I must admit, your approach seemed far-fetched the first time I looked at it, but it's been a boon to our research to use your approach."

As they were distancing themselves from the bully, Christopher squeezed Ayla's hand. "I hope that will inspire that guy to open his mind," he said. Ayla raised Christopher's hand to her mouth and kissed it. *How could he know what to say?* she thought. She hadn't told him much about her time there. She chose to let that thought go, happy to leave that place.

They walked toward Ayla's home, following the same pattern as before in the car, using a convoluted route to make sure no one was on their tail. As they grew more confident that they were not being followed, Christopher told Ayla more about the village in India that could welcome them.

CHAPTER 17

After a day spent deciding where each plank of wood was to be placed, Engella looked at the work she had accomplished, admiring her new shed-house with love, proud to officially be a part of the community. Seen from the outside, one could think the village was a cult with a rigid set of rules, when, in fact, each person there was free to come and go as they pleased and led the life they thought best for themselves. Engella was told this could cause some strife on occasion, but a well-organized public forum was planned every week in the park at the center of the village. At the forum, any person who spoke was to adhere to the truth and stay true to the situation. Any personal interpretation or opinion was to be silenced if it didn't constructively add to the discussion. This usually resulted in a fair compromise for both parties, although sometimes the discussion could take a more vehement turn.

Some people have come and gone, unable to connect with their true inner self, keeping a foot in the "civilized" world by way of social media, or grasping at their past life, letting it haunt their souls with regret. They are never kicked out. Everyone can be who they are. But these people always reach a breaking point and leave, unable to absorb what the village can offer, obscuring the present with an unhealthy attachment to a long gone past, or unnecessarily dreaming of a Utopian future. By staying true to their inner feelings and sharing them, most people at the village found companionship, friendship, sometimes love. Some stay, even if they never find a way to fully integrate the emotional spectrum, keeping a distance from everyone, a part of their lives staying private. But they still take part in the everyday activities required to keep the village going, finding fulfillment in those moments, even thriving from them. Each person is assigned a task according to their abilities and interests. Depending on the needs in the village at any given time, someone is tasked with fulfilling that need. That approach had helped the village stay true to its nature as its inhabitants adapted admirably to the changes that have occurred over time.

Night had settled on the region, and since she had recovered her capacity to see, Engella was itching for a night run. She had grown to love the idea of discovering a new area at night. Each time she was in a new place, she would feel the same nerves she felt the first time Rafael took her night running. She went to a stream that passed near her house and bathed her bare feet in the running water. Engella was surprised at the coolness of the stream. The day had been blisteringly hot, and the evening was barely cooler, but the water running over her feet felt cool, almost cold. Thiago came along, a blissful smile illuminating his face as he strolled along, deep in thought. He noticed Engella and sat next to her.

"Cooling your feet, I see? Good way to bring down your body temperature. It won't get much cooler over-night. I suggest you sleep on your roof tonight; it will be more tolerable that way."

"In fact, I'm getting ready for a night run," Engella said as she rubbed her feet with a cloth to dry them off.

"What's that?" Thiago had a Portuguese accent, but Engella couldn't tell if the origin was European or Brazilian.

Engella saw a clean-shaven and long-haired man that was proud of his appearance. But he seemed to wear it well, as the pride in his appearance didn't overpower the vibe that emanated from him. He carried a sense of contentment everywhere he went, happy to be the person he was. Surprised he didn't know about the night runs, she explained as best she could.

"It's something I learned a long time ago. To be able to find a connection to the surrounding land, I must go running in the forest at night. This way, I can learn of its nuances, its hidden powers. It helps me focus and stay centered. I'm washing my feet so I can feel the ground under them even more." Thiago looked at Engella, perplexed.

"You go barefoot? At night?" His face had lost all trace of blissfulness as he seemed genuinely worried.

Engella smiled at his worry. "It's not as dangerous as you might think. Once I reach a complete state of meditative connection with the world around me, I can see the forest, and I let my energy guide my steps. It hardly ever fails. In a worst-case scenario, I scrape my knees and elbows." Engella looked at Thiago. Isn't this something that's practiced here?

"No. We use group meditations to center ourselves and feel connected to one and other. Travel deep in the forest is something reserved for the hunters and gatherers. I guess they might be able to tell you if they know of this. Personally, I'll take the occasional daytime walk in the forest, but I like to stay available for whatever is needed in the immediate vicinity of the village. If it's workers in the kitchen that are needed, I'll go there. If it's traveling to neighboring towns for trade, I will do that. I keep to immediate and necessary village activity. I don't like the idea of walking in the forest." He put a hand on her shoulder. "Be careful, Engella. This forest holds secrets of a deadly variety. Stay alert, and don't go too far. She found his worrying endearing, wondering how someone who's afraid of the forest could live here."

"Don't fret Thiago. I'm safe doing this. Once you learn to see, there's no difference between night and day. Plus, I've already met the tiger; it approached me when I reached the edge of the forest and brought me here. In my book, that tells me that it and I are on the same wavelength." She got up and began looking around, deciding which way to go. "See you at breakfast," she told Thiago and took off running.

He waved at her, smiling at the strange practices of the new villager that was Engella. He then took a sip from the stream by cupping his hands and continued his evening walk.

Engella entered the forest at full stride, her mind ready and excited, her body filled with adrenaline. The aromas in the air hammered her olfactory senses, the perfume from the flowers mixing with the evening dew to create a strong, thick wall of pollinated incense. But she kept her rhythm, following the ground's variations with ease, breathing in the new environment with deep, deliberate inhalations. The green hue pulsing from the ground seemed thicker somehow, perfumes rising from it in waves, invading the air she was breathing. With her heart rate getting a little out of control, Engella slowed her pace, wanting to take in everything she could from this run. She sensed something observing, even following her. Engella ducked behind a tree and waited for her pursuer to show himself. Sounds of heavy foot-steps accompanied by low grunts preceded the beast's apparition in the moon's glow.

Engella saw a beautiful sloth bear appear from the trees in front of her in a small clearing in the forest. It stopped and looked in her direction, seeming to wait for her to follow. Its dark coat shined in the moonlight, the rays of light shining off each hair like stars spread all over its body. She got out from behind the tree and began to walk toward the bear. Satisfied by this, it began to walk toward a clearing, keeping an eye on Engella to make sure she was following. In the clearing, it circled a large object, then disappeared into the dark forest. Engella reached the large object and went to touch it. A bolt of ethereal energy traveled from her fingers to her toes, passing through every single particle in her body, down to the smallest molecule. Within seconds, millions of images traveled through her mind when the energy bolt invaded her.

Engella tried to concentrate to see at least one image clearly, but as soon as the energy bolt reached the ground, passing through her feet, she was brutally pushed back and found herself sitting on the ground, three feet away from the object. The images had passed through her mind so fast she wasn't certain what had happened. She got up, eager to return to the village, curious from the experience. When she reached the village, no one was in sight, so Engella climbed up to her roof to look at the stars and meditate on her encounter. As she was getting ready to settle into her mantra, Jolan arrived.

"Hey there. Can I come up?"

"Sure. There's a rope ladder on the side." Engella was disappointed she couldn't meditate, but Jolan might be able to enlighten her on what had happened.

"I saw you run into the forest earlier. I guess you still apply Rafael's training regimen. Do you think you would be able to teach it to the villagers?" Jolan almost seemed to be pleading.

"I guess." Engella quickly changed the subject. "Can we talk about something I observed in the woods a moment ago?"

Jolan seemed a little surprised. "Sure. Are you okay?" He looked genuinely worried.

"Yeah, I'm fine," Engella said, waving her hand. "I crossed paths with a sloth bear that guided me to a clearing in the forest. There was a large object in the middle of the clearing, and when I touched it, a jolt of energy mixed with millions of indiscernible images traveled through my mind before the energy pulse propelled me away from it. Do you know what that might be?" Relating the event almost made Engella relive the moment, her body still pumped with adrenaline, and her brain drowned in dopamine.

"You came across our tree of life. If a bear showed you the way, that means you're probably already in sync with its energy. All we need to do now is share our knowledge of the tree with you before you can return to connect with it once more." He seemed genuinely excited. "It's taken some people years to be able to approach the tree, let alone touch it." His eyes beamed in the dark, reflecting the moonlight. "Yes, Engella Iblis, I believe we are at a crossroads in our existence, and you're an important part of this."

CHAPTER 18

Christopher and Ayla were walking down an alleyway three blocks from her apartment. He stayed ahead of Ayla, his senses fully unrestrained, the blood in his veins running cold as he stayed on the lookout for any sign of an ambush. He was alarmed by the eerie calm that enveloped them, making Ayla a little nervous as well. This part of the city wasn't the most active, but on any day of the week, the activity level created a certain amount of noise that was absent, the only discernible noise coming from the leaves dancing in the light breeze—no cars, no pedestrians, nothing else.

"We'll wait here," Christopher said, crouching behind a trash container.

"Wait for what?" Ayla wanted to get her documents and leave that place.

"I called Zorina from the allegiance; she should be here soon." Christopher relaxed a little, satisfied they were safe for the moment. "You can give her a key to your place when she gets here. That way, she can clear your apartment before we enter."

Ayla sat on the ground next to Christopher, crossing her legs and leaning on the wall to get comfortable while waiting. Christopher had told her about a village deep in a national park in India, where a group of people lived according to the rhythm of nature. A village governed by all, under the guise that all human life deserves respect, that all must accomplish the tasks required to keep the village going, that freedom of thought is primordial to evolution. He went on and on about the place, and Ayla couldn't contain her excitement to get there, her eagerness to retrieve her documents so they could leave almost overpowering the need to stay put. She heard footsteps approaching and jumped out to greet the reinforcements. She found herself face to face with Dr. Frank Cutler, who was flanked by three "bodyguards" who were at a complete standstill, awaiting instructions. Christopher stayed behind the container, hoping they hadn't seen him.

"Happy to see you," Cutler said. He wasn't smiling. "I had no doubt we would meet again. I had hoped we could settle this in a more peaceful manner, but you have given me no choice. A new world order is upon us, and you're in my way. Now, you will kindly go with my associates to your house to retrieve your research; then, you will give me everything you have, after which my associates will take care of you." Cutler looked at her with stern eyes. "I warned you before. And that stands for the both of you." Cutler finished, stretching his neck, so Christopher understood he was busted.

With one nod from Cutler, Ayla found herself physically incapacitated by one of the bodyguards as he grabbed her arm and performed an arm lock before trying to push her ahead. From afar, this probably looked like an arrest, as people walked by, virtually ignoring what was going on, even trying to widen their path to avoid the situation.

Christopher was surrounded by the two other bodyguards, each grabbing an arm and lifting him up, pulling him ahead with his feet barely touching the ground. He remained calm, his eyes revealing a confidence they could find a way out to Ayla. This helped her focus, as she began to concentrate on the grip the bodyguard had on her arm, looking for a way to loosen it to get away. The pressure he was applying was constant, but with each step they took, there was a brief instant that his grip waned. Ayla focused on that rhythm, certain she could tear away at the right moment, although she wasn't sure what she would do after.

"You disappointed me, Ayla," Cutler said. "I thought you understood the grandeur of my plan. Your research will do nothing but hinder my project, which is why I need to keep you quiet." Ayla looked over at Cutler, gauging him for any sign of humanity, to no avail. Cutler's gaze was cold, unflinching.

"Would you at least consider looking into it? I'm certain there's some information there you can use for your project." Ayla said, trying to buy some time.

She noticed a small glitch in Cutler's stone-faced demeanor. He ordered his bodyguards to stop and placed himself squarely in front of Ayla. Christopher was forced to his knees by his two tormentors, one of them pressing down on his head to keep him immobile.

"My dear, I've studied your research, and it's a problem for me. The one thing I can do with this problem is to make it disappear. All I wanted was your research, but now you've shown me that you will be a nuisance. I have tomorrow's key to a better future for all, and there's nothing you can do about it. The group Christopher speaks of has been decimated, no one can help you. Your resistance will only result in death unless I decide to reprogram you to do my bidding." His smile sent shivers down Ayla's spine, which strengthened her resolve.

Cutler was so filled with pride during his rant to Ayla that he didn't notice Zorina approaching them from behind, the bodyguards oblivious to her advance. Cutler had programmed their focus to be on Ayla and Christopher, overly confident that no one would come to help them. Zorina got squarely behind the man holding Ayla. She glanced around to make sure she hadn't been spotted. Ayla, who had noticed Zorina's approach, discreetly nodded to her that she was ready to pull out of the grip the bodyguard had on her. She had slid her thumb away from the turning point that gave the bodyguard leverage on her to a position where she could escape from the hold without breaking her arm. Christopher gave Zorina a signal he was ready to break out of his hold as well by blinking twice. Zorina dug in her feet, making sure she was well grounded to pounce on the guard holding Ayla. Christopher started counting down from three with his hand hidden alongside his leg. Cutler, still unaware of the imminent ambush, continued his rant.

"Humans need order to be able to function properly. They need direction. Any other way of thinking automatically leads to disorder, social unrest. Your suggestion that humans can reach a higher level of consciousness on the condition that mystical and scientific options merge into a single line of thought is a pipe dream that will achieve nothing. At best, it will possibly prolong humanity's tedious existence by a couple of generations. I offered you the chance to join me and ensure your comfort in the new order, but now it's too late."

As Cutler finished saying this, Ayla broke the hold the bodyguard had on her, twisting her body counter-clockwise to release the arm lock. At the same time, Zorina grabbed Ayla's captor by the neck and applied pressure, putting him to sleep in seconds. Christopher stood up abruptly, whispering something in his captors' ears, making them both slump to the ground. Christopher dusted himself off, the two hypnotized guards lying either side of him, and looked straight at Cutler, now defenseless. The guard who had been choked to sleep by Zorina began to awake, groggy from the bear hold he just suffered.

"Protect!" Frank Cutler barked at his soldier, as he took off in the opposite direction, leaving his bodyguard to face the three accomplices.

Christopher and Ayla stood on either side of the bodyguard, waiting for a reaction on his part. "Calm down and rest," Christopher said to the guard. He didn't react to the order, meaning he had a different shutdown command. The bodyguard was trying to figure out who he should immobilize first but was becoming more and more aggravated, unable to make a choice. By staying on opposite sides, Christopher and Ayla kept the hypnotized soldier at bay, as he tried to figure out his next move, unable to act, his mind frozen by the indecision. He would focus on Christopher for a second, then Ayla, not able to decide who to neutralize first. Zorina took off after Cutler, seeing that her two friends had the situation under control. But she was already too late; he had disappeared.

Ayla and Christopher had tightened their circle around the hypnotized bodyguard. If the hypno-soldier went for one of them, the other would punch the guard in the ribs, which would incapacitate him long enough for them to neutralize him. Christopher saw Zorina return without Cutler. This meant backup could be on the way soon. Ayla understood the situation and punched the bodyguard behind the knees, forcing him to the ground. Christopher pressed down on his shoulder to keep the man down.

"I'm really sorry, man, I'm sure you're a nice guy when you're not hypnotized, but right now, I need to get as far from you and your friends as I can."

Christopher brutally pushed him to the ground, face down in the dirt. Ayla climbed on his back and dug a knee into the bodyguard's back, right between the shoulder blades. She held him there while Christopher tied him up. Zorina helped them carry him behind the trash bin.

"The hypnosis will cause him to do everything in his power to liberate himself, so he should be okay before the next trash pickup," Christopher told Ayla, thinking she might be worried about the man. She was already on her way to her apartment.

"What? Yeah . . . sure . . . fine. Come on."

They entered the apartment as quietly as possible, making sure no one was waiting for them. As they reached Ayla's office space, a desk and file cabinet in the middle of the living room, Christopher continued his search of the place while Ayla retrieved her documents. Once she backed everything up on the computer, she cleared her hard drive. Christopher returned, visibly satisfied they were safe.

"Have you backed everything up?" he asked.

"Yup, and I reset it back to factory settings."

"Not enough."

Christopher began to unscrew the computer's cover. After revealing the innards of the machine, he proceeded to rip out all the chips and threw them in the micro-wave. When he started the oven, the inside of the oven became a spectacular show of lights, with sparks and flames emanating from the dying computer chips. As the microwave ended its destruction, a stench of burnt plastic and rubber filled the apartment.

"Now it's erased," Christopher said. "Do you have everything?" He was already at the door, ready to go.

"I think so," Ayla said, still going through the filing cabinet. She pulled out more documents, then filled the bottom drawer with random papers, all unrelated to her current research. "Now, I'm ready." She told Christopher.

"Let's go," he said, opening the door.

Ayla looked around her apartment one last time to make sure they hadn't forgotten anything before following Christopher out the door. As they turned the corner, Ayla took Christopher's hand, feeling their luck was starting to change for the better. As they moved further away from her former life, Ayla's thoughts went to Engella. She hoped they would meet at the Indian village. Engella did tell her she was leaving for a while, that could be where she was going to.

"This village in India, where did you hear about it?" Ayla asked, realizing she had not asked Christopher before.

He hesitated, not sure his explanation would hold up.

"I dreamt it." He looked at Ayla sideways, gauging her reaction. "But it wasn't a normal dream. I felt present and conscious in it. A brown-haired woman showed me how to reach this place, showed me their way of life, told me they needed protection. She was luminous and dark all at once, the light she emitted was enveloped with a shadow that seemed to contain the power her light harbored." His description filled Ayla with joy.

"That was Engella. I'm sure of it. This means she knows about this place." Ayla let out a cry of joy, starting to skip along the sidewalk, pulling a confused Christopher along.

• • •

They reached the airport without a hitch and purchased two one-way tickets to Bhopal, India. As they waited to pass through airport security in the central waiting area, Ayla noticed a woman standing near the entrance. The woman had the same stance as the club bouncer they saw at the university. Ayla noticed she hadn't yet spotted them and proceeded to sneak around the waiting area so she could go around behind the bouncer woman. Once she was close enough, Ayla whispered, "Calm down and rest," in her ear. The woman wavered a little, then fell to the ground with a thump, Ayla getting a surge of excitement from the woman's reaction. This attracted the attention of everyone in the waiting area, causing a major commotion as airport guards called for medical help amidst the sudden chaos of travelers running around, fearing a terrorist attack.

Christopher, seeing Ayla next to the fainted woman, understood what had happened and began to scan the room for other hypno-soldiers. He spotted a man and a woman scanning the room as well, and they spotted him at the same time. Christopher did what he could to disappear in the chaotic crowd while still looking for Ayla. Keeping an eye on the two targets, he slipped behind a column. He saw they had lost track of him, so he made sure to stay at a safe distance from them. Ayla had seen them as well and chose to stay low, waiting for Christopher to look in her direction so she could signal him to follow her through security. Their flight was in four hours, but it seemed prudent to access a more secure area of the airport at that point.

Christopher's eyes found Ayla's, and she waved him over with her head, keeping the two pursuers in her line of sight to stay out of theirs. They were searching in the opposite direction, so this was the perfect time to slip away. The commotion around them was calming down, and paramedics were helping the unconscious woman. Christopher managed to reach Ayla without being seen, and they strolled discreetly towards the security area, where a massive line was clogging access to the customs officers. The general atmosphere was a little calmer on that side, but there was still an excited fever in the air, everyone in a rush to get beyond the gate into a "safe zone." Ayla tried to take advantage of it, slipping into the middle of the line unnoticed, disappearing from sight between two travelers who were carrying massive amounts of baggage, still unnerved by the fainting hypno-soldier.

Christopher stayed near the wall, keeping his back to it as he scanned the line for anyone suspicious. They advanced at a snail's pace, and the energy in the place had people around them, screaming bloody murder because of the delays. Christopher couldn't see the two pursuers anymore but stayed alert; they couldn't be far. Ayla passed the gate rather quickly as the customs officers, feeling the rush to let as many people through as they could, didn't ask many questions before stamping her passport. She then slipped to the side to wait for Christopher. She spotted the two hypnotized soldiers beyond the main security access, still searching in the wrong direction. The hypnotized woman Ayla had put down was getting up, visibly confused about her presence at the airport. The paramedic tried to get her to board the ambulance, but although she couldn't confirm her identity, she refused to go to the hospital and left the airport before the police could question her more on her lack of identification. Finally, Christopher came through the gate without a hitch. Certain they had escaped, Ayla and Christopher awaited their flight, their minds more at ease.

They kept an eye open for any potential danger, but no one around them showed any sign of being hypnotized, which helped them to relax a little more before boarding the plane. An announcement calling for their flight over the public address system finalized Ayla and Christopher's escape as they smiled and boarded the plane hand in hand, both smiling broadly.

CHAPTER 19

Engella settled at the lunch table with her plate. Today was a "whatever's left day," meaning the kitchen team created a meal with everything that was scrapped from other recipes. A cream of discarded vegetable pieces, cooked in a broth made with the bones of the week's hunt, was the main course, accompanied by a wondrous choice of cheese and yogurt obtained from trade with neighbors. The regular income of wheat from their fields guaranteed there was always bread available. That day was naan bread, but there was a rotation, as most types of bread were offered over a two-week period. She thought back to her discussion with Jolan after she found the tree. Her sleep had been dreamless, even if she tried to connect with her dream self. Since Rafael had taught her the way to access the dream realm, she had never had any trouble entering her own dream, except for the night before.

Absent-minded, she sipped away at her soup, letting her thoughts wander. She thought about her time in Yaqui Territory, the time she spent with Ayla at the university, the time she taught Dwight in high school summer classes, her trip with the nameless taxi driver, the thoughts and memories associated with these events all merging together as if they were becoming the memory of a single, larger experience. Her capacity to place an event in time had always been iffy, but those moments all felt directly related as if a giant synchronicity permeated her life and had brought her to this village. She interpreted the fact that she couldn't dream the night before as a sign that there was a new evolution required on her part. The fact her mind went to these specific events, pulling them together as one, indicated to Engella that she was following the right path. She suspected that the energy bolt given by the tree was probably the main reason she couldn't dream. So, she needed to gain the necessary knowledge to evolve to her next phase and connect with the tree's energy.

Since leaving Rafael, the stagnation of her evolution left her doubtful that she could ever reach a higher level of understanding, even abandoning the belief that she could reach this higher knowledge in her lifetime, as her time in populated parts of the world had obscured her capacity to go beyond what she already knew. The amount of energy flowing in city centers in the dream realm was too opaque for Engella to be able to rise above it and explore her waking dreams satisfactorily. She concentrated her efforts on maintaining her capacity to have simple, lucid dreams, unknowingly strengthening her presence in this realm during that time. When Rafael told her that her energy had grown exponentially, she felt emboldened.

Encouraged by the fact that her subconscious mind was able to analyze and absorb information without the help of her conscious brain, Engella felt the urgency to reconnect with her subconscious. Being able to create a link to the tree was now the sole focus of her life. She knew the village had group meditations on a regular basis and thought she could use that as a springboard to return to a higher state of consciousness.

While she mused on her immediate future, a group had formed around her. Jolan sat at her table, accompanied by Naina. As the group formed around them, everyone wanted to listen in on the coming conversation. Jolan sat in front of Engella and waited. Naina stood next to the table, arms crossed. It flustered Engella, as neither Jolan nor Naina were smiling. Their faces were deeply serious, bordering on angry.

"Um, is everything okay?" Engella said, unsure of the reaction to expect. "If I did something wrong, I apologize, I'm still adapting to the way of life in the village." Engella waited to see if that would calm them down. Naina spoke first, her jaw clenched from either anger or fear; Engella couldn't tell.

"We are in danger. You need to speak with the tree. We must open the gates before it's too late."

Naina was speaking in the direction of Engella, but through her as well, her eyes glazed by a strong, negative emotion. She didn't ask Naina about what she meant by "opening the gates," fearing it would only exacerbate the tension.

"I will. But first, I need to learn its language; match its vibration." Engella spoke as softly as possible, trying to calm Naina in the process.

"That's where I will help you," Jolan interrupted. "I would have preferred taking more time to help you assimilate this knowledge, but we must move faster now.

Some people are motivated to erase us from existence, and we can't identify them, their energy is hidden or invisible. But if you can do what I believe you can, it won't make a difference if we disappear. A new phase of existence will already be in motion."

Jolan looked around; everyone was evading his glance, looking like a class of primary school children caught doing something wrong. He continued. "They are scared," he told Engella. "We have some defensive capacities, but nothing that can withstand what I believe is coming. You can precipitate events. Rafael is a great guide; I know he has shown you how to overcome your limitations. We need that now. From this moment forward, that is your sole task at the village; you're not to participate in everyday chores, we will all cover for you."

Engella looked at the group around her and began to worry about their motivations. She risked a question, trying to probe their intentions. "The tree of life's energy is for every human, plant, animal, or rock that populates this planet, right?" The group nodded in unison. "Will you try to influence its energy flow after I establish a connection with it?" Her question was direct in hopes of getting a reaction. A quiet chuckle came from the group.

"You overestimate us, Engella. How could we think about influencing the energy flow of the tree if we can't even get close to it?"

Jolan seemed calm, but Engella noticed she had pressed a button asking that question. "We are much more worried about the possibility of being attacked and seeing the tree destroyed forever." He looked around for support, but everyone kept their heads hung low, ashamed they were succumbing to the feeling of fear.

"You shouldn't worry too much," Engella said. "I met a warrior in a dream and asked that person to come here."

Christopher's subconscious energy had crossed Engella's during a recent lucid dream, and she had sensed she needed to show him the way to the village, as she populated his dreams with images of this place, not knowing why she felt the urge to do it. Sitting there with the villagers, she knew why. Jolan looked at Engella with an intrigued look, a smile emerging from beneath the strain of fear that permeated his face. "And how do you know he is a warrior?" Jolan asked.

"The energy's color, its intensity, and other variables help me recognize who is before me when I visit that plane of existence. This person is powerful and trustworthy. That, I'm sure of." Engella leaned back on her chair, trying to give out a more relaxed vibe to calm the group.

"You say, person. Is this warrior a man or a woman? How will we recognize this combatant when he arrives?" Jolan's impatience surfaced in the cadence of his speech.

"I don't know the sex of a person in the dream realm, but you will recognize the warrior the same way you recognized me." Engella understood at that moment that the villagers were not ready for armed confrontation, even if they had a small group of people dedicated to the eventual defense of the village. She hoped the warrior she met in her dreams would come. They needed an injection of optimism.

Jolan got up and invited Engella to follow him. They went to a large barn hidden behind thick bushes and lush trees, a windowless mixture of wood and bricks that turned out to be filled with books and ancient documents, a soft yellowish light flooding the room from different sources. There was a large hanging lamp in the middle, and small table lamps spread around. The junction between the roof and walls let a little light into the room but was mostly for aeration purposes.

Jolan took out books from a shelf, holding them out for Engella. She took the books and set them on the table in the middle of the room.

"Thank you. I know you want to help, but I must first listen to the silence of the room before I can start." She gently waved toward the door, indicating to Jolan that she wanted him to leave. "If I'm to learn to speak to the tree, I need to listen for it."

Jolan left without saying another word, visibly relieved and excited.

CHAPTER 20

Dr. Cutler was seething. Ayla's escape meant there was a possibility his plan could get derailed. Although the potential she had to interfere could appear infinitesimally small to an outsider, Frank couldn't leave anything to chance. Anything that could contradict his research could be the seed needed to mount a resistance, making the operation that much more difficult. He promised an easy transition to the initiative, and during an operation as sensitive as this one, no detail could be ignored. He had been informed of her travel to India with Christopher Saddleton. He needed to find their trail and end the threat they represented to him.

Frank mused on his twisted notion that the pursuit of self-realization among the people has never yielded any other result than confusion and violence. He felt a surge of pride, knowing that this idea will be a thing of the past with his intervention. Humans will be confined to follow the path assigned to them and will be happy about it. Frank knew why human history constantly repeated itself and knew he could correct the anomaly. All Ayla and that dastardly group of bleeding-heart light-bringers were doing was accentuating the divide between individuals without attacking the core of the problem, our parasite encrusted DNA. His mind returning to practical notions, he thought about India being such a big place; he would need more soldiers to canvas the country. He sent a group of his personal soldiers to gather people from the Indian community so he could hypnotize a small army he would send all over India in search of the thorn in his side. As the hounds brought in subjects, Frank submitted each individual to a complete brainwash, erasing anything that could interfere with their chase from their minds.

With each hypnosis, Frank felt his anger swell, unable to understand why Ayla, or anyone else for that matter, would reject his offer. Humanity has designed its society in a way that requires that a select group define the path to follow for the masses. Humans weren't equipped to confront the horror of freedom. They needed beacons to mark out the boundaries which represent the limits of their independence. Without those borders, most people spread themselves so thin they end up voluntarily choosing to limit themselves, becoming ascetic and close-minded as they try to protect their individuality. Frank was impressed at how the initiative managed to convince the people that they could find comfort in the notion that a heavy workload and a large debt would help them uphold a balanced existence. The system made it so that it was easy to spot those who were able to navigate this freedom unblemished. They were commonly recruited by the initiative to be shaped into tomorrow's rulers. If a person refused to integrate the halls of power, their reputation would be destroyed by any means necessary, the resistor being reduced to living anonymously on the outskirts of society, barely scraping by.

Regrettably for Ayla, those who refuse to take part in the change this time around will be eliminated by way of death or psychic destruction, *death being the best of the two options*, Frank thought to himself. The hounds began to return with their prisoners. As Frank settled a newly captured recruit into the hypno-chair, two men entered the laboratory—designer suits, head held arrogantly high, gold cuff links adorning their dress shirts beyond the suit sleeve. *Lawyers*, Frank thought to himself. He gestured to the panicked man in the chair to wait a moment by miming the shush sound, and after making sure the straps were tight, went towards the lawyers, who were both opening their briefcase in a synchronized gesture. The blond-haired one spoke first.

"Good day, Dr. Cutler. It has come to our attention that you have been having trouble with a certain individual who could cause the project to derail. The consortium would like to know if this will have any bearing on the procedure that will be implemented soon." The brown-haired lawyer remained fixated on Frank, giving him a "be careful what you answer" look. Frank cleared his throat.

"If there's an impact, it will be minimal. I'm making sure of this as we speak. You can go back and reassure the initiative that the plan is on track."

Frank felt confident this meeting was nothing more than a courtesy visit designed to show Frank he's under surveillance. The brown-haired lawyer dismissed that thought in an instant.

"If any doubt lingers on the feasibility of this enterprise, the group will not hesitate to shut down the project. Rest assured, we are still fully invested, but should this problem persist, we might be obliged to look at you as a potential problem—a loose end to be erased." He looked straight at Frank, "I believe you know what happens to problems."

Both lawyers stuffed whatever documents they took out back into their briefcases, wished Frank a good day, and left. Right before leaving, one lawyer turned back and added, "You're certain we can't go ahead without their elimination?"

"I'm certain," Frank replied stiffly. "But don't worry; I'm in control of everything." The lawyer gave him an unconvinced look and left.

As the laboratory door clanged shut, Frank was a little bemused by the visit. For the first time since meeting with a council of representatives from the powers in place, he felt threatened. Up to this point, his project had created excitement and hope of a better, more powerful tomorrow for the dark matter initiative. But they were having doubts, and Frank found it essential to quell these doubts as soon as possible.

He returned to the man in the chair, who was in a complete panic and began to apply the hypnosis procedure, adding in a propensity for violence to make sure no one got away. Frank believed that had the preceding hunters been infused with a little more violent inclinations, Ayla and her helper wouldn't have managed to escape. As he completed the process, the man's eyes confirmed to Frank; it was the way to go. The man was looking at Frank with a steely-eyed focus, ready to take on his mission. Frank kept him under a couple more minutes, adjusting certain social traits, so he could get through customs and circulate in society without being targeted by enforcement officers who could be attracted by his threatening look. The result fascinated him each time, as the man emerged from the hypnosis

visibly itching to get going, pulling on the straps holding him down. Although he was eager to get going, he
remained in full control of the pulsing anger that Frank
had infused in the hypnosis. As Frank untied him, he
seemed bigger somehow. The man got up from the chair
and headed straight for the exit. His demeanor was
confident and strong. Frank congratulated himself on
the new level of hypnosis he was able to infuse, certain
this time it would be enough to complete the task.

Frank felt he was as close as ever to attaining his
goal to fix the human DNA and became more and more
obsessed with the need to tame any encouragement
toward self-reliance in the world, which would help
to ensure the final procedure's full implementation.
Happy about the new level of hypnosis he had achieved,
he decided to send out violence-infused hounds to
the four corners of the world to confront and eradicate any person that preached any form of ecological
or psychological equilibrium to find happiness. Their
teachings could encourage some people to forgo the
DNA procedure, which would do nothing more than
create a different kind of social inequity, unquestioned
happiness versus search for self. The lawyer's visit had
shown Frank that nothing less than a 100% transformation of the people would be considered acceptable
to the initiative. He didn't want to become a problem
to the group, that much was certain.

The hounds he sent out began a crime spree that
resulted in most cities' murder rates going up, the wave
of violence they ignited spreading like wildfire. With
help from the controlled media outlets, the majority of
the earth's population began to see the proponents of
a life based on the search for the true self as dangerous
to society. The systematic murder of any person who
preached self-reliance, which was presented in the media

as proof that they were dangerous and violent, created a notion that the cleanup was necessary. Some preaching practitioners were chased down and eliminated by the hounds, others denounced by their neighbors or co-workers, sometimes even their own followers. Frank took this development as a sign that humans were more than ever ready to be instructed in what to think and what to wish for. He decided to help amplify the developing notion that freewill was dangerous. He released some research made by Dwight Como about the existence of pillaging and violence throughout human history. Frank prepared clean, crisp documents for the media, twisting Dwight's research to show that all who were prone to a life based on self-reliance, sharing, and community organization are nothing more than dangerous false prophets who must be silenced. Their teachings have done nothing more than make life more miserable than it needed to be. That addition to the campaign helped unearth more false prophets, as the hounds pillaged their way through every city, town, and village.

The path toward happiness lies in the dictate Frank will implant in everyone's DNA. Society's hierarchy will be established and accepted by all—even celebrated. Frank believed that the injected DNA strands would create a natural leveling of the society, as each class level would stay within its social borders, having no wish to mingle with others who didn't share their desires. In this new world order, should the leading strata need an injection of fresh DNA, a person will be extracted from a lower caste, and his or her DNA will be modified to fit with the wants and desires specific to the highest caste. Frank couldn't help but feel his ego bulge with pride as he saw his plan come to fruition, with the exception of the small detail called Ayla Karemi and her research.

Even if the collective unconscious allegiance was almost eliminated, the remaining members of the group couldn't get their hands on this research; it would do nothing more than embolden their resolve. He couldn't understand Ayla's refusal to accept the truth. Most humans need direction, rules, limitations. He always saw anyone who believed in humanity's capacity to evolve on its own as cloud chasers. And with his plan almost complete, the belief had turned to certainty. Frank picked up his phone and called a representative from the group who had been building the transformation laboratories to make sure construction was on time, itching to start playing with people's DNA. Satisfied with their answer, he continued programming soldiers for the hunt in India.

Reassured the laboratories would be ready on time, Frank returned to his research, wanting to go through it once more to make sure no detail was overlooked. He spread some documents on his desk, bringing up more information on his three computer screens, then settled into a meditative-like state and went over the research's minutia. As he reviewed the work, finding no flaw, he was fully confident he was on point. Besides Ayla, his main worry was the two-year transformation period. This was a long enough timeframe for a resistance to form. Although his soldiers were hard at work cleaning up any potential problem, assisted by the initiative who used their population control tools, Cutler couldn't help but be a little paranoid. From police authoritarianism to forced psychiatric internment, the initiative assisted the hypnotized soldiers in rounding up the potential resisters as much as they could. But he still didn't like the fact he wasn't in full control. His other main worry was the competence of the doctors who will carry out the procedure around the world. He had taught the basic method to about a hundred doctors so far and felt confident most of them had the know-how to achieve the desired goal, but he had some reservations. Not as much about their competence than their palpable doubt about this procedure. Frank had advised the initiative to set up surveillance on the doctors to make sure they stayed true to the plan but had received no news since relaying this information. He made a note to speak to someone about it before the start of the transformation program, unaware of the initiative's plans for him once everything was complete. They had agreed to his demands, but only verbally. His pride was blinding him from seeing that they would erase him from existence after everything was done.

CHAPTER 21

When the steward opened the cabin door of the plane, Ayla and Christopher were instantly floored by a wave of Bhopal heat invading the plane cabin as they exited. As soon as the humid air reached him, Christopher felt his shirt stick to his skin as sweat began to pearl on it. Ayla joyfully breathed in the heat, taking deep breaths, thanking mother earth for this humid, enveloping warmth. She had spent most of her life either basking in or dreaming about the heat-filled days of summer. Her love of the heat had been a part of her essential being for as long as she could remember. Any time spent in a winter setting was pure torture for her, and she relished the heat, wrapping itself around her, even more, when she stepped out of the plane onto a hot tarmac. The airport was a beautiful little building filled with windows all around, Ayla hoping the heat of the sun would reach inside once they entered. As the door slid open to let them in, an air-conditioned wall of cold hit them, Christopher taking advantage of this to air out his already wet shirt by flapping it by pinching parts of it while Ayla began to shiver as she accelerated her walk to get out of there as quickly as she could. She filled out the custom's form and went to the next available window. The customs officer went through the motions at a snail's pace and asked her every question on the form she filled out. Ayla felt the cold air of the airport penetrate down to her bones, and she shivered more intensely, the customs officer continuing down the list of questions.

"Do you have more than five thousand dollars in foreign currency?" the officer asked in a perfect British accent.

Ayla laughed, exasperated by his insistence to ask every question on the form, even though she had already answered every one of them on paper. "Not at all. I have twenty-five hundred dollars to exchange into rupees as soon as I can reach the exchange counter over there," she said, pointing her finger.

The last question on the form asked about any personal possession that has a total value of more than ten-thousand dollars. The officer had the decency to skip that question and stamped her passport. "Welcome to India," he said as he gave the passport back to her and turned to the next passenger.

Christopher had already passed through and had time to find transportation while Ayla crawled through the gates, held back by her sloth officer. Ayla exchanged her money into rupees, eager to rejoin the outside heat, and just about ran to join Christopher. He was waiting next to a Toyota-looking car with a brand logo Ayla didn't recognize on the front grill.

She bathed in the heat of the sun as she regained control over her shivering muscles. Realizing Christopher was suggesting a taxi, Ayla spoke up. "Isn't it a long ride for us to use a taxi? I mean, the train is a real experience in this country, and it's certainly cheaper." She wasn't tight with her money, but it seemed to her a five-hour taxi ride would cost more than they could pay.

"It's a hundred-rupee difference," Christopher said, "in exchange for more comfort and a personal tour guide."

The driver looked at Christopher with pride. "You know how to sell this ride, my friend," he said with a melodic accent.

"Just repeating your sales pitch," Christopher said with a smile. He felt a connection with the driver as soon as they began to speak, like meeting a kindred spirit, and was happy to work at convincing Ayla to make the trip in a taxi. She placed her suitcase in the trunk of the car and took a seat in the back without further debate, surprised at the small difference in price. The driver and Christopher shared a fist-pump, happy to have convinced her. Christopher took his place in the front seat, a tourist-like excitement lighting up his eyes as he looked around. He was simultaneously taking in the smells and the view, having never traveled much in the past. As he sat in the taxi, he proceeded with the introductions.

"I'm Christopher. This is Ayla," he said, pointing to her with his thumb.

"I have no use for names, sir. They are nothing but administrative tools. I choose my clients based on feeling, and I liked your energy. So, I approached you. That's enough for me." The driver looked at them sideways, measuring the impact of what he said.

Christopher and Ayla shared a look, surprised by his answer, but didn't make a case out of it and shrugged their shoulders in unison. "Alright, then; let's get going,"

Christopher said to break the silence that followed the driver's declaration.

As they pulled out of the airport parking area, Ayla's mind was already slipping away into vague daydreams about what might happen once they reach the village. Christopher gave a vague description of the village to the driver, using his dream experience as if it had been an actual meeting with someone.

"That's funny. I went there with a woman not long ago!" the driver said.

"Woman?" Ayla asked, sitting up in her seat, wondering if it could have been Engella.

"How did she seem?" Christopher asked. He was afraid Cutler's hypno-soldiers had beaten them there and that they would be ambushed somewhere along the way.

"A nice woman, I must say. Said her name was Hand Jella or something like that. Do you know her?"

"I do," Ayla said, smiling at the driver's interpretation of her name.

The new information helped her relax as she laid back into her seat. She fell asleep, and a wave of relief surrounded her, creating a void that she slipped into joyfully, letting the slumber take over. They left the city in silence, Christopher taking in the scenery and Ayla slipping into a deep sleep, riding the bumps like a rocking chair. The city spread out before them, Christopher marveling at the combination of modern and traditional architecture. Some beaten-down houses appeared as blemishes at irregular intervals, revealing a dark past that was being gradually erased by time. They stopped at a red light. A small family was crossing the street, and Christopher noticed one child with his eyes missing. Skin covered the space where you would normally see an eye. A little girl, apparently the boy's sister, was next to him and had one arm smaller than the other. Christopher shuddered a little seeing this.

"Poor buggers," muttered the driver as he stepped on the gas at the green light. He turned to Christopher; his face darkened by angry sadness. "Thirty years ago, there was a massive chemical accident. A pesticide plant had a giant gas leak that polluted the water for twenty-four hours straight. Nearly 4,000 people died that day, plus another 30,000 over the following years. To this day, children are being born with defects like that family[9]." As he spoke, the driver's jaw clenched.

"A handful of company employees received a two-year jail sentence for negligence, and some money was directed towards the problem to quell dissidence, but the site still exists to this day, companies coming and going without any real clean up being done. They repaired the leak and have continued their business as if nothing had happened. The equipment hasn't been modernized, so the same thing will happen in time." The driver looked over at Christopher, his sadness replaced by anger.

"You know, years of litigation was necessary to get the convictions for the seven employees. Jail sentences were received in 2010. The accident happened in 1984. It took so long, one of the employees died before sentencing." The driver's knuckles were turning white on the steering wheel.

Christopher didn't know what to say. He wasn't aware of the disaster that plagued the city and couldn't understand how this could stay silent for so long. He reached back, searching for Ayla's hand, needing some human contact. This woke her and seeing Christopher's face so sullen and the driver looking so angry; she thought they might have had an argument while she slept. She sat up straight, fully awake, ready to mediate any situation that might have occurred. Christopher proceeded to explain what he had seen, along with the history of the city over the previous thirty years. The 4,000 deaths, the 30,000 that followed, the half-million deformed children born over the years. Unable to contain his emotions, Christopher began to cry. Tears silently streamed down his cheeks. His shoulders bounced a sad rhythm, causing Ayla to cry as well. The driver gave Christopher a friendly tap on the thigh.

"Keep your head up, man. We have one weapon—life itself. All we can do is continue living the best we can. They have already taken our past; they will not take our future."

"All we control is our own actions, after all," added Ayla from the back seat, leaning forward and wrapping her arms around Christopher. She felt the depth of his anger, his body tense, his shortened breaths.

This put a smile on the driver's face, as he gave Ayla an approving wink in the mirror. Christopher regained some composure as the taxi drove away from the city, the highway engulfing them into anonymity. At Christopher's request, and after spending an hour on the main highway, indistinguishable from any major highway in the world, the driver turned onto a secondary road. He explained that it would prolong the trip by a good two hours, but both passengers agreed the scenic route was the best choice. Christopher asked the driver if he had any music.

"I have a Telugu movie soundtrack CD or the radio." The driver smiled at Christopher while holding the CD, hoping to influence his choice.

"Telugu?" Christopher had obviously never heard the term before.

"It's like Bollywood, but from a different part of the country." Christopher grabbed the CD and shoved it in the player. He turned the volume up, and the taxi was filled with a loud, magical, rhythmic sound that got Christopher and Ayla dancing in their seats. The music was a perfect mix of classical Indian sounds and a modern beat using traditional drums. The driver sang along with the songs, as the two passengers bobbed their heads to the beat, snaking their bodies back and forth on their seats to the melody of the singers. It went on for the duration of the CD, eating away the kilometers. The radio had no new songs to offer, so they turned it off. Ayla requested a stop for snacks and a bathroom break. But they drove another ten kilometers before finding a small town with a market. By then, Ayla was ready to explode. The road had been bumpy, adding to her discomfort. As the car came to a halt, Ayla jumped out in search of a public bathroom, or anything she could use to relieve herself. She ran into the market and went straight to the checkout.

"Is there a bathroom I may use?" She realized as she asked the question that they might not understand English. If not, there was a good chance she would pee her pants right there.

The cashier looked at her curiously then called over a colleague. They spoke for a moment in Hindi; then, the colleague turned to Ayla. "What do you need, madam?"

Ayla repeated her question, her bladder had expanded to its limit, and the colleague pointed her to an outhouse behind the market. Ayla ran behind the market, her knees glued together for bladder support. It made for a comical scene to anyone who saw her. She turned the corner and froze for a second, unsure of where to go. There were two sheds leaning precariously against the market wall. Neither seemed suitable to house a bathroom, throwing Ayla's bladder into full panic, shivers and tremors announcing to her that the urine will start to flow regardless of her actions in the next minute.

She weighed the possibility of hiding in a corner and relieving herself but decided to first check the sheds.

She went to one of them and pushed the door. She was surprised to find a decent looking bathroom behind the decrepit walls of the shed. She went in and did her business, the relief washing over her as the pressure subsided. The walls were nothing more than discarded pieces of wood, but the toilet and sink were functional and modern-looking. She washed her hands, surprised to get hot water from the tap. She emerged a new woman, ready to continue the adventure when she noticed something out of the corner of her eye. There was a woman standing in front of a vendor's booth bearing the club bouncer look they had encountered at the university. Ayla slipped back into the taxi as discreetly as possible, staying behind the tree line along the sidewalk. When she reached the taxi, Christopher and the driver were already in the car, frantically waving her over. She climbed in the back, and the driver took off as fast as he could, within the legal limits, trying to blend into the dense traffic. Although it seemed like a small village, its location made it an important activity hub in the region, regularly causing traffic jams.

"You saw something too?" Ayla asked.

"Yup. Told you these hounds were unrelenting." Christopher's physiognomy was now hard and almost aggressive. He was scanning the area for any sign of trouble, while the driver remained focused on staying hidden in the traffic.

"Have you ever met a hypnotized soldier?" she asked, surprised the driver understood the gravity of the situation.

The driver glanced at her in the mirror. "I didn't know they were hypnotized, but I knew to stay away from the red-eyed people. They harbor a devil in them." While

he spoke, the driver used the same tactic as Christopher
had. He sneaked out of the traffic using side streets,
weaving his way through small alleys, keeping an eye
on his rear-view mirror.

They emerged from an alley using the highway
on-ramp a hundred feet away from them. They were
on their guard, unaware that the soldiers they saw were
in fact looking for Dwight Como. The taxi crawled along
a garden wall on a gravel path before reaching the road.
Moving at slow speed, they managed to avoid attracting
attention as they passed, since they didn't raise any dust
as they rolled by. As soon as they hit hard pavement, the
driver stepped on the gas and rejoined the highway as
fast as he could, not worried about raising dust anymore,
confident they could disappear in the highway traffic.

Christopher kept looking out of the back window
of the car, searching for suspicious-looking vehicles.
Ayla tried to calm the adrenaline rush the situation
caused with deep-breathing exercises. She had hoped
they lost their pursuers after leaving for India, but she
found herself confronted by the reality that they would
be pursued to the ends of the earth. She was ready to
fight but wasn't sure what would be required from her
if there was a battle. Christopher began to relax after
they put some distance between them and the hounds.
The rest of the trip was completed in silence. They had
turned off the radio and traveled with the windows
open, letting the sound of the wind be the music. They
reached Satpura National Park as the sun was going
down. The driver stopped the taxi along a small road
at the same spot he dropped off Engella.

"Here we are. The village you seek is that way." The
driver pointed toward the forest bordering the field.

Ayla paid the driver, adding a generous tip for his efficiency in the escape from the dark matter initiative soldiers. "Thank you. Be careful on your return," she said.

Christopher tapped the roof of the car and turned to begin the walk to the village. The taxi took off, the driver waving out the window as he disappeared behind a hill on the road that would take him back to his relative's hotel. Christopher and Ayla walked towards the edge of the forest, both a little unsure of the path to follow once they got there. As they approached the trees, Ayla noticed some movement behind a nearby bush. Two small mirrors were reflecting the light coming from the adjacent farmhouse. Ayla froze. Christopher took a couple more steps before realizing Ayla's sudden stop. He turned and saw Ayla in fear, instinctively crouched to get out of sight of whatever was freaking her out. He crawled back to her, tugging at her shorts for her to crouch with him. Her legs turned to jelly, and she slumped down awkwardly, keeping her gaze fixed on the shiny eyes.

"I think I can see their eyes now," she whispered. "But how could they already be here? We left no clues along the way, did we?" Ayla replayed their trip in her mind, trying to remember something that could explain the presence of a hypnotized soldier in the bushes.

"Hold on; what did you see?" Christopher was trying to keep a level head, but he was feeling his muscles tense up as the adrenaline pumped blood, ready for battle.

"Two shiny eyes in the bushes." Ayla began crawling towards the sighting, no longer able to see anything. Christopher stood up a little, searching for any sign of movement. Losing sight of Ayla, he moved ahead to follow, still unable to see any red-eyed soldier.

"What color were the eyes?" Christopher asked, still unable to see Ayla, asking basic questions to keep his mind calm.

"They had a golden glow," she said. "Its gaze was fixated on us, following our movement."

The answer came from the dark ahead of him. Ayla stopped moving as the bushes went silent. Christopher felt the tension leave his body, reassured this wasn't an ambush.

"Their eyes can only be red," he explained. "The hypnosis they suffer translates to red eyes for those who can see it."

"Then, what was it?" Ayla startled Christopher as she appeared right next to him. "Could there be a golden-eyed, special-ops kind of hypnosis?"

Ayla's question raised the tension once more, Christopher pondering the possibility they had managed to perfect their hypnosis techniques. He crouched down and continued to advance. As they edged closer to the forest, a loud grunt shocked them both. Ayla turned and saw a tiger standing next to her, its warm breath spreading down her neck and back. It grunted again, bobbing its head as if asking them to follow and began to walk into the forest. Ayla felt at ease with the beast. Even if it had come close enough to kill her, Ayla felt it wanted to help.

"I think we need to follow it," she told Christopher standing to follow it.

"Hope they have fresh undies over there," joked Christopher with a half-smile, his skin pale and transparent from the scare he suffered.

CHAPTER 22

Engella had slipped into a deep meditative state as she absorbed the vibrations that surrounded her. She began by taking in the silence, listening for nothing, hearing everything as she heard the breeze pass through the opening in the wall. She could perceive the people's footsteps passing by outside the tent, and the leaves dancing in the trees in the forest. This transitive state lasted for a moment before Engella let herself slip into a meditation-induced waking dream. Sensing she could leave her physical body, she raised her spirit toward the ceiling to float around the room, observing the energy emitted by the different documents, searching for a specific signature.

The different books and maps were strewn around chaotically, each one emitting a pulse that Engella felt at varying intensities. She was feeling for anything related to the history of the tree. Her spirit body floated about the room, sensing the vibrations, searching for a signal.

She had a significant attraction to one book; its pulse was golden, reassuring, strong. She instinctively knew the book would bring new information to light that would help her. Her first touch with the tree had been too intense, out of control. She needed to strengthen her essence to be able to accept the energy it had to offer. Engella remained in her transitive state for a couple of hours, happy to let her physical body rest. The sense of freedom she felt when in this state was joyful, decadent, like a long, wandering orgasm you never want to stop, and she hadn't felt this in a long time. Feeling a connection to the core energies that govern our existence has always been Engella's favorite element in her spiritual quest, and she never missed an occasion to wallow in the weightless freedom when she could. But recent events had made it difficult. She wanted to stay in this state as long as possible, unsure she could return soon.

Obligations being what they were, she unwillingly began to reintegrate her spirit-self back into her physical body—each time, feeling the weight of gravity like a giant steel boulder being delicately deposited on her shoulders. She initiated a specific breathing sequence designed to bring her mind back to the uncompromising laws of physical reality. As she emerged from her meditation, the village beyond the door seemed abuzz. Engella went to the book she selected during her meditation, admiring the quality of the binding, the thickness it had in her hands. The book smelled of dust, time, and knowledge, as she ran her nose from top to bottom, inhaling its age-old dust. She coughed and hacked out the dust that invaded her larynx for the next five minutes, smiling broadly as she seemingly coughed up her lungs and laughing at herself. She sat back down at the table and opened the book to handwritten pages.

The calligraphy was spectacular. Engella found it hard to read as she lost herself in the sheer beauty of the script.

The book had been dictated by a village sage to a group of scribes dedicated to documenting the knowledge the villagers had accumulated for generations. Its contents were an incoherent mishmash of ideas and musings on the existence of the village, and by extension, humanity and its relation to the tree of life. It spoke of the role the tree held in our existence, the necessity to protect it. Making sense of the incoherent nature of the book, Engella understood that the tree serves as a connection with the universe to our dream state, our spirit-self. The outreaching branches channel the chaotic energy from the universe, allowing us to integrate new knowledge, new ideas into the collective unconscious of the planet. The energy absorbed by the tree isn't confined to the human unconscious psyche; it doesn't privilege any being before another. It merely exists. The energy it absorbs is offered to every single living molecule on the planet. It does not consciously select information to be integrated; it indiscriminately absorbs any form of energy that passes the earth at any given moment. Should the tree be destroyed, the disconnection will cause humanity to become dependent on a parasite that pollutes our DNA for survival, during which time the earth would continue to evolve independently. This could mean humans would end up going to war with the planet. Engella froze at this. She began to look for the book's publication date. How could the ancients of the village know about DNA? There was no formal date printed anywhere, but the binding and calligraphy had to be at least 400 years old. Plus, there was no mention so far about the origin of the information contained in it. This could be a transcription of older knowledge passed down orally. She pushed aside her modern notion that ancient minds couldn't possibly be in possession of knowledge that is new to us and kept reading.

There's more than one tree of life in the world, and they each share the load of absorbing the universal chaos. Beyond the physical obligation, our need to sleep is related to the existence of these trees. It's during sleep that our subconscious can communicate with the tree's signal and absorb or exchange information with the energy emitted by it. Without the connection, our tether to the universe is severed, and we spiral into a single-minded path toward destruction as instructed by the parasite that inhabits us. The book stated they had come to the unfortunate conclusion that we are inhabited by a destructive force simply by observing human behavior. Their interpretation was that the parasite was, in fact, nothing more than pollution created by our tendency to confine our existence to individualistic desires. It resulted in divisions within varying groups of people, which evolved into class separation. The main motivators being individual pursuits, humans have dug the chasm that has separated them from nature themselves.

When attuned to the tree's energy input, empathy and creativity become the main motivators. That creates a sense of community that can develop beyond geographical confines. Rafael had told her about these trees, that some had been destroyed over the years as despots and expansion-obsessed leaders cleared the way for industrial or housing projects destined to fulfill immediate urges at the expense of staying connected to our profound nature. But he had nothing more than second-hand information about them.

Engella continued reading and found that the village's existence became focused on the protection of the tree. It lasted for generations until the tree was reduced to a stump, leaving a hole in the forest ceiling where it once majestically stood. Text written on a piece of paper was slipped into the book. It explained that before the region was declared a national park, development promoters wanted the territory to build a whole city. The villagers resisted the offers of money and didn't fear the intimidation tactics brought on by the developers. After many unsuccessful attempts to chase the villagers away, they had thought that by destroying the tree, the villagers would disperse, giving them free rein to build.

The text in the book had become typewritten from that point, continued by different members of the village after the destruction of the tree. It stated that the stump that remains still lives, although its power has been greatly reduced. Some have tried to communicate, or at least preserve the connection to the tree, but most who try, end up living in a confused state upon their return, unable to fathom what they have experienced. For a time, the village leaders withheld permission for anyone to approach the tree stump until they understood what they could do to better prepare the participants. Engella, eager to learn more, put the book back where she found it and went to find Jolan.

"The book says most of the people who tried to connect with the tree have lost their grasp on reality when they return. Are there any of these people still alive, and can I speak with them?"

Jolan cocked his head sideways. "Alive, yes, but speak to them? Our inhabitants have peculiar habits that could be interpreted as having lost their grasp on reality to a certain extent. I will need more information." His broad smile told Engella he was playing with her.

"Take me to them, please," she said. I'm a little tired from studying." Her direct tone told Jolan he had better do as she asked, fearing there would be retribution if he pushed his joke any further.

He brought Engella to a wooden house hidden behind some trees, a short walk away from the village. The house was once painted a bright yellow that had faded to a brownish hue, the humidity and time taking their toll on the paint. It looked like a North American suburban house, making it one of the biggest homes in the village. Two large bay windows flanked a white wooden door, a short stone path leading to the front door. The windows were dressed in flower arrangements that were visibly left to fend for themselves but were beautiful nonetheless. A bluish flower had become the dominant plant, as it had spread to every planter box along the front of the house.

Jolan turned to Engella. "Before we go in, please try to keep a calm demeanor. They have seen beyond our capacity to understand, so their ramblings can seem incoherent, even scary."

"If I'm to communicate with the tree, I must study every aspect of it before I even try. My mind is as open as ever for new information, and this meeting will help me appreciate the extent of the task ahead." Engella's matter-of-fact attitude reassured Jolan, and he knocked on the door.

A bug-eyed woman opened the door. She looked at the two visitors with a penetrating look, eyeing them from head to toe. Then her focus went right to Engella, taking small steps toward her with her feet dragging on the floor as she began to smell the visitor's odors much like a curious dog would. The closer she got, the more her face was turning to an expression of joy. As she reached Engella, she was trembling, seemingly unable to contain the emotion brought on by the visit. The woman wrapped her arms around her and began to cry. Thick, bouncing sobs made it hard to understand what she was saying, or if she was speaking at all. Engella welcomed the embrace by hugging her back as hard as she could. They stayed there in the entryway with Jolan awkwardly standing next to them, waiting in silence.

"I knew you'd come. I saw it," the woman said as her sobs subsided.

She had become almost liquid in Engella's arms, who picked her up and carried her into the house. She was way too light, Engella thought, having lifted the woman with more ease than expected. "Are they fed properly?" she whispered to Jolan as they went into the house. He nodded, throwing his hands up as if saying they decide how much they eat, no one can force them.

They entered a living area cluttered with two large sofas and cushions covering the floor, leaving no space to walk. Engella tried to lay the woman on the sofa, but she kept her arms and legs wrapped firmly around Engella, refusing to let go. Engella chose to sit on the sofa with the woman on her lap like a baby. Two other residents walked into the room, both as bug-eyed as the first woman. They gave the visitors the same look as the woman before, both edging toward Engella as their faces began to light up the closer they got.

"They undeniably see something," Engella said to Jolan as she prepared to get crushed by a three-person group-hug any moment.

"We're aware, but we can't make sense of what they tell us. All we have managed to understand so far is related to the state they're in since their return, but without any clear explanation about what they saw." Engella was being hugged by the three inhabitants of the house, their cries and laughs obscuring any chance of a normal conversation.

Engella stayed with the three explorers, sending Jolan away with a wave as he returned to his duties, happy to leave. After he left, the house fell into a tired silence.

Engella felt her three partners getting heavier as sleep was beginning to overcome them. The calmness of their breathing lulled her to sleep as well. She slumped her head back, trying to concentrate on her conscious mind to make sure she entered the dream world awake. As always, she awoke in the dream realm looking at her hand. Engella willed her spirit energy to advance, taking a moment to celebrate her renewed capacity to travel in this realm, and began to look for her three new friends right away. She raised herself toward the sky to see as far as possible in the darkness of the dream realm, searching for any sign of a different energy signature, an out-of-place element.

The landscape before her was overwhelming, millions upon billions of energy masses representing every person's subconscious in the world. During her absence, she had forgotten about the sheer size of that world. She took a moment to reacquaint herself with it, taking the time to see the energy flowing all around her. Engella was convinced she could communicate with the three inhabitants of the house there, as words represented but a part of the communication in that reality. Scanning the strange horizon before her, the millions of balls of energy seemed to merge together, making it look like lava. She then noticed three small balls of energy flowing together, apart from the mass, seemingly dancing in the air, almost like an air show demonstration. They bobbed and weaved across the sky, joyfully engaged in some sort of dream state.

As Engella willed her spirit-self to follow the dancing lights, she found her energy was naturally attracted to them, as if an invisible cord was pulling her. Growing closer, Engella saw a thin strand of light connected to them from above, disappearing into the sky. The light strand, as thin as it seemed, was responsible for tossing and throwing the three balls of energy around. Engella's spirit-body rose as high as she could but couldn't see the end of the light strand as it disappeared into the murky sky, into deep space. She followed the strand back to the three explorers. When she reached them, she could hear the chaos that dominated their minds. She couldn't make out any specific element, still surprised she could even hear something in this realm. She had always thought that everything that happened there could only be on a psychic level. The sound was like nothing Engella had ever heard. It had a point of origin, which were the three dancing lights, but came from all around as well. Unsure of how to continue and beginning to feel the strain of being far from her physical body, Engella chose to propel her energy toward one of the three rest home inhabitants. Thinking she would break through the noise emitted by the strand to speak to the person inside, Engella found herself unequivocally thrown back by the energy contained in it. For an instant, her mind was saturated with images and emotions emanating from all forms of life in the universe.

Engella awoke, startled, sunken into the sofa, her three companions still deep in sleep. Her arms were numb from the pressure they were exerting on her blood vessels, which gave Engella a serious challenge to pull herself out. She desperately wanted to return to the library. She thought she had an idea about what they suffered from but needed confirmation. Engella managed to wiggle out without waking anyone, and once the feeling returned to her arms and legs, she returned to the library. She retrieved the book and searched for information about the tree's conception. She learned that ancient botanist sages had found a way to integrate DNA molecules from each category of living beings—human, animal, plant, aquatic, into the tree's seed. That generated a monstrous tree that reached to the sky, becoming a connection to the universe. What Engella saw when she was shoved back in the dream realm showed her that the three residents of this house might be directly connected to the universe's influx of information, causing their intense confusion. They are the link to the universe, receiving the input destined for the tree, except there's too much information to absorb, and it muddles their mind. Engella felt the time had come to start the ceremony Jolan had spoken of and went to find him.

CHAPTER 23

Frank had received a message from the lawyers that came to see him. They wanted more assurances that the latest escape wasn't a sign of him losing control over the project. The lawyer said he would return to the lab soon to see what was being accomplished, and Frank had to find a way to spin something in his favor. He put away his research to prevent any chance the lawyer might have to steal some documents. On days like that, he questioned his association with the group. He knew the initiative was generally overly cautious, but this fixation on one element of the potential resistance was confusing. Didn't they wield enough power to subdue this threat?

Frank noticed the religious branch of the group was especially inquisitive, planting the seeds of doubt in the minds of their partners. It appeared they were afraid of being thrown out of the group and wanted to show their worth. Frank had to find a way to reassure them, so he could continue to work without further hindrance. As he was shutting down his main computer, he came across a statistical analysis of the hound's capacities to track someone. The graph he pulled out was concentrated on their hunt of the collective unconscious allegiance members. It showed a 95% success rate. He had finally perfected the hypnosis level of his bloodhounds, making Frank confident he could sell this statistic to the group and keep the level of confidence he needed from the powers in place to continue the project. The light above the access door to the lab lit up, indicating someone was waiting at the door. Frank looked at the security screen and saw the lawyer was already there. He buzzed him in, armed with the statistical proof he could use to keep his administrators happy. The lawyer approached Frank with his usual look of disdain, placed his briefcase on the desk without uttering a single word, and opened it. He pulled out a large brown envelope and handed it to Frank. Remaining silent, evading Frank's gaze, he closed his briefcase and left. Frank was flabbergasted; he was ready to argue his point but found himself holding an envelope without anyone to debate with. He sat at his desk and broke the seal. Inside was a letter from the religious administrators of the initiative.

Dr. Frank Cutler: It has come to our attention that two resistance agents have escaped your grasp. This is unfortunate. After deliberation, we consider that the resistance agent you let escape must be silenced before we can move ahead with your plan. Her research gravely undermines the pillars of our philosophical foundation, and that is unacceptable to us. Her presence in the population during a two-year transition period would be fatal to the completion of the task, as she may disrupt our efforts. Even the mere existence of her research will be a problem. You have two weeks to find and silence Ayla Karemi, after which we will rescind our support for the project if you are not successful. Our current position in the world is satisfactory to us, and so far, you haven't proven anything outside theoretical argumentation.

Frank was beginning to shake as he read on.

You may consider this letter a first and final warning. Be aware that should we rescind our support, our colleagues in the initiative will follow suit. It's imperative that you succeed in this enterprise. As a show of support, we can supply all the soldiers you need to complete this task.

The letter was signed by a representative of each main religion that governs the world, along with a mention that the letter was copied to the Initiative. Frank was floored. There had been no sign of any doubt from the initiative, and within days he found himself first visited by two lawyers carrying veiled threats, then being placed on a deadline. Rage rose from the pit of his stomach as he turned his computer back on to track the progress of his hounds. They all had landed in Bhopal, and from the twelve sent by Cutler, two of them went north. But all the others seemed to be following the same general direction to the southeast. It was a good sign. It meant they had a lead. Ayla had chosen to hide in the Indian wilderness, and that reassured Frank, as her capture could be accomplished without any witnesses. Looking at his screen, he felt his confidence slowly returning. He began dreaming about the punishment he would inflict on Ayla. DNA transformation was no longer enough. She had evaded him twice, and this was highly insulting to him. Although a small part of him respected her for her capacity to constantly fall through the net he was casting; he couldn't wait to begin experimenting on her. He would push her mind past the breaking point, then analyze the result. Breaking Ayla Karemi's mind and tracking its descent was then the sole purpose of Dr. Frank Cutler's life; his sanity depended on it.

As he paced around the lab trying to calm himself down, he received a phone call from one of the hounds that went to the north. He told Frank he found a taxi driver that had brought the escaped fugitives to the edge of a national park called Satpura National Reserve. Frank ordered the hound to pressure the driver for more information and then dispose of him.

"He's a polluted mind; he can no longer be trusted to follow protocol," Frank told his agent.

The hypnotized soldier submitted with a grunt and hung up. Frank was certain everything would be wrapped up within the next day or two, as he began to pace around the lab again. He always felt a swell of pride when one of his interventions yielded results, feeling like the only capable human on those occasions. "No one can equal my resolve!" He screamed at the empty laboratory, although a twinge of panic was still present in the pit of his stomach.

He never coped well with deadlines, but he had to keep his head on straight to get through this one. He needed the support given by the Dark Matter Initiative for his project to see the light of day. Text messages began to arrive from India. The agents who went north of Bhopal relayed information to the other soldiers on the direction the fugitives took, which meant they had managed to squeeze out some information from the person they detained. The other hounds responded one by one to the text, confirming they were headed for the indicated coordinates. Frank also received a personal message confirming the taxi driver was no longer a threat, unaware they had been provided with false information. The driver sent them on the opposite side of the national reserve, where he left Ayla, Christopher, and Engella.

The 202 square mile park was elongated, which meant the driver had sent the hunters 200 miles off course, hoping it would be enough. Frank sent an order to his hounds to report any findings, then sat back and waited. He chased away any stray thought that brought him to imagine the punishment that would be dispensed should he be unable to find the fugitives. He still couldn't believe they threatened to cut financing; this project carried the possibility of ensuring their hold on power for generations. But if they went as far as cutting him off, that would also mean they would need to make him disappear, which Frank couldn't let happen.

Turning the recent events around in his mind, he came to believe they were testing his capacity to work under pressure. It made sense because the transformation period would be intense. He held on to this thought as it helped him calm down. He went back to studying the protocol that would be in place when they start to inject the people's DNA with their own moral codes. Everyone would need to be on the same page to bring the project to its full term. *The challenge imposed by the initiative to find and neutralize Ayla Karemi is nothing compared to the pressure that will permeate the world during the transformation period*, Frank thought. The CRISPR[10] device is designed to work on one person at a time, and with the DNA transformation taking at least two hours per person, plus a three-month re-adaptation period, it would take at least two years to infect the whole population, and that's if every laboratory worked at full capacity. Frank understood the need the initiative might have to test his resolve, but he was still destabilized by the lawyer's visit, trying to understand how the initiative could have more doubts.

What he was offering humanity was beyond necessary; the DNA transformation he was proposing was the
only way humans could avoid extinction. The solution
was elegant and simple, but it would be tricky to circumvent the beliefs humans have about their individuality.
There would certainly be some form of resistance to the
procedure, but by eliminating or silencing any source
that could feed the resistance, it should be simple enough
to work around it. The Initiative was already hard at
work as web sites of historical writings in philosophy and
history were being silenced or converted. The same was
happening in physical libraries, the book collections in
them being transformed into non-threatening types of
literature, designed to entertain without reflection. Any
activist with a following, no matter how small, was to be
silenced or converted. Being a member of any resistance
would guarantee the chance to be the first humans to
receive the DNA transformation. When the procedures
start, there would be little to no information accessible
to nurture any form of rebellion, which would ensure a
smooth transition.

Frank felt a sense of self-importance to be part of
such a large undertaking. For a short period, he might
be perceived as the incarnation of evil, a mad scientist.
But by the end of the project, people will realize he
ushered in a golden age for humanity. With the people's
deepest desires under control, no one would feel out of
place. Everyone would have their personal routine, and
everyone would work toward the greater good without
question. All they would need are orders to follow,
which is where the dark matter initiative comes in.
There might be adjustments to make along the way,
but Frank wasn't worried. He could easily reprogram a
person's DNA to fit varying parameters.

CHAPTER 24

Christopher tripped and fell with almost every step, the dark moonless forest yielding no visual information to help him see the ground. He was trying to keep up with Ayla and the tiger, but after stumbling his way through the first ten feet, he decided to let them go and track them using the hunting skills his mother had taught him. He stopped to clean his wounds at a small brook. He stepped in and fell. Ayla's footsteps were becoming more and more distant. She seemed to weave through the forest as if in broad daylight. He had to ask her how she did this. Christopher splashed fresh water on his knees and cleaned his hands before continuing his trek, listening for Ayla's movements to keep track of the path he should follow. He continued as her steps were becoming almost inaudible. With his hands out-stretched in front of him to protect himself from stray branches, he cautiously placed one foot in front of the other, feeling out the ground with the tip of his foot before stepping down. He was moving at such a slow pace; within minutes, he couldn't hear Ayla's movements.

Christopher decided to find a shelter and wait until morning, unsure of his ability to follow a straight line in the dark. He climbed a tree and found a large branch to lay upon through the night, surveying the surroundings for any sign of danger. An hour passed in silence, the occasional bat echo-locating its flight breaking the stillness of the forest, the short shrieks they emitted to guide themselves divulging their presence. Christopher wondered where the night-stalking animals could be until he saw two golden eyes looking straight up at him from the base of the tree. The tiger had returned and was waiting for Christopher. The adrenaline rush he felt guaranteed there would be no sleep for him, his heart racing. Christopher made sure he was safe on the branch, not wanting to fall. The tiger's heavy breathing kept him on edge. Hours passed without incident. Christopher felt the weight of sleep taking over and dozed off. He laid his head on a knot in the branch, and sleep came almost instantly. His last thought before falling asleep was the realization that there could be snakes in the tree. This filled his dreams with chases and battles with strange, powerful beings, making his sleep agitated as he turned all night on his branch, almost falling off multiple times.

The first light of the morning splashed Christopher's face with warm rays, waking him. As he opened his eyes, he saw the tiger sitting on the branch he had slept on, up against the tree, waiting for Christopher to wake up. Christopher tried to contain his panic, and he kept his eyes straight ahead on the animal as he inched his way further along the tree branch. The tiger ignored the panic and stretched lazily before jumping down from the tree. It looked back up at Christopher, appearing impatient as it walked in a circle, grunting and pawing the ground. Christopher, feeling more at ease with the beast, accepted the invitation. He dexterously descended the tree, and as soon as he set foot on the ground, the tiger took off into the forest. Unsure at first, Christopher ran after it, following the sounds as the tiger made no effort to be silent. The quiet bustle of a waking village began to filter through the leaves. Christopher thought he heard people talking, although he couldn't make out what they were saying. The tiger came back toward Christopher, freezing him in his footsteps for an instant.

Was it all an elaborate trap set by the animal to bring Christopher into more inviting terrain? It came walking toward Christopher, brushing past him, slightly rubbing its side on his hip as it passed, pushing Christopher off-balance as it began trotting back to the forest. Christopher watched the tiger disappear, then turned back to the sounds he heard. He still couldn't make out what the people were saying, but as he got closer, the sound of the voices became obstructed by the sounds of music, a rhythmic and melodious jam session filling the air. He stayed put for a moment, crouched in the bushes that marked the edge of the village to analyze what he heard until the smell of food reached him. That caused his appetite to roar for mercy, hunger becoming the exclusive thought on his mind.

He decided to follow the smell. He walked into a winding path, wooden huts and tents randomly placed, creating a quiet chaos that he would come to learn later is called "the residential district." The complete lack of urban planning caused the walkway to follow a convoluted pattern with no discernible direction. Christopher kept a lock on the magnificent smells that occupied every olfactory cell in his nostrils, turning left and right, then left again. The smell became stronger as he emerged on a terrace of tables where people joyfully chatted as they ate. A beautiful smile appeared on Ayla's face when she saw him. She motioned him over to join her. A wave of relief came over Christopher, happy that she had made it safely. He joined her in the food line and was handed a plate. He let himself get lost in the beauty of her face, thinking back to the way she looked sitting on the porch of the house dressed in leaves. Christopher's heart swelled with love, and he was almost crying as he realized they had reached their goal. But he couldn't dwell on those emotions. The odors given out by the food had become unbearable. Christopher's hunger was in complete control of his actions.

"I was afraid I'd have to go back to look for you when I saw you weren't able to follow me in the dark," Ayla said. "Glad you made it."

She nudged him with her elbow, still shy about her feelings toward him. She felt his love when he looked at her, but she wasn't sure how he would react to a show of public affection.

"Hmm," Christopher answered, his hunger forcing him to ignore her.

He was able to see the choices offered on the buffet table, and his mouth watered as he licked his lips with anticipation. Ayla wasn't fazed by his demeanor and went on to introduce her new friends to him.

"This is Naina. She'll help us with the construction of our home later." Unable to contain her excitement, Ayla grabbed Christopher by the shoulders. "We've found it! Engella's here!" She shook him at every intonation, excited that they had made it. This temporarily shook Christopher out of his hunger dream.

"Yeah," he smiled. "It's the same place as the one in my dream, except it's even more beautiful than I expected."

They moved a step closer in line, and Christopher's hunger came rushing back when it was his turn to choose. There was some Doro Wett, an Ethiopian chicken recipe, and eggs Benedict served with avocado and candied turnips. But there was a ten to fifteen-minute wait for this one as they were cooked to order. He splashed his plate with the chicken recipe and ordered some eggs as well, certain his hunger would not be satisfied with a single plate of food.

When they sat at the table, Christopher engulfed his food with glee, filling the void in his stomach as fast as he could. He barely chewed as he swallowed the food whole, a mixture of lime and ginger grazing his taste buds as the food passed by. His plate empty, he sat back to let the food settle in his stomach while he waited for his eggs. The taste of lime and ginger lingered in his mouth, making him ponder the possibility of grabbing another plate of chicken before the eggs so he could appreciate it a bit more. Then he noticed everyone looking at him slack-jawed, visibly surprised by something he did. Christopher, feeling a little uncomfortable, turned to Naina.

"Did I do something wrong?" He rubbed some crumbs off his chest as he asked.

His naive disposition as he asked his question broke the awkwardness, and the room filled with laughter. This made Christopher even more uncomfortable, still unsure of what had happened. A cook yelled his name. His eggs were ready. Happy to remove himself from the awkward moment, he got up and went to pick up his order. He felt all eyes on him, which made him self-conscious about his walk. He never understood where that feeling came from, but whenever Christopher was the center of attention, he felt self-conscious about the way he walked. Fully concentrated on returning to the table without dropping anything, he sat back down with Naina and Ayla. His hunger was still present, although not as dominating. This time, he took his time, savoring each bite, impressed such high-class meals could be obtained so deep in the forest.

"Your capacity to swallow so much food at once is fascinating," Naina said. She was observing him intently, looking like a nature explorer observing a new species of animal.

"Well, thank you . . . I guess."

Christopher regained some of his poise as the hunger waned away, although the feeling of awkwardness hung around. He had never liked being in the spotlight, such as it was at that moment. Naina continued. "What I mean is that I admire the resolve you had to gratify your hunger. That kind of determination is to be applauded. She smiled as she began to get up. We must talk more. But for now, take the time to finish your meal, and we'll help you install you're home afterward. We have plenty of time to get to know each other."

"Not as much as you'd think," Christopher said, his mouth full of eggs.

The relentlessness of the hypnotized hounds that were after them had popped up in his mind now that the hunger had been satiated. "There's a group of people coming," he continued. "They're armed with the conviction that they alone have the truth. Do you have people who can fight in the village?" Christopher's gaze had become hard and cold as he spoke. His reply threw a cold blanket over the group at the table.

"You're the warrior Engella told us about," Naina said. She sat back down, wanting to know more.

"Is she near?" blurted Ayla. As excited as she was to hear Engella had found the village, Ayla knew the hounds pursuing them would find them at some point.

She felt a pang of regret at this, feeling responsible for attracting them here.

"She is, but she can't be disturbed. She has begun the connection ritual and needs to devote her time to that."

"Connection ritual?" Christopher asked. With everything that had happened of late, he had learned to trust his gut. He felt comfortable since arriving there, but his gut still felt a bit of a cult vibe. The attraction everyone had toward him and Ayla was a little unnerving to him.

A man spoke up. "Among the tasks bestowed upon us by our ancestors, there's a tree of life in the forest we must nurture and protect." Jolan stepped into Christopher's line of sight.

"I've heard of these before, but isn't it nothing more than a mystical allegory?"

"Not at all. The tree exists. There's even more than one in the world, but ours is weak, it's nothing but an energy-infused tree stump. That's what Engella is working on."

Jolan sat at the table, squarely facing Christopher with a serious look. "We need you to train us. There's a battle coming, and although we try to train to be able to face most situations, we have no real defense if someone chooses to attack us with real weapons. A group of fifteen people has volunteered to be part of our militia," Jolan said, emphasizing with air quotes. "You would be their general." Jolan kept looking straight at Christopher, his demeanor very business-like.

Christopher finished his meal in silence, observing the people looking at him around the table, unsure of what to say. He realized there was one element missing for this place to be a cult—uniformity. A true cult would have some sort of identity marker to show the member's allegiance to the belief system imposed on them—not the people in front of him. Their personalities shone through the clothes they wore, each person proudly displaying who they were. He counted about fifteen to twenty people around them, beginning to understand this was probably his army to train. A Japanese woman stepped forth, tan-skinned and tall. She stood proudly, her short brown hair framing her face, her intense gaze the only indicator she might be a warrior and a fierce one at that.

"My name is Pawa, which means power in Japanese." The way she said it left no place for a reply as she fixed her gaze on Christopher.

"I guess it does. Nice to meet you. My name is Christopher." He gave Pawa his best possible smile, hoping it would break her intensity. She smiled back, which softened her face somewhat, but it didn't reduce the strength of her presence in any way.

"I'm honored. Get settled promptly; we need to start the training." She walked away without waiting for a response. Christopher felt some relief to have actual combatants to train. If the other volunteers are half as eager as Pawa seems to be, they might be okay.

"There might be hope after all," Christopher muttered, sopping up the remaining mixture of sauce and eggs with some bread.

"Hope for what?" Ayla asked while sneaking up from behind. Christopher jumped a little at her presence.

"Beat the hounds." He looked at Ayla lovingly. "We don't have to do it alone anymore," he said, tears beginning to drip down his face. For the first time since being pulled into this strange adventure, he believed they could find a way out. They hugged to celebrate, holding the embrace for a long moment.

The rest of the day was dedicated to settling into their home, meeting the villagers, and learning about life there. Christopher's wariness about the villagers being a cult had evaporated. He could see everyone remained there by choice and could come and go as they pleased. No one philosophical line of thought was imposed on the villagers. If there was one compulsory philosophy, it was the obligation for everyone to follow their own path, their own soul. As they settled in for the night, Christopher was asleep before his head hit the pillow, his mind filled with questions of how to continue. He slept a dreamless night.

CHAPTER 25

As Jolan finished explaining the process she was about to undertake, Engella's excitement was getting hard to control. She was ready to get started, her life's chaotic past merging with her newfound balance for this one momentous task. She thanked Jolan and went to the tree at once, using breathing exercises to calm herself as she walked into the forest. Approaching the clearing where the tree once stood, Engella felt a wave of emotion, thinking back to the first time she met Rafael. That one single event changed the whole course of her life, and every moment that followed that meeting was designed to bring her here. Engella took a deep breath and moved ahead.

She waited in the clearing that harbored the stump of the tree. The glade was a clean, flawless round circle in the middle of the trees in the forest near the village. Engella was amazed at its perfection, wondering how this could have been accomplished. The circle of trees was a magnificent one, with the giant stump in the middle. The distance to the edge of the forest from the stump was equal all around. She had found the clearing at night, so she could fully appreciate the magnificence of this place, which gave her a sense of ease and peace that she seldom felt in her life. Was the sensation coming from the sunlight bouncing off the top of the trees, or the smell of the flowers that cover the ground around her? She didn't know or care. Wild blue nightshade flowers mixing in seamlessly with multi-colored lotus flowers and purple impatiens, with red hibiscus closing the circle at the foot of the trees all around the circle, gave the place a temple-like feel.

There was a giant tree stump in the middle, where Jolan told her she needed to stay near for the next two days. Here she was, in the middle of India, in a tribe known to a select few people, being asked to sit and meditate for two days in a clearing where hungry tigers might roam, although she sensed she would be okay for that last part. She settled at the base of the stump, sitting with her legs crossed slackly, leaning her back on the stump for some measure of comfort. She realized she was touching the tree but that nothing happened. This worried her a little. She wondered if the touch she had before caused some sort of disconnection. Her worry ignited a pang of hunger, which raised her anxiety level that much more. Someone was to bring her water, but she was not allowed anything else for the two days she was to meditate there. The connection to the tree is to be accomplished in stages, and Engella needed to ignore any and all physical signals so her spirit may roam free. Thinking back to her training with Rafael, Engella decided she would adopt the mindset she used for the high noon meditations in the sun she had to endure during her initial training. This helped her calm down. She was able to take deep breaths as she prepared for the next phase of her evolution. The thought of going hungry didn't disturb Engella anymore. She felt a sense of ease, trepidation even, feeling she was near something big.

She had spent years traveling and learning as much as she could from the different belief systems that permeate our world, whether religious or mystical. From established religions to obscure tribal beliefs, she was searching for an answer to a question she didn't know. The question had appeared to her when she visited the Yaqui Indians in Mexico. But since the revelation she had eight years ago when Rafael made her drink his red potion, nothing of note had been added to her newfound knowledge. She had often found herself looking into the dream realm as if sitting in some invisible grandstand, watching from a spectator seat, which made her wonder how she could have strengthened her power there while doing so little. Since arriving at the village, she mastered the art of displacing her energy in the dream realm, the pressures imposed by the physical proximity of many people around her rendered irrelevant. When she reconnected with Rafael in her dream, it ignited her desire to master the ability to freely move her spirit-self. When she left the Yaqui Village, he had told her she would need to find him before they could continue her quest, but she didn't realize it meant meeting in the dream realm.

Upon her arrival at the Soochit Karana tribe, she fell in love with the community. There, hierarchy had no meaning; there was no clear chief, each person responsible for their own duty, assuming it with diligence. After a week spent with them, she saw that everyone worked together to achieve the goal of fulfilling the needs of the community. It resulted in a clear line between wants and needs in the community. Everyone worked toward meeting civic needs, but no one was forced to ignore their own wants. That reality resulted in a great variety of arts and crafts appear in the village since each person was free to pursue what interests them when they are not working for the community. Every person lived in respect of his or her neighbor, as well as the plants and animals that populated the surrounding forest. When they harvested the plants for food, or kill an animal for their sustenance, they thanked the planet for the bounty by sharing their spoils. For example, they would either leave a carcass for the scavengers to feast on or gather the seeds from the plants to feed the birds. According to this community, we are nothing but microbes, insects living on a larger being. In the village belief system, a planet is a living entity, as are all the stars above us, and it's our responsibility to respect and love our creature, so we may prosper and raise our souls toward the stars.

With that idea as the basis of their existence, centuries before, the community became aware of the energies that surround us all. In her conversations with the people, they told Engella about the duality that inhabits us, about the notion that if you want to prosper into the light, you must accept the darkness. If not, we would be blinded, unable to see as the darkness helps to define the shapes present in the light. It's the same with the darkness; if we turn to it without light, it will be pitch black all around, and our soul would be unable to rise, as the light from our soul defines the depths of its darkness.

Engella felt that this voyage was the one that would take her deeper into understanding the energies that dictate her thoughts. After a month with the community, she felt at home, with no wish to leave. She had immersed herself into the tasks needed by the collective by working in the kitchen to help prepare the food for all before being ordered to connect with the tree. She once went on a hunt for meat, cutting off a large piece from a boar's thigh to leave some for the tiger that was watching them. When she participated in the harvest in the wheat field, there was a family of elephants close by. Engella and two other villagers prepared some bails of wheat and gave it to them. It was all accomplished without question. The result of that way of life was that the notion of regret didn't exist in the community, as all were free to pursue their interests outside the community obligations, which created the balance needed to make the society work properly.

They had taught her the difference between wanting and needing—what incites us to search in dark or in light. Their definition of a need is all that is related to giving us the chance to live another day. It incorporates the notion of eating, sleeping, and reproducing. Those are the elements that were needed to survive. Wants are outside elements we integrate into our lives to help us flourish as individuals. They're based on our personal tastes and desires, which develop according to a person's life experience. Being aware of this difference and applying its principles to everyday life helps a person to define what his or her wants are, leading to a balanced mind.

Leaning against the stump of the tree, letting the sun warm her skin, Engella thought back to a meeting that had happened a while back when she had just arrived. Unaware of the realities of the village, she had asked about their education system. A lively debate exploded when she explained the tenants of the education system she had been raised in. Some people at the meeting were afraid Engella would try to impose the construction of a schoolroom where the children would be imprisoned. They argued that the children, although free to pursue their interests, had to learn basic skills like reading and counting, that discipline was as much a part of their life as the freedom they learned to master. No child was forced to follow an imposed rhythm, as they each had a different learning curve. They kept throwing arguments at her until she managed to tell them she was only curious, nothing more. Knowing she wasn't there to impose anything, Engella marveled at their ability to argue, thinking it would be next to impossible for someone to impose anything on them. She smiled at the memory of that conversation as she tried to settle herself against the tree stump, testing for a more comfortable position. She was trying to empty her mind of the clutter that distracted her from the task at hand when a young girl came into the clearing carrying a jug of water. No more than thirteen years old, the girl had carried the jug as if empty, although she was encumbered by the size. She placed the jug next to Engella.

"Someone will come to replace it every twelve hours. Make sure you drink it all between each refill; you will need it." The girl turned and left without saying another word.

After she left, Engella let the silence of the clearing around her wrap her up like a blanket. The only noise she could perceive was the rustle of leaves in the trees under the breath of a light wind and the occasional insect flying by. She took a sip from the vessel, thinking to herself a jug this size would be more than enough. Within seconds, a feeling of lightness and bliss came over her; her conscious thoughts were pushed aside by an immense chasm of delight and joy. She decided to take a bigger gulp of the water, suspecting it had to be laced with something that would help her, guide her through the two days. Sleep then came to her as she fell to her side, eyes half-open.

She felt her body starting to float, or its essence, since she could see herself lying down next to the tree, somehow continuing to sip water from the jug as her conscious spirit continued elevating itself toward the sky. Engella watched and observed, her conscious mind fully awake, as her body became smaller and smaller, constantly sipping away at the jug. She felt nothing but bliss at this point, getting lighter and lighter, her spirit-body entering a quantum state as she rose. She watched her physical body disappear, as her spirit kept climbing higher. Reaching the sky, the view before her was awe-inspiring. She could see what looked like energy flows traveling between the clouds, seeming to follow patterns, the same way water or wind does. As her spirit rose, she saw that the patterns had colors. It had the same look as a weather pattern seen from a satellite. Engella also saw bursts of energy popping up everywhere on earth, then rising and joining the currents of energy, much in the way a tornado lifts dirt from the ground. Beautiful spirals rose to the sky, joining currents that almost seemed painted on the face of the earth by a master watercolor artist. The whirlpool of colors merged perfectly into one another, offering images of pure beauty for Engella to watch.

When she reached the top of the earth's atmosphere, a spasm of fear set in. Engella realized she had no real control over her spirit's movement. She became scared of floating into deep space, never being able to return. It created an immediate shift, as the bliss and the lightness abruptly switched to deep anxiety, causing her spirit-self to start falling back to earth, gaining speed as if her physical weight came into play. As she gained momentum, she felt a paralysis take over every aspect of her being, each cell stricken by fear, her heart beating hard and fast. The ground was coming at her faster and faster, the colorful currents of ethereal energy replaced by real mountains and forests, and they were approaching fast. Engella was unable to gather even a thought, let alone a scream. She came into view of her body, and she was closing in at a high rate. When she was about to crash into herself, and by extension the earth, Engella managed to muster a loud scream, heard by no one.

She woke up coughing and gasping for air, her back in pain from the position she had slumped to, and her bladder ready to explode. It took Engella a minute to regain her thoughts. Night had fallen, and the clearing was lit by a sliver of moon, creating long shadows on the ground. The sheer beauty and magnificence of the clearing in the pale moonlight almost made her cry from the joy it kindled in her heart. The flower's colors were whitewashed by the moon's light with the shadows dancing beautifully under the mist of the evening dew that was floating above the flowers, undeterred by the light breeze caressing Engella's face. She looked around for a spot to pee, feeling her bladder would soon let go if she didn't do anything about it. A woman returned with a second jug, which intensified Engella's need to go. The woman was elderly, and at first glance, someone would think she was frail and weak, but she was carrying the jug over her shoulder as if the container was a foam cut-out. It meant Engella had been out for twelve hours. She shook her current jug and realized she had emptied it. As the woman approached, Engella felt desperate.

"Where can I go?" She was standing and dancing around while squeezing her knees together to make her message clear. The woman pointed to her left, smiling wryly. Engella ran there, spotting a small indenture in the ground that seemed slanted the right way to guide the urine down the hill. She peed for what seemed like an eternity, and her mind gradually found a sense of balance as the pressure subsided. She returned to the woman feeling exhausted—her mind reeling from the experience. With the Yaqui Tribe, she saw a world that was different, fantastical but still anchored in our plane of existence. This time, she felt she could've left earth forever to travel the universe, and that scared her beyond anything she had ever felt. She thought back to her Yaqui teachings, trying to find something she could grab a hold of to stay sane. The feeling of bliss, as well as the anxiety she felt during the travel, was far beyond anything she had ever experienced at any moment in her life. But she knew the dangers going in and thought back to the residents of the rest home. She needed to do this for them. As Engella returned for the second part of her experience, the woman stayed silent, seemingly waiting for Engella to speak.

"Can I decide where I go?" Engella asked, a little apprehensive about continuing the experience.

"First, you needed to be born; now, you may start to learn. What you felt was the same feeling a newborn goes through as he enters our world. In the womb, the baby is in bliss, floating freely, then he is propelled into our world. The trauma they feel at that moment is temporary, as they begin their journey in this plane of existence with us. It's the same for you. We believe you will start to see more, feel more of the universe now that your birth has occurred. Be aware that the bliss and fear you felt came from both the light and the dark in your soul. I cannot tell you what your light or dark consists of, as it's different for you than it can be for me. But you must learn to love and accept them both to be able to advance further." The woman got up to leave.

"Am I in danger?" Engella said.

"Only if you want to be." The woman walked away.

CHAPTER 26

Oblivious to outside stimulation, Devi Gotra was no longer master of his thoughts since being hypnotized by Dr. Frank Cutler and sent to India in search of the two resistance elements considered dangerous to the program. His unique goal was to find these two fugitives, his mind unequivocally programmed to fixate on that single task. Going through customs went well as Devi recited the text Dr. Cutler made him learn. When the customs officer asked him the reason for his travel to India, Devi recited his text.

"I am visiting. My father grew up in Bhopal. I want to see where he lived and visit his grave." Devi's speech was jerky, but the customs officer accepted his explanation without question and stamped his passport, welcoming him to India.

Devi stepped out of the airport along with three others like him, who, unknowingly, took the same flight. With his senses heightened by the hypnosis, he began to track the pheromone smell left behind by the two fugitives, which still lingered in the air since their passage through there. He followed the olfactory trail to the taxi stand, the smell getting stronger as he approached it. Two other hounds joined him, following the same trail. From there, the scent went in two opposite directions.

"We will track to the north; you go south."

The two other hounds left without another word, leaving Devi alone. He began to trek south, following the trail left by the two fugitives. A third person had joined the target's pheromone dump, but Devi ignored it, his mind entirely focused on the task assigned to him. Unbeknownst to his conscious mind, the hypnosis created a shift in the brain that gave Devi a wolf-like sense of smell. He was able to track the thinnest thread of someone's scent. But the programming had an unfortunate side effect, as it caused a major limitation in the bloodhound's capacity to use the cognitive functions of his brain. Devi was able to send a text message when he wanted to communicate something related to his quest, but that was about it.

Before his capture by the dark matter initiative, Devi Gotra was a quiet man, content to live his life in the confines of a simple routine. On the day he was kidnapped, Devi was going to his son's dance recital. Those activities were the highlights of his days, his three children being the pride of his life. Sometimes, his kids were the sole motivation that kept him going. The man he had become under Dr. Cutler's supervision couldn't be more distant from his true personality. His conscious mind reduced to an empty shell, Devi was only motivated by a single thought, capture Ayla Karemi and Christopher Saddleton. As thoughtful and empathetic as he was in his life, always thinking of others before himself, the hypnosis had turned him into a sociopathic hunter, devoid of emotion—his social filters turned off. He was ready to draw blood if it came to that.

Traveling by foot at first, Devi followed his trail, bumping into people along the way, ignoring traffic lights. As he was attracting more attention, the people around him pondering the possibility of calling the police, Devi found an unsupervised scooter with the key in the ignition and took it. Christopher and Ayla's scents were weak, and Devi had to stay wholly concentrated on the thin thread of pheromones he was following to be able to keep his bearing, which caused him to provoke some traffic accidents as he proceeded, unaware of the trail of chaos he was causing.

Once out of the city, he found a quiet road and continued undisturbed, guided by the inflexible orders coming from his hypnotized subconscious. His conscious self would have cherished the chance to visit his parent's country of origin. They had told him and his brother a legion of colorful stories about their childhood. Devi would have appreciated the chance to absorb some Indian culture at the source. Born in the United States, he heard his parents' stories and read books about India, but never got the chance to travel here, his budget never aligning to allow the journey. The programming imposed by Dr. Cutler obliterated any chance that he might have to remember the trip. So, Devi drove on his scooter oblivious to his surroundings, keeping track of the trail left by his two targets, obsessed by the thought of capturing them for his master.

Hours had gone by when Devi's phone vibrated. His airport colleagues sent a text message. The text contained new coordinates for all the hounds to follow. Devi took the next available road and went in the direction of the coordinates. But the closer he got to his new destination, the weaker the scent of the two fugitives became. His programming didn't tolerate any form of deviation from directives, but the weakening pheromone trail raised some doubts in the hypnotized mind of Devi Gotra. The scent had grown stronger at first, and now the fact the pheromone thread was weakening caused him to try to find an alternative. In his condition, it was a monumental task. The only thing he knew, the only thing he felt was that the thread of pheromones was getting weaker. No other thought could form in his mind as he focused on holding on to the fugitive's scent. Entering a small village, the main road looked more like a market than a street. Devi stepped off his borrowed scooter and went into a store. Indian hip-hop was blaring from the speakers, the employee sitting behind the cash register bobbing his head to the beat. Devi brandished a photo of Christopher and Ayla at the employee.

"Have you seen these people?" He asked in the jerky speech pattern his hypnosis caused.

The employee shook his head. Devi looked around the store and decided to show the pictures to everyone he saw. The employee started spewing insults and curses in both English and Hindi at Devi, ordering him to stop. As Devi went around to the customers, the employee left his counter to grab Devi by the shoulders and shove him out of the store. Unfazed, Devi continued showing the photos outside the store until someone said they had seen them.

"Where are they?" He asked with his robotic cadence.

"I don't know," the person said. "But they spoke of a village in Satpura National Park. I crossed paths with them as I was traveling here."

Devi went back to his scooter to return to the intersection that had brought him there, convinced it was the right path to follow. Excited about his discovery, he sent a text message to the others, sharing the most recent development. As he reached the intersection, the scent was growing stronger again, bolstering Devi's resolve, confirming his obsession, which created a dopamine surge in his brain. He rejoined the road he was following earlier with a deep sense of excitement. Besides bolstering their tracking abilities, Dr. Cutler had also programmed the hope for a reward in his hounds' minds, which he thought would guarantee their relentlessness. Dr. Cutler was so worried that the conscious brain of his army could derail the plan, that he basically destroyed a person's psyche while reprogramming them. Although the hypnosis was temporary in most cases, when the hypnotized person awoke, an empty mind awaited them. Hospitals had been overwhelmed with cases of amnesia and dementia as the soldiers that are discarded after use by the initiative found themselves aimlessly wandering the streets. Dr. Cutler and the group preferred it that way. It made the soldiers easier to control. They would soon receive the implant of DNA anyway, so there was no reason to worry about their safety.

After a couple of hours, Devi found himself riding along a country road, the pheromones of his targets thick in the air. Devi felt he was getting closer. As he came across some farmhouses, he stopped to show his fugitive's photos once again to the people living there.

"I saw a taxi drop off two people down the road in the middle of my fields." The farmer pointed to an empty space in the road. "They went into the forest in that direction," he said, adjusting his aim.

Unsure of what he saw before, the farmer thought Devi might be part of an undercover police operation. Thinking the two people he saw might be dangerous fugitives, the farmer was happy to direct Devi in the direction they went. He had always refused to do business with the village, saying he only did business with companies that paid him money. So, he was unaware of their peaceful philosophy, even going as far as giving them evil intentions to comfort his own refusal to have any dealings with them. Devi left the farmer without saying thank you and started across the field diagonally, stepping on the crops as he went.

As Devi reached the edge of the forest, he was overwhelmed by a new scent, this one more powerful and menacing. He stopped for a second to analyze which direction he should take. Before heading in, he texted the group, signaling that he'd arrived at his destination. As he stepped into the forest, Devi was unaware of the tiger observing him. His last hour on earth had come, as the tiger began to track him as prey, waiting for the best angle of attack. As Devi progressed into the forest, the tiger circled him three times, causing confusion in the hound's scent trail. The tiger had created a barrier, causing Devi to stop as he tried to make sense of the direction he needed to take. That was the moment the tiger chose to jump him, killing Devi instantly by breaking his neck with one swift bite. As the tiger ripped out Devi's intestines to feast, some scavenging birds and bugs began to gather. The tiger, once satiated from the intestines, left the rest of the body to the scavengers and went to clean himself off.

Dr. Cutler received the message from Devi and began to dance around his lab, ecstatic at the idea he would soon be able to undertake his ultimate task of freeing humanity from the clutches of supposed free will.

CHAPTER 27

Engella watched the woman that carried the jug disappear behind the trees, unsure of what to expect next. The bliss and the trauma she experienced earlier drained her energy to a point where she honestly doubted that she would be able to complete the ceremony. Would she end up being parked in the house with the other explorers, unable to communicate what she saw, her brain broken? Would her spirit energy be tortured by the universe for the rest of her life? She looked at her jug, every part of her mind and body wanting to sleep, or at the very least rest before continuing. The fatigue rendered her immobile, numb, unable to think. Engella felt she didn't even have enough strength to lay herself down as she kept staring at the spot where the woman disappeared, unable to do anything else. Shaking herself out of her immobility, she compelled herself to take a sip from the jug. She knew she would come out of this with greater understanding, maybe even some answers, but she wondered if the physical toll would overcome her willingness to continue. The physical training imposed by Rafael was being tested to its limits, Engella giving herself a mental high five for maintaining the exercise regimen since leaving the Yaqui village. Her muscles weak from fatigue, she looked at the water vessel, somehow hoping she could will it to move with her mind, which did not happen. Raising her arms to pick it up, she felt as though she was lifting a piano, her arms so heavy she wasn't sure she could do it. As she touched it, a prickle of the bliss she felt earlier jolted from her fingers to every part of her in an instant. She took a big gulp to get going. The energy was returning, she was fully ready to explore the next phase.

As her spirit being rose to the sky once more, Engella sensed that her bliss had a more conscious, palpable feeling. She was able to process her thoughts more distinctly, although they were still swirling in her psyche, each errant thought stopping for a millisecond in her waking mind before moving on. While her spirit body continued to rise to the sky, Engella concentrated on understanding and acknowledging each thought that came to her. As she reached the edge of the atmosphere, she realized how far she had climbed, and a pang of fear seized her once more. Consciously trying to push it back, she managed to focus on one of the thoughts swirling in her mind; "what do the colors mean?" As she concentrated on the question, she was propelled toward the currents circling the earth. As she fell toward the watercolor infused energy currents, she noticed she was in control of the speed of her descent that time. It gave her a feeling of liberation beyond anything in her life. She dived headlong into the watercolor currents, oblivious to the assaults her mind and soul were about to sustain.

When her spirit body reached the whirling tips of the currents, she marveled at the way they looked like drawn waves. This elation lasted for a millisecond as Engella found herself thrust into an ocean of thoughts and emotions coming at her as one giant swell—happy thoughts, sad emotions, angry thoughts, joyful emotions. Everything every person has thought or dreamed or felt was coming straight at Engella, who was unable to avoid the onslaught. Her mind was overwhelmed by the amount of energy assailing her. Her spirit self became wedged in the middle of the strongest current, a swirl carrying her spirit body away, making the assault even more intense as the emotions came crashing on her, invading her every thought, overcoming any independent thought she might be able to muster. To Engella, it looked like millions upon billions of fireflies coming at her. She felt the pang of fear still present in the pit of her being, inhibited by her force of will alone. She made a conscious effort to acknowledge the fear amidst the chaos in her mind and managed to liberate it. Her spirit body began to fall back to earth the instant the fear filled her mind, but before Engella could leave the influence of the currents, she was mentally raped by feelings of fear and anger and despair so deep it seemed to carry the weight of her spirit body, stopping her fall as she once again began floating in the miasma created by the currents of energy.

She tried to weave her way down as if she was swimming in water, desperately trying to leave the dark gorge, now murky and thick with fear and anger, unsure she could withstand any more. She pierced a hole through the obscurity surrounding her as her hand created an opening, revealing the earth beneath. Her spirit-self was sucked through the cavity, and she abruptly started to free fall the same way as before toward the earth, picking up speed as she descended. She accepted the growing velocity of the fall with glee. The fear was still present, her heart beating fast and hard, but Engella had developed a form of respect toward it. The feeling of respect toward her anxiety gave Engella peace as she entered her physical body at full velocity.

She awoke as if coming out of a deep sleep, her eyes opening slowly, feeling heavy. There was a man sitting next to the tree stump, waiting. She felt stiff the first time she woke up, but this time her whole body refused to move, extenuated by the experience. "This is probably what it feels like when you finish a triathlon," she whispered to herself, her mind frayed. The need to urinate wasn't as strong this time, although she had once again emptied the whole jug.

"I don't know about that. You're only halfway through the race," the man said. "But what I do know is that you have gone further than anyone before. Do you have any questions before you continue?"

The man sitting on the stump had a familiar presence, but a thick beard and long, scraggly hair hid his face enough for Engella to wonder who he might be.

"Yes, two of them, she said. "First, how come I've never seen you before? It's a small community and, I feel I see everyone else at least two times a week. My other question is, have we met before? I recognize your energy, but for some reason, I can't place it in my mind."

The man smiled at Engella. "For your first question, I come and go, but mostly go. It's my task to search the world and explore it far and wide and report my findings to the tribe so we may follow human evolution from a distance. The news I bring helps us measure the state of the collective unconscious. For your second question, yes, we have met. The man cleared the hair away from his face."

"Dwight Como!" Engella shouted, suddenly recognizing his smile through the thick hair on his face. Her fatigue abruptly disappeared. She felt spry and ready to go. She sprung to her feet. "Since when are you a resident of Soochit Karana? My god, you've changed!"

Engella had trouble containing her joy. Dwight's presence there with her was another element that proved she was following the right path.

"A while now, I guess." He said. "I stopped counting time ages ago, so I'm not sure. Thing is, I would love for us to reminisce, but you still have two more jugs to drink." He handed her the water, picked up the empty jug, and started to walk back.

Engella felt a twinge of frustration as she watched him walk away, wanting to talk more with him. Looking to prolong their meeting, she asked him a question that was bothering her since the beginning.

"What's in the water?"

Dwight stopped and turned, happy to continue their conversation. "Nothing. Just water. It's the place, not the water. We don't want you to dehydrate. That's all."

"Yeah, sure." Engella then changed the subject. "How long are you here for this time?" She planned to drill Dwight with questions the next time they meet.

"I'll hang around for a while. We can catch up when you're finished if that's what you're wondering. I need a break from travel anyhow," he said. "Plus, I'm curious to know what your journey is like."

"What do you mean?"

"The residents of the resting house didn't even make it to the second jug, and we're barely able to piece together fragments of information since their minds are so broken. Anything you do from this point on is new territory for everyone." Dwight turned back to leave and disappeared into the forest.

CHAPTER 28

Christopher awoke with Pawa standing over him, eager to get started. "We don't know how long we have; we must begin."

Pawa's voice was seemingly coming out of nowhere, her thick accent making it look like a poorly translated movie, her lips seemingly saying something different than her mouth. But her firm tone and the sun hitting her from the back gave Pawa a bigger than life aura. Christopher crawled out of bed, a little intimidated.

"Gimme a minute; need coffee," he grumbled. Ayla, lying next to him, gave Pawa a sleepy nod. Pawa blurted something in Japanese and left the tent in a huff.

"Man, she's intense," Christopher whispered to himself. "I wonder how the others will be. If she's been the one training them, it should be interesting."

Pawa came back, armed with a full coffee cup. "Here," she said, sticking the cup in his face.

Christopher broke out laughing at her impatience and grabbed the cup. Pawa stepped out of the house, mumbling something inaudible and waited outside.

"Let's go then," Christopher said as he got up. He gulped down his cup of black coffee, pleasantly surprised at the quality, and stepped out to join Pawa.

She guided him to a small, enclosed space where his so-called security team had already gathered. Ten-foot fences closed off a small courtyard, which was equipped with straw dummies and wooden targets. Christopher looked around, wondering what kind of weapons they used. Save the dummies and targets, the grounds were bare; all he could see were slingshots in a basket and homemade bows and arrows strewn on the ground in a corner. His heart sank. This was an armory for children. No hound could be stopped with a slingshot, and the bows and arrows both looked way too primitive to be useful. Trying to hide his disappointment, he asked the would-be warriors to give him a demonstration of where they stand in their capacity to use these weapons. Pawa grabbed a slingshot, and three comrades followed suit. They lined up four abreast and began to stretch the elastic of their slingshot, each aimed at the same wooden target. They were armed with a small rounded stone. On Pawa's cue, they let go, each hitting the target in the exact same spot, making a machine gun sound as each rock hit the bullseye a fraction of a second apart, tearing a hole in the thick piece of wood. In a coordinated movement, they bent over and reloaded by picking up a rock from the ground, ready to repeat the exercise. Christopher's mouth was agape; he didn't expect such a violent and satisfying result. A combination of awe and fear filled his mind, awestruck from the demonstration. Pawa smiled, proud of her group. They deposited their slingshots.

Pawa nodded at another group, signaling them to pick up some bows and repeated the demonstration, aiming at a straw dummy. The seemingly weak bows and crooked arrows all connected with the head of the dummy, which consisted of an empty coconut shell, splitting it in two. The arrows hit the face in a straight line down the middle of the head, which created two equal pieces. Christopher let out a loud yelp of joy. "Whoa! You guys are serious!" he said, smiling like a kid at Christmas.

It hasn't been that long since he began fighting the hypnotized hounds, but it felt like such a long time. It seemed like he would never be able to see the end of the war. Up to that point, he had been forced to react and defend himself. With that team he could go on the offensive and cripple the initiative's plans for real. All his new militia needed was some strategic help. Pawa had helped them master the art of using their weapons with deadly force, but should an attack happen on more than one front; they would be overwhelmed. With his knowledge of the strategies used by the bloodhounds and Pawa's army by his side, he knew they could withstand an attack from Dr. Cutler's soldiers, even inflict some real damage.

The day went on in a joyous atmosphere, the trainees alternating between practice and theory. While half took shots with the available weapons to perfect their precision even more, Christopher went over the map of the village with the others, showing them how they could withstand an attack from any direction. They would place a lookout at the three entry points of the village and provide three other patrols of three or four people who travel from one entry point to the next. Christopher thought this should prevent a surprise incursion into the village, although the thickness of the forest did play against them. The remaining soldiers, along with Christopher and Pawa, would stay in "the barracks," on alert. The lookouts are to be relieved every eight hours to prevent mistakes that could be caused by fatigue. When an attack happens, the soldiers are to move in groups of three. The slingshots would stay at ground level while the archers would set up their shooting positions in the trees when possible. The preparations excited Christopher. Certain the hypnotized hounds would eventually find him and Ayla, Christopher wanted a fierce and violent response when they did. He wanted to send a message to Dr. Cutler and his backers that this village is ready to offer true resistance. He wanted the tide to change, and he believed he found a way for that to happen.

As Christopher headed to the cooking area to propose a new recipe of his making to ensure full protein intake for his soldiers, he noticed Zorina Smith speaking with Jolan. Christopher's heart sank a little. As well-intentioned as they were, the Collective Unconscious Alliance had a way of investing themselves in the decision process when they were interested in something. Despite their desire to spread happiness, they generally did little more than cause confusion. This village didn't need the misplaced ambitions of the allegiance. They had shaped a functioning society where freedom and responsibility are synonyms, where choice is a truly a personal matter, a place where people are never judged for what they've done, are accepted for who they are and respected for what they do for the village. If the collective unconscious alliance set foot in this place, they could derail the whole system with their notion that the darkness of the soul must be eradicated, that exclusively following the light in our soul is humanity's salvation.

The people of the village have learned to live with both the light and the dark that inhabits us. It's the balance we achieve between the two that defines us, not the annihilation of one or the other. Christopher had remained faithful to the collective because of Zorina. Her honesty and her support are the main reason he didn't go crazy at first. But he also stayed the course based on the idea that their pursuit of the light within all was way more positive than the Machiavellian plan being implanted by Dr. Cutler and the initiative. Except that since he met Ayla, Christopher's perspective had changed drastically. His outlook had evolved from the idea that we need to guide the people in a specific direction to achieve happiness, to the notion that we each have the responsibility to accept and love who we are and those around us. Since his arrival at the village, he understood that our personal connection to the universe is the saving grace for humanity to overcome its destructive patterns. He stayed out of sight, waiting for Zorina to leave before going to Jolan to warn him about the collective's tendencies.

"What did she want?" Christopher asked bluntly.

"They are offering their help," Jolan said.

Christopher cut him off.

"Don't. I'm sorry. They're good people, but they have a way of taking over a place when they invest themselves in it. Their intentions are good, but their methods are contradictory to the intentions. They will install a hierarchy in the village, and their way of thinking will cause trouble. They believe in the notion of a leader to guide the flock." Christopher tried to calm himself. "I mean, they're not as destructive as . . ." Jolan cut him off.

"Calm down, young man," Jolan whispered. "I refused their help."

Christopher was dumbfounded. "Oh! Well then . . . Good." Christopher stood there looking awkward as Jolan laughed.

"The surprised look on your face is entertaining. Thank you for that. I needed to laugh a little." He looked at Christopher. "You know, they aren't the first group who want to merge their ideals with ours. But most want to use the village's knowledge to further their personal agenda, fill their own needs, even if it's done with good intentions. Anyone who approaches us with a petition to merge our beliefs to theirs is typically turned aside."

"Typically?" Christopher asked.

"You have a quick mind," Jolan said. "Over the course of our history, we have crossed paths with higher minds who have helped us overcome certain limitations. When this happens, we accept any new knowledge that helps us grow. It's typically a single person who integrates into the family. Much like the arrival of Engella Iblis." Jolan looked at Christopher. "Your arrival is also a prime example. Your strategic ability was the missing element to our capacity to defend the village from ill-intentioned groups. Military knowledge has never been a priority, but our needs changed, and within months, both Pawa and you have arrived, each armed with a piece of knowledge essential to our survival."

"How do you know I won't skip out when trouble comes?" Christopher was looking for a reaction from Jolan but wasn't expecting the one he got.

"If you so choose, we won't stop you." Jolan turned to leave. "But, I believe you will stay." He walked away.

CHAPTER 29

Meeting Dwight in that place, combined with the realization that their roads always seemed to cross at crucial times in their lives, gave Engella a boost of energy, most of it coming from the dopamine release in her brain. She felt ready to undertake the next phase. Her body had gone way passed tired and was deep into exhaustion, but Jolan had explained that the connection needed to happen all at once, within the same forty-eight-hour period. She was grateful for the energy her meeting with Dwight gave her, but she was worried about her mind's capacity to absorb any more assaults from the universal energy wrapping itself around the earth. There were two more trips to go, and even though she had a better understanding of what to expect in the ethereal energy realm, she was genuinely worried that her physical body and conscious mind couldn't take much more. "The show must go on," she said to no one in the clearing, picking up the jug to drink.

Before Engella took a sip, she realized she didn't pee this time, although she had emptied the jug a second time. She paused; there was nothing, even the hunger was gone. Trying to settle herself into a more comfortable position, Engella hoped to obscure a part of the physical pain she felt when she returned by getting more comfortable. She noticed the apprehension she had felt before starting this journey was replaced with excited anticipation of what lies ahead, her exhilaration growing as she brought the jug to her lips. As the water entered her body, there was no bliss this time around, but no fear either; all she felt was nothing, as her spirit body began to rise once again. The feeling of nothingness was so complete, Engella didn't know what to make of it. And she didn't care that she didn't know. The calm carried in by the surrounding emptiness brought on a sense of serenity so strong, Engella could effortlessly direct her spirit body toward the energy currents. In the void, she was capable of a single thought at a time. As hard as she tried, Engella couldn't produce more than single commands to her spirit self; go, stop, turn. Realizing she had some control this time around, she entered the energy currents willfully. The emotions and thoughts carried by the energy field that assaulted her the previous time did nothing more than bounce off her. The fireflies, still feverish and excited, danced around her presence but were unable to penetrate her thoughts. She was able to travel through the watercolor masses of energy with ease, dexterously flowing in the currents like a swallow playing with the springtime wind. It gave her time to see the flow, then observe and analyze its contents as she tried to understand its function. She saw that she was navigating through a massive energy field created by the humans, the animals, the plants, everything that lived on earth, including the earth itself.

Where she had before seen an indiscernible mass of energy that invaded her being and raped her mind, she now saw herself before a billion little specs of energy that were traveling together, each following its own path, each carrying its own burden, its own elation. Engella could almost feel their caress as they floated by, contouring Engella the same way water swirls around a rock in a river. This gave Engella plenty of time to analyze what she saw. Her logical mind was fully present, which bolstered her confidence. She tried to grab a speck of energy that was passing by, but it dissipated into her skin instantly, showing her a moment in a person's life, as if she were watching a movie preview. She looked around and found different looking specks of energy, trying to figure out the color-coding, the meaning of these little bursts of thought and memory.

That's when she noticed a silhouette lurking in the current—an enormous shadow, obliterating from sight anything behind it. It seemed stationary, but Engella couldn't ignore the fact she felt watched, probed, even. She could almost make out a face in the middle of the shadow but was too busy holding back the fear that was encompassing her spirit body to concentrate on what she saw. The dark shape then appeared to move toward her, encasing Engella in place, not by fear this time, but by an outside force alien to her being, like invisible hands holding her by the shoulders, keeping her in place. She thought she had met her doom as she was engulfed in the shadow with nowhere to run. As it closed in on her, she realized it contained her own thoughts and memories—her past as well as her future. Before the shadow engulfed her, Engella thought she had gained some control over her conscious mind in that realm. She thought she had reached a point where she could absorb what was happening with a calm analytic mind, then return to the village to ask questions and learn more. But with her whole life story bearing down on her, Engella acknowledged the failure of her mind with calm and serenity, letting the madness take hold without offering any resistance. Thoughts and memories began to reach her, passing through her randomly, one-by-one. Engella saw flashes of the contents, her mind spinning in every direction, causing her focus to waver. The joy of learning to ride a bike popped into her mind, although all she could *see* was the joy itself; there was no image to go with it. All she knew was that it was the time she rode her bicycle with no training wheels for the first time. Then a jolt of emotion shook her to the core. As sure as she was that the other flash of energy was from her first bike ride, she knew the jolt she felt came from the feeling provoked by Dwight dying in her arms. Waves of sadness and rage overwhelmed her as she cried at his death. This threw Engella into a spiral, her conscious mind refusing this new information with ardor, her fear taking over. Desperate to find a way out, she seized control of her fear, channeling it to open up the sky, Engella willing her spirit-self back into her physical body.

She opened her eyes to a pitch-black night—the moon hidden behind the clouds. She was fine; no lumbago, no pain, a little tired, but not exhausted. Except the need to urinate was back with a vengeance. Engella wondered if she could pee near the tree stump. There was no way she could find her way to the indenture she saw before in this darkness. For some reason, she couldn't see the dark like she does when she goes running at night. The voice of Rafael then popped into her mind. "You don't need to see your surroundings to be aware of them." She remembered the countless times he had her taking the most rugged paths to help her learn to feel the ground. The helplessness she felt in those moments was the same as the feeling she recognized now. "Embrace your helplessness," he would say.

These thoughts helped her regain some focus, and although she still couldn't see the forest, her senses were strong enough for her to find her spot. Engella got up and let the smell of the flowers fill her nostrils. It instantly created an image of the clearing in her mind. She walked to the spot where she would relieve herself with the dread of Dwight's future death lingering in the back of her mind. The emotion she felt was visceral as if something violent had happened. As she returned to the stump to continue her journey, she noticed a slight glow emanating from it. The shimmer was hard to perceive, but a light pulse was enough to make it clearly visible. Engella heard someone approaching, the breeze carrying the woman's perfume ahead of her.

"Hello, Ayla." Engella was surprised she remembered Ayla's perfume.

"Hello Engella," she whispered, smiling in the dark.

"It's been a while," Engella whispered, not questioning the need to keep their voice low. She was now sitting at the base of the stump, leaning against it.

"I know. I thought I would find you as soon as I arrived, but you were already preparing for this, and I couldn't see you right away." Ayla paused. "So much has happened since the last time we met, I can't wait for you to meet Christopher. He's the one you spoke to in his dreams." She placed the water jug next to Engella. "I volunteered to bring you this last jug because I wanted to tell you that I love you and I've missed you."

Engella was overwhelmed by emotion. From the moment she met Ayla, Engella had always felt a connection between them—an implicit acceptance of who they are, which helped them build a strong relationship. The psychological strength exhibited by Ayla while she was being ridiculed, combined with her acute intelligence, prompted Engella to train her towards "the dreaming arts," and their relationship grew even more from there. Even if they haven't seen each other in a long time, it felt to Engella like they had spoken only the day before.

As much as Engella wanted to continue the conversation, tell Ayla about her newfound knowledge of the future, she had to stay concentrated on the task at hand. Her mind was looking for a reason for Ayla to stay, trying to find anything that would allow them to talk some more. But there was one more jug to drink, and Engella was curious to see what happens after completing the journey. Would the experience create an all-out social upheaval in the world? If Jolan was right, Engella was working to rejuvenate the tree, which, if successful, would cause it to fill everyone's subconscious with cosmic energy. The influx of new energy could provoke massive changes in people's habits as fresh information gets absorbed in their dreams.

Or would it be something more private with each person awakening to his or her own new reality—still causing a social shift, except at a slower rate. The one thing she was certain about was that she needed to speak with some theoretical physicists after this to see if they could incorporate her experience into some sort of mathematical formula that would help define the limits of her experience. The exhaustion long gone, she silently celebrated her body's capacity to withstand everything that had happened in the last day and a half. The glow coming from the stump grew stronger, telling Engella she was close to completing her task. She lassoed her mind to concentrate on the next part of her assignment, ready to finish her journey.

Ayla had always thought of herself as a conscious being. She had been at peace with her existence since childhood. But since her mentor had directed her toward Engella to help with her thesis, Ayla's life had drastically veered away from normality, testing her need for logical explanations as she found herself exposed to an almost outlandish reality. Engella had introduced her to a world where mystical phenomena lived in harmony with scientific realities. She had helped Ayla reach the understanding that the world that surrounds us is all-encompassing. To be able to understand and assimilate the knowledge that governs our existence, one had to accept that there's science in mysticism, and there's mysticism in science. Everything is inhabited with a light-versus-dark duality, and our responsibility is to learn to accept both as truth and embrace it all. Engella had pushed Ayla to train her body to be strong enough to withstand the energy drainage caused by a visit in the dream realm, after which she showed her a glimpse of the other realm, much like Rafael did with Engella. After the time they spent together, they had followed the path destined for them. Ayla, unable to master the art of the waking dream, corresponded through text and email to keep in touch. For Ayla, Engella had always been the one who pushed her to confront her beliefs and enticed her to go beyond the questions her modern mind could muster. This is the reason she loved her.

Here they were, in the dark forest of Satpura National Park in India, the tree stump glowing stronger than ever, its glow having become strong enough for Engella to see Ayla's facial features. Engella was startled looking at her, her mind flashing to the eyes of the shadow that carried her memories in the ethereal energy currents. She took a deep breath, reminding herself that she was in the clearing with Ayla.

"What do you think the glow means?" Engella asked.

She knew the answer but wanted to be sure her mind was back in reality, and asking an obvious question was one way that often worked for her. Ayla responded, nonetheless.

"The link with the universe is activating itself. This is the place on earth where the cosmic energies can be absorbed and then join our collective unconscious," explained Ayla. "Or, that's what Jolan told me you were doing," she added. "When the tree was complete, its branches touched the sky, guiding the flow of energy toward the earth so humans could be aware of the duality within every one of us. The tree has been nothing but a stump for centuries. Nonetheless, what remained has continued as a link to the energy field, albeit a weak one. What had changed was the fact that the tree was now unable to reach into the field and properly filter the information being directed to our subconscious, making the dream realm a dark and confused place."

Engella stayed silent during Ayla's explanation, even though she had already gotten the lesson from Jolan, not wanting to take away the pleasure Ayla had from sharing the information. As Ayla was talking, the tree stump started to pulse more and more, its light growing stronger still. They both took it as a sign. Engella needed to continue her journey.

"That's your last jug of water," Ayla said, pointing to it. She was clearly visible under the powerful glow of the tree.

"It's all true," Engella said, nodding her head. As Ayla got up to go back to the village, Engella stopped her and said, "Wait! What's in the water?" Ayla cocked her head sideways.

"Nothing. Water from the source, that's it. I asked the same thing to Jolan as we were filling the jug, but he told me the tree is the guiding force." Ayla gave Engella a serious look. "I thought you already figured that out."

"I did, I think. But I guess I didn't want to believe it." Engella leaned on the tree and took a large gulp. See you in twelve hours.

CHAPTER 30

The first three hypnotized hounds to arrive at Devi Gotra's coordinates didn't notice the human remains on the ground as they passed by, their focus solely on the scent of the two fugitives they were pursuing. When one of them stepped on some bones and got one stuck on his shoe, he barely slowed down to see what was wedged on to his foot, impatiently shaking it off with a kick in the air. They walked through the forest, unaware they were being watched by a massive tiger who was following them on a parallel path. When the sounds of life from the village reached them, they stopped. One of the hounds scouted a little further to confirm they had reached their destination, while the two others sent a report back to Dr. Cutler reporting their latest advancements. As the scout returned, four more hounds joined them, eager to move into action.

"Confirmation," the scout said as he returned from his village analysis. "They are present. We must first surround the village to limit any chance of escape."

Lifting his head from his phone screen, another soldier spoke. "Dr. Cutler has ordered us to spread out and take notes for now. More reinforcements will arrive soon." He gave the orders in short, concise phrases. The hounds spread out in search of a well-hidden observation spot as soon as he finished speaking. They were to report anything they saw to Dr. Cutler, with the exception that should they be in a position to capture one of the fugitives, they were not to hesitate.

Frank Cutler, already imagining the accolades he would receive as the creator of a new tomorrow, was getting regular updates from his hounds. The information was a little troubling to Frank. The place his hounds were describing seemed to show there might be more resistance than anticipated from his two fugitives. Frank congratulated himself for following them with zeal. They had brought him to a place he might not have found on his own. His hounds had found the two fugitives, but they had also found a place that could harbor a strong resistance and needed to be erased from existence. The news would serve him well with the Initiative, a new development sure to re-establish the confidence needed between him and them.

Gathering his thoughts as the information came in at a fast pace, he sent an update to the Initiative, presenting the new developments as a quasi-victory, staying silent about the fact that he had no idea what he was up against. He said that after this operation, they could start the procedures. Within minutes, his email box was filled with replies from the different divisions that composed the dark matter initiative. They all said that on his signal, the security and enforcement elements of the initiative would swing into action. The incarcerated population, along with the spiritual leaders that had already been silenced, would be the first to be modified. To Cutler, this meant they accepted his message as a done deal and that their confidence had been restored. A message came in after the others, the initiative stating they're now fully invested, and should the procedure go through some growing pains, he had their full support. But Frank, exuberant at the expectation of finishing it with Ayla Karemi, was positive there would be no more problems. He had revised the theory countless times, created millions of simulations; nothing could go wrong. All that was needed by then was the silencing of the two thorns in his side to quell the doubts brought forth by the initiative.

A fleeting memory of his family flashed in his mind, which Frank readily pushed aside. His past life had nothing to offer but pain and regret and dwelling on his past could only slow him down. In a way, he was relieved that he could give his family a life they could love and appreciate without the torments supposed free-will can breed in one's mind. Although he had trained many doctors to do the procedure, he wanted to make sure he would personally implant the changes in his family to ensure their future happiness. They had refused to follow him in his dream, fighting for his attention when he was deeply entrenched in his research. They began to resent him for isolating himself from the family, and he began to resent them for not understanding the importance of his research. Frank had grown apart from his family because of this, but he didn't hold a grudge against them and understood what they were longing for. He wanted to make sure they received the best transformation options possible. His wife and children wanted a simple nine-to-five life—a family routine entrenched in the uncompromising dictate of a schedule, which he would grant them. That way, the memory of his passage in their life would be a distant mirage, as if from a stranger. But he was curious to see what their reaction would be like when his wife and children see him, part of him worried they might react emotionally, afraid he might break down if that happens. Forcing his mind back to the present, Frank went back to his phone to see if there were any new messages.

Back at the village, the hounds had positioned themselves around the village either by climbing up a tree or digging into a bush, so they could analyze the movements in the community without being detected. One of them had to circle the whole village before settling in. As he climbed up a compact grove of bamboos, he was too obsessed with his mission to marvel at the fact that those lean sticks of wood could lift him without collapsing. He also couldn't appreciate his luck that the harvest of the grove wasn't due until the following month. But he did pick up on the person returning from the forest carrying an empty clay jug. Ordered to do surveillance first, the hound remained silent, unevenly balanced in the bamboo grove. He took note of the direction the person came from for future reference, and once alone, settled in his grove more comfortably. He then sent a message to his associates to send someone to his side of the village to investigate further into the forest.

By then, a small army was gathering at the edge of the village. Dr. Cutler's soldiers were ordered to spread out in groups to join the scouting parties. Two of them joined the bamboo grove hound. As they climbed into the cluster, making themselves as invisible as possible while they await instructions, the first hound climbed down and went in the direction the person carrying the jug came from, as requested by Dr. Cutler. As soon as he entered the forest, his augmented sense of smell picked up on the scent of Ayla Karemi. He hid behind a tree, looking for his target, ready to pounce. Walking the forest with some villagers, Ayla passed within ten feet of the hound, carrying empty baskets into the forest. They were looking for mushrooms or fruits they could bring back to the village, each person concentrated on scanning the ground in front of them as they walked in silence. Ayla stopped and looked around, feeling watched. One of the villagers, a slingshot expert assigned to protect the group, stopped with her.

"What's up?" He asked, thinking she had found something.

"Don't know, I feel like someone's watching me." Ayla said. She scanned the surrounding forest. Nothing seemed out of place, but the feeling lingered.

"You're nervous," he said, trying to reassure her. "The people pursuing you may be relentless, but Christopher trained us well, you shouldn't worry."

The villager spoke while petting his slingshot, looking eager to use it. He then pulled her along to rejoin the group. As they went back to their companions, the hound followed at a distance, certain he would receive a great reward for capturing a target all on his own. But to apprehend his target, he needed to find a way to isolate her from the group and then make her disappear quietly. The deeper Ayla and her acolytes got in the forest, the more the hound's artificially enhanced hope for reward became his unique focus. The moon was bright, and the games its light played with the shadows helped the hound get closer to Ayla, who had stopped and seemed to be waiting for something. A tiger appeared next to the hound, the warm breeze of his breath sliding down the hound's back. In one swift, silent move, the tiger grabbed the hound by the neck and crushed it, not giving it time to react and canceling any chance to call for help. The sound of the cracking bones was no different from a branch snapping under someone's foot, so no one from the group of gatherers paid any attention. As the body of the hound hung lifeless from its mouth, the tiger walked away from the group, carrying the body to a spot where scavengers could fight over it. The tiger then went to join Engella's lifeless body, awaiting her return.

While the unlucky bloodhound was being torn to pieces by the forest scavengers, more of Dr. Cutler's soldiers were gathering near the village. Their battle strategy was basic; surround the target and close in. Their programming needed to be as simple as possible for Cutler to be able to control their actions, which meant any elaborate strategy was condemned to fail since they couldn't hold a thought long enough to adapt their approach. The one strategic moment would be when the go-signal was transmitted. In those moments, the hounds reacted as one, the group tightening their noose on their target in hopes of creating fear in their minds.

By then, all thirty-five psychopathic bloodhounds sent by Dr. Cutler had arrived. They segmented into four groups to join the lookouts, taking a wide berth, being careful to stay invisible to the villagers. As each group reached their destinations, they spread out and hid in the bushes or climbed up a tree. But there was one lookout missing. The group attached to the missing sentinel sent a message to Dr. Cutler, unsure of the path to follow. Their inability to improvise had always been their biggest weakness, and the confusion about the missing colleague attested to that.

"God damn it!" Cutler growled to himself when he received the text. He sent back an order. *Spread out and get ready to move!* But his anger didn't cloud his mind enough to forget about the missing bloodhound. He sent a private message to the hound's phone.

In the empty forest, a telephone lit up on the ground, ringing for no one. Hyenas and vultures were feasting on a human carcass lying nearby. Getting no answer, Cutler slammed his phone down on his desk. Christopher and Ayla had been thorns in his side for long enough; it ended today.

Unaware of the villager's preparation, the hounds didn't see Christopher's army, nor did it interest them. From the moment the first hound arrived, sentinels posted around the village had set off the silent alarms they had prepared, and the village's army sprang into action. They were strategically set up, slingshots and bows in hand while they awaited the hound's first move.

CHAPTER 31

This time, Engella concentrated her thoughts on the water entering her body, taking the time to feel it spread to every cell of her being, lifting her spirit toward the atmosphere. It was the last jug of water, and as she was rising to the sky, she joyfully flew in loops as she rose. She let her spirit body rise above the atmosphere, feeling an irrefutable need to explore, her fear well contained. For a short moment, a slight panic set in when she felt herself begin to float uncontrollably when she reached outer space. Surprised that the weightlessness of space affected her spirit body as well, she pushed aside the fear that had tried to grab hold of her. Instead using the energy emitted by her unrest to gain control over her movements. She willed her consciousness to focus on the incomparable beauty of space, as she could now observe it without the veil of the atmosphere. She could physically feel the vastness of the universe as it pulled at her, trying to split her spirit into a million little pieces and spread it across the universe. Seeing space without the filter of the atmosphere was almost too much to bear for Engella, who was using every ounce of her energy to remain whole, as she tried to find a way back down towards earth, her particles being too small for gravity to take hold. She let a pang of fear grab her, thinking it might create the same descent as before, but she stayed above the atmosphere the fear trying to seize her conscious mind.

Engella was aware that if it happened, the panic induced by the fear would cause her to split into a million atoms and neutrinos, dissipating into space. Her head was on the verge of exploding when she spotted a dust-like cloud floating toward earth. It looked like a dust devil in the desert, bouncing head over heels in the emptiness of space—closing in on the earth. Where an earthly dust devil dances and moves while staying anchored to the ground, this mass of particles seemed anchored in the emptiness of space, bouncing off invisible walls as it edged its way onward. Engella's fascination with this phenomenon concealed any sense of confusion or fear, as she let her urge to get closer take over. A mixture of fear, anxiety, excitement, and curiosity filled her mind, which somehow helped her stay focused on the swirl of particles. She began to wave her arms in a swimming motion, striving to approach the cloud. She realized travel in space was easier than traveling within the atmosphere, her spirit body entirely free of resistance.

Someone could get lost forever here, Engella thought, feeling the weightlessness of space supported by a thick, invisible force that wanted to pull her into its unfathomable depth. As Engella approached the spatial dust devil, she noticed the particles it contained looked like the same specks of energy that composed the earthly collective of unconscious energy spirals. As the cloud was about to touch the earth's atmosphere, Engella tried to dive into it. But she was stunned by a powerful blast of energy penetrating her spirit body, splitting her apart. If she put together every orgasm, every time she opened a Christmas present, every happy moment she celebrated, then joined it with the energy contained in every sad, difficult moment that happened in her life and put them together, it would represent but one percent of the energy she felt in this cloud. Engella, overwhelmed by the sheer brutality of the cloud's vigor, felt her spirit body expanding, ready to split into pieces. She managed to keep her focus on one single speck of energy floating around her like a confused firefly and reached to grab it. The power contained in it exploded in her hand, and Engella instantly found herself in front of a star, somewhere deep in space.

A swell of emotions came to her, but she didn't have time to react to any of them as the star began to expand, swelling more and more to the point where it touched Engella's quivering spirit body. Unable to move or think, she watched as the star grew closer. She thought she would feel the heat coming from the expanding star, but it only became brighter, blinding her. As the star reached her, it exploded, propelling her ravaged spirit body and the resulting neutrino cloud the explosion produced, through the universe at light speed toward the earth. Engella briefly lost her connection to her consciousness, unaware she was passing through planets and stars as she approached earth. She awoke with her spirit floating aimlessly in the energy currents that surround the earth, left to wonder if her spirit had stood witness to the death of a star or if it had been a strange dream provoked by the energy contained in the speck of light she touched.

Sensing something was a little off, Engella realized the shadow which contained her life was wrapping her up, keeping her afloat. She felt comforted by the spectral mass encircling her spirit and floated aimlessly, waiting for her mind to recover. She accepted the shadow's presence, and this time the walls of the shadow didn't close in, the specks of energy seeming slower within its borders as if they were plowing through invisible mud. Engella tried to see if she could recognize specific elements of her life story as she emptied her mind, ready to absorb any new information. There seemed to be fewer specks floating around, but Engella ignored it and focused on one bit of energy that was floating toward her, seemingly aiming itself at her. She braced herself as it reached her spirit body.

She not only felt the moment; she was propelled into it. Her adult, conscious mind was hidden in the teenage girl she was at that moment. The memory was from when she found herself lost in the woods during a school outing. Engella was mesmerized, unsure of what to do, feeling like she was physically in her own body so long ago. She remembered everything about that night—how cold it had been—how helpless she felt. Her panic had caused her to make bad decisions during this ordeal. If the search had taken but one more day, Engella would have surely died from hypothermia. During the outing, she had separated from the group during a class expedition, and after realizing she was disoriented, she had wandered aimlessly, not drinking enough water, not eating anything, as she was unsure of what might be poison. She felt the panic in the mind of her younger self; she had to do something. She spoke out, hoping to reach the mind of her young self.

"It's going to be okay. Find shelter. Find food." Engella repeated this mantra over and over, hoping the teenage her would hear the chant. As she was repeating her mantra, the memory of that moment began to shift in her present mind. She remembered hearing the voice in her head, at the same time as she was sending her thoughts to her younger self. She took a mental note to look back to this moment in her life when she returns to the physical realm.

It worked. Engella felt the panic subside as her younger self began to look for shelter, shifting her focus to survival instead of despair. Engella was then instantly expelled from the memory, as she found herself thrown back into the flow of energy. The shadow had evaporated. The spatial dust devil had also disappeared, but she could still feel its presence, as the neutrino cloud seemed to permeate everything with its energy, generating a pulse that excited the specks of energy contained in the flows that carried them. Trying to see through the dancing fragments twirling all around, she spotted a nearly invisible cloud that was feverishly descending to earth, pushed by an invisible wind. She felt an urge to follow it and directed her own spirit body towards the cloud. Approaching the mass confirmed to Engella that this was the same ball of energy that had carried her through space, flashes of the exploding star popping into her mind as she got closer.

When she reached it, the cloud had become cone-shaped, a tornado-like funnel. Engella felt herself being pulled in as the power of the phenomenon spread to the surrounding particles, sucking everything in. She resisted for a second but then dove in willingly, getting pulled into the swirl unceremoniously, her spirit body stretched to its limits once again as she was swallowed whole. The swirl contained everything and nothing all at once. When she was sucked into the vortex, Engella found she could understand the vastness of the universe, accepting the infinitesimal nature of life, celebrating the uniqueness of every cell, and applauding the harmony of it all existing at once. But her moment lasted but for a second, as the tip of the tornado touched down on the tree stump in the clearing. Engella deftly thrust herself out of it and into her physical body as the funnel exploded in a loud crackle of lightning, disappearing in a flash.

Engella found herself at the foot of the stump with the tiger sitting on it, looking at her. A burst of adrenaline exploded when she saw it, aware that its savage nature could return any time. The tiger was looking right at her with intent, its eyes locked on her. Even immobile, the tiger bestows a raw energy that can strike fear in the most hardened people. *The definition of strong and silent*, Engella thought as she focused on her breathing to calm herself down. The tiger had been at her side since she arrived and didn't show any signs of wanting to kill her, making her laugh at her own fearful reaction when she awoke. Her heart rate came back down. The tiger reacted to the laughter by lying down; he began to lick his paws, ignoring her. She got up and sat on the edge of the tree stump, wondering if the tiger would let her pet him. He was calm, busy cleaning himself up, and didn't flinch as she approached. She was so close; she felt its heat—a soul comforting, powerful warmth. She laid next to it and instantly fell asleep, feeling its breath on her neck as the tiger laid on its side for her to spoon it.

Engella woke up startled, raindrops falling on her face. She still felt the heat of the tiger next to her, but it had returned to the forest as the rain went from a drizzle to a full-blown storm in seconds. Engella stayed in the warm shower as she laid back on the stump, amorously letting the rain get her wet, happy to be back in the physical world. What she had experienced was the consecration of all her travels, the ultimate discovery. She knew that. Her understanding of the universe was so short and fleeting. She also knew she would need to leave the tribe to begin to explore the academic and scientific world to search for common ground with her own discoveries.

Her final task would be to share her experience at the next village round table, and then she would return to academic life. With that thought, Engella began to cry profusely, the exhaustion and sadness combining to make her cry more than she ever had in her life. She had found a home she loved but couldn't stay. Her tears flowed with the rain—her cries dampened by the sheer volume of water falling. Then, as fast as it arrived, the rain stopped. Engella was still submerged by her sorrow, lying in a heap next to the tree stump when a group of people from the village approached. They circled her, Engella realizing she was on the ground, lying in the flowers, her face buried in the grass. She perceived the presence of the villagers around her and began to emerge from her weeping. She had never let out so much emotion at one time. She was feeling emotionally drained beyond reason, her eyes unable to produce any more tears. Engella always found that emotional exhaustion was way more daunting, her conscious mind unable to seize a single thought, completely frayed. The group picked her up by the shoulders to help her get back to the village, wrapping her in a blanket to carry her as paramedics would, using tree branches tied together with leather straps as a stretcher. Engella began to slumber during the return, letting the movement of the stretcher rock her to sleep.

Engella woke up in her home. Confusion clouded her mind. *Was this all a dream?* she thought, looking around to find out what day it might be, not seeing anything that could tell her how much time had passed. She thought back to the time she got lost as a teenager, and the memories felt jumbled as if something had changed. Had she really influenced the outcome? Was she genuinely in her own mind?

Ayla walked into her room. "Well, well. Look who's awake." She was carrying a bucket and a sponge.

"Thank you for looking after me," Engella said, still fighting with the idea everything could have been some mental fabrication.

Ayla blushed a little at this, uncomfortable with the idea of being thanked when she was doing something she saw as normal. "It's no problem. It's hot out. You needed to be refreshed somehow. I was going to cool your forehead and arms with the water, but now you're awake, so I guess I'll leave the bucket here." She bent down to deposit the water-filled bucket.

"Did I dream the last couple of days?" Engella felt a spasm of dread saying this, hoping it wasn't the case. She was afraid the whole experience was nothing but a dream— a fabricated reality from her subconscious.

"Of course not, silly. You feel like this because you slept ten straight hours when you returned, which is fogging your mind." Ayla paused, looking at Engella with love. "As soon as you're ready to meet the tribe, we need you to share your experience; something majestic happened when you came back."

Engella, still emerging from her sleep, thought Ayla was talking about the tiger. "I know. Feeling its power so close to me truly made its mark on me."

"What do you mean?" Asked Ayla, cocking her head sideways as she always did when she asked a question.

"The tiger, isn't that what you're talking about?"

"The what?" Ayla almost choked,

"The tiger," Engella said. "It sat on the stump, waiting for me to return."

"The people will want to know about this for sure," Ayla said.

"What were *you* talking about? I thought a tiger that lets me lie next to it is pretty big news."

"Lie next to it!" Wow!" She tried to gather herself. "Is there anything else?"

"Plenty. I'm sure we'll see what comes up at the round table. What I am certain of is that when I awoke in the clearing, the tiger was sitting on the tree stump, watching me. It let me lie next to it, and I fell asleep. It's the rain that woke me up, but by that time, the tiger had returned to the forest. What is it you were talking about?"

"Lie next to it," she whispered to herself. "Wow . . . okay . . . well, when we came to pick you up, Dwight noticed a small leaf had begun growing from the tree stump, right where you leaned on it. While you slept after returning, it had already grown into a small branch. It's not a coincidence and means we will have the capacity to usher in the next evolution for humankind."

Someone popped their head into the house. "The round table's starting soon."

Ayla ran out of the room to corral the villagers, Engella needing a gargantuan effort to get out of bed, feeling the fatigue pulling her back down as she tried to get up.

CHAPTER 32

At the first sign of strange-looking men arriving near the village, Christopher had set his village defense plan in motion. Isolated as the place was, these strange men could only be the bloodhounds sent by Dr. Cutler and the initiative. He dispatched his scouts to keep an eye out for them while making sure all of his sling-shooters and archers were ready and their weapons operational. Christopher and Pawa patrolled the outskirts of the village together. Christopher was hoping to confirm that the strange men were part of a bloodhound invasion attempt. He was itching to get the battle going. Those hounds were in for a surprise. He did feel a bit of a twinge of regret knowing he was about to kill decent human beings who have done nothing more than being kidnapped and brainwashed. He took comfort in the knowledge these people would never be able to rejoin their life—their brains having been scrambled forever. The best-case scenario for these soldiers of fortune was to spend the rest of their life in a confined space in some psychiatric ward. Christopher convinced himself he was doing them a favor by killing them, though that didn't stop the nightmares he always had after a bloody battle.

Although the forest was quiet, Christopher stayed focused on the bushes, looking for red dots through the leaves. Pawa scoured the trees, trying to see through the branches. She didn't know if she would be able to see their eyes, so she tried to peer deeper into the interlocking branches above her head, using the moon's rays for light. They passed by each hound more than once during their rounds, the closest one being three feet away at one point, sitting above them on a banyan tree branch, impossible to spot without climbing the tree. Christopher was preparing himself for a sleepless night, not aware that the bloodhounds in place were waiting for the arrival of more soldiers the next day. As the evening was pushing on, Christopher took up a post on the far side of the village, in the treehouse they had built for surveillance. As soon as it was built, the children used it as their den in the daytime, which meant there were always toys to clear out when it came time to use it for the night watch. Pawa set up at the other end of the village, leaning against a large tree, making sure she kept a wide vantage point to survey.

The villagers went to bed one by one as the evening music session died down to a respectful whisper. A small group of villagers finished a jug of wine by singing some songs around the dying fire, almost whispering the words, trying to stay as quiet as possible. Within hours, the village was blanketed by a tranquil serenity. Pawa always relished these moments, walking around in the village as it slept. She knew they had reached a turning point in their existence, that within the next week, life would not be the same in this place. She took in the silence intently, listening to its boundless void, not knowing when she would have the chance to do it again, if ever. A snore coming from a nearby tent broke the silence, provoking a giggle from Pawa, surprised by the sound, a single tear streaming down her cheek. She felt like there was a shadow of death hanging over the village.

Dawn broke with no unusual activity to declare. Pawa and Christopher regrouped, unsure of what to expect.

"Nothing to declare?" Christopher asked.

Pawa shook her head. "Even the animals were quiet."

That worried Christopher. The hypnotized bloodhounds, as efficient as they were to track someone, typically weren't the most discreet. If Dr. Cutler had managed to perfect his hypnosis technique, there might be more trouble than anticipated. Villagers began to emerge from their homes, each person looking as groggy as the next. A group meditation was scheduled, but Christopher and Pawa didn't want to leave the village without surveillance during this time.

"You should take part; you'll feel good after," Pawa said, pushing him to go right away.

"Will you be okay?"

"Yeah, I'll keep a couple of scouts with me. We'll come to get you if anything happens." Pawa nudged him along and turned to the members of the security team who were present. "Who wants to come with me to patrol?" Four of them joined Pawa, but nothing happened during the group meditation. The patrol stayed close to the group to make sure everyone was safe.

***

As Christopher settled himself into his cushion, he felt at peace more than ever in his life. He let his mind wander back to the speed date evening where he met Zorina, and by ricochet the collective unconscious allegiance. At first, he thought he had found a calling, to help this group usher in a new era. But his time with that group had turned out to be no different from the rest of his life. While supporting the Allegiance in their resistance against the Dark Matter Initiative, the chronic emptiness that was the void in his life still couldn't be satiated. No matter how hard he tried, the best he could do was mechanically carry out the tasks that were asked of him, his only solace being the knowledge that he left his old life behind. The deepest relationship he was nurturing before meeting Zorina was with the friends who challenged him to the speed date. His family was dead; he had no girlfriend and had a job he hated. So, leaving all that behind was a relief more than anything. But even though the allegiance showed him more knowledge on the energies that govern our lives than he could have imagined even existed, he was still unable to do anything else than wallow in a repetitive loop where he could only react, never act. He didn't question his time with them, holding on to the hope they would find a way to use their knowledge to go on the offensive. But nothing prepared him for what would follow in his life.

He met Ayla Karemi, who transported him to a world that challenges our senses, bulldozing his thin grasp on reality. From the moment he saw her at Dr. Cutler's lab, he knew she was different. When she exited the car in the ditch during their escape, he knew his destiny was linked to hers for the foreseeable future. Her presence, her insights, brought Christopher to an all-new level of understanding of everything around us. She helped him understand the duality that inhabits us all, teaching him to appreciate and love every aspect of his soul. Her capacity to live in the present moment had guided them there, and he thanked her for it.

"The light is useless without the dark, its brilliance renders us blind," she would tell Christopher when he felt regret—about the joy he felt when he violently dispatched the bloodhounds who were on their trail.

Here he sat, fresh from the group meditation, his mind clear, and his focus entirely directed on the task at hand. Sensing the coming battle, he gleefully acknowledged the blood beginning to go cold in his veins, his mind covered in a shroud of violent thoughts. His vision became clearer than it had ever been, giving him the sensation that he could see through walls. His muscles were tensing up in anticipation of the impending fight. The newfound love for the darkness that inhabits his soul was the single most liberating thing he could have ever done for himself. He could peer into his own darkness without fearing what he would find. With this newfound knowledge, he was able to control the impulse his darkness generates.

He looked up and saw Pawa, standing in the middle of the village, awaiting the battle. A feeling of brotherly love warmed his heart as he looked at her. She was standing tall. The tension in her face gave her features a fearsome look. He could have insisted for her to take part in the meditation, but her offer that he do it felt more like an order, which left no room for arguing. Christopher was grateful to have her on his side; she would be a fearsome bloodhound he wouldn't want to confront. During training, he saw her chop down a small tree with one swoop of a machete during a harvest. She had humbly thanked the blacksmith for a well-sharpened tool after her accomplishment, but Christopher knew no one else could duplicate what she did, sharp blade or not. What she did then was a snapshot of her character. He would trust her with his life any day. She looked back at him, apparently noticing that he was daydreaming while staring at her. She shot back a mean glare.

"Stay focused!" She barked, then turned her attention to something she heard.

Her order shocked Christopher back to the task at hand, his heart skipping a beat at the surprise. Pawa then crouched and moved toward the back of a house, disappearing into the dense bush without making a sound as she moved through the branches. Christopher felt a swell of pride, seeing that his plan would be called into action. At the first sign of movement, Pawa was to join one group of militias, and Christopher was to join another. The third group of village guards was to stay in the central part of the community and serve as the backup to either of the other groups should there be a need for it.

Christopher joined his group of militias, who were ready to jump into action. One of the sling shooters was playing with his munitions, twirling three rocks in one hand, the other hand firmly grasping the slingshot in its holster. Christopher nodded to the group, indicating that something was happening—to be ready. The hypnotized soldiers thought they had a slight advantage when looking at the village's defensive setup, thinking the villagers had overlooked different entry points. As the order to advance came in, they began to close in on four fronts, two hounds from each group now intentionally showing themselves hoping to create fear and confusion. Unable to properly analyze what they were surveying in past days, they were unaware of the sentinels hidden in the trees, waiting for their advance. Slingshots extended and ready to fire, the village soldiers remained hidden in the bushes. Christopher had established the importance of letting the hypnotized hounds make the first move, so they knew how many of them they would need to confront. Their single-minded demeanor should drive them right into the traps set by the village battalion.

CHAPTER 33

Engella, groggy from a deep sleep, got out of bed. After splashing her face with water and wolfing down two oranges, she arrived at the round table meeting to a noticeably eager crowd. They all stopped talking upon her arrival, making her feel a little uneasy, like an intruder for some reason. She was offered the middle seat at the main table, as she would be central to the discussion.

Dwight began. "It's been our hope that the returning person relates his or her experience. Up until now, we have welcomed back broken minds unable to communicate what they saw. You have survived the whole ceremony. So, if you will, in your own words, share the details of your four travels to the energy field."

Engella began to report what she had experienced, trying to include as many details as possible, each person hanging on her every word. As she narrated her experience, she noticed some people began to lose interest, seemingly unimpressed by her accounts. She continued to recount her travel, wondering if Ayla might have gotten a little excited and that nothing that spectacular had happened. The people of the village were attuned to the energies that flow around us, so she wasn't telling them anything they didn't already know or feel. Then, Engella told them how she floated beyond the atmosphere and saw the neutrino "dust devil." It got everyone's attention. The murmur that was beginning to hum in the room stopped instantly. She told them of the feeling of being in space, the neutrino mass floating toward earth, the jolt of energy it made her feel and see, her moment in time with herself, and her return in the spiraling tornado, down to the tree. She added that the tiger was waiting there for her, that she spooned the animal on the tree and slept, the rain that woke her up, and the emotions that spilled out. Perfect silence greeted her final words. The people were in shock, taking in the new information with wide-eyed wonder. Engella waited for someone to say something.

"You let yourself go into space, and you came back?" Engella heard the voice but couldn't see who was asking the question.

"Yes—with the help of the energy cloud I described. I believe it to be the remnants of a supernova. I also believe the energy of the exploded star carried me to its point of origin to witness its end. The darkness of space around me was different, somehow lighter as I saw the star swell, then explode, propelling me back to earth. The tornado funnel I descended on was the energy from this supernova pulling me down, along with thousands upon millions of specks of earthly subconscious energy. Specks from humans, plants, rocks, all being propelled to earth by this tornado-like energy."

Sensing no one was able to muster a question, Engella changed the subject. "I think I had the privilege of being in the right place at the right time—nothing more. You said a leaf had begun to grow where I leaned on the tree stump? I would like to see it." No one contradicted her, as a small group volunteered to join her.

Engella left with the group, and they went back to the clearing to look at the branch. As they walked toward the clearing with Dwight leading the group, a profound silence accompanied them; even their foot-steps were muffled. Engella was battling a deepening sadness, sensing that once they visit the clearing, she would have to leave. The experience showed her that she had reached the final destination in her mystical quest. She must turn to science and merge her new-found knowledge with it. Although years had passed since she started her thesis, Engella felt younger; more complete. She accelerated her walk to reach Dwight ahead of the group.

"Nobody else went beyond the atmosphere?" She asked bluntly, breaking the deep silence.

"Some texts in the library speak of others who made it to space, but it's said that they didn't come back, so we don't know if it's true." Dwight was pensive, talking to no one in particular.

"Yeah, I can confirm it's tempting to let yourself float away," Engella said. "Without the energy cloud to pull me back, I might still be out there. What happens to the bodies if someone doesn't return?"

"The old texts say they placed the bodies in a crypt where they waited for their spirit to return, but we hav-en't found anything. As for our more recent attempts to connect the tree to the universe, you've met the inhabitants of the house. All we can do is keep them as comfortable as possible, in hopes their minds will return at some point." Dwight looked over at Engella and paused—a slight smile appearing on his face. "But now there's hope. The leaf that appeared on the stump will grow into a branch, the branch will reach for the sky, and the tree will once again feed our collective unconscious."

Somehow, Dwight didn't seem overly excited by this, talking flatly, his mind visibly elsewhere. Engella wanted to talk about her life-changing moment when she visited herself, so she pushed on. "When I woke up today, my memories of the time I got lost in the woods as a teenager felt different. I still remember the panic setting in, but then there's nothing but random snippets and flashes."

"You changed the outcome," he said. "The memory will settle over time. Your brain is presently busy finding a resting place for those new recollections. It's a kind of time-lapse jetlag for your brain." Dwight picked up the pace as they grew closer to the clearing.

"When you saw yourself inside your young mind, you were actually there. An old text shows that they tried to influence the energy currents in the past, hoping to rebuild a better future when the tree was first cut down. They hoped they could subvert the tree's weakened state and preserve the connection to the collective unconscious energy field. Thing is, they discovered that time does what it needs to do regardless of our interference or meddling. The tribe's people noticed they weren't helping to support the connection, only altering individual moments. That's when they decided we cannot meddle with time; it's its own master as well as the master of all. That's why the memory you have changed is floating in your mind without an anchor. The rest of your life had a course to follow, and it did. Over time, you might discover some moments in your life that have been altered due to the change you operated, but the basic timeline that is your life has remained intact. All I can say is that it takes some time for the memory to reconnect with your mind." Dwight stopped. "We're here." His serious tone indicating to Engella that the conversation was over.

Engella walked up to the tree stump, eager to see the leaf. What she saw was already a sizable branch, with many new sprouts coming from it. She felt a wave of emotions wash over her; the joy, sadness, despair, and bliss she felt during the connection ritual all coming back at once. The branch seemed to be pulsing like a beating heart, the glow that had appeared on the stump now visible in the daytime. Engella reached down to touch a leaf on the branch, and the moment the tip of her finger touched the leaf, she was flooded with the same energy she felt in the tornado. She pulled her hand back, shocked.

"How can this be?" Engella could feel her waking mind struggling to make sense of the sensation the leaf was carrying, refusing to accept the reality before her, refusing to admit her actions precipitated this. The group that accompanied her gathered in a circle. Some sat, while some remained standing. She looked at them, thinking they wanted her to say something.

"What?" She barked, not wanting to give a speech. But no one reacted to her annoyance. They had gathered to contemplate on the day's events together and weren't expecting any grand gesture. No one spoke for some time until Ayla broke the silence.

"We are at a turning point. This branch is the rebirth of our tree, humanity's tree. It's still weak at the moment. How will we be able to protect it?"

"We can't protect it, only nurture it," the young girl said—the one who brought Engella her first water jug.

Engella looked at her, seeing a young girl but feeling an old soul, her facial traits reflecting wisdom and peace. "If we choose to nurture it, the tree will grow. If we choose to protect it, we will feed a destructive path and attract violence, and it will die, this time forever."

The young girl's intervention tossed a cold blanket over the group, but no one left. After a moment of silence, conversations turned to the needs of the village, which could change with this new reality. As the conversations picked up around her, Engella was relieved that they weren't expecting a speech. She let the surrounding discussion become a low hum in her mind as she navigated the meanderings of her inner self. She tried to apply basic meditation techniques to drown out the noise and concentrate on her innermost thoughts, to no avail. Her waking mind pulled her back again and again.

"Neutrinos. You need to learn about neutrinos." Was she whispering in her own ear like she did in the woods so long ago? Pulling herself back to the present, Engella noticed the conversation in the group was directed toward the organization they needed to create to properly nurture the tree. A decision was also reached that they won't let anyone travel within the tree's connection to the universe until they know more. A group meditation was planned for that afternoon as a starting point toward the village's new future. As everyone began to stand, ready to return to the village, Engella saw the tiger at the fringe of the clearing, watching her with the same fiery intent as it did when she returned from her ethereal travels.

"The tiger is here to protect the tree," Engella said out of nowhere. The tiger turned away, looking satisfied. No one else had seen it, so its presence didn't cause a commotion.

"Good to know," Dwight mumbled, unaware of the beast's presence. His mind was already back at the university offices, but he knew there were a few more things to do first. Raising his voice for everyone to hear, he continued. "Everyone that has a scientific task outside the village will need to get going. This is a moment in history that far exceeds anything that has occurred in humanity's existence so far, and we need to explore this with enthusiasm."

"I believe it's as important as the formation of the first multicellular beings," Ayla added. "This marks the beginning of a new era."

Dwight looked at Ayla, a little annoyed that she cut him off. "We may be on the verge of reconciling beliefs and mysticism with knowledge and science." He was walking faster like he was late for something. Even if he was pulling ahead of everyone, he continued, a little out of breath. "That would be a first in the history of mankind." He started running. "I need to speak with Dr. Cutler. I need to tell him we can rid ourselves of the parasite that clouds our unconscious judgment without outside intervention." He was talking to himself at that point, far ahead of the group, unaware of Frank Cutler's plans for him.

Upon their return, the village was abuzz with the preparations for the group meditation. Dwight had disappeared into his home without acknowledging any of the salutations, the rustling noises that started as soon as he entered indicated to everyone that he was packing.

Engella did the same, wondering what it would be like to go back to civilization armed with this new knowledge. If she didn't experience any major shift of her urban existence after her time with Rafael, she knew it would be different the next time around. A part of her wanted to shout this to the world, but Engella knew that the only way for the collective unconscious to be properly re-established was to let humanity evolve on its own within the new reality.

Ayla began to organize the group meditation, including the children in her quest for cushions and carpets. The ruckus heard all over the village was celebratory— giddy even. Engella could hear her neighbors laughing aloud, the village chef calling his assistants to prepare a feast of feasts, the children running all over the place looking for cushions and carpets. It all made her smile. At no moment in her life had she felt more at peace than with the Soochit Karana tribe, and she would miss them terribly.

She knew that staying in the village also meant giving up on her own quest, as she must find a link to her experience within the knowledge accumulated in the higher learning centers of the world. Her new goal was to find common ground from which she can build a case showing some commonality between science and mysticism in the study of particles, which could help people realize and feel the newly established connection between them and the tree of life. She knew that much of what she learned during her travels could be explained, at least in part, by particle science. But her grasp of certain aspects of the science is weak, and she didn't know if she would be able to find the common link. Ayla would be able to help, and Dwight also told her about some colleagues of his. She especially wanted a chance to meet the Dr. Cutler she's heard about from him and from Christopher and Ayla. If there was any proof of a link with our subconscious, Engella believed she could find it using the existence of the DNA parasite Dwight told her about as the basis for her research.

As the afternoon pushed on, everyone converged on the group meditation that was scheduled to take place.

Engella felt a swell of emotion rise as the people gathered, knowing this was the last group meditation she would have with her village brothers and sisters. She didn't believe she would ever return. The villagers gathered in the meditation circle, each picking a cushion or carpet randomly. They each settled into their preferred position to begin meditating. As Engella reached the group, many were already deep in contemplation, and she could feel a warmth emanating from the circle. She lowered to her knees on a red velvet carpet, her butt leaning on her feet, and closed her eyes.

Hours passed before the first person emerged from the meditation, looking replenished and rejuvenated. That generally marks the awakening of the group, as the circle of deep thought is disturbed. When this happens, everyone awakens within five minutes, but this time, each person awoke one at a time over the next two hours. Everyone had the same feeling of rejuvenation, and the more people woke up with this sentiment, the more everyone knew the meditation was successful. Engella awoke last. She opened her eyes to empty cushions, as everyone had returned to their occupations except Dwight, who was sitting next to her, reading. She embraced the feeling of completion in her soul that the group meditations gave her, letting her mind wander as a deep sense of peace enveloped her like a blanket. Her logical mind was fighting for control as she laid on her velvet carpet, the voices in her head screaming for her to explain her experience, giving Engella the reassurance she was headed in the right direction. Where her mind went after meditation was always of capital importance to her, since, according to her, the mind's wanderings following meditation confirmed the demands the universe had for her.

Looking at Dwight, she couldn't refrain from the wave of love she felt for him. Her love was akin to the love of a mother for her son, although she didn't know if it was the same for Dwight. Trying to refrain from the need to hug him, she asked, "What does the group session bring to you? For me, it's a sense of completion."

"Balance," he answered, stuffing his book in his bag without marking the page. "It gives me a sense of balance, knowing that the world is a continuing exercise of equilibrium on an invisible string. When we meditate together, I feel I can walk freely on that string. Ready to go?" He asked, jumping to his feet, his hand already extended to help Engella.

As they looked around the village one last time, wanting to take as many mental photographs as possible, Engella saw Christopher pass by, accompanied by villagers who were armed with slingshots, advancing cautiously. A chill went down her spine.

CHAPTER 34

Engella and Dwight almost seemed to be skipping when they left the village together, both promising to keep in touch. Too much time had passed since their last meeting, and even that one had been short. As they walked away from the village, busy making plans about their return to civilized life, they were unaware a hypnotized soldier had seen them and had become interested in Dwight. The soldier had been reconditioned to pursue Christopher and Ayla, but he was still nurturing the command to kill Dwight Como on sight, having been on that mission until he was reassigned. Because he hadn't been awakened from his original hypnosis before being reprogrammed, the command to kill Dwight remained unsatisfied and dormant in the back of his mind. Forgetting about the command he received to seize the village and end the threat, he made a beeline toward Engella and Dwight, his hypnosis carrying orders to be careful to stay out of the target's line of sight, helping him remain unnoticed. He easily approached them, since the two friends were oblivious to their surroundings, absorbed by their conversation. The bloodhound felt a sense of excitement rise within him, as the memory of the command to kill Dwight Como flooded back to him. Staying crouched, he moved closer, his heartbeat steady, his focus unclouded. The bloodhound felt his ears burn from the excitement of being on the verge of accomplishing his task, but his focus remained steady. He pulled out a small knife, then froze, as Engella turned to look back. The hound stood as still as possible, not knowing if there was enough brush around him to hide his presence.

"What is it?" Dwight asked. He saw her face change from joy to worry in an instant, thinking she must be sad to leave the village.

"Probably nothing, but I feel as though we're being followed," Engella said, trying to hide her feeling of dread. She looked around, and although she didn't see where it happened when she had the vision of Dwight's death in her ethereal travels, she knew this was the place where he dies in her arms. Submerged with emotion, she put her hands on her mouth, trying to hold back the rising sobs. She couldn't find a coherent way to tell Dwight about her vision of his death, not even certain herself of what she had experienced. Engella had her eyes closed, taking deep breaths trying to center herself. Satisfied they hadn't seen him, the bloodhound preyed on the manifest confusion before him to get closer to his target.

"Engella, what is it?" Dwight was worried, watching her seemingly melt down right in front of him.

"I'm sorry. This is where you die in my arms, and I don't know how to stop it."

"What the hell are you talking about?" Dwight was almost laughing, thinking she needed some reassurance. The experience she went through would floor the strongest shamans; she could be having some kind of PTSD thing. He wrapped his arms around her to comfort her.

"No, you don't understand!" She pushed him back. "It happens today." Her eyes peeled, looking at their surroundings, she regained her composure and looked at Dwight, her eyes now fierce, determined. "Unless we change the outcome, let's go." She got up and grabbed Dwight's hand to pull him up with her and leave. No memory is unalterable, and they still might be able to escape and create a new timeline. But she had nothing to lean on from the memory flash she had about this moment and didn't know which way to go. Should they run, hide, confront whatever is about to happen? Her mind still reeling; they were standing in the middle of the road when she saw the hound pounce out from the bushes behind Dwight, brandishing a knife, diving toward his target.

"No!" Engella screamed, vaulting herself toward the attacker.

"What?" Dwight turned to look behind him and received a knife in his eye. The hound then ground the blade in place, a strange satisfaction glowing from his eyes as he pushed down on it.

Engella tackled the hound, wrapping her legs around his chest with her knees on his arms to hold him down and began to punch away, screaming. The hound took the punches, his head flapping from one side to the other under the impacts of her beating, swaying in and out of consciousness. Engella then grabbed him by the ears and started pounding his head on the ground, screaming like an enraged animal, until she crushed his skull, blood spilling from the back of his head. The red puddle that was forming was spackled with white pieces of bone from his skull. Out of breath, she tossed the one ear that stayed in her hand into the bushes and turned to Dwight. Villagers began approaching, led by two of Christopher and Pawa's soldiers. They were attracted by the sounds, which caused their approach to be cautious, as they hugged the side of the road, some of them crouching to try to stay out of sight.

Dwight was lying on the road with the butt of a knife sticking out of his eye, his body sporadically jumping from spasms caused by the knife digging into his brain. Engella knelt behind him, cupping his head on her lap. The knife had pierced the skull, and he was leaking brain matter out of his eye. As he laid there, her mind went back to the summer class where they met. Engella recalled how she had been attracted to him because of his unbridled curiosity. The young man she met was thirsty for knowledge in a way she had seldom encountered, and she had felt a need to nurture that. Although their meeting that summer had been a brief teacher-student relationship, it had been meaningful enough to plant the seeds for them to develop a parallel relationship. When they had met at the club not so long ago, it felt to Engella that their destinies had been linked in time somehow, that their lives would progress and evolve in the same direction. Looking at the blood still spilling out of his eye, Dwight's head lying heavily on her lap, it seemed to Engella that he was trying to speak. But he was merely making guttural sounds from the blood spilling into his mouth coming up in bubbles as he tried to breathe.

Engella felt a deep rage build within her, obscuring any thought other than finding the man named Dr. Frank Cutler. Dwight and Ayla had spoken to her of this man, and from the information she had gleaned from them, she knew he was trouble. If she thought the Collective Unconscious Allegiance were misguided in their approach, they at least have a base in the search for harmony, as they try to find the answer to humanity's happiness. From her rare meetings with members of the allegiance, Engella knew she could show them the virtue of accepting the duality that inhabits us, and they would be able to adapt to a new reality. But what she had heard from Dr. Cutler placed her before the obligation to destroy his plans by any means necessary.

Amidst the raging confusion in Engella's mind, Dwight released his last breath, a sputter of blood bursting from his mouth and leaking down his cheek in the process, after which his body became limp. She stayed with him and cried, her tears spilling onto his face, mixing in with the blood. Some villagers formed a circle around her to try to comfort her and let her evacuate the outflow of emotions the death of her friend had caused. Engella went from sadness to rage to discouragement in waves. Part of her wanted to scream at the villagers to leave, that his death was all their fault, while another part of her wanted to crawl into her house and forget about everything and everyone. Engella felt she was losing her sanity, unable to focus on one single thought. The energy from the circle of villagers had a calming effect on her mind, as she felt the control of her consciousness returning. Letting the raging darkness rise from her soul, she focused her attention on finding Frank Cutler, which freed her mind, her focus now crystal clear. Before the tree could gather enough strength to have a real influence on the earth's collective unconscious, Dr. Cutler needed to be silenced. The villagers who stayed to comfort Engella helped her pick up Dwight's body and bring it back to the village for a proper ceremony.

CHAPTER 35

His eyes still focused on the oncoming initiative soldiers, Christopher heard rustling sounds coming from behind the nearby trees on the edge of the road that leads away from the village. A bloodhound that was close by jumped toward the street, attacking Dwight Como. It caused Christopher's blood to make a single turn in his veins, becoming ice cold. He wanted to spring into action. Pawa had also witnessed the attack and sent a call to the sentinels around the village by imitating owl hoots. Christopher couldn't help but admire the strength of her voice while she hooted, her hands cupped around her mouth. He couldn't see her from where he stood, but it sounded like she was right next to him. The power of the sound that emanated from her impressed him every time. But he couldn't dwell on his impression of Pawa's call. The owl hoot meant *load your weapons; trouble is near.*

Christopher gave his group the signal to spring into action while Pawa activated her team, both itching to get going. If Christopher was motivated to end it with the bloodhounds, Pawa had her own reasons to want to confront these brainwashed soldiers. After listening to Christopher's description of the bloodhound's methods and modus operandi during the training, she had reached a definitive conclusion that these beings were responsible for the disappearance of her brother, a political activist. She believed his penchant for socialism, along with a growing following, is what caused his disappearance. Christopher's description of the way they moved around was a perfect match with the two men Pawa saw right before realizing her brother was missing. She knew blood would be spilled, the rage in her soul fighting to burst out and destroy the Initiative's army of hypnotized soldiers. She hoped Christopher had given them enough insight to make sure the spilled blood would be that of the hounds.

Their strategy was based on the lack of discretion the hounds manifested when attacking, but despite having guards posted around the village, there was no visible activity in the forest during the days prior. That worried Christopher. Had they managed to sneak in close to the village without being spotted? If so, how many of them were there? And why were they so quiet? Making a quick scan of the grounds, Christopher saw three hounds headed their way. He froze as the hounds approached, realizing they barely made a sound as they walked. Their eyes were normal, no redness, although he could perceive a slight glow in them. The initiative had perfected their hypnosis techniques, that much was clear to Christopher. The hounds continued to advance and broke his fixation. He gave the sling shooters the signal to tense up their elastics. The archers had set up in the trees to back up their comrades and awaited their orders. Christopher flicked his wrist, upon which the sling shooters let go of their munition, a round of polished stone the size of an average adult's big toe. The stones made a hissing sound as they pierced the air. Then the three hounds stopped in their tracks, a surprised look on their face as they fell one by one, each slumping to the ground as if their bones had left their bodies, each one the recipient of a brand-new hole in their forehead.

Silence followed for a moment. Christopher kept his eyes peeled in the direction where the first hounds came from, unaware that he was facing a new breed of soldiers. He had underestimated the capacity Dr. Cutler had to breed these newly designed soldiers and didn't see the five hounds that had flanked him and his militia as they evaded the sentinels charged with slowing them down. Before anyone realized what was happening, the lead hound managed to reach one of the sling shooters and deftly broke his neck, the body becoming limp in his arms after making a loud cracking noise. The soldier had a gleeful look as he let go of his victim—his eyes darting around looking for a new target. One of the archers spiked an arrow through his skull as the hound advanced on another potential victim. Two sling shooters and the other archer turned their attention toward the direction that the hound came from and saw four other enemies heading their way, the same gleefully violent look in their eyes. One slingshot and one arrow connected, leaving two hounds charging the militia group.

The saving grace for the village militia was the slow speed at which the bloodhounds advanced. It gave Christopher time to slip behind a bush and move unseen toward the incoming enemies. After the first salvo from the slingshots, he jumped out, ready to confront any remaining hound. He found himself in front of two of them, and just as one of them lunged at him, Christopher heard one of his militia scream out. "Get down!"

He threw himself to the ground, and a split-second later, he heard the hound's forehead crack open. He fell back from the impact of the expertly shot piece of rock. The last one hesitated, something Christopher had never seen in them. He advanced on it with his shoulders squared, ready for anything. He grabbed the hypnotized soldier and wrestled him down, surprised at how easy it was to neutralize him. Christopher then quietly strangled him, apologizing to the person underneath the hypnosis. While he was doing this, the archers mowed down four more hounds who were acting much more in line with what Christopher expected of them, a zombie-like march with no effort made towards concealment. That meant they had developed some sort of elite soldier. That's probably why they managed to stay out of sight while preparing for this. Pawa needed to be informed before it was too late. Christopher left his group with the order to shoot all hounds on sight and ran to Pawa's post to warn her.

Pawa reached her group at the same time a couple of hounds raised their heads, surveying their surroundings, seeming to be looking for an alternate entry point to the village. Pawa picked up right away on the fact they weren't the single-minded creatures Christopher spoke of. She grabbed two sling shooters and proceeded to flank the hounds by taking a wide berth around them to create an element of surprise. As they crossed the road to reach the spot she had chosen for her surprise attack, one of her shooters slumped to the ground, lifeless. There was no blood, but Pawa saw that her dead comrade had a knife skewering her through the neck, holding in the blood, making it pool in her throat instead, choking her. Pawa felt a burst of raging adrenaline as she dived to her colleague and pulled her to the side of the road. She pulled out the knife, letting the blood flow out in slowly weakening bursts. She tried to compress the injury as much as possible, knowing she couldn't stop death from coming. It wasn't long before the warrior's heart gave out from the lack of blood. Pawa tried to ease the final minutes of her friend and sister in battle by caressing her forehead, singing a bedtime song Pawa remembered from her childhood. She stayed with her battle sister to the last breath, all the while, keeping her eyes peeled on the bushes around them, looking for a clue, anything that could give her the exact position of the killer.

With her heart beating heavily and her mind focused on revenge, Pawa noticed a slight movement in the bush right in front of her. She left her dead sister and ran to it, screaming bloody murder. Two steps inside the bush, she ran right into a hound, toppling him over with the finesse of an NFL linebacker. Staying on top of him as they fell, she let her weight fall squarely between the hound's shoulder blades, forcing his face into the ground as they slid at least a meter. Without giving him time to recover, she turned him around. "Is this yours?" she asked, shoving the knife in his face.

The man seemed dazed from the tackle, and before he could muster any reply, Pawa pulled the knife from his face and dug buried it in his chest, between the fourth and fifth ribs, piercing the heart, while looking him straight in the eyes. The hound's eyes widened for an instant, then became empty and glazed before rolling back in his skull. Although disappointed, she couldn't see any humanity in the creature's eyes; Pawa felt satisfied to have seen his last breath and searched the immediate surroundings for more enemies.

She looked around for her sling shooter while trying to measure the level of danger they were in. She got her answer as a hound fell to the ground behind her, his forehead pierced. The sling shooter gave Pawa a wink from behind a tree and advanced, seeming to have spotted new targets. Pawa called him back. They needed to return to the others so she could warn Christopher that the hounds seemed to have better tactical knowledge than anticipated and to warn everyone to be extra vigilant.

CHAPTER 36

Oblivious to the rising sounds of battle all over the community, the villagers had wrapped Dwight's body in a cotton sheet and carried him away on their shoulders with a line of four people supporting the weight. Engella watched them walk away, trying to assemble her thoughts as she battled the rage and sadness weeping from every pore in her body. After all those times they crossed paths, after living parallel lives for so long, she and Dwight had a chance to try to build a relationship by being present for one and other. The pain pressed down on her chest, making it difficult to breathe. The scene replayed in her head over and over, Engella trying to understand what happened.

She decided to let the rage burning her up from the inside rise and permeate her every thought. As it spread throughout her mind and soul, the rage turned her blood cold. Every thought she had was focused on the destruction of Dwight's real killer. She would find Dr. Frank Cutler. She could talk to Christopher to get more information on his whereabouts, but from what she's gathered so far, this man was pretty much unapproachable in this reality. Her one weapon at that point was her ability to travel the dream realm, where she would call on the lost souls to help her. She knew doing that would be a risky proposition. She couldn't be sure if any of the lost souls would care enough to help. There was also the danger that she could become the target. Engella was confident she could resist their power up to a point, but if they decided that she's their preferred target, she would vanish forever, sucked into the dream realm permanently, her subconscious absorbed to nourish their ethereal energy. She leaned her hopes on the fact that the lost souls were human first. Although they have chosen to stay in the dream realm and to some extent, become nothing more than quantum energy, their origin is human, which Engella would try to cultivate to convince them. If all else failed, she could try to convince them that their very existence was endangered by this man's projects, which wasn't entirely false.

But chaos had enveloped the village, and Engella ran back to help any way she could. Following the main road, a dirt path wide enough for two small vehicles to pass, she saw Pawa and her militia in a battle with the invaders. Engella could see Pawa was in complete control as she slid past, unseen. She then spotted three hounds, undoubtedly tracking something. She noticed they were headed for the main house where most of the villagers had retreated. Engella ran to circumvent the hounds and warn the villagers in the house. As she reached it, Engella was almost struck with a slingshot bead as it zipped past her ear with a whistling sound. She felt the air displacement as it whizzed by, prompting her to throw herself to the ground.

"Whoa!" She screamed, "I'm with you!" The door opened, and Engella crawled into the house.

Two sling shooters had set up on the roof. The one who shot at Engella opened the trap door to the roof and peered in. "Sorry about that. My grip on the leather pouch slipped when I saw you and tried to pull back." The militia seemed repentant enough, but Engella wanted nothing to do with an apology. She felt a drop of blood on her neck and touched her ear to find it had been lightly clipped. She looked at the blood on her fingers, surprised she didn't feel it more than she did.

"Keep your eyes open, three of them are coming here," Engella shouted. "And don't just clip their ears this time." She spoke with her teeth clenched, and her eyes dark with anger, giving the militia no possibility to reply. He shut the trap door and went back to his position without saying another word. Engella went to a window to track the hound's approach.

• • •

Ayla knew they were coming for her. She wondered if Christopher was okay. Pawa's battle cries were heard from inside of the house as she directed her troops. Ayla was confident Christopher had the upper hand on his end but knew she would be worried until she saw him. She went to Engella, needing to feel her presence near her own. Engella wrapped her arms around Ayla's shoulders as they looked out of the boarded window through a small opening. The three hounds Engella had seen were standing out of reach from the sling-shots, seemingly aware of the danger but uninterested in hiding. Hidden by the gable above the front door, the other sling shooter on the roof managed to signal an archer, who approached in silence, climbing up a fig tree, staying in the hound's blind spot while she moved. She armed an arrow in her bow and released it. The arrow pierced a hound in the neck, throwing him sideways under the impact. The two other hounds reacted by bouncing ahead, turning their back on the house to see where the arrow came from. That was enough for the two sling shooters to place a small bead in the heads of the two remaining hounds who collapsed, their bodies falling in unison. Engella took this as a cue and left the house, ordering Ayla to stay inside until the battle is over, like a mother speaking to her adolescent child.

Exiting the house, Engella made a beeline towards the tree. She needed to be sure it hadn't been besieged. As soon as she closed the door and made sure there were no other enemies in sight, she started running, making no effort to be discreet, wanting to reach the tree as fast as possible. She saw Christopher, who gave her a recognition nod as she passed him in full flight. Engella ran as fast as she could to the tree, ignoring the scrapes the branches made on her skin along the way. When she approached the clearing, Engella saw two sloth bears sitting on either side of an imaginary entryway. She didn't slow down, and they barely acknowledged her passage, one of them giving her a short grunt as she passed.

The clearing was bathed in sunshine, the flowers covering the ground, exploding with color. The tiger was lazing on the newly reborn tree stump, licking his paws, looking like a house cat lying in the sun. Engella stopped in her tracks as the tiger looked up, giving her a mean, determined look. She didn't understand. It had been helpful each time they met so far. It had waited for her at the tree. Why would it turn on her now? The tiger rose to its feet and began to walk toward Engella, belly to the ground, ready to pounce at any moment. She felt her heart beating in her throat as the tiger approached. She was unable to move or breathe, hearing the two bears shuffling around in the flowers behind her. Then she saw that the tiger's gaze was fixed on something behind her and risked turning her head, not knowing if this would be the last moment of her life.

She saw the two bears flanking two bloodhounds that had followed her. The bear's behavior seemed natural, as they looked like they were scrounging for food, the hounds not paying them any attention. The tiger came up to Engella's feet and laid there, apparently waiting for the bears to be in position. She could see the tiger's backside dancing as it set its footing, ready to lunge at any moment. Satisfied the tiger was still here to help, Engella began to breathe again, turning to face the hounds, confident the animals would help. Simultaneously, the two bears got to their feet, a signal the tiger took as confirmation they were ready, as it moved ahead without a sound, disappearing into a bush. Engella was amazed a 300-pound animal could move with such stealth, as she watched in wonder at its capacity to zero in on the two hounds, who were oblivious to its presence. The bears closed in on either side and within seconds, all Engella could hear were screams and growls. Ten or twenty seconds passed, and the clearing was silent once again, the tiger returning to the tree stump to clean up the blood on its snout. Relieved the tree was safe, Engella decided at that moment that she would sleep there that night and then put an end to Dr. Cutler's project.

CHAPTER 37

Christopher saw Engella running past, in the direction of the clearing, not sure if he should follow. Before he could decide, another wave of hounds came down on his position, preceded by a thrown knife that dug into the tree, inches from his face. The thud of the blade in the wood snapped him back to the moment at hand. As he grabbed the knife and turned, he witnessed at least ten hounds bearing down on him and his militia. He had never seen more than five of them at once, which told Christopher this invasion was major, and it needed to be defeated, neutralized, annihilated. The number of soldiers attacking them convinced Christopher that a victory would severely weaken Dr. Cutler's ambitions.

While studying the Dark Matter Initiative's methods to know what he was up against, Christopher had noticed that the easiest way to erode their resolve was to create uncertainty. It's like kryptonite to them. By repelling the attack, he was sure the initiative would retreat and reconsider, which would give the tree time to grow. If enough time passes, humanity will have rekindled its connection to the universal collective unconscious, prompted by the influx of information brought on by the tree. It would produce the emergence of a new tomorrow, which would be independent of the influence exerted by the initiative, weakening their hold on humanity a little more.

But their victory needed to be complete and unequivocal for this to happen. Christopher crouched to watch the group of bloodhounds as they approached. He saw that the four hounds leading the pack were coming at them in the manner Christopher was accustomed to; straight ahead, no strategic effort to hide or be cautious. Christopher raised his hand, showing four fingers to his hidden militias to indicate the number of attackers, then proceeded to go around the oncoming hounds, having noticed that two of them seemed to oversee this group, barking orders and acting as though they had full possession of their minds. They walked around alert and conscious of their surroundings, meaning they might be actual soldiers.

As Christopher moved to attack the two leaders from behind, he didn't notice two other hounds breaking off from the group to pursue Engella, keeping his focus on the pack leaders. The first four hounds stopped in their tracks following an order from one of the two captains. Two more of them stayed close to the leaders, *probably acting as bodyguards*, Christopher thought. He was still too far to make out what they were saying, but as he got close enough, he saw the two bodyguards bend down and crawl ahead to scout the surroundings. Christopher raised his hand above the bushes and signaled to his militias that two hounds were crawling toward them by showing the international heavy metal sign then pointing his thumb down.

His blood racing in his veins, Christopher edged close enough to propel himself at the two leaders, coming at them from behind, stabbing one in the back of the neck with the knife that he pulled from the tree. He then turned to the other hound and invited him to hand-to-hand combat, feeling the urge to make this fight last a little longer before ending it. The hound seemed surprised as he stood there, appearing not to understand the situation. Christopher made it clear for him as he lunged at him, leading with a direct punch, his fist crushing the hound's nose. The hound fell back, blood spilling out of his nose, an angry leer appearing in his eyes. His look surprised Christopher, who had never seen any emotional reaction in the bloodhounds that pursued him in the past. The initiative soldier stayed low and dove into Christopher's legs, toppling him over. Using the inertia, the hound climbed on Christopher and pinned him down with his knees leaning heavily on Christopher's elbows, searching his pockets for something. Not interested in waiting to see what the hound was searching for, Christopher thrust his pelvis upward, hoping to destabilize his aggressor. It worked enough for Christopher to reclaim some leverage, and he rapidly turned his hips, releasing the hold the hound had on his arms.

Christopher was in the perfect position to throw uppercuts and proceeded to pound the hound's chin with some well-placed shots. The third punch was enough to force the hound off him, and Christopher threw himself at his target, eager to finish it. He let his rage take full control of his consciousness as he managed to neutralize his adversary, pinning him face down on the ground, wrapping his arms around the hound's neck and applying pressure. The hound kicked around at first, but his legs quickly went limp, giving out spasms at bigger and bigger intervals, until they stopped, the hound's dead body heavy in Christopher's arms. He rifled through the hound's pockets and grabbed a knife. He then stood up and stared at the dead body on the ground. Christopher felt a twinge of sadness as he looked at the man lying dead before him.

Before Dr. Cutler and the initiative got their hands on him, this man had a life, possibly even a family. Each hound Christopher killed had come back to haunt him at some point, causing nightmares when his anxiety acted up. He often felt the same sadness he was feeling now when he killed a hound, but he never felt regret when freeing these men from their mental prison. Christopher cleared his mind then turned back to his team, who were standing around him, waiting for orders, looking for new targets. An eerie calm fell over the village as the realization they had resisted the assault began to dawn on them.

The sounds of people coming out of hiding gave new life to the village. Pawa and Christopher rejoined in the central meeting area. The militias followed suit; their energy drained by the emotional crash that follows a murderous battle. One of the militias returned carrying the body of his sister, who was killed during the assault. His face was wet with tears as he held her in his arms, her bobbing head indicating her neck had been snapped. He fell to the ground upon reaching his team, letting his sister fall to the side. "I didn't want the scavengers to feast on her," he said curtly.

No one dared contradict him as he sat next to her body with a transfixed gaze mixed with anger, sadness, and despair. Pawa sat next to him. "We'll have a proper ceremony for her and the others as well," she said softly, rubbing his back as she spoke.

It brought the militia back from his despair a little, as he turned to look at Pawa. Even when comforting someone, she had a fierce look to her, which broke him down, and he started to cry, hiding his face in Pawa's shoulder while she squeezed him in her arms. Stroking the hair of her aggrieved brother, Pawa turned to the others. "Let's begin to clean up. We can group the ones we have lost here so we may hold a ceremony for them later. The invaders' bodies are to be carried into the forest for the scavengers to feast on their corpses."

Her orders left no place for discussion and even seemed to instill new energy in the group, as everyone instantly moved into action, the rest of the villagers joining in to help in any way they could.

CHAPTER 38

With the sun going down on that historic day in the existence of the Soochit Karana community, Engella was genuinely proud of the setup she had managed to create for herself at the foot of the tree. She had made a bed by lying palm leaves on the ground, using dead branches to create a triangular shelter that she covered by overlapping more palm leaves that she tied down with ivy branches to protect her in case it rained. She worked at keeping an even mental state while she built her shelter, trying to control the anger that was just below the surface. The anger painfully constricted her face, her furrowed brow causing cramps in her forehead. She believed the lost souls would not help her if they suspected her motivations were guided by anger and revenge.

Although their survival instincts bring them to absorb the unconscious energy of a person for sustenance, Rafael told her that they never acted on the impulse of anger. To be able to convince the lost souls, Engella would need to insist on the fact Dr. Cutler is motivated by a self-righteous need for power—that his plan would endanger the existence of this realm since his work would disconnect every human from the collective unconscious and that he must be stopped. She couldn't predict their reaction to her demands. Rafael had warned Engella that the lost souls would act on their behalf alone. They had no propensity to offer any help or interact with anything, always on the hunt for new prey. They are much like predators in the wild, scouring the dream realm for vital energy to feed on, and will not hesitate to suckle on her energy if she calls on them. They will not see an equal being looking for counsel; they will see a potential meal. She needed to be alert, ready for anything.

Engella settled into her makeshift dwelling and began to concentrate on her hand as she had always done to be able to awake conscious in the dream realm. She kept her gaze fixed on the center of her hand, forcing her conscious mind to stay focused on that spot as her body became drowsy and sleep overcame her. At that point, she needed to have clear intentions; the lost souls do not give second chances. As she began to slip into sleep, Engella felt the tiger's heat at her feet. It had laid on its side near the shelter, guarding her against intruders. She didn't hear the two bears who were there before but presumed they were still nearby, patrolling or resting or both. Engella smiled, thinking of the relationship she had developed with the beast. She knew their connection would stay feral and instinctual, but the love she felt for the tiger was nonetheless real.

Her mind wandered into amazement, thinking of the intricate web her life had been to bring her to this moment. She wondered if she would be there had events been even slightly different, knowing the answer. Different decisions in life would invariably lead to different outcomes. She leaned on this saying to center herself when the pangs of regret showed themselves, making her question her life. She would remind herself that she made the decisions she did based on the knowledge she had at the moment, and nothing could change that. The tiger growled at her, placing its paw on her foot, a stray claw scratching a toe, waking her instantly. It provoked an intense adrenaline rush, Engella believing for an instant she was under attack. The tiger looked at her disapprovingly, calling her back to the task at hand by bobbing its head up and down, as if it was telling her to focus.

"Thanks," she told the tiger. "But be more discreet next time. Now I have to calm down before being able to sleep. You startled me." The tiger looked at Engella and laid its head on its paws, uninterested in her complaints.

After an hour to get the adrenaline back down to normal levels with breathing and reflective meditation, Engella began once again to concentrate on her hand. She saw it in her mind, focusing her gaze on the middle of the hand, all other thoughts shunned away as sleep crept up on her. The sounds of the tiger's breathing, the raindrops falling on the shelter, the forest bat's echolocating shrieks all dwindled, replaced by perfect, exquisite silence. Engella opened her eyes, her hand still before her. She lowered her hand and took in the view.

Each time this boundless, enigmatic plain appeared before her, Engella had to take a minute to readjust. It felt like finding yourself in space, with all points of reference relating to a gravity-ruled world thrown out the window. Masses of energy clustered together to look like galaxies, with wide zones of darkness between the clusters, single photons floating freely in the dark spaces. Rafael had told Engella to be wary of lost souls when traveling near oceans of darkness, as the cloak they used to hide blended in with the pitch-black darkness. She started by looking for such oceans, working hard to contain the anger she felt from the death of Dwight. Free-flying specks of light spread all over the expanse like stars in the universe, each speck representing a person's energy. The space between them varied from complete darkness to vein-like strands of light that spread unevenly across the landscape from one cluster to the next. Engella concentrated on the dark spaces, looking for any variation in the blackness that would reveal the presence of a lost soul. Their cloak would sometimes make it so the darkness they envelop themselves in will waver slightly, revealing their presence.

Engella began to lift her spirit energy to what could be called the sky, although, in this realm, the surrounding cover was murky, an almost liquid cloud that worked at retaining the unconscious energy in that place. She felt her energy suddenly get compressed as she flew too near, the liquid clouds taking hold of her energy. Engella panicked a little at this, knowing that any piece of energy that encountered the cloud cover was slammed right back to the ground to reintegrate the energy flows of the unconscious. When this happened, the sky would briefly fill with what could only be compared to lightning, as the repelled energy was returned to its point of origin with a bang. As spectacular as they were, these flashes of lightning were commonly the result of infinitely small specks of energy reaching upward, basically psychic dust.

Engella had raised her entire ball of energy up to the edge of those clouds to get a better vantage point of the area but misread how close she could get as she felt her energy being sucked in and compressed, setting it up for a violent descent to the ground. Pain was different in this realm but was surely as real as in the physical world. The difference was that although your physical body doesn't suffer the consequence of the event occurring in the dream realm, the mind feels it as though the body did suffer the injuries. Engella tried to wriggle out of the entrapment, attempting to will her energy downwards, but the clouds had a hold on her, crushing her entirely as she saw herself swiftly reduced to an infinitesimally small, single-cell element of light. She felt her memories, emotions, and knowledge, all being crushed into one single quantum space. Paradoxically, the more her soul was reduced to its simplest state of existence, the more her mind extended its reach, giving her the sensation that she could touch the edge of the universe with her thoughts. That feeling went beyond anything she had experienced in her life, including her travel to the supernova, and she was reveling in its magnificence. Seconds before being propelled to the ground, Engella realized she was going to be separated into infinite specks of light, becoming a big bang of herself, forever dispersed in the universe. Deploying more effort than she even knew she had, Engella concentrated on each thought, memory, piece of knowledge she possessed to try to preserve the entirety of her being and braced for the impact.

The peaceful dream realm was rocked by a nuclear level explosion. A gigantic ball of light exploded on the ground, stretching to illuminate everything, revealing every nook and cranny this realm had to divulge. It revealed a desolate land, the oceans of darkness showing themselves as barren mountains, devoid of any energy, any life. The displaced clusters of energy were all attracted to the remaining sources of subconscious vitality like a thirsty traveler who hears the call of an oasis in the desert. Engella absorbed the shock of the landing with surprising ease, as she managed to keep her energy intact, her mind then liberated from the compression caused by the clouds, its contents intact.

The light she discharged on her landing had revealed the position of the lost souls, as they scrambled like cockroaches to reactivate their cloak, their camouflage bulldozed by the force of Engella's landing. Her thoughts and memories felt a little scrambled as they returned one by one to their original place in her mind, causing her focus to waver. Engella fought off the exhaustion triggered by her compression and explosion and went straight to a lost soul, willing her energy to it. The lost soul saw her coming and decided to stand its ground. Absorbing someone as powerful as Engella would sustain it for years. But as Engella grew closer, the lost soul felt suddenly helpless, unable to absorb her energy. Rafael had taught Engella a technique designed to withstand an attack from the lost souls, but she didn't know how long it would hold. As the light from the explosion grew dimmer, Engella reached out to the lost soul with her thoughts.

"Can you help me?" She thought, sending the energy from her question toward the lost soul. The lost soul didn't seem to understand as it remained immobile before her. A long moment passed, then it vibrated.

"What do you want?" Its answer sounded like a scream in Engella's mind, a wave of energy splashing over her and at the same time, pushing her back. She was barely able to contain herself from bolting, the vibrations coming from the lost soul chilling her own soul beyond comprehension.

"Remove a common enemy," she managed to send back, her mind stretched to its limits.

The lost soul remained immobile. Engella wasn't certain she could keep this up for long, having pushed herself far beyond her limits. She was in unknown territory and didn't have a barometer to measure her capacity to resist long enough to convince the lost soul. As they faced off, the lost soul still working to regain his energy absorbing faculties, Rafael appeared next to Engella. His appearance instantly gave her strength; he was nourishing her with his own energy. She felt her power replenish as she let her light shine as brilliantly as possible to try to attract more lost souls. She kept her focus on the one before her, and with harmony returning to her thought process, coherence re-established its dominance in her mind. She continued sending her thoughts to the lost soul.

"This common enemy will destroy this realm if he can carry out his bidding. He carries enough energy to sustain every one of you for decades." Engella bombarded the lost soul with every argument that came to mind. "His beliefs endanger this realm; its existence is threatened by his desire to cut off the people's subconscious energy from this realm."

"Enough!" bellowed the lost soul. Engella and Rafael froze for a second before the amount of power displayed, but Engella kept her composure.

"Follow me. I can show you," she added, hoping her arguments were convincing enough.

More lost souls were arriving, their almost invisible energy filling the sky above them. Rafael had told Engella the lost souls can communicate as a hive but had never verified this fact, always staying as far as possible from them. As hundreds of lost souls began to obscure everything surrounding them, Rafael found himself praying to the universe for his survival. Engella stayed focused on her prisoner, hoping he could persuade the others, unaware she was speaking to each one of them at once. Her hold on his powers to assimilate energy had spread to all the lost souls through this hive connection, and she needed to convince them to follow her before she lost control of their power.

"Will you follow me?" she asked again.

Rafael stayed as immobile as possible, afraid they had stepped too far and would soon be absorbed. The lost soul began to vibrate once more. "Your energy can sustain us for as long or more; we can feel your power." The voice was calmer, giving Engella hope that she was softening them.

"True, but with nowhere to exist, what good will I be to you?"

A low hum followed this argument, the lost souls seemingly debating among themselves. "We can help." The voice was almost whispering at that point, the wave of energy coming from them feeling like a soft summer breeze on Engella's spirit body. "But be aware this is an exceptional situation. We will continue as we always have after this."

"I understand the warning," she said almost immediately. Engella wondered if they would turn on her as soon as Dr. Cutler was removed. She continued to "speak," still unsure if they would cooperate. "Be aware I understand your motivations. I believe your presence in this realm is essential to the ecosystem."

It clearly surprised the lost souls, as Engella noticed a glimmer of light dancing like a wave on the dome they formed around them. "Take us to him."

The lost soul's dome raised up as they formed a large, single entity, its shadow darkening everything around, even though there was no light source strong enough to cast the shadow from, reminding her of the shadow that enveloped her before, making her physical body shiver in the tent. They remained there, waiting for Engella to lead the way.

CHAPTER 39

Frank Cutler was waiting for the confirmation that the operation was complete, feeling agitated, pacing in his empty laboratory, ready to push on to the next phase of the program. He had been getting brief reports from his team leaders at a regular interval as they advanced on the village until everything had stopped all at once. No more messages, no more updates, complete silence. Frank's stomach turned as he prepared for the worst. His natural disposition had always been to prepare for the worst, hope for the best. It served him well over the years, but he knew that if this mission went sideways, his head would be on the chopping block, as the members of the Dark Matter Initiative are not known for their patience.

Unable to wait for his soldiers to send him information, Frank began to send messages at a furious pace, inquiring about the advancements, conscious his army might be too occupied to answer, but sending the messages anyway. He walked in circles in the lab, sending out messages with a series of question marks, followed by more messages exposing his impatience, ordering them to answer. Then two men entered the lab, surprising Frank, their grim faces indicating trouble. Frank knew he had to do something fast to save his skin; the initiative had lost patience. Acknowledging their presence, he indicated to the two men that he needed to go to the bathroom and ran out of the lab, heading for the furthest facilities, looking to put some space between him and the men. He entered the bathroom and locked the door behind him. Sweat was streaming down his back as he found himself unable to contain his nerves. His hands were shaking as he clumsily pawed at the window lock, needing to get outside. Then, his phone buzzed.

"At last," he whimpered, tons of pressure lifting from his shoulders all at once.

He picked up his phone, and the pressure that had lifted seconds ago came crashing down, pressing down on his shoulders, shutting down his mind. The phone display showed the number calling was from his strike team, but the message was from Christopher Saddleton. It read, "Better luck next time," with a wink emoji. He saw the message had been transmitted to all. Aware the initiative received the same message he did, Frank knew there was little hope they would interpret this message in a positive light. He took a second to gather his thoughts, then cracked open the bathroom door to see if the two men were coming for him. Seeing they were heading for the bathroom next to the lab, Frank congratulated himself for choosing the furthest one. He locked the door once more and went to work on the window, his hands feeling more stable. Frank cursed himself for installing locks that needed a special tool to open. He had thought this up when his paranoia was at its peak, wanting to make sure that anyone who was moved to the lab couldn't escape. Now he found himself caught by his own invention, the window lock needing an Allen key to open. Naturally, the key was in his desk in the lab.

For a second, Frank thought he would be able to go back to his desk without getting caught but quickly changed his mind. He heard the two initiative agents searching more intently now, the sound of their footsteps going in opposite directions. Frank's eyes darted around the room, looking for something with which to break the window. He decided on a soap dish that felt heavy enough in his hands and propelled it toward the window, cursing his parents for not letting him play baseball during his youth. The soap dish weakly bounced off the window without even leaving a mark, then came crashing to the floor with a loud bang as it bounced on the tile. Panicked, Frank picked up another dish, wrapped his hand with his jacket to protect it from the glass, and proceeded to punch away at the window. He slammed his soap dish reinforced hand on the window, producing little more than a knocking sound. It took three good hits before the window started to give way, a small crack appearing at the point of impact as the soap dish broke in half in his hand, cutting him deeply in his palm. His eyes filled with tears from the panic. He continued to whack away at the window, the dish digging deeper into his hand at every punch. While one of the agents was jiggling the bathroom door, Frank managed to break the window and slip out. The agent was banging on the door as Frank took a deep breath of the outside air, still undecided on what to do next.

He decided his first order of business would be to get as far as possible from this place. Frank hugged the building walls, trying to stay out of the camera's field of view to get away as fast as he could before the agents got a bead on him and chased him down. He had originally hatched an escape plan in case the project went sideways, but he didn't expect to need the getaway and gave it little attention, as the main plan seemed to be on track, a golden life waiting for him around the corner.

He reached ground level without triggering the alarms, sweat pouring down his spine from the tension gripping his body. His mind was fixated on his survival. When he stopped to see if he was still being followed, Frank wrapped his cut hand in a piece of cloth that he ripped from his shirt while trying to find a path around the cameras to the garage. He had a small car hidden in the back of the garage that he had prepared for his escape. The car was filled with clothing, a slew of false IDs, and enough cash to survive at least five years. He realized the only way he could circumvent the cameras would take too long; the agents would have time to circle back to the garage by the time he could go around. He had to sprint through the open territory between the lab entry and the garage. He took a deep breath and crouched a little, looking a little like a track and field athlete settling in his starting blocks before a race.

Frank had pretty much ignored any form of physical exercise in his life, making this sprint look a little comical as he plundered across at a snail's pace, giving one of the initiative men time to notice him on the surveillance monitors. The agent called his colleague, and they both headed for the garage. Frank thought he had made it without being detected, and as he turned to look toward the main building to make sure he was safe, he saw the two agents heading his way. Frank felt a twinge of panic, but the elation he felt as he got in his car was too powerful for the fear to settle. He congratulated himself for having the presence of mind to make the preparations and turned the key to start the car. Nothing. He turned the key repetitively, getting no reaction. Then he noticed the hood was ajar, and his heart sank.

They had disabled all the vehicles in the garage before entering the lab, one step ahead of Frank. He tried to get out of the car, his mind racing to find a solution, but one agent slammed the door closed, the other agent sticking his head in from the other side.

"You will need to follow us, Dr. Cutler," said the agent on the other side of the car, pointing a strange-looking gun at Frank.

The other agent opened the door and grabbed Frank's shoulder to pull him out of the car. They dragged him away to their waiting vehicle, Frank offering no resistance.

"Really? A black SUV with tinted windows?" Frank scoffed, trying to defuse the situation. "Come on, guys; why not plaster Dark Matter Initiative in red letters across the side while you're at it?"

His comment was greeted by silence as they unceremoniously shoved him in the back seat and drove away. Frank, desperate to find a way out of this, sat back in silence, letting his mind meander in search of a way out of this.

When they reached the highway, Frank was reeling, his mind all over the place, unable to focus on anything. How could two people derail such an extensive plan? Why did the initiative desperately need these two out of the picture to move ahead? What was that place his soldiers found? Nothing made sense to him as they sped down the road toward his demise. The agent in the passenger seat was turned to face Frank, pointing the strange pistol at him. It looked like a boosted stun gun, designed to send an electric string that wraps itself around the victim, exponentially raising the electrocution level, which canceled any possibility to wriggle out of his bindings, certain he would be neutralized before being able to free himself.

The agent compounded that thought by saying that any movement would be perceived as an escape attempt that will be neutralized at any cost. Frank's last hope was to pass through the city at some point. He could then find a way to attract attention and disturb the transport enough for Frank to find a way out of the car. As if fate had intervened, Frank saw the horizon changing, as its silhouette transformed from farmland to a distant city skyline. He tensed up in his seat, still unsure of what he could do to attract enough attention to provoke someone to intervene. The windows were tinted, so anything he could try wouldn't be visible to anyone else other than the two agents in the vehicle, who would certainly shoot him with the stun gun. The front windshield was the only two-way window, which meant Frank would need to find a way to leap to the front fast enough to create a scene before they could neutralize him.

As they approached the city, traffic began to slow them down, giving Frank a little time to prepare his jump. He discreetly moved his feet to be able to apply the right amount of pressure to push him to the front when the time came. He would need to time his jump perfectly, knowing he would only have one chance at it. The highway merged into a large boulevard, as houses and small buildings were occupied most of the view. They reached an intersection and stopped at the red light. Frank looked around, but all he could see out of the windshield were half-empty parking lots. They were in suburbia somewhere. He needed to bide his time and hope for a more clustered environment where his actions would have more impact.

His hopes were rewarded when the car turned towards the city center, the large boulevard turning into a smaller street, and the buildings becoming higher around them. He thought they were certainly heading for the basement of a building or public parking lot, meaning Frank had minutes left to do something. They stopped at a red light, and he noticed two pedestrian officers patrolling. Without hesitation, hoping the surprise of his move would give him enough time to attract the attention of the officers, Frank propelled himself to the front, and as he was about to let out a scream, the passenger side agent pushed him back in one swift movement of the elbow, then shot Frank with the stun gun, immobilizing him in an electric harness. The electricity shot through him like nothing he had felt in his lifetime; each muscle was contracted, cramps popping up in his legs, abdomen, and arms all at once. As the pain reached intolerable levels, Frank fainted, going limp in the seat. The agent shut off his stun gun and sat back, happy to relax a little.

Frank had been propelled into unconsciousness so fast, he found himself caught in a strange limbo, as he could still see the two agents inside of the car and the city out the windshield, but unable to move a muscle or even utter a sound, his breathing limited to the point where he wondered if he was dying. At the same time, he found himself awake in the dream realm, the dark expanse that is the collective unconscious spreading out before his mind's eye, as his waking mind battled to stay in control.

Frank physically felt his mind break down, the information before him too chaotic to make any sense. He thought he had found the truth to our existence, but saw everything slipping away fast, the expanse before him proving his theories were flawed, his life's work voided. Ayla Karemi's work spoke of a place called the collective unconscious. Frank felt like a fool for not delving deeper into these theories. He had always considered himself to be a complete scientist, never omitting any detail, covering every angle. He knew he could have avoided this situation if he had only read Ayla's research with more vigor. Alone and vulnerable, he was somehow relieved that no one was witness to his demise. As he was beginning to let go and accept the impending doom, his unconscious mind saw a large ball of translucent energy flowing towards him, led by a bright, opaque light that beamed in all directions with radiance and power. Their approach blinded Frank's view of the unconscious expanse.

CHAPTER 40

Sensing an impatient vibe coming from the cloud of lost souls, Engella raised her newly energized spirit body toward the dark, murky sky, careful to stay below an acceptable altitude. She felt the lost souls' luminescent mass behind her and around her all at once, creating an ambiguous view of the dream realm. The mystical waves present in the lost souls' cloud distorted the view of the expanse, generating a foggy view because of the translucent swell the lost souls carried with them. Engella wasn't entirely certain where she could find Dr. Cutler but knew she could home in on someone's energy signature if she thought about that person long and hard enough.

As they floated aimlessly for some time, Engella kept her full concentration on localizing Frank Cutler, hoping the souls would be patient enough for her to find their common enemy. Time is a constantly changing variable in this realm, making it impossible to know how much time had passed when present in this environment, which worried Engella. She was still looking for Frank Cutler's energy signature, becoming more and more anxious as time slipped away. Engella knew she needed to hide her anxiety from the lost souls, but it became harder and harder to do so.

She then noticed an impossibly thin yet intensely bright strand of light that shot from the ground to the sky. Its position seemed to mark the middle in the dream realm, a central point of reference, something that wasn't there before. For Engella, since she discovered its existence, this realm was an expansive and flexible entity that did not offer any bearing to guide you when traveling through it. She guided her energy to flow in the direction of the light strand, curious to see what the point of origin of this new phenomenon was.

Engella loved the way travel in this realm resembled swimming in water if it offered no resistance at all. One swift movement of the arms could carry you across vast distances, and as she approached the strand of light, its emanation seemed to release infinitely small bits of energy all along its slim stem. The light strand was spewing photons, the same way a tree spews pollen, in the guise of subconscious energy disguised in infinitesimally small specks of pure energy. The area contingent to its origin was becoming colorful and alive as the bits of energy merged into clusters of pure light. As the clusters grew, the same kind of watercolor waves that she saw when traveling in the tree's energy flow began to appear, flowing in a tight circle at first, then slowly expanding. Other specks of energy floated away, while some fell to the ground, like leaves from a tree in autumn. As they landed on the ground, it widened the available space for the light to connect. The accumulation of photons at its base created a foundation for the strand of light to grow.

As it gained a stronger foothold in the realm, its energy began to shine more brilliantly, lighting up the darkness that had become humanity's unconscious. Engella felt the same energy she did when she was traveling in the collective unconscious and instantly knew this strand of light was the emanation of the tree in the subconscious dream realm, its connection to the universe now re-established. Her energy filled up with joy and relief for a brief instant, disturbing the cloud of lost souls around her.

"What is this?" they asked, visibly perturbed.

"A new reality," Engella said.

Understanding she was in immediate danger of being absorbed as the cloud above her closed in, Engella willed her energy away from the light strand and went back up to get a better vantage point of the area. It seemed to be enough to calm the lost souls as they chose to continue to follow her without question, releasing the pressure they had begun to apply near the light strand. As Engella started to doubt her capacity to find Dr. Cutler, a small explosion occurred in the realm that caught her attention. The lost souls veered in that direction without waiting for her, almost racing Engella to make it there before her as she desperately swam as fast as she could, feeling they had found their target.

Approaching the mass of energy that was unceremoniously sent to this realm, Engella recognized the signature she was looking for. Dr. Frank Cutler's light was dim, its emanation so weak it was absorbing some of the surrounding darkness. As they got closer, Engella slowed her approach, wanting to make sure it was the right person. The lost souls followed suit. They held back as she let her ball of energy graze Cutler's half-unconscious mind, picking up some memories as she did so. She settled before Dr. Cutler's vibrating ball of dim light and waited for a reaction. The absence of any response showed them that the energy before them was not entirely present. Engella could almost make out images of the physical world beyond Dr. Cutler's conscious mind.

"Are you present?" she asked, not anticipating an answer.

Sensing that the energy before her was unable to communicate, she noticed the energy ball quiver slightly, as if something within was trying to emerge and respond. Engella could see the ghost of a city skyline reflected in Frank's energy and wondered what could be happening to his conscious mind for this image to transcend the realms. She turned to the lost souls.

"It's him," she told them, not sure what to expect next.

The lost souls didn't react, their cloud remaining static. Engella then began to feel a quiver coming from the lost souls, discreet at first, becoming more and more intense with each second. It sounded as though they had a drum, the beat going from a distant, almost indiscernible echo to a resounding bang within seconds, the sound created an opaque bubble that grew with every beat. As it reached Dr. Cutler's energy source, he reacted, his unconscious mind apparently trying to let out a scream of psychic terror as the lost souls launched their absorption ritual on him. His scream came out as a weak whimper, Engella deciding to pull back, afraid she would be included in the ceremony if she stayed too close.

The scene fascinated her, as the translucent cloud became opaque, then turned into a frothy mass. It closed in on Dr. Cutler, his own energy beginning to dissipate as if pulled in by a vacuum cleaner under the pressure imposed by the lost souls. Engella stared at the display of power, morbidly fascinated by the frenzy before her. She saw Dr. Cutler's energy being sucked into the frothing cloud, his light broken down into photons that were then stretched and absorbed into the cloud. It became even more frenzied as the lost souls feasted; their resolve emboldened by the amount of energy given to them by Cutler's subconscious mind. Engella began to worry that they wouldn't be able to contain themselves once they had absorbed Dr. Cutler, that their frenzy would overcome any restraint they might need to leave her alone. They were then feasting on Dr. Cutler's ball of energy with an unapologetic, gleeful joy, absorbing every ounce of his subconscious energy with vigor. Cutler's energy was almost entirely transparent; his existence almost erased. A thought crossed Engella's mind.

"Wait!" Shrieked Engella, pushing all of her psychic energy into the scream.

The cloud mellowed down to its original translucency rather fast, which surprised her. The lost souls stayed close to Dr. Cutler's almost dissipated energy, as it quivered meekly, almost not emitting any light at all.

"Can I take possession of one memory?" she asked. Engella wasn't sure about their reaction to this kind of request, but abruptly felt she needed the information.

"Your soul is still attached to your body; you will not be able to absorb the energy contained in the memory." The reply was soft-spoken, almost apologetic.

"I must try," she responded, hoping they would accept.

A long silence followed, Engella unsure of which course of action she should take, ready to run away in case they tried to attack her. There was no hum, no activity in their translucent cloud, Engella feeling like they were staring at her silently, sizing her up.

"If such is your true wish, we accept. It's possible your mind will explode, so consider yourself warned. What is it you need to know?"

Engella focused her thoughts to be sure to ask the right question. "Who did the physical body work for?"

"The memory is yours." The lost souls released a small, imperceptible speck of light out of their grasp. It floated aimlessly for a moment before turning towards Engella. It glided to her unhurriedly, her energy petrified in place by an invisible force.

"As it enters your consciousness, the memory will need to find a place in your personal history. It will cause great pain at first, but it should subside over time." As the lost soul said this, the speck of light reached Engella.

As soon as it touched her spirit body, Engella felt submerged by a massive wave of energy. The little speck of light carried more power than Engella felt she could sustain; her mind being ripped apart by a psychic explosion. Dr. Cutler's memory of his associations leading to his venture to disengage humanity from its subconscious exploded in her mind, causing her own thoughts and memories to be displaced with apocalyptic force. She panicked, as her mind had become a barren wasteland, her whole life history disengaged from her mind while the new memory was seeking a compatible space to merge into. She managed to gain some footing on her jumbled mind by adopting an observer's point of view, using the knowledge she acquired while traveling in the tree's energy. With her consciousness and subconscious stuck in a confused limbo, Engella couldn't focus her attention to start organizing the influx of new information. The only thing she could do was bear witness to her descent into madness. Then she felt something release her spirit body; the memory had integrated her mind completely.

"Be safe, Engella Iblis," bellowed the cloud of lost souls. "Now our association is over. Should we meet again, be aware we may still be hungry."

They turned back to the remains of Dr. Cutler's unconscious energy and absorbed the rest of the energy in seconds. The lost souls stayed there for some time, like a predator digesting his catch before moving on. After they had released her, Engella was able to concentrate enough will to force her mind to restore her memories, using every ounce of power she possessed to return them to their original place in her mind. As her psyche gradually returned to normal, she knew she would need to adapt to new memory connections in the waking world but felt she had managed to absorb the energy from Dr. Cutler's mind and could use its information. The lost souls were still there, apparently observing her, and Engella feared she could be next; on top of her exhaustion, they outnumbered her far beyond her capacity to withstand an assault. The lost souls spoke once more.

"Your power is greater than we had anticipated, Engella Iblis. We have decided your existence is as crucial as ours for this realm to continue to thrive; you will be excluded from future hunts."

Within seconds, every single lost soul had disappeared; the low hum of the new light strand emitted by the tree was the only sound. The lost souls' disappearance happened so fast, Engella's ethereal vision had to adjust to the lack of translucency around her. She let her spirit body float back to the tree's strand of light, imbibing the pollen photons emitted by it. Their light was filled with energy from the universe, filling Engella's mind with the same visions as the ones she saw when she was absorbed by the particle dust cloud, except this time she saw it as a movie, not an assault.

Along with it came a sense of calm, the visions creating a feeling of fulfillment in her soul that she had never felt. The fulfillment was complete, unobstructed by conscious thought, spreading to every molecule in her being. Engella understood that as the tree of life grows in this realm, more humans will become aware of a personal sense of fulfillment, bringing on a new era for humanity.

Over time, as each human connects with his own subconscious, they will bear witness to the disappearance of negative sentiments like jealousy and greed and the appearance of more sharing and empathy. With the conscious and subconscious connected properly, every person will follow their own path without carrying judgment on someone else's journey. Those thoughts elevated Engella's soul to levels of happiness she couldn't imagine existed. She stayed near the light strand for a moment, ecstatically flowing through the photon pollen, absorbing its vital energy.

CHAPTER 41

Stuck in limbo between his waking and unconscious mind, Frank was helpless to stop the mass of light from advancing on him. He understood it wasn't a normal dream but couldn't decide if what he was seeing was a fabrication of his mind or not. He was unable to communicate in either realm—his muscles cramped up by the spasms caused by the stun gun keeping his conscious mind neutralized. During that time, his unconscious mind was entirely focused on finding a way to absorb the pain caused by the electric shock without his heart stopping. As the ball of luminescent energy reached his unconscious mind, Frank was doing everything he could to awaken, sensing that the thing approaching him was not there to help, nor was it a fabrication of his mind. As it hovered near him, seeming to survey and analyze the situation, Frank noticed the translucent cloud behind it begin to merge, becoming opaque, somehow burning through him with its invisible eyes.

"Are you present?" bellowed the ball of light before him, the echo carrying far beyond what Frank could envision about this place.

The words uttered by the mass of light pushed Frank's mind deeper into the madness that had become his life. He knew this was more than a hallucination. The entity in front of him was there, and it represented another person; he was certain of that. The cloud of translucent energy was also genuinely there, floating menacingly above him. Frank had based his entire program on the notion that humans are slaves to their conscious mind, everything else being a fabrication of some underlying factors our brains try to compartmentalize. He had refuted all theories evoking any notion of a connected subconscious, convinced he held the key to unlock the human potential. He saw the theories exposing the existence of that reality as elaborate lies created by humans to reassure themselves of the existence of free will, of independent thought. Frank cursed himself for not delving deeper into these notions, thinking he might know what to do if he had taken the time to enrich his knowledge about this plane of existence. Had he studied these theories, he would have a plan for what was happening. Tears began to stream down his face in the physical world, his conscious mind aware of his coming demise.

"It's him," said the entity of light, the reverberation of the voice once again carrying to unfathomable distances.

On those words, the echo still perceivable in this expansive and dark land, Frank saw the opaque cloud become a frothing mass under the beats of a distant drum, then advance on him. He didn't know his subconscious was about to be destroyed but still desperately tried to communicate something to the oncoming mass of doom, hoping to establish some sort of dialogue. He thought he was screaming for mercy—unaware his cry was nothing but a whimper. As it bore down on him, Frank felt his mind being severed into millions upon billions of particles as memories, thoughts, and secrets were being separated from one another, becoming independent entities. His energy source became a fragmented cluster of photons absorbed into the frothing cloud, dissipating into pure energy; the memory, thought, or souvenir, no longer present in Frank's mind.

Desperate to alert anyone, Frank tried to emit a cry for help to alert the two agents in the truck that something was going on, but as had happened in the dream realm, all he did in the physical realm was moan, the agents in the car not even noticing. As he was being absorbed, Frank couldn't do anything except witness his mind being shattered, his life getting sucked out of him one memory at a time. The frothing cloud seemed to be feasting on his mind with unapologetic pleasure. Although they emitted no sound other than the beating drum, he felt their presence inside him. It felt as if millions of insects were eating away at his mind, each taking a small part of him and flying away. Frank could see and feel the memory get pulled out of him, float around aimlessly, and then disappear as it was absorbed in an instant, a sharp stabbing pain shooting through his head every time a memory was absorbed. The second the photon carrying his recollection disappeared into the frothing cloud, Frank found himself wondering what he was looking at, before focusing once more on a passing memory and repeating the same exercise, over and over. A deep, empty chasm was forming in the pit of his soul as his life was methodically sucked out.

"Wait!" There was a loud shriek, and everything stopped.

Frank was barely able to support a coherent thought with so little information left in his mind, but a glimmer of hope gave him enough energy to focus on the ball of light and the frothing cloud. He couldn't interact with them in any way but hoped they were finished with their punishment, and he could begin to rebuild his mind, unaware the lost memories were gone for good.

To his dismay, the reason they stopped was to share the spoils of their victory, and within seconds, Frank Cutler no longer existed in the dream realm. He found himself back in the waking world, looking out of the window of a car he didn't know, seeing a city he didn't recognize. He looked at the two agents quizzically, wondering why one of them was pointing a pistol at him.

They pulled into an underground garage. The passenger-side agent noticed Frank's eyes were glazed and empty. He wondered if the stun gun had done more damage than expected, unaware of the destruction that had been perpetrated on his mind.

"Think we hurt him?" he asked his colleague. He was worried they might get punished for damaging the goods. The driver looked in the rear-view mirror.

"Looks like it," he said, looking back at a vegetable where a man was sitting. "But I don't care, as long as we receive our reward for delivering him."

Frank couldn't appreciate the level of sophistication the initiative had attained in hypnosis. The DNA experiments were still stalled at the initial stage, as every test to graft a new line of thought had failed miserably. Each test subject either disappeared in a psychotic void or simply withered away and died, which rendered the implant project unusable for the foreseeable future. But during the process, the initiative became very interested in Cutler's techniques in hypnosis. They had built a Soldier Development Center adjacent to Cutler's and did experiments of their own. They had programmed the men who apprehended Cutler to act solely on the promise of money, which worked beyond their wildest dreams, the initiative now planning to include hypnosis in the training of their security corps to see where they could go from there.

Cutler sat in the back seat oblivious to all of it, the only thing remaining in the shell that was once his mind was the automated commands present in his brain to breathe and blink his eyes. The agents parked the vehicle, the passenger-side agent opening the back door to let Frank out. An auditory response caused Frank to turn his head, but he didn't know why the agent opened the door and looked at him, eyes glazed by the emptiness behind them. The agent reached in and pulled him out of the car, Frank falling to his side, unable to align his movements to match the force applied by the agent.

Lying on the ground in a heap, stuck between two cars, Cutler was unable to command his body to make specific movements to help himself up. His body was instinctively trying to get a little more comfortable, appease the pain caused by the fall, not reacting to the brain's attempts to get up. The agent didn't wait for him to understand how to stand as he picked Frank up by the shoulders and held him there. His legs spontaneously stiffened as the agent released his grip. Frank found himself standing next to the agent, wobbly and unaware. The other agent walked around the car, and they both grabbed Frank by a shoulder and pulled him along. They looked like two guys helping a drunken friend with Frank's feet dragging behind them. A security guard at the building's main desk noticed them on camera as they disappeared behind a door. The security guy smiled, seeing this, reminiscing about his own drunken adventures.

The agents followed an underground corridor that came upon a large metal door. They left imprints of their passage on the dust covering the ground, with footsteps surrounding two draglines along the white, gloomy corridor. One of the agents flashed a badge at a small hole in the wall, and the door unlocked. Frank would have loved to see the level of sophistication they had reached, as the trio emerged in an ultra sophisticated laboratory. He would have probably resented the fact the initiative had this equipment. No one will ever know, as the husk he had become stood in the middle of the room, the two agents keeping his balance for him. He was unaware, empty, basically dead.

A man came out of one of the offices and walked toward the three men. He sported a wild head of short dark hair that contrasted with his clean, black suit, giving the two agents a wide smile as he approached. His eyes were slightly hidden by his bangs, randomly moving around his face as he walked, and they were not smiling.

"What happened here?" he asked as he saw Frank's glazed look.

"We're not sure. I had to stun him when he tried to escape, but when he woke up, this was the result."

The agent reported the situation with a cold, matter-of-fact tone. The wild-haired man looked at the agents, assessing the situation in silence.

Well, you can't lie; we know that, he thought. "Okay, the money will be deposited in your account today, thank you for your service. We will be in touch if we need you in the future. Stay available." He gave them an absent-minded wave, and they left without hesitation, leaving Frank unsupported. He crumpled to the floor, unable to control his muscles enough to stay upright. The wild-haired man laughed.

"Well, someone took care of you," he told the empty lump on the floor. "Guess we can dispose of you now. I'll be taking over the research."

Dr. Travis Lawrence had been secretly studying Frank Cutler's research and was able to take over the operation, guaranteeing a brighter future for the initiative, as they gained full control of all the research. It erased the last potential interference the initiative faced in the foreseeable future. Unceremoniously, Frank Cutler was placed in a shipping container that was dispatched at sea a week later, ending his life in the depths of the Atlantic Ocean.

Dr. Lawrence was unaware Engella had taken the memories related to this operation and began to celebrate the initiative's victory, popping a bottle of champagne upon receiving the message that Dr. Cutler was no longer among the living. Tomorrow would be a new day for the initiative, but for today celebrations were in order. The Dark Matter Initiative had managed to guarantee generations of dominance for their group, possibly even more.

CHAPTER 42

The villagers were busy cleaning up and preparing for the funeral ceremony that evening. From afar, the flurry of activity would seem like there had been a big party the night before, and the cleanup was underway. But if someone were to look more closely, the scars caused by the fighting would be clear. Dead bodies aligned at an altar, puddles of blood staining the ground at irregular intervals, the grave look in the people's faces, all indicated something tragic had happened. Christopher and Ayla were entwined in a hug in the middle of the village, both sobbing, the tears and snot spilling on to each other's shoulders as they both squeezed hard, not wanting to let go, freeing themselves from the stress caused by the combat one tear at a time.

Pawa approached them with caution. The fierceness in her eyes had dissipated. She seemed almost apologetic about bothering them in their embrace. She stayed close to them, waiting for a sign that she could interrupt.

Christopher and Ayla felt a presence near them, which broke their concentration, and both turned toward Pawa at the same time, their eyes puffy and bloodshot from the tears, maintaining their embrace as they looked at Pawa while standing cheek to cheek. Seeing them in that state melted Pawa's heart, as she felt tears welling in her eyes also. She joined their embrace and let go of all the tension she was holding in since the start of the battle. With Christopher and Ayla on each side of her, Pawa cried harder than she had ever experienced in her life. The flow of emotion was so intense; she was worried she wouldn't be able to stop, as the tears, cries, and screams came out in uncontrollable waves.

"It's okay," whispered Christopher as he stroked her back. Let it all out. It all needs to come out.

"As if I had a choice," Pawa mumbled through the tears.

That made Ayla smirk. The smile that appeared on her face, although nearly invisible, gave everyone the chance to take a breath, allowing Pawa to regain some composure. The feeling of despair that enveloped her not a second ago abruptly became a fading memory, and she could once more breathe freely. She felt light, happy, the tears drying up, and a powerful sense of accomplishment rising in her, swelling her chest with pride. She felt more waves of emotion coming up, this time filling her with joy and relief. Pawa and Ayla looked at each other and began to dance, hand in hand. They spun around in a circle, holding both hands as they hopped around gleefully.

Some villagers joined them, and soon, the whole village was in a celebratory mood, even though the reality of what had happened was still present, the smell of death still dominating the air. After an hour or two of wild dancing and crying and laughing, everyone had let go of their emotions, and cleanup was in full swing. Some prepared the funeral reception, gathering the necessary seating and properly dressing the dead brothers and sisters at the front for the final farewell that evening. Jolan was busy preparing an incense mixture he might use during the ceremony while gathering his thoughts to preside over the event with dignity for the lost villagers. He felt a swell of anger rise in him each time he thought about the reason for their death and knew he needed to contain it. The ceremony needed to be respectful, anger and resentment had to be minimized for the occasion.

Christopher took a team to retrieve the bodies of fallen enemies and carry them deeper into the woods for the scavengers to feast on. He traced his steps back to where he had fought, still a little unsure that the battle was over. He had been separated from his old life for so long; he wasn't sure he could return to a "normal" life. Since his first meeting with Zorina Smith and the Collective Unconscious Allegiance, his life had been nothing but running, hiding, and fighting. Could he return to a routine where the biggest concern would be lack of milk in the fridge, or that the dishes needed to be cleaned? Distracted by his thoughts, Christopher tripped on the body of a dead initiative soldier and fell spread eagle on the ground. Looking back at the dead body, Christopher knew he would be okay. He had done enough fighting for two lifetimes; the war was over. Getting up and dusting himself off, Christopher loaded the corpse onto a cart they had brought for the purpose. The smell of death was all over him; the dead soldiers already beginning to decay in the heat, forcing Christopher to breathe through his mouth to prevent him from throwing up.

He led his team to the forest with five bodies on the cart. As they dug deeper into the brush, hyenas had encircled them, waiting for the corpses to be dumped, vocalizing their impatience with a creepy, laughter-like sound. The trees were also filling with ravens and vultures, so Christopher decided they were deep enough in the forest and dumped his cart unceremoniously, the bodies piling on each other in a jumbled mass of arms and legs. As they turned back, the hyenas didn't wait for them to be out of sight as they bore down on the banquet offered by the villagers, growling and pulling at the meat, while the ravens and vultures eased in closer, hoping to steal some scraps for themselves. As Christopher walked away, the sound of bones crushing under the growl of the animals was somehow melodic in his ears. He smiled all the way back to the village, loving this newfound freedom. He knew the Initiative would find a way to regroup, but for the time being, everything would be okay. And by the time the initiative got their act together, humanity might already be on a different path, eliminating them from existence.

Despite everything that had happened the day before, the village had returned to its original, peaceful state. The only remnants of the tragedy were the coffins lined up at the altar for the funeral ceremony and the occasional puddle of blood still seeping into the ground. Jolan waved Christopher over to the altar when he saw him return from the forest.

"I need you and Pawa to be at the front for the celebration," Jolan told him. "Without you two, there would have been more bodies lined up here, and we would probably all be part of them."

Christopher was surprised at the request but was honored nonetheless. "Sure. Is there anything special you need me to do during the ceremony?"

"Be present." Jolan turned away and continued to tend to his set up for the evening.

Christopher stood there for a second, watching Jolan make his preparations, fascinated at how he seemed to be integrating elements from varied beliefs to the ritual. A pang of hunger brought his mind back to the present, and Christopher headed to the food court, hoping there would be something available. The buffet table was bare except for a large salad bowl in the middle. Christopher grabbed a plate and dug in, discovering a plentiful salad that was chock-full of veggies and nuts, covered with a discreet yet fragrant vinegar-based dressing. As he sat to chow down, Zorina Smith sat in front of him, arms crossed, her wonderful smile lighting up the whole village with its naïve looking beauty.

"That was something else," she said. "You seemed to be in sync with your dark side during the battle. I've seen you neutralize hypnotized zombies before but watching you during that battle yesterday was a little unnerving, the violence coming out of you was impressive. How is it you're not a slave to it now?"

Christopher looked at her with a twinkle in his eye. "I think you've been here long enough to know the answer." His mouth full of salad.

Zorina smiled at his reply. "I do. That's why the Allegiance has chosen to rewrite its definition based on what we've found here."

Christopher stopped eating, his fork halfway between the plate and his mouth.

"Seriously?"

"Yup. The allegiance has recognized that the existence of our duality is what defines us as humans. This new position actually helps us understand what went wrong in our earlier attempts to influence the collective unconscious. We are but children before this knowledge, and we need the village's help to deepen our under-standing before we can move ahead." Zorina looked at Christopher with pleading eyes.

"You'll need to speak at the round table," Christopher said as he started to fill his mouth with the salad once more. "All major decisions come from there."

"When's the next one?"

He looked around, seeming to assess the situation. "Don't know. With everything that's happened, the one thing I know for sure is that the funeral is this evening. It's been generations since the village has lost members to tragedy, so it's important that we do this properly to honor their deaths. You can stick around; we don't refuse people, only ideologies." Christopher gave her a wry smile, and Zorina burst into laughter as they both celebrated the allegiance's new stance with a glass of freshly pressed mango juice.

***

While the cleanup was going on at the village, mem-bers of the Dark Matter Initiative were scrambling to salvage anything they could from the failed experiment, erasing any trace of their involvement, worried they could be accused of forming illegal militias. Although the project wasn't yet abandoned, it had been reduced to exploratory research. Dr. Lawrence, who had been tasked with learning Dr. Cutler's research, would over-see the development of a new plan for the technology. The necessity to force the whole population to undergo the procedure had been trashed, hoping they could selectively apply the method to different population groups. That would still guarantee a hold on power, as they believed they could shape the leaders of tomorrow with this transformation.

CHAPTER 43

When Engella opened her eyes, it took her a moment to realize she was back in the physical realm. She was lying on her back, unable to move, exhaustion and the full weight of her body anchoring her to the ground. She stared up at the makeshift roof she had built, letting her mind regain its hold on reality. Confusion reigned in her mind as she tried to make sense of her new memories, now an integral part of her. The conversations Dr. Cutler had with different members of the Dark Matter Initiative were bouncing around with the other memories in her mind, creating a sense of unease as she tried to focus on individual moments in her life, trying to make sure her own memories were still present. A touch of panic set in when she could not remember Rafael's village location. She focused hard to retrieve that information, feeling an irrepressible urge to go there and see him in the flesh.

While she was fishing for that information, she noticed her memories were displaced, some of them seeming to float aimlessly in her mind with no attachment to any specific time or place. She became fascinated with the situation. She felt the memories were hers, but unable to place them in time caused Engella to question their existence. The lost souls might have caused more damage than she originally thought. She opened her energy to their power, and that could have caused her mind to split into different parts, looking to defend itself from the injection of new information. In a flash, Rafael's village location came to her, and she held on to it, focusing all her attention to that single thought, deciding at that moment to let her subconscious make sense of the rest. It gave her enough of a surge of energy to get up. The tiger was no longer there, giving Engella a sense of relief; if it had left, it probably meant the danger had passed. She crawled out of her makeshift shelter to the raucous sounds of a loud celebration coming from the village through the branches. Her legs felt shaky as she stood, so she waited for her balance to return before going back to the village.

She almost felt drunk; some of Frank Cutler's memories were floating around with her own, looking for a place to settle in her mind, causing her to waver as she walked. The list of names was long; Engella would need to find the leaders of this list, so she may understand how to dismantle the group that fed Dr. Cutler's delusions. The dimness of his energy told Engella he had spent his life focused on his conscious mind, ignoring all signals emitted by his subconscious. That meant the Dark Matter Initiative was most certainly a group inclined to concentrate on animalistic power struggles while staying hidden in their opulent offices. It made them hard to reach in the physical world, which meant she would need to contact the lost souls once again.

She would need Rafael's help to carry it out, and the thought gave her enough motivation to get going. Her walk became more stable as she accelerated her pace. As she was walking through the forest, the three inhabitants of the resting home came to her mind. Engella made a beeline toward the house, and entered without knocking, curious to see if their state had changed with the tree regaining some power. The house was quiet inside. As she made her way through the rooms, Engella found the three inhabitants ensconced in their beds in a deep, restful sleep. She was relieved for them but wondered if they would be capable of returning to a normal way of life after having been the universe's connection for so long. Will they remember what happened? Will they reject the normality of everyday life and try to return to their former state?

Engella had promised herself to keep an eye out for them in the dream realm; if their adaptation to physical life is difficult, they could be tempted to join the lost souls. She thought she could help them acclimate to the physical realm by contacting them in the dream realm. Trying not to disturb the residents, she left the house as discreetly as possible. As she headed to the village center to bid farewell to everyone, Engella froze in her tracks. She noticed Ayla and Christopher withdrawing from the feverish activity and wanted to go toward them but found herself unable to move. Ayla noticed her and waved, but Engella's feet were mired in some invisible cement, forcing her to stay put. She felt unable to face a goodbye, so she blew a kiss to Ayla, and that liberated her to move as she turned, heading for the forest that would lead her back to the road. Engella didn't look back to see if Ayla was following and disappeared in the trees, thinking she might never return to the village.

When she reached the fields, Engella heard a grunt in the bushes and stopped to look. The tiger had come to bid farewell, doing so by approaching her and rubbing his body against hers, like a house cat asking for food. It laid itself down, and Engella crouched, grabbing the tiger's head and looking at it straight in the eyes. She could feel puffs of its breath on her face while it tried to rub its forehead on her as a sign that they were friends. Engella's eyes filled with tears as the tiger, satisfied with the goodbye, got up and left, disappearing in the bushes in an instant. She picked herself up and headed for the road, hoping to find transportation.

A taxi was parked on the side of the road, and Engella ran to it, thinking she recognized the car, excited to find the driver that brought her there. A woman was there instead. She saw Engella running and waved her over as if expecting her. Engella was surprised that it wasn't the same driver but approached the taxi anyway and saw that she did recognize the car. It had the same stickers in the window, the same rips in the seats.

"Who are you?" The question came out faster than Engella anticipated, and she apologized for her bluntness.

"No problem," the driver said. "I am Akshaya, Sanjay's sister."

"Sanjay?" The driver who brought her had left without giving her his name.

"The driver who brought you here . . ." Akshaya paused, a smile appearing on her face. "Oh! I see; he gave you the administrative purpose of a name speech, didn't he? Many people know my brother, but not a lot of people know his name, it's a game he liked to play."

Engella was happy to hear about the taxi driver; she felt they had created an interesting bond. "And why is it that you're here, waiting?" Engella felt a comfortable energy emanating from Akshaya, feeling confident she was there to help, but couldn't help asking the obvious question.

"My brother spoke to me in a dream not long ago and said to wait for you here, that you might need help to leave promptly. Since he's dead, I took this as a message from beyond and have been waiting here for about two days."

"He's dead?" Engella felt her heart sink.

"Tortured and killed, to be more precise." Akshaya's voice carried a melancholic tone, her eyes glazed over with deep sadness. Engella grabbed her by the shoulders.

"I'm going to take care of this. Let's go." She was looking to snap Akshaya out of her sudden downswing, which worked.

"Let's go then," Akshaya blurted as she returned to the driver's seat.

She drove with purpose, as they headed back to Bhopal airport much faster than it took to get to the village in the first place. Engella didn't dare ask Akshaya to slow down since she was concentrating on her driving, eager to get to the airport, and didn't want to distract her. Engella grabbed hold of what she could in the car to reassure herself they would be okay, tugging at the seat belt on occasion to make sure it was still secure. Akshaya picked up the pace when they reached the main highway, much smoother than the country roads they came from. Engella felt her heart float near her throat the whole way as they zigzagged through the traffic into Bhopal. When they reached the city, Akshaya slowed down.

"I have to watch my speed around here; the police are more active," she said, seeming disappointed that they had to slow down.

It gave Engella a chance to catch her breath as her heart returned to her chest, chasing the jelly out of her legs. They made it to the airport with plenty of time for Engella to catch a flight to Mexico. Akshaya pulled Engella's bag out of the trunk and gave it to her.

"You know, in the dream, he also told me you would guide humanity to its next evolution, and he showed me the existence of different planes of reality. I know I spoke to him for real in my dream, which is why I accepted the mission to wait for you. But doubt still clouded my mind; the conversation I had with him was nothing but a dream after all. When you showed up, I was almost at the limit of my patience, ready to leave and forget this ever happened. Now, I don't know how I will be able to go to sleep without hoping to talk with my brother again."

"You'll see him again." Engella hugged Akshaya without knowing if what she said was true and left to enter the airport.

CHAPTER 44

The villagers were gathering at the funeral ceremony, everyone sporting a solemn look, the joyous cleanup session replaced with a more somber mood. The villagers stood around, waiting for the ceremony to start, reminiscing about the lost brothers and sisters.

"He was so generous with his time," one said.

"She always knew how to adapt to a situation," said another.

"We planned on having a baby," mumbled yet another, his voice broken by emotion.

That last comment drove home the notion that their friends were dead, as the conversational buzz died down, sharing the emotions of the weeping man's lost family. Most of the people there gathered around the grieving man, and a group hug formed around him. The group remained almost immobile, each person holding the next by the shoulders, their breathing becoming synchronized as the hug lasted for a long moment.

Jolan then arrived, joining the hug before commenc-
ing the ceremony. Others who arrived also joined in
on the embrace. The group grew to fifty people as
some friends from adjoining villages came to pay their
respects after hearing about the clash. Even the farmer
who had directed the hypnotized soldier was present,
feeling they, and him, had been victims of governmental
madness. The group hug raised the mood a little, and
Jolan separated from the group to head to the front and
begin the funeral. As he settled at the front, the group
cuddle broke, and people began to spread out, some
sitting and some standing. Silence fell over the assembly
as everyone waited for Jolan to begin the ceremony. He
stood at the front, looking out to a point on the horizon,
his arms crossed on his chest in deep reflection. The
altar had been erected on a small wooden stage, and
the bodies were lined up, side by side, covered in white
cotton sheets. Some villagers had picked flowers from
the forest and scattered them on the lost brothers and
sisters. Beliefs and rituals were a constant moving target
there, so no specific belief was placed at the forefront.
Instead, the altar attractively recreated the surrounding
nature, the white cotton sheets covering the bodies a
true representation of their simplicity. They also integrated artwork and other elements that would create
an illustration of the history of the deceased.

Jolan had agonized over the best approach for the
ceremony. Normally, when their own death becomes a
real possibility, the villagers can choose the ceremony
they want for their funeral. But on that day, Jolan had
many bodies to grieve, and the one common desire was
that they all wanted cremation. Spiritual beliefs in the
village were volatile, prone to change under the impulse
of each individual's adaptation, and Jolan wanted to
pay proper respects to the lives of each person for the

sacrifice they made. Someone coughed in the crowd, looking straight at Jolan, which prompted him to begin.

"My friends, what happened here is far worse than anything we could prepare for, the sudden disappearance of our brothers and sisters exposing us to the darkest reality life has to offer. We find ourselves exposed to the finality of life today, and nothing I can say will change that." Jolan paused, looking around the improvised chapel they had set up, seeing angry faces where he thought he would see sadness.

"Let's all remember that their sacrifice was not made in vain. We have rekindled the tree's connection with the universe, and we have saved the village from doom. Their contribution to all our lives will never be forgotten," he said, pointing to the coffins. "Their impact will be celebrated for generations, not for the blood that was spilled, but for the lives that were saved. I propose we each step up and share a moment spent with one of our deceased kin. A recording of this ceremony will be stored in the library for future generations to understand the sacrifice made on this day. I believe this will help us begin to overcome the grief." He looked around, but no one seemed to want to speak.

After a few moments, Christopher walked to the middle of the funeral shrine. Standing before the group, he didn't yet know what to say. He felt awkward standing there, with no other knowledge of the fallen villagers than what he knew about their abilities to shoot a bow or a slingshot. The urgency had forced them to train intensively and quickly, obscuring any chance Christopher had to establish a real relationship with his soldiers.

"They followed *you*!" Yelled someone in the crowd. Christopher felt his shoulders sink at that comment. Jolan intervened.

"His presence may have accelerated the timeline, but yesterday's battle was destined to happen. Our tree is possibly the last one." Jolan looked at the group as if talking to one person. "You know this. Don't let your grief take control of your thoughts; it will do nothing more than drive us down a dark, endless road filled with rage and discontent. With Christopher's help, we have limited the damage inflicted on the village, and we can continue our existence in peace. That much is true. Because of his help, we now can hail the beginning of a new era."

Feeling his anger rise, Jolan tried to calm himself down before continuing. "But all this is beside the point. We are here to celebrate our deceased compatriots. Please. Let's concentrate on that. It will help us deal with the emotions more constructively."

Jolan's intervention seemed to center everyone's thoughts, and people began to approach the shrine to wait their turn to speak while the others settled in more comfortably in their seats. All eyes turned to Christopher, making him feel like the shy child he once was, his brain freezing up, limiting his capacity to think coherently. He stood there trying to find something to say, everyone's stares feeling like little daggers.

"What can I say?" His voice was already cracking from the emotion. "The army that attacked us chased me here. Had I chosen a different hiding place, your friends, brothers, and sisters would still be alive. Had I chosen to ignore the dream that brought me here, they would still be alive. But I didn't, and they're dead. All I ask of you is forgiveness, so we may remember our brothers and sisters as the heroes they are."

Christopher stood there without saying another word, waiting for a reaction, a comment, anything that would break the awkwardness he felt. But everyone remained silent, looking at him, seemingly waiting for more. He took a step sideways, indicating he wanted to leave the stage. The silence was then broken by a salvo of claps, as some villagers pushed Pawa to the front, so that everyone could celebrate today's bittersweet victory. She stood at the front next to Christopher, who wanted nothing more than to slink his way off the stage. Pawa grabbed him by the shoulder and began to speak.

"As members of the village's defense team, we all shared a belief." Pawa's eyes darted from one person to the next. "With the knowledge that our actions might one day bring our lives to an end, we adhered to the notion that our lives are expendable, but not our memories. It's our responsibility to ensure that their deaths have not been in vain."

Christopher stood next to her, thinking to himself that this was the strangest funeral he had ever seen.

Pawa continued. "To be able to do this, we must overcome our egos and our impulse for revenge. We must overcome our soul's emotional despair. We must celebrate the lives they have lived and not the deaths they have suffered." She paused, letting her words sink in.

Another villager stood in the middle of the congregation. "I know my brother Sven wanted a party at his death," he said, his face streaming with tears. "Music, dancing, all that."

Another villager stood. "My sister, Katie, hoped we could make a group painting in her memory. A large canvas is already set up for the occasion next to her home for those who want to take part."

As the final wishes of the departed began to be revealed, a sense of calm returned to the village.

Another villager stood to speak. "Let's celebrate the rebirth of our tree with our departed brethren.

Tomorrow, we can undertake the distinct wishes they have shared with us."

Then, a villager pulled out a harmonica and began playing. The music was sad at first, with long melancholic notes. But as others joined in with different wind and string instruments, the tone gradually picked up, until exploding into a full-blown jamboree as the drums joined in, taking the music to a level of euphoria. They all began to dance and sing along with the music. A dance circle formed around the departed villagers' remains, the people in the circle exchanging stories about their dead siblings, laughing, crying.

Christopher had left the stage and was looking for Ayla as the funeral turned into a full-blown party. He needed to hug her, feel her close to him. She had been the one person able to touch his soul the way she had. Having prided himself on being an independent person in his life, he still felt a strong need to be close to her as often as possible, her presence near him creating a balance in his mind and soul no other person could produce. Scanning the party to find her, he saw that she was dancing her heart out in the middle of what one could describe as a peaceful mosh pit, her arms in the air, her eyes closed, hopping and dancing around. Christopher stayed to watch her, feeling so much love for her at that moment; he thought his heart might burst.

Ayla swayed and weaved her way around her dancing cohorts to the sound of the music, releasing pent-up anger, anxiety, and sadness. Her eyes were filled with tears of joy as she danced away her negative emotions, filling her soul with the bliss that surrounded her. Random memories from her past overpowered Ayla as she glided around the dance floor, unaware that she was being watched by Christopher, her vision blurred by the tears that filled her eyes. As she spun around the dance floor, she found herself getting closer to him, and as she was about to slip out of the dancing frenzy, needing to drink some water, she felt a hand in the crease of her back. Christopher was inviting her to a cozier dance as he pressed her body against his. He wiped away Ayla's tears with his thumb. She grabbed him by the neck, squeezing as hard as she could, feeling overwhelmed at the onslaught of emotion. Locked in their embrace, Ayla and Christopher slowly danced in the middle of the frenzy, by then in full swing around them as the drums had taken over the music, pushing the energy up another notch.

The celebrations lasted through the night, the dancing making way for more docile remembrance conversations, laughter and crying mixing together as the villagers spoke of their lost loved ones through the night. Christopher and Ayla had stepped to the side and were lying on their backs, staring at the sky.

"What happens now?" Ayla asked after lying in the grass for hours, contemplating the stars.

"Good question," Christopher said. "All I know is, whatever happens next, I'd like it to be with you. I've never met anyone like you, and I'm sure I won't again. But that's what I want, what would you wish for?"

Ayla looked at him, her heart filling with love. "I'd also like it to be with you," she whispered. Christopher's heart filled with unabashed joy.

CHAPTER 45

Engella passed through customs at General Ignacio Pesqueira International Airport in Hermosillo, Mexico. As she exited through the front door, she was still undecided if she would walk or take some other form of transportation. She walked up and down the front of the airport, looking for a surprise connection like the one she found with her taxi driver in India. The airport, itself, had a Home Depot vibe, with its large orange band circling the building near the roof, which, for some reason, prompted Engella to walk to Rafael's village. It would take her three or four hours, which would be plenty of time to get her head straight.

She purchased some water before setting off, leaving most of her belongings in a locker so she could travel as lightly as possible. The airport was on the outskirts of the city, so Engella chose to head in the opposite direction from the city and reached the Sonoran Desert countryside rather quickly. An expansive, lush landscape awaited her, spreading beyond the horizon. The land was bursting with color, the recent rains having given the plants a chance to flourish. The region spreading out before her had a desert-like feel, with a sporadic tree popping up here and there, casting shade around it, the rest being rocks and sand. Blooming bushes of flowers were scattered randomly across the horizon, the bees buzzing all around Engella, eager to extract the pollen. The colorful flowers gave depth to an otherwise monochromatic scene as she took in the flat, endless horizon studded with small, rocky hills.

Engella climbed one of the hills to get a better vantage point to make sure she was headed in the right direction. Snakes and lizards scurried as she climbed a rock, bringing a large smile to Engella's face, her mind flashing to the lizard that visited her every day when she lived in the village in India. Then a rattlesnake shook its tail, jolting her out of her daydreaming and warned her that she was too close. Engella stopped and looked around to see where she could step without being bitten. The snake was hiding in a crevasse right in front of her. She couldn't see it, but heard the rattle, which was enough for her to change course. She reached the top of the hill and surveyed the land. Her heart filled with love, almost bursting out of her chest. She had felt welcome and at home in the Soochit tribe village, but this was her true home.

She spotted some rooftops she recognized as houses from the village in the hazy mist dancing on the horizon. A massive wave of emotion hit her; relief, happiness, and contentment. She knew she had arrived. She descended from the rock, wanting to get to the village as fast as possible so she could take Rafael in her arms to thank him for his help with the lost souls. A thought popped into her head, and she froze. What if the lost souls absorbed Rafael as well? He was almost burnt out when he gave her his energy and could have been adrift in the dream realm for some time. She pushed away the fear and ran toward the village.

• • •

Ayla and Christopher were standing in the middle of the village, bags strapped to their shoulders, surrounded by their new friends. Everyone was standing around, no one wanting to instigate the goodbyes. An awkward silence hung over the group until Pawa broke the silence. "If you visit us on occasion, we'll let you go," she said with a half-smile.

Pawa cursed herself for being so corny, but her intervention was enough to break the awkwardness as Ayla and Christopher got around to hugging and kissing everyone. The general feeling went from sadness to a joyful goodbye, as each person wanted their moment with the two departing members. Ayla and Christopher progressed through the goodbyes, hugging, kissing, and promising to keep in touch or to visit.

Pawa lingered at the end of the line, waiting her turn. As Christopher locked eyes with her, they both converged toward each other in tears, the surrounding clamor becoming invisible. They locked in an embrace and stayed there, both immensely grateful to what the other had brought into their life. They hugged for a long moment, until Jolan broke it up with a tap on Christopher's shoulder, wanting his turn. Pulling away from Pawa, Christopher turned to Jolan, putting a hand on his shoulder.

"It's been something, hasn't it?" Christopher never knew how to have a normal conversation with Jolan, and the same underlying awkwardness was still the same.

Each time, he felt like a child trying to have an adult conversation with his father.

"That it has," Jolan replied in gentleman-like fashion. Then, he stood in silence, his hand out for a shake, until Christopher pulled him in for a hug, which felt right to both of them.

Ayla and Christopher reached the edge of the forest and turned back one last time to wave goodbye. The group of villagers had already begun to scatter as they turned their attention to the day at hand. It made Ayla smile as she realized at that moment how relaxed and free of cumbersome negative emotions she was. Looking at the villagers going back to their lives as quickly as they were doing then gave her hope that she could keep this new sense of equilibrium going for as long as needed. She looked back at Christopher, but he had already disappeared into the forest, walking with purpose. Ayla ran after him, and together they reached the neighboring village where they found transportation to the airport.

Ayla and Christopher slept through the whole flight, each well taken care of by the flight attendants while they dozed. They took a flight to New York, neither of them noticing the stop in Delhi that lasted a good three hours. The wheels of the plane touching down in New York awoke them both as the plane shook heavily upon landing. Both their eyes popped open instantly, their minds still programmed to evade capture or death. Although the flight lasted over nineteen hours, their sleep had brought little relief to the sense of exhaustion they carried with them.

They slowly exited the airplane, following the flow of passengers to the luggage carousel. A strange feeling overwhelmed Christopher as they were waiting for their baggage. He had no desire to return home, feeling a need to explore his duality further. But he wasn't sure

how to proceed, the reality being so new to him. Until
he met Ayla and Engella, he thought any dark wish
we may dream up was to be obscured and forgotten
because its existence was considered evil. But here he
stood, feeling more complete than he could have ever
imagined. By acknowledging his soul as a whole being
within his physical self, it felt like tons of anxiety had
left his body. Like his conscious mind, his soul was governed by the same contradictory forces that dominate
our waking lives. He realized how tiring it had been
to fight against something that will exist, nonetheless.

"What next?" Ayla asked. She had noticed his mind
was preoccupied.

"I don't know, but I feel like I've got a lot more
to learn about the energies that govern our lives," he
answered absentmindedly.

"I'm up for it," Ayla said, smiling. "There's nothing
for me at the university anyway."

Ayla's reply relaxed Christopher a little. He turned
and looked at her. "I love you, but I'm never sure where
to place my feelings for you. It's intense, but where is
it coming from? My soul, my light, or my darkness?"

"Why do you ask?" Ayla asked, coyly. "Any ideas?" She
looked at the restroom nearby. Christopher chuckled
at this, her capacity to live in the moment once again,
pulling his mind back.

"You little horn dog." He grabbed her by the hand,
and they headed for the restroom, keeping an eye out
for security guards. They slipped into the restroom
and made love in a stall in silence, both exulting in
the present moment, their bodies welded together in
the cramped space, leaving little room for movement.
Someone walked into the restroom, breaking the bubble they had created around themselves for an instant.
Both stayed as immobile as possible while the person

did her business. After the person left, the moment had passed, so they returned to the baggage carousel, a little embarrassed by their sudden urge.

"Getting back to your question," Ayla said, trying to break the awkward silence, "sexual attraction emanates as much from our dark as our light. That is why some people end up in either extreme of the spectrum, puritan or perverse. Grey is the true color of sexual impulse."

"Makes sense." Christopher turned to look at the sky through a window in the ceiling. "It would have been nice to say goodbye to Engella, though," he said, changing the subject.

"I saw her when we went to watch the stars; she blew me a kiss and walked away. With her, you'll have to learn to accept that she appears and disappears in your life according to her own needs."

"Yeah, I kind of got that feeling when we met," he said unperturbed. Their bags arrived on the carousel, and they picked them up and left the airport.

• • •

Having hit her stride, running full steam through the rocky landscape, Engella spotted a feline observing her from a distance, atop a hill a little further ahead. She didn't slow her run but kept an eye on the big cat. Her first impression gave her the same vibe she had with the tiger, but she knew it could be wishful thinking on her part, and she needed to stay alert. She couldn't be more than fifteen minutes away from the village, which meant she might come across some people soon, alleviating some of the stress she felt as she saw the big cat climb down its hill, coming in her direction. She kept her rhythm, maintaining a good pace, trying to contain her excitement to meet Rafael face to face for the first time in way too long. Her mind was abuzz with memories of her last time there. She wondered what would have changed since then. She didn't expect much change since their way of life was still dictated by the idea of self-sufficiency that had been instilled in them from childhood. They are governed by rituals that don't need any adaptation to what is commonly known as modern life.

Her mouth began to water at the thought of having some cheese broth, the local specialty. She spotted something out of the corner of her eye and turned, seeing a jaguar coming right at her, stomach to the ground, ready to pounce. Engella stopped as the jaguar ran right past her, attacking a snake that was coiled and ready for her passage. They disappeared in a cloud of dust, and within seconds, silence fell over them. As the dust settled, Engella saw the jaguar with the snake in its mouth, chomping away at it, sucking the juices out, purring loudly. She walked away, keeping an eye on the jaguar, which was then oblivious to her presence. She said thank you using sign language and walked away, letting her heartbeat slow down.

As she approached the village, the distinct smell of the cheese broth she so desperately wanted to eat came to her, pulling her along. Coming over a small ridge, she saw the village and was overwhelmed by a wave of emotions. Every moment, every challenge, every conversation she had since leaving came back to her, causing her to pause and sit. That village had become her anchor. She sat and watched the people go about their business, her heart filled with pure joy, her smile so wide it hurt her face. Rafael's face popped into her head, prompting Engella to get up and find him.

She ran to his house, pausing when she saw that the blinds in the windows were pulled. She went to the door and knocked, not expecting an answer. Rafael had always insisted on the importance of daylight, that you must expose yourself to it as much as possible. So Engella thought he must be somewhere else if the blinds were still down. The door opened, which startled her. A sullen-looking man was there. His eyes carried the dread of despair, the dark circles under them witness to sleepless nights. Moving to the side, he let her in. They went to a room where Rafael was lying in bed, unconscious.

"He's been like this since going to help you," the man said.

There was no accusatory tone in his voice, but Engella still took it like a dagger to the heart. She held on to the thought that if the lost souls had absorbed him, he would have awakened, although empty. If he was still unconscious, it meant there was still hope. Feeling her heartbeat in her throat, Engella sat on the edge of the bed and took Rafael's hand. The result was powerful and immediate. He opened his eyes and took a deep breath, his chest swelling suddenly as he breathed in as if recovering from a near-drowning. The man who had opened the door jumped back, as though he had seen a possessed man.

Engella placed her hand on his forehead, trying to share the sense of calm that inhabited her the same way he did when she first took some dreaming broth. They stayed like this for a long moment, Engella ordering the man to bring water. Engella dipped a cloth in the water and squeezed it in Rafael's mouth, causing him to cough as the water reached his dry throat. As Rafael was regaining some control over his consciousness, he looked around the room. Confused at first, he gradually came to the realization he was back home, his respiration calming down as the reality sank in. He looked at Engella, his eyes filled with pride and love.

"It took you long enough," he said with a wry smile.

Engella couldn't help but give him a gigantic hug, kissing his face, repeating "thank you," over and over. Rafael pushed her away like a child evading an overbearing aunt.

"Easy... we did what was necessary." He wiped away the kisses with the back of his hand, although he was touched by her emotional response to his awakening. His face then became serious. "What about the lost souls?"

"Gone for now, but we will need them again."

"How so?" He felt a shiver go down his spine, anticipating the answer.

"They let me take possession of Dr. Cutler's memories of who was working with him to obliterate the collective unconscious; we must take care of them."

Engella's look was fierce, determined. Rafael knew she would take action. Nothing he could say would change that. He desperately wanted to ask her how she took another person's memory but kept silent. "All right then; what do you need from me?" He asked.

THE END

A very special thank you to my wife Karine, without whom I never could have finished this book. Her steadfast confidence in the process was the island of peace from where I could fully concentrate on the creation my story.

NOTES

1 Wolfgang Pauli, a theoretical physicist and Carl Gustav Jung, an analytical psychologist, worked together on a theory that Jung coined a "synchronicity," which holds that events are "meaningful coincidences" if they occur with no <u>causal relationship</u> yet seem to be meaningfully related.

2 A thermophilic extremophile is an <u>organism</u> that thrives in physically or geochemically <u>extreme conditions</u> that are detrimental to most <u>life on Earth</u>. It's believed in certain circles that when the planet became capable of sustaining life, the first signs of life came from these organisms since they possess the ability to transfer DNA from one cell to another cell, followed by integration of the donor DNA into the recipient cell's chromosome.

3 The **Collective unconscious** is a term introduced by psychiatrist Carl <u>Jung</u> to represent a form

of the <u>unconscious</u> (that part of the <u>mind</u> containing memories and impulses of which the individual is not aware) common to mankind as a whole and originating in the inherited structure of the <u>brain</u>. It is distinct from the personal unconscious, which arises from the experience of the individual. According to Jung, the <u>collective</u> unconscious contains <u>archetypes</u>, or universal <u>primordial</u> images and ideas.

4 The double-slit experiment is a demonstration that light and matter can display characteristics of both classically defined waves and particles. The experiment was first performed with light by <u>Thomas Young</u> in 1801. In 1927, <u>Davisson and Germer</u> demonstrated that electrons show the same behavior, which was later extended to atoms and molecules.

5 The Pauli-effect is a term referring to the supposed tendency of technical equipment to encounter critical failure in the presence of certain people. The term was coined after mysterious anecdotal stories involving <u>Austrian</u> theoretical physicist <u>Wolfgang Pauli</u>, describing numerous instances in which demonstrations involving equipment suffered technical problems only when he was present. One such incident occurred in the physics laboratory at the <u>University of Göttingen</u>. An expensive measuring device, for no apparent reason, suddenly stopped working, although Pauli was, in fact, *absent*. <u>James Franck</u>, the director of the institute, later reported the incident to his colleague Pauli in Zürich with the humorous remark that at least this time, Pauli was innocent. However, it turned out that Pauli had

been on a railway journey to Copenhagen and had switched trains in the Göttingen rail station at about the time of the failure. The incident is reported in <u>George Gamow</u>'s book Thirty Years That Shook Physics, where it is also claimed the more talented the theoretical physicist, the stronger the effect.

6 Since the early 1900s, physicists have postulated that the number 137 could lay at the heart of a <u>grand unified theory</u>, relating theories of electromagnetism, quantum mechanics, and, especially, gravity. According to Neils Bohr, a Nobel winning physicist, the innermost electron of an atom with $Z = 137$ would be orbiting (just below) the speed of light, and the next element ($Z = 138$) would be «impossible».

7 Soochit Karana means to enlighten in Hindi.

8 The tree of life is a widespread myth or archetype in the world's mythologies, related to the concept of a *sacred tree*. The tree of life connects all forms of creation and is said to be born from the cosmic tree. It's portrayed in many variations in several religions and philosophies.

9 The Bhopal disaster, also referred to as the Bhopal gas tragedy, was a <u>gas leak</u> incident on the night of 2–3 December 1984 at the <u>Union Carbide India Limited</u>(UCIL) <u>pesticide</u> plant in <u>Bhopal</u>, Madhya Pradesh, India. It is considered to be <u>the world's worst</u> <u>industrial disaster</u>. Over 500,000 people were exposed to <u>methyl isocyanate (MIC)</u> gas. The highly toxic substance made its way into and around the small towns located near the plant.

10 The CRISPR device is a genetic engineering tool designed to identify and replace malicious strands of DNA to reinforce the immune system. Its name is an acronym for Clustered Regular Interspaced Short Palindromic Repeats. The CRISPR-cas9 machine is currently being used in genome alteration research.

Other notes:

Rafael's explanation to Engella in chapter 4 is loosely based on the writings of Carlos Castaneda relating to his training in shamanism with a Yaqui "Man of Knowledge" named don Juan Matus. Chapter 6 is loosely based on "the art of dreaming", also by Carlos Castaneda. These writings permeate Engella's quest throughout the book.